THE
Courageous
BRIDES
COLLECTION

Compassionate Heroism Attracts Male Suitors to Nine Spirited Women

THE
Courageous
BRIDES
COLLECTION

Johnnie Alexander, Michelle Griep, Eileen Key,
Debby Lee, Rose Allen McCauley, Donita Kathleen Paul,
Jennifer Uhlarik, Jenness Walker, Renee Yancy

BARBOUR BOOKS
An Imprint of Barbour Publishing, Inc.

Print ISBN 978-1-63409-777-2

eBook Editions:
Adobe Digital Edition (.epub) 978-1-63409-872-4
Kindle and MobiPocket Edition (.prc) 978-1-63409-873-1

Published by Barbour Books, an imprint of Barbour Publishing, Inc., P.O. Box 719, Uhrichsville, OH 44683, www.barbourbooks.com

Our mission is to publish and distribute inspirational products offering exceptional value and biblical encouragement to the masses.

 Member of the
Evangelical Christian
Publishers Association

Printed in Canada.

Contents

The Healing Promise

by Johnnie Alexander

Dedication

For Dawn Lahm and Audrey Cravatt,
treasured friends from our Nebraska days.

Acknowledgments

Special thanks to Gayelynn Oyler for sharing her expertise on horses.

Thanks, too, to the other authors in this collection who shared historical tidbits
and resources, and also to my Imagine That! critique partners
and Kindred Heart Writers.

As always, love to my children: Bethany Jett,
Jillian Lancour, and Nate Donley.

He giveth power to the faint;
and to them that have no might he increaseth strength.
Isaiah 40:29

Chapter One

Neligh, Nebraska
Tuesday, May 22, 1877

The tawny rabbit, its soft fur the color of a newborn fawn, squirmed beneath Marcy Whitt's gentle grip. She repositioned him on the examining table then cleaned the dried blood from his injured paw. Hopefully, Copper would be her most difficult patient in Doc's absence.

"Shh," she murmured as she cleaned the wound with an alcohol-soaked cotton ball. "It only stings a moment."

"Will he live?" Sadie Ellison's red-rimmed eyes darkened with worry, but at least she wasn't crying anymore.

"To a great and respectable old age, I should say. As long as he stays out of trouble."

"Are you sure?" Sadie's voice cracked. "I don't want him to die."

"Have you never scratched yourself?" Marcy asked in pretended surprise.

"I suppose."

"Yet here you are. A thriving young girl." Marcy dabbed at the last of the blood then examined the slash again. "It's not a very big cut, but it needs a bandage. Will you help me?"

"What do I need to do?"

"Sit in that chair and hold him tight. Can you do that?"

Sadie nodded, and Marcy placed the rabbit in the girl's lap. She retrieved cotton and a strip of bandage from the apothecary jars then knelt in front of Sadie to wrap the injured paw.

"I wish he hadn't gotten out of his cage," Sadie said. "Then he wouldn't have tangled in that dirty ole barb wire."

"Hopefully he learned his lesson."

"What lesson is that?"

Good question.

Marcy focused on wrapping the bandage then smiled at Sadie. "Sometimes it's safest to stay at home. Especially if you're a rabbit."

Sometimes even if you're not. Perhaps she needed more time in this bustling frontier town for it to feel like home. A sigh pressed against her throat. Time wouldn't change anything. No matter how long she lived here, Neligh, Nebraska, would never be home. That special place was hundreds of miles away in Cincinnati.

"I wish Joel didn't have none of that barb wire." Sadie's pouting voice interrupted Marcy's thoughts. "Then it wouldn't have mattered if Copper got out."

"He probably needs it to fix the fences."

A slight movement behind Sadie caught Marcy's attention. Joel Ellison had entered the parlor, the room where people waited to see Doc, and now filled the door frame.

Brown hair curled low on his brow and against the collar of his homespun shirt, tempting Marcy to pick up her scissors and give it a much-needed trim.

"Naw," Sadie said, jutting out her jaw. "He doesn't care, that's all."

"You talkin' bad about me, missy?" Joel's lighthearted tone took the sting from his words, but Sadie practically jumped out of her skin. She clutched her pet so tightly his eyes widened.

"Only saying what was on my mind."

Sadie bent her head over Copper so Joel couldn't see her surly expression. Hiding her amusement at Sadie's spunk, Marcy concentrated on tying the bandage and securing the ends. Of course a child could get away with saying things a twenty-year-old couldn't. Though perhaps Marcy would be outspoken, too, if life had been as unkind to her as it had been to the Ellison family.

Joel was doing as well as could be expected—at least that's what everyone said. Marcy only saw him in church on Sundays and occasionally at the general store. He had a farm to run, a child to raise, and seemed to have little time or desire for socializing.

"You're not bothering Miss Marcy with that silly old rabbit, are you?"

"She's no bother," Marcy said before Sadie could answer. She patted the little girl's knee. "I'm all done. And don't worry. Copper is going to be just fine."

Marcy rose and pumped water into the enamel basin. Doc once told her folks had laughed when he put the pump inside his house, but it sure was convenient. While she washed and dried her hands, Joel entered the room and bent beside his sister.

"He hurt his paw," Sadie said.

Joel stroked the rabbit's head. "How did he get out of his cage?"

She shrugged her shoulders and mumbled something unintelligible.

"Were you careless about the latch?"

"Maybe." She raised her eyes to Joel. "But he's not going to die. Miss Marcy said so."

A weight seemed to settle on Joel's shoulders, and an unexpected sensation fluttered in Marcy's chest. She wanted to do something, to say something to ease his burden. But no words came.

"I'm sure Miss Marcy fixed him up real good." He pressed his palm against Sadie's cheek. "Now he needs you to make sure he can't get out of his cage again."

"I will." Sadie nestled her head against Joel's shoulder. "I promise."

"That's my girl." He prodded Sadie from the chair as he rose. Apparently the brotherly gesture was all Sadie needed to forgive him. She leaned into him while cuddling Copper.

"Bring him by tomorrow," Marcy said, "and I'll take another look."

"You'll be here tomorrow?" Joel asked.

"I can be."

"Where's Doc?"

"He's gone to Norfolk."

"When will he be back?"

"Tomorrow, maybe. If not, the day after."

Joel's facial muscles constricted, and his eyes darkened with worry.

"What is it?" Marcy asked.

Instead of answering, Joel touched Sadie on the shoulder. "Tell Miss Marcy thank you, then go wait for me by the buckboard. It's out front."

Sadie ran to Marcy and gave her a quick hug. "You make everything better. Thank you."

"You're very welcome."

"Go on now," Joel urged Sadie. His gaze followed her until after she left the room. Not until they heard the soft sounds of a door opening and closing did he turn back to Marcy.

"She loves that rabbit. Don't know what she'd do if something happened to it."

"Nothing will."

"Folks around here say you've got a way with animals." He stared into her eyes as if taking her measure. "Do you have a way with people, too?"

The intensity of his gaze unsettled her. What he said was true—she seemed to have an innate gift to soothe aches and pains. Sadie wasn't the first child to bring her a sick or injured pet.

Something in his expression, though, told her he wasn't impressed. Deeper than that, he found her wanting.

But why?

"Doc trusted me to look after things while he's gone," she said, her eyes fixed on his. "But my only medical training is what I've learned from him."

"A child needs tending."

"Who?"

Joel hesitated, as if reluctant to speak. "You'd help a child, wouldn't you? No matter who it was?"

At first, her mind refused to accept the strange questions. Then it rushed through all the possibilities, recalling then dismissing each child in the community. He surely couldn't believe she'd refuse to help any of them.

"Why wouldn't I?"

"She's a Ponca child," he said as if he'd read her thoughts and known she hadn't considered anyone outside of Neligh.

"They sent for Doc?" An odd thing if so. The Ponca were friendly with the settlers but also aloof. They rarely came to town.

Joel shook his head. "They're camped about a mile from my farm. The agent who's with them asked me to fetch Doc. One of their little ones is feverish."

"So it's true. They're being forced to leave."

"The army is taking them to Oklahoma Territory."

"In this weather?" Every day brought more rain as if the dark clouds were water-laden ships speeding toward them from the Pacific Ocean.

"Right now the sun is shining."

"But for how long?"

Joel shrugged. "Will you come?"

"I'll come." Marcy scanned the shelves of medical supplies and focused her thoughts. Doc had taken his medical bag with him, but she had the basket of mending she'd brought from home—something to occupy her time if the good people of Neligh had no need of her skills. She emptied the contents onto the table and filled the basket with medical supplies.

When Joel took the basket from her, Marcy reached for her shawl. "I need to let my pa know where I'm going."

"We can send Sadie."

"She's not coming with us? I don't mean to the camp, but home. Your home." She pressed her lips together to stop the rambling. Nerves, she supposed. Cleaning an injured rabbit's scratched foot was one thing, but caring for a sick child at an army camp was another thing entirely.

"I already asked Betsy Taylor to look after her. Thought it best for me to stay at the camp in case Doc needed a hand." He glanced away. "Didn't expect I'd be taking you out there."

"Did you honestly think I'd refuse to help a child?"

"We need to go." He took long strides toward the door, leaving Marcy scurrying to catch up.

Once outside, she locked the house and tucked the key into the pocket of her gingham dress. By the time she reached the buckboard, Joel had placed her basket beneath the wooden seat. Sadie sat inside the wagon bed, head bent while she softly sang a lullaby. From her vantage point, Marcy couldn't see Copper, but the child obviously held her cherished pet in her lap.

Joel grasped her elbow to help her onto the seat. Once she was settled, she tied her bonnet beneath her chin. Her movements were smooth, practiced. But her thoughts were spinning like a springtime tornado.

The Ponca were leaving, and a child was sick.

Father, please don't let it be the Beloved Child, she silently prayed. *Please not her.*

Chapter Two

After Joel helped Marcy onto the wagon seat, he folded his arms over the wagon bed near Sadie. Her eyes were still red, but at least she wasn't crying. He pulled out his bandanna anyway and made a pretense of drying her tears. "How's Copper?"

"He's better."

"Good enough for you to do me a big favor?"

"I guess so."

"I need to drive Miss Marcy out to the army camp. Don't know how long we'll be gone."

"Am I going, too?"

"Miss Taylor said you could stay awhile with her. You'd like staying with your teacher, wouldn't you?"

"She likes rabbits."

"That's good. But first I need you to go by the lumber mill. Tell Mr. Whitt where we're going so he doesn't worry." He playfully pulled her braid. "Can you do that?"

"Can Copper go with me?"

"Don't see why not." Joel lifted her from the wagon bed, and Sadie ran toward the river, Copper clutched tightly in her arms. "You'll make that rabbit sick," he called after her. Sadie slowed to a walk, albeit a fast one.

Joel shook his head then climbed onto the high seat beside Marcy. Toward the west, little swirls of dust kicked up as the breeze quickened, died, and quickened again. Dark clouds sped toward them, chasing away the blue skies. "Storm's a-coming."

"Will we reach the camp before it hits?"

"I think so." Joel released the brake and made a clicking noise as he lightly tapped Toby's broad back with the reins. The horse trotted along the familiar road leading toward the farm.

"He's going to be mighty disappointed when I don't turn into the barn," Joel said with a wry laugh.

Marcy didn't respond, and he gave her a sideways glance. The bonnet hid most of her face but not the set of her jaw.

"Hope I didn't take you from anything important," he said.

She turned to him, her blue eyes boring into his. "You didn't answer my question."

"What question?"

"Why you thought I wouldn't come."

Joel exhaled and stared toward the horizon. "Some folks aren't sorry to see the Ponca go. Thought you might be one of them."

"Why would you think that?"

"Because I know what people close to you've been saying."

"My pa is friendly with the Ponca. He built a fine table for Chief Standing Bear."

"I wasn't talking about your pa."

She didn't reply, but he sensed her posture tense as she clutched at her shawl. It might not be fair, but he couldn't help his misgivings about her. Everyone in town knew Benjamin Hollingsworth's views on the Indian question. And everyone knew Benjamin was Marcy's beau.

They drove for a few moments in silence. Joel had never been good at small talk, and Marcy's feminine proximity made it even harder to think of something to say. He didn't suppose he'd ever be good at courting. Not that he had the time. After Pa died, the farm had been his to keep, and Sadie had been his to raise. He was determined not to lose either.

Five years had passed since he'd buried Pa, and so far Joel had managed to hold on to both. The farm did as well as any of the others near the prairie town, if not a slight touch better. And Sadie brought him a joy he'd never expected to find this side of heaven.

He'd grieved for his mom when he was eleven and for his stepmother when he was twelve. Pa had wasted no time finding a much younger replacement after Ma died—a gal only a few years older than Joel. She'd been more like an older sister than a mother. For her sake, he'd held on to Sadie when Pa died instead of giving her over to an orphanage. That's what folks told him to do. But he never considered it.

"How old is the child?" Marcy's voice, as refreshing against his ear as a spring breeze in the twilight, interrupted his thoughts.

"The agent didn't say. Only told me that they had a sick child. A girl."

Marcy stiffened beside him. Or maybe he imagined it.

"Why didn't he bring her to town? Or send her with you?"

"Her pa wouldn't allow it."

"Why not?"

"Maybe he worried about trusting her to the enemy."

"Enemy." Marcy repeated the word, almost as if she were trying it out, feeling its sharpness against her teeth. "I'm surprised he asked for help."

"You can't blame him for being suspicious. Not after everything that's happened."

"You mean the treaty." She sighed heavily. "Why couldn't they just fix it?"

"That would take brains. Something those muttonheads back East don't have."

"It has to be for the best. They'll be safer in Oklahoma Territory."

Joel slapped the reins against Toby's back more to express his frustration than to goad the horse into a faster trot. Despite her willingness to help, Marcy wasn't much different than the other girls in Neligh—more interested in the new fabrics and doodads at the general store than what was going on around them.

"You disagree?" she asked.

"A few of the Ponca already went there. They came back because they couldn't find a decent place for the tribe."

"I didn't know that," she said, uncertainty in her tone.

"What do you know?"

"Pa said someone back in Washington gave the Ponca land to the Sioux during their treaty negotiations. Now the Sioux are trying to drive out the Ponca."

"Your pa's right." Joel peered at her under the brim of his broad hat, but her expression showed genuine concern. "I'd be suspicious, too, if my farm was taken away and I was sent packing."

"I still don't understand why they don't fix the treaty."

"I don't have the answer to that. I don't suppose anyone does." Joel sympathized with the Ponca, even felt anger toward the tall-hatted men in Washington who made their laws and signed their treaties with little regard for those they were supposed to protect.

But he didn't like to think about the treaty too much. At one time, all the land around the Niobrara and the Missouri Rivers belonged to the Indians. What if the treaty was overturned? And then another and another? Would he have to give up his farm? The land where his parents and Sadie's ma were buried?

He'd worked alongside his pa since he was knee-high to a grasshopper, and then he worked alone. That work meant something.

Course it meant something for the Ponca, too. They'd been settled at the Niobrara long enough to build homes and grow crops and gardens. They weren't a roaming tribe, not anymore.

Beside him, Marcy sat quietly, her gaze fixed on the far horizon. Her thoughts hid behind eyes narrowed with worry. He couldn't read her mind, but her expression told him she wasn't thinking about what to wear to the town's next social event.

Maybe he'd misjudged her.

◆　◆　◆

Marcy stared across the horse's back toward the edge of the broad prairie. Joel's words echoed in her thoughts, as dark as the clouds filling the sky.

I wasn't talking about your pa.

He meant Benjamin. And he was right.

After Pa told her about the mistaken treaty, she'd tried to discuss it with her fiancé. But he'd laughed away her concern. His future wife didn't need to worry her pretty little head about such affairs.

Benjamin didn't think she needed to be spending time with Doc, either, or giving Pa a hand in the lumber mill when he needed it. "Once we're married, you'll be too busy for any of that," he'd said. More than once.

Though he'd never been clear on what she'd be busy doing.

But he loved her, and she wanted to be a dutiful wife. So she heeded his mother's advice on posture and poise and learned the rules of etiquette that guided the family's social events. High-falutin' nonsense, her pa called it. But Marcy appreciated the elegance the Hollingsworth family gave to the frontier community. One day soon, Benjamin's parents would announce their engagement. Then she'd belong to that elegance, too.

Lightning flashed in the distance, and Marcy grasped Joel's arm.

"We'll be there soon," he said. "Sure hope your pa doesn't tan my hide for taking you out to the camp in this weather."

"He'll understand." Dread settled in the pit of her stomach. Pa knew she couldn't ignore a sick child. Benjamin must know that, too, though he hadn't been pleased when she went with Pa to deliver Chief Standing Bear's table.

"I went to the Ponca village once," she said. "Shortly after I moved here."

"That so?"

"It wasn't at all what I expected."

He glanced at her, an amused smile playing at his lips. "You expected tipis and scalps?"

"I didn't expect wooden houses and vegetable gardens."

"But that's what you found."

"Yes." She'd also found a friend. "I met a woman there. She was about my age, but she already had a baby. A little girl who was teething and crying and making her poor ma miserable."

"Don't tell me. You held the baby, and she stopped crying."

"She went to sleep in my arms." Marcy smiled at the memory. "Her mother didn't speak English, but her husband called the baby their Beloved Child."

"Their firstborn. It's a Ponca tradition."

"It's a lovely thought, isn't it?"

"I suppose it is."

"She'd be about eighteen months old now," Marcy said. "I always meant to go back."

"Why didn't you?"

She opened her mouth to respond then closed it again. What could she say? She didn't have a reason—at least not one that mattered. The days had sped by as she got used to living with Pa after being separated from him for so long. Their neighbors had welcomed her into the rhythms of the small community—the quilting bees, the church dinners, the harvest festival.

And then there was Benjamin. He'd swept her off her feet, leaving her breathless with his charm and his lavish gifts. He made sure she spent most of her free time with his family.

She snuck a peek at Joel beneath the brim of her bonnet. He'd been at the mill on the day she arrived in Neligh, and at the time she thought he liked her. But after she met Benjamin, Joel seemed to avoid her.

Her thoughts returned to her only visit to the Ponca village. Even though they couldn't communicate, the women had been gracious and welcoming. Their children, smiling and curious, had stared at her blond hair and took turns wearing her best Sunday hat.

These same women and children were being forced from their homes because of a bureaucratic mistake.

"Is this the only answer?" Marcy's voice startled her. She hadn't meant to ask the question out loud. Apparently, Joel was surprised, too, given the wide-eyed look he gave her before turning his attention back to the trail.

"What are you talking about?"

"Why won't the army protect the Ponca from the Sioux?"

"They're following the orders they've been given."

A crack of thunder prevented Marcy from answering, and large raindrops pelted the wagon. She pulled her shawl closer and subconsciously leaned closer to Joel.

Toby picked up speed, following the track as it curved past a grove of trees. Joel's house and barn appeared, and he tightened his grip on the reins to control the horse.

"Not going home yet, boy," he said.

Toby neighed in protest and shook his head, but Joel directed him past the farm. Marcy silently prayed the wagon wouldn't get stuck in the thickening mud or, even worse, tip over.

Finally, ghostly images appeared in the blur created by the steady rain. The tents and crude lean-tos of the encampment.

Chapter Three

Inside the dimly lit tent, Marcy huddled beside the feverish toddler. She placed a cool cloth on the small forehead and smoothed back the child's long dark hair. Moon Hawk knelt on the other side of the pallet, rocking back and forth as she muttered desperate prayers for healing. Marcy gave her a slight smile, but the gesture meant little. Not when her baby girl, her Beloved Child, was so ill.

Marcy removed the mustard poultice from White Buffalo Girl's bare stomach. She grimaced at the small blisters appearing on the skin. If only there was another treatment—one that didn't cause harm of its own.

But she'd tried a tonic when they first arrived, and there'd been no improvement.

With careful movements, she replaced the poultice with another one, almost too hot to touch, from a kettle hanging over a low fire. White Buffalo Girl stirred and tried to swat away the pungent cloths.

"That's it, little one," Marcy cooed as she placed a worn blanket on top of the poultice to keep in the warmth as long as possible. "Fight."

The flap opened, and a rain-soaked gust blew into the tent. Except for its chill, Marcy welcomed the fresh air. Joel entered, carrying blankets and a stew pot. Black Elk, Moon Hawk's husband, followed closely with a large basket.

Disgusted by the lack of supplies he could scrounge up from the army—though to be fair, the soldiers were as much in need as the Ponca—Joel and Black Elk had ridden through the downpour to his farm. He'd gathered as much as he could spare.

Joel hung the pot over the fire then helped Marcy cover White Buffalo Girl with a few of the blankets. He placed a patchwork quilt over Marcy's shoulders, and she gave him a quick smile of thanks.

Black Elk handed Joel the basket and knelt by Moon Hawk. The fire cast shadows on his strong cheekbones and bronze skin. His eyes darted from White Buffalo Girl to his wife. He said something to her, but she didn't respond.

Marcy adjusted the blankets around White Buffalo Girl and moistened the child's lips with a damp cloth. If only Doc were here. Surely there was something else she could be doing. Should be doing.

As soon as the stew bubbled, Joel ladled it into bowls, giving a couple to Black Elk then handing one to Marcy. She shook her head.

"You have to eat."

"I'm not hungry."

"At least try. It's not bad if I do say so myself."

"You made this?"

"Sure did."

She took the bowl, grateful for its warmth in her cupped hands. Dampness seemed to permeate the tent, and the fire radiated only a small circle of heat.

Black Elk murmured something to Moon Hawk. He appeared to be pleading with her, and she leaned her head against his shoulder but still refused to eat.

"You can feed a little to your daughter if you'd like," Marcy said. "Only the broth."

Black Elk translated for his wife. A moment passed while Moon Hawk took in Marcy's words and found in them a glimmer of hope. Marcy raised the little girl's head while Moon Hawk pursed her lips and cooled a spoonful of liquid with her breath.

White Buffalo Girl swallowed a few tiny mouthfuls then coughed. Momentarily strengthened by the broth, the child mumbled something Marcy didn't understand. Moon Hawk grasped her daughter's hand and repeated the same word, a Ponca word.

"She asks for her doll," Black Elk said. "We had to leave, and the doll was lost."

Moon Hawk spoke quickly, her words tripping over each other. When Black Elk replied, he kept his voice soft, his words few. Moon Hawk didn't answer, but anguish accentuated the fear in her dark eyes.

Marcy didn't need to know their language to understand Moon Hawk had expressed her dismay, perhaps even disappointment in her husband, that White Buffalo Girl didn't have her cherished toy to comfort her.

"I'm sorry," Marcy said.

Moon Hawk's nod was barely perceptible. She spoon-fed more broth into her daughter's tiny mouth while shrinking within herself. Her fear hovered in the shadows, another presence inside the dismal tent.

◆　◆　◆

During a lull in the storm, Joel drove the wagon the short distance back to his farm. He wiped down and fed Toby then saddled his mare. Buttermilk, the color of her name, nuzzled his hand as he slipped the bit into her mouth. "You ready for a ride, girl?" he asked. "Sorry to take you out in this weather, but I need to check on Sadie."

Buttermilk whickered her eagerness, and Joel chuckled at her willing spirit. But she was always one for an adventure no matter the weather. He had found her several years ago, a young colt standing over the body of her mother, and brought her home. His inquiries had gone unanswered, and now he no longer worried someone would claim her. Whatever happened on the prairie remained a mystery.

He shrugged into his oilskin duster, adjusted his hat, and then led Buttermilk from the barn. The late afternoon sun, barely visible behind rain-heavy clouds, might as well set for all the good it was doing. He'd have to hurry to get back to the camp while there was still light enough to see.

Miss Taylor invited him in, but he declined. No need to drip water on her floor. Sadie showed him the embroidery sampler her teacher had given her to work on, and he dutifully admired her stitching.

"How's that rabbit?" he asked.

"He's sleepin' on the back porch," Sadie said. "I think he had a rough day."

"I think he did, too." If only a rabbit's injured paw was the worst thing the day would hold. Somehow he didn't think it would be. Marcy had seemed reluctant for him to leave her, and he'd offered to bring her home. She'd gathered her resolve and refused. Seemed she had more spunk than he gave her credit for.

But she was afraid. He'd seen it in her eyes.

Joel tapped his hat against his leg. "I gotta go back to the camp. As soon as I see Mr. Whitt. Let him know Marcy is fine."

"Don't worry about Sadie," Miss Taylor said. "She can stay here all night if you need her to."

"Thank you, ma'am. I think we better plan on that."

"We'll see you tomorrow then."

"Tomorrow."

He nodded good-bye then rode to the lumber mill. A carriage stood nearby, and Joel blew out air in frustration. The last person he wanted to see.

Benjamin Hollingsworth.

Joel sheltered Buttermilk beneath a three-sided pole barn then entered the mill.

Thad Whitt emerged from an inner office and limped his way across the sawdust-covered floor. He was one of the lucky ones—at least he'd survived the war. Benjamin followed behind, and both men looked past Joel.

"Marcy at the house?" Mr. Whitt asked.

"She's still at the camp."

Benjamin glared, a grim expression on his face. "You left her out there? Alone?"

"She's not alone."

"Of course not. She's with a bunch of no-good Indians who are being sent away from here. About time, too."

"That's enough, Benjamin," Mr. Whitt said quietly and turned to Joel. "My girl all right?"

"She's fine, sir. But the child. . . I'm not sure Marcy can help her."

Benjamin made a harrumphing noise and stepped closer. "Then she doesn't need to be there, does she?"

Joel kept his eyes on Mr. Whitt. "I offered to bring her home, sir. She wouldn't leave."

Mr. Whitt wiped his forehead with a large bandanna. "No, I don't suppose she would. Not as long as there's a chance."

"Not even when there's not, I'd say."

Mr. Whitt met Joel's gaze and slowly nodded. "You're right, son." Weariness softened his voice. "Not even when there's not."

"Did she say anything about our plans?" Benjamin demanded.

Joel slowly turned toward him. The man reminded him of a tiresome nag his pa once had. Cantankerous and out of sorts when things didn't go her way. "Plans?"

"My mother is hosting a dinner party this evening."

"In this weather?"

Mr. Whitt made a strange noise, something between a snort and a cough, then turned away and seemed to choke. "Sorry, fellas," he finally said.

"The date was set weeks ago," Benjamin said. "No one could have predicted this storm."

"Or that a child would need medical attention." Tired of Benjamin's petulance, Joel turned to Mr. Whitt. "I need to get back to the camp. Just wanted you to know Marcy is fine."

"You'll stay with her," Mr. Whitt said. "You'll take care of my girl?"

Joel glanced at Benjamin, expecting he'd want to take that responsibility.

"I told you," he said petulantly. "I've got plans. So does Marcy."

"So she does." Joel clenched the brim of his hat with both hands as a slow burn filled his gut. He shifted from one foot to the other, resisting the urge to grab Benjamin's bolo tie and haul him out to the buggy. Only a low kind of man cared more about a dinner than his gal. To show that kind of disrespect in front of her father sank him even lower.

Mr. Whitt stepped between them and gestured toward the door. "There's Marcy's coat. Take it with you. Do you need anything else?"

"I don't think so, sir."

"I'll see you out then."

As they headed for the door, Mr. Whitt grabbed Marcy's coat from a peg and handed it to Joel. Once they were outside, Mr. Whitt closed the door behind him. "Once he leaves, I'll join you. Tell me what you need."

"We've got blankets. Food and shelter. There's no need for you to be out in this weather." Joel eyed the horizon. The sun touched the rim of the world, and more clouds scurried toward the town. "It'll be dark soon, and more rain's coming."

"That girl's all I've got."

"I'll take care of her, sir. You can count on me."

Joel didn't waver under Mr. Whitt's measuring gaze. Finally the older man nodded.

"God be with you, son."

"With all of us."

Chapter Four

Joel slipped between the flaps of the tent and paused to give his eyes time to adjust to the dim lighting. He knelt beside Marcy, who seemed oblivious to his presence until he gently touched her shoulder.

"Your pa wanted you to have this," he whispered as he placed her coat about her shoulders.

"How is he?"

"He wanted to come, but I talked him out of it."

"I'm glad."

"How is she?"

"She's still crying for her doll." Marcy glanced at Moon Hawk then stood. Joel rose beside her, his hand sliding down her back before falling to his side. They huddled together as far from the little family as they could in the confined space and spoke in soft whispers.

"Black Elk told me the army didn't give them time to pack anything. White Buffalo Girl was already sick, and he begged the captain to let them stay in the village." Her voice quivered. "But he wouldn't allow it."

"What can I do?"

"Will you. . .please. . .just stay with me?"

Her simple plea shot like an arrow into his heart. In the wavering light of the smoking fire, he'd have done anything she asked.

"Of course, I will."

"I'm not sure I can do this."

"I know you can."

"She's going to die."

"With people around her who love and care for her."

Marcy's eyes misted, but beneath the tears shone resolve and courage. Had he given her that?

"Thank you." She knelt beside White Buffalo Girl and cooled her forehead again with the damp cloth. Joel settled slightly behind her. From his vantage point, he could see her gentle expression as she tended the toddler.

Marcy Ann Whitt. She'd taken his heart the first day they met outside her pa's lumber mill. He thought she felt the same, but then Benjamin Hollingsworth had claimed her attention. And Joel had let her go.

After all, no girl in her right mind would choose a farmer raising his little sister over the banker's son. Benjamin could offer her a life of privilege, something Joel couldn't.

22

Though Benjamin certainly had made his priorities clear tonight. And Marcy wasn't at the top of his list. What would he think if he could see her now? Strands of blond hair fell from their pins, and her cheeks were streaked with ash, probably from where she'd warmed her hands at the fire.

To Joel, she'd never looked lovelier. The girl in front of him wasn't a mere doll to dress up and show off at fancy dinner parties, but an admirable young woman with a caring heart. Joel should have seen that before now. And he shouldn't have given up so easily.

He could tell her about Benjamin's refusal to come to the camp. Show her the kind of man she had chosen. But that's not how he wanted to win Marcy's heart.

What was he thinking? Having given up before, was it too late to try again? He squirmed uncomfortably as one thought filled his mind. If he were in Benjamin's shoes, Marcy would already be wearing a gold wedding band on her finger.

Joel shifted again. He'd promised to stay, and he wouldn't break his promise. But doing nothing wasn't his usual routine. If only there was something else he could do. Something that would help Marcy heal White Buffalo Girl. Only one thing came to mind.

He closed his eyes and prayed.

◆　◆　◆

Marcy bent low, her ear pressed against White Buffalo Girl's nose. Not even the slightest breath, the quietest sigh, escaped the child's colorless lips. Marcy removed the blankets and slipped her hand under the poultice. The unmoving chest, still warm from her futile treatment, no longer held life.

Leaning back on her heels, Marcy clasped her hands within her apron. Her prayers had gone unanswered, as if they couldn't rise above the roar of thunder and clash of lightning that surrounded her beyond the clammy tent.

Across from Marcy, Moon Hawk let out a keening gasp before collapsing across her daughter's small body. Alarmed, Marcy leaned forward and awkwardly embraced Moon Hawk. She didn't know how long they stayed like that—Moon Hawk embracing her Beloved Child, Marcy embracing the mother. It might have been hours or perhaps only seconds before Joel bent beside Marcy and pulled her close to him. She rested her cheek against his chest while he wrapped his arms around her.

Only then did she taste the salty wetness on her lips and realize that tears streaked her face.

On the other side of the makeshift pallet, Black Elk wrapped Moon Hawk within his blanket.

◆　◆　◆

Joel swallowed the pain that threatened to swamp him. For only a moment, he wasn't inside the dim tent but in his parents' room. It wasn't a small Ponca child whom death had claimed, but his mother. The little boy he'd been wanted to scream and cry and throw things at the unfairness of life, at all the unanswered questions that tormented his heart.

He squelched the feelings by reminding himself he'd made peace with God a long time ago. Not that he had found fairness or the answers to his questions. But he'd found a faith that made it easier to live with the pain.

Sickness had taken White Buffalo Girl's life, but now she was snug and warm in her Father's arms. She'd never know sickness or hunger again. And she'd never have to wrestle with life's difficult questions.

He silently prayed that her parents would eventually find the peace they needed to survive her loss.

"Let's leave them be," he whispered in Marcy's ear.

She nodded, and he helped her rise. They stood near the tent's flap, unable to give the grieving parents any more privacy than to turn their back on them.

"I failed them," Marcy said.

"There's nothing else you could have done. She was already ill before they got here."

"Why couldn't the army have let them stay in their home? They killed that child as surely as if they'd put a bullet in her heart."

"Shh," Joel cautioned as her voice got louder. "You may be right, but fixing blame on the army won't do anyone any good. It won't bring her back."

"I've never. . ." Marcy's voice cracked, and new tears flowed down her flushed face.

She didn't need to finish the sentence for Joel to know what she meant to say. She'd never tended anyone who hadn't gotten well. But neither had she ever been called to the sickbed of someone already so close to death.

If this was anyone's fault, it was his for bringing her out here. When he'd learned Doc was away, he should have returned to the army camp. He hadn't needed to tell Marcy about the child.

Why had he?

The answer stared him in the face, and his neck burned with the embarrassment of truth. His motives hadn't been totally altruistic. He'd secretly hoped for a chance to spend time with her away from everyone else they knew.

Full of his own desires, he hadn't thought ahead of what sorrow the night might bring to her.

"I'm sorry, Marcy," he said quietly. "I should never have asked you to come out here."

Her gaze snapped to his, the shimmering blue of her eyes appearing dark as night as she huddled in the shadows.

"I'm glad you did. I shouldn't have stayed away from them for so long." She hesitated, and somehow he knew she was facing her own unwanted truth. "I think they frightened me a little."

"The Ponca? They've always been a peaceful tribe."

"Pa said the same. But. . .other people said other things." She glanced over her shoulder at the unmoving family tableau at the rear of the tent. "I should never have listened."

She turned her face into Joel's shoulder, and he held her close. Her head fit perfectly in the space above his heart, and he wanted her to stay there forever. Snug, safe. Seeking his comfort.

He loosened his hold, forcibly reminding himself that, at least for now, she belonged to another man. A despicable man. But that was her choice—not his. It wasn't right for him to prolong this moment when he should be getting her home.

Though that wasn't really an option with the storm raging around them. They couldn't even leave the tent to allow Black Elk and Moon Hawk to grieve in private.

Morning would be here soon, and the storm had to end sometime. He'd take Marcy back to her pa, back to her beau.

But he wouldn't ignore her anymore. He wouldn't stand by while Benjamin molded her into his own creation.

And he'd pray she found him to be the better man.

◆　◆　◆

Marcy had thought sleep impossible, but it had enveloped her sorrow into restful oblivion. At least for a couple of hours.

She awakened as if from a bad dream, but any details slipped away, leaving her with only a sickening despair. Near the back of the tent, Moon Hawk lay next to the pallet. Black Elk sat beside her, his back stiff and upright as he watched over all of them.

Seeing her awake, he nodded. "Thank you."

"I didn't save her."

"You tried. You cared about her. For that, I thank you."

He stood, and Marcy rose, too, groaning at the stiffness in her body from sleeping on the ground. Black Elk opened the tent's flap and ducked through the entryway.

Marcy pulled her shawl around her shoulders then glanced at Moon Hawk. Even in sleep, the young mother's face was stricken with grief.

"I'm sorry," Marcy whispered before stooping between the flaps to exit the tent. The rain had temporarily ceased, but more was coming. The Ponca couldn't travel in this weather.

Again Marcy's heart screamed. *Why couldn't they have stayed in their homes?*

No answers came from the heavens.

Joel came toward her, carrying a mug of steaming coffee. Suddenly self-conscious, she rubbed her palms against her apron and quickly re-pinned the long strands of hair that had loosened during the night.

Immediately after White Buffalo Girl died, Marcy had sought comfort in Joel's arms. Now the memory embarrassed her. What would Benjamin say if he knew she'd cried on another man's shoulder? More than that, she had felt a stirring unlike anything she'd ever known. A sense of belonging, of rightness.

But that had to be her imagination. The result of being emotionally distraught and vulnerable.

And yet. . . Marcy tried to imagine if it had been Benjamin who had learned of the sick Ponca child. How would he have responded? Would he have sought help?

The answer stared her in the face, daring her to admit it.

Shame engulfed her that she'd never realized this flaw in him before. She'd been too blinded by his wealth and standing in the community. Too proud to admit she didn't really like him even though she'd persuaded herself she was in love with him.

"It doesn't taste very good, but it's hot and strong," Joel said as he handed her the coffee. "I brought back the wagon this morning. We should probably get back to town during this lull."

She cradled the mug, breathing in its warmth. "I'm ready whenever you are," she said wearily.

"Let's pack your supplies."

Cloths. A tonic that hadn't helped. Her coat. A poor trade for a daughter's life. But perhaps useful to the Ponca on the long trek to a new home.

"Leave them."

Chapter Five

Gray clouds covered the skies with the promise of more rain as Marcy maneuvered around puddles of mud on her way to Joel's wagon. Like her, he'd left his belongings—the basket, the stew pot, blankets—with Black Elk and Moon Hawk.

He was about to help her into the wagon when someone called her name. Black Elk and Mr. Jarrett, the Indian agent, hurried toward them.

"Your father?" Black Elk made a whittling motion with his hands. "He carves wood, yes?"

"He does."

She waited for Black Elk to continue, but instead he glanced at the agent. Mr. Jarrett removed his hat. "Miss Whitt, we'd like to ask your pa to make a cross. For the child's grave."

Filled with compassion, Marcy reached for Black Elk's hand. He stiffened slightly at her touch then wrapped her hand in his. His calloused fingers felt cold but strong. "Your father will do this?"

"He would be honored."

"I'll ride back to town with you then," Mr. Jarrett said. "Give me a few minutes to saddle my horse."

"We'll wait for you." Realizing she hadn't consulted Joel, Marcy turned to him. "You don't mind, do you?"

"Why would I?"

"I didn't mean to speak out of turn."

"You didn't."

She read the unasked question in his eyes, soft and brown as they gazed into hers. The strange sensation returned, and her cheeks warmed. She couldn't tell him that Benjamin expected to arrange such things—and he wouldn't like Marcy usurping his place. It never bothered her before, but now she found Benjamin's overbearing attitude embarrassing.

Joel's different demeanor shone a harsh light on her judgment. What she had accepted as Benjamin's strength was nothing but swagger. Worse, she had allowed what he had—status, money—to blind her to his faults.

Another rush of heat burned her cheeks, and she turned away from Joel's searching gaze.

◆ ◆ ◆

Joel halted the wagon in front of the lumber mill then gazed at Marcy, who slept fitfully beside him. He hated to wake her—and not only because she'd been up most of the night. Something about the way her head pressed against his shoulder pleased him. At least for a little while, he could imagine she belonged beside him. If not for the agent riding horseback beside the wagon, Joel would have been tempted to slow Toby's pace. Perhaps even let him stop to graze for a while.

But now they had arrived. The dreamlike quality of the past several hours diffused before the stark reality of the river, the lumber mill, the Whitt family's adjacent house.

Again he fought the feelings rising in his heart and nudged Marcy's arm. "You're home."

She murmured senselessly then smiled at him. "I'm sorry."

"For what?"

"I'm not sure."

"Nothing to be sorry for." He hopped out of the wagon and reached up to help her down. His hands enclosed around her slender waist, and he couldn't help smiling when she gripped his arms.

"Marcy!" Mr. Whitt called from the doorway of the mill. He wiped his hands on a stained cloth then limped toward them. "Welcome home, child."

Marcy hiked up her skirt and ran to meet her father. After they embraced, Mr. Whitt cupped Marcy's face in both his hands and examined her closely. "You look worn out."

"I'm fine, Pa."

Jarrett dismounted beside Joel. "Is that Mr. Whitt?"

"The one and only."

"Why the limp?"

"Civil War."

"Union or Rebel?"

"Does it matter?"

"I guess not." Jarrett looped his reins around one of the wagon wheels and moved toward Marcy and her pa. Joel started to follow when a movement behind them caught his eye.

Benjamin Hollingsworth stood in front of the mill, feet apart and arms crossed. The men glared at each other.

Joel looked away first. The fight wasn't between them—at least not yet. Marcy had given him no indication she felt anything for him other than friendship. Unless she decided otherwise, their days would probably fall into the same routine as before. Formal nods at the general store. Perhaps a greeting at church.

What happened at the camp bound them together, but only in memory.

And not a pleasant one.

Perhaps even the polite nods would be a thing of the past. Would Marcy want to stay away from any reminders of what had happened at the camp? That's what he would be to her—a reminder of a child's death. The child she could not save.

Mr. Whitt caught Joel's gaze over Marcy's head, and Joel shook his head. Before Mr. Whitt could respond, Jarrett introduced himself, shifting to make room for Benjamin as he joined the group. "I have a favor to ask of you, Mr. Whitt."

"What would that be?"

"The child's father has requested a cross to mark the grave."

"You'll do it, won't you, Pa?" Marcy asked. "I already told Black Elk you would."

"Black Elk?" Benjamin practically spit the name. "Sounds like you all got real familiar out there. Guess that happens when you spend the night with Indians."

"You disapprove," Marcy said, her voice flat.

"You should never have gone out there. What if you get sick? No telling what kind of diseases they've got."

Before Marcy could reply, her father pulled her close. "I'd be honored to provide the cross. When do you need it?"

"As soon as possible," Jarrett replied. "The captain has agreed to wait till after the funeral to resume the march, but he doesn't wish to delay any longer than necessary. The grave is already being dug."

"Guess I better get to work then." Mr. Whitt patted Marcy's cheek. "Go to the house, daughter. Get some rest."

"I'll rest after the funeral."

"You're not going to that," Benjamin said with a snort.

She looked at her pa and the other men, her eyes wide with alarm. A flush crept up her throat and face as her gaze settled on Joel. "You won't go without me." It was part question, part statement.

"I need to check on Sadie, but I'll be back for you if you're sure that's what you want."

"It is." She graced him with a smile and headed toward the house.

"Guess I better get started on that cross," Mr. Whitt said. "Thanks for bringing her home, Joel."

"Happy to help out, sir."

Mr. Whitt and Jarrett headed for the workshop. Once they were out of earshot, Benjamin rounded on Joel. "You shouldn't encourage her in this foolishness."

"It's her decision. Not mine and not yours."

"My future wife does not socialize with Indians."

"You and Marcy are engaged?"

"We have an understanding." He took a step closer and lowered his voice. "I should string you up for taking her out there. Letting her stay there the whole night. Though perhaps you had your own reasons for that."

"You could have been with her. If you'd gone to the camp yesterday, I would have stepped aside."

"Already told you. I had other plans."

Joel pressed his lips together and tamped down his rising anger. When he spoke, his voice was low and soft. "You should be proud of her. She tried real hard to save that child."

"But she didn't. So there was no need for her to have tried, was there?"

The man had no decency.

Joel's thoughts whirled then cleared with startling clarity.

Benjamin didn't love Marcy.

He wanted her, but he didn't love her.

The revelation calmed Joel's spirit. Turning on his heel, he headed for the wagon. If he could see it, surely Marcy could, too. All he had to do was wait.

Chapter Six

After Joel climbed onto the wagon seat and drove away, Marcy let the curtain drop. She wished she'd heard the conversation between him and Benjamin. From their expressions, it hadn't been a good one.

She shouldn't have asked Joel to take her to the funeral. Pa would go to be sure the cross got set correctly. She could go with him. Or if she wanted a different escort, then why not ask her fiancé?

Asking Joel had simply seemed right. Perhaps it was because he had been with her throughout the long evening and night. He'd been the one to comfort her when White Buffalo Girl died. It was only fitting for them to attend the funeral together, too.

She glanced out the window again. Benjamin stood in the front yard, arms crossed as the wagon disappeared from sight. He glanced at the house, the lumber mill, and back at the house. In a few short strides, he was knocking at the door.

With an inward groan, Marcy joined him on the porch.

"You look tired." His voice was kind, his eyes warm.

"I'm fine."

"You've been through a horrible experience, Marcy. You need to rest. To get your strength back." He drew her into a tender embrace. "The funeral can go on without you."

"I need to be there."

"Why?"

She didn't have an answer, not one she could put in words. But deep within her soul she knew she had to see Black Elk and Moon Hawk again. She had to be there when their Beloved Child was laid to rest.

Benjamin had never lost anyone he loved. He would never understand.

"I know what it's like to lose a parent. To lose a child," she shuddered, "I have to be there."

Benjamin pushed her from him and closed his hands around her upper arms. "I forbid it."

"You can't stop me."

"You're not needed there, Marcy."

"Let go of me."

"My parents will not approve. Do you think my mother will be there? What will they think of you?"

The words echoed in Marcy's head—she'd heard versions of them so often. Too often. Always before she'd given in when faced with Benjamin's tiresome argument.

But not this time. She was too weary to care what his parents thought. Bone weary. Soul weary.

She pulled her arms from his loosening grip and rubbed the sore spots. "Surely your parents would feel the same compassion for the loss of a child that I do."

"An Indian child? I don't think so."

His callousness cut into her heart. Joel's reaction had been so different. He hadn't hesitated to do all in his power to help the Ponca.

The contrast couldn't have been greater between the two men.

"I'm going to the funeral, Benjamin. Your parents' opinion of me won't change my mind."

He stared at her, his eyes turning from bluish-gray to a hard steel. She could almost see the wheels turning inside his mind as he considered her unexpected rebellion.

"What about your father?" he finally said, his voice quiet.

"Pa doesn't mind if I go. He understands."

"Will he understand if it costs him trade?"

"What are you talking about?"

"My father sends a great deal of work his way, you know."

"He does?" Momentarily puzzled, Marcy's mind flipped over the commissions her father had in his workshop, the ones he'd worked on in recent months. It was true that he was sought after for his carpentry work. But. . .

"People come to him because he's good at what he does."

"People come to him because they owe my father a favor. Or because they want to ingratiate themselves with him."

"I don't believe it."

"Your belief doesn't change the facts." Benjamin reached for Marcy's hand, but she backed away. He smiled as he gave her a conciliatory look.

"You stood me up last night," he said. "Make it up to me now. Forget the funeral, and we can go on a picnic. You'd like that, wouldn't you?"

"In this weather?"

"If it's not too bad for standing at a grave, it's not too bad for lunch by the river."

"I can't, Benjamin. Not today."

His face smoldered. "Go then."

"I will."

"I'll give my parents your regards. My father will be especially interested to know that your father is making a cross instead of working on the desk he ordered."

"And my father will finish your father's desk when he's good and ready."

"We'll talk about this again later. When you've come to your senses."

Before Marcy could reply, he turned his back to her and headed for town. She waited till he reached the boardwalk, then went inside the house. Shaking with anger, she splashed cool water on her face from the porcelain basin. After unpinning her hair, she pulled the brush through the long strands, yanking at the tangles.

All the while, Benjamin and Joel occupied her thoughts.

She blamed herself for Benjamin's confidence in his ability to bend her to his will. Since the first time they met, she'd allowed him to dictate practically everything she did—the books she read, the events she attended, even the thoughts she had. His mother lavished her with clothes and made Marcy feel guilty when she protested. Eventually the hints, the tacit agreement that she was being groomed to join the prominent family allowed her to take the expensive gifts with a clear conscience.

But months had slipped by, and a formal engagement still had not been announced.

Maybe that was a good thing.

If only Joel hadn't been the one looking for Doc, the one who accompanied her to the army camp. Benjamin suffered by comparison with the compassionate farmer. But why had she never noticed it before?

Because she'd enjoyed Benjamin's attention? Because he made life easy for her?

Because he shielded her from the injustice occurring only a few miles away, from the knowledge that the Ponca were being harassed by their enemies and the army planned to unjustly remove them from their homelands.

She'd been so willing to allow his opinions to be her own.

No more.

Not when she'd seen their suffering with her own eyes. The Ponca loved their home. They didn't want to leave all that was familiar and good.

And they shouldn't have to.

If only there was something she could do to stop them. But what?

She entered her bedroom, an addition Pa had built onto his two-room house shortly before her arrival. The rear window, framed by her grandmother's heirloom lace curtains, overlooked a gentle slope leading to the river. A few trees grew along the bank, their branches vibrant with rain-sprinkled leaves.

Marcy resisted the urge to stretch out on the pastel quilt covering her bed. As tired as she was, she might fall asleep and not waken till tomorrow. Instead she sat on the edge and gave a silent prayer of thanks for the blessing of this comfortable room in this snug little house.

It still didn't feel like home, even though she'd brought her treasures with her on the long journey west.

Her treasures.

The beloved china doll Ma had given her on her sixth birthday. The cedar box, the size of a small valise, that held packets of ribbon-tied letters. All the ones Pa had sent her in what she now thought of as the gray years.

War had been declared, one that pitted family against family, and Ma had moved in with her widowed mother while Pa marched off with the others in his unit. He expected to return home within a few months, but the battles raged on, one after another after another.

By the time he returned, wounded and distant, Ma was buried in the churchyard next to her father. Eight-year-old Marcy didn't recognize the emaciated, limping stranger who'd been gone half her lifetime.

Unable to settle down, Pa soon headed west. Marcy refused to go with him. He wrote her faithfully every week, but she threw the letters away, unopened and unread. Grandma saved them, though, placing each one in the cedar box. When Marcy was a teen and recovering from a serious bout with the influenza, Grandma had handed her the box.

Marcy read the letters and discovered her pa, the wounded carpenter, had a poet's heart. She wrote to him, eagerly awaited his replies, and forgave him all her childhood grievances. When Grandma died, Marcy packed the things she cherished most, sold the rest, and traveled west to join Pa on the Nebraska frontier. Except for missing Grandma terribly, Marcy never regretted the move. But that didn't mean she never got homesick for the southern Ohio hills she loved.

Her move had been her choice. She was free to return if she wished. Or to move somewhere else.

She held the china doll in front of her. "Why don't the Ponca have the same freedom?" she asked. The doll's blue eyes stared. "Why did White Buffalo Girl have to lose her doll?"

What if I could find it?

The thought, a mere whisper, rooted in Marcy's heart. "That would mean going to the village," she whispered. "Pa would never allow it."

Pa didn't need to know.

She rose from the bed and walked to the window. The broad river appeared gray beneath the slate-colored sky, as if all nature mourned the Poncas' loss of their child and their homeland. The rooted thought sprouted, and Marcy knelt on the floor in prayer, her doll clasped in her arms.

"Father, my Lord. A thing is never a substitute for the ones we love. But when Ma died, it kind of helped to have something from her to hold on to. Moon Hawk has nothing. Nothing from her home. Nothing belonging to her precious daughter." Her voice cracked, and she paused to steady her thoughts.

"I'm not sure I can do this, Lord. But the Bible says 'to them that have no might he increaseth strength.' Pa wrote that to me in one of his letters. You gave him the strength to start over out here in this hard country. I'm asking You now to increase my strength. Give me the courage to search for White Buffalo Girl's doll. Give me a plan."

She sat in silence, her knees tucked beneath her skirt, listening for God's still voice. An indescribable peace filled her spirit, and her lips curled upward. She knew exactly what she needed to do.

Chapter Seven

Inside his farmhouse, Joel pulled on a dry shirt and rotated his shoulders. After spending the night in the damp tent, it felt good to be moving his muscles. If only he could rid himself of the ache inside his soul as easily. But he wasn't even sure what caused it—sadness over White Buffalo Girl's death certainly. And also the unfair treatment of the Ponca by high-falutin' officials a thousand miles away who knew nothing about the situation here on the prairie. Who didn't care that the Ponca were the only tribe who had always maintained friendly relationships with the white settlers. Who never caused any trouble to the army but were pestered by warrior tribes.

Yet if those griefs were the only reason, he'd know how to handle them. Something else caught at him like a burr under a saddle.

He only had to close his eyes to know what it was. Every time he did, he saw her face. *Marcy.*

In the few hours he'd tried to sleep, his dreams had been filled with her. Her good-natured laugh as she fixed the bandage on Copper's foot. Her intensity as she did everything she could to save White Buffalo Girl's life. Her grief and helplessness when she failed.

Closing his eyes, he relived the memory of holding her in his arms, of her tears dampening his jaw. It had taken all his self-restraint not to kiss them away and promise he'd never leave her to grieve alone.

◆　◆　◆

As soon as Joel halted in front of the Whitts' home, Marcy came through the door, carrying an oilcloth bundle. He jumped down from the wagon to take it from her. "What's this?"

"A few canned goods and a bag of flour for Moon Hawk. I wish I could do more."

"Almost everybody is contributing something. Word's gotten around, and folks are giving what they can." He placed Marcy's bundle under the wagon seat and went inside the mill to help Mr. Whitt.

At the cemetery, Joel stood beside Marcy as Mr. Whitt packed the rain-soaked dirt around the base of the simple oak cross.

Many of the townspeople, hearing of the child's death, had come to see her buried. It seemed as if everyone was here except the children. They were in the schoolhouse with Miss Taylor. The Hollingsworth family was also conspicuously absent.

No surprise there.

The women dabbed at their eyes with their embroidered handkerchiefs, and more than one man cleared his throat of an unfamiliar lump. Everyone seemed genuinely sorrowful at the loss of the Ponca couple's Beloved Child.

"Moon Hawk isn't here," Marcy whispered.

"Jarrett told me she was too distraught to come," Joel whispered back.

"I'm worried about her."

"She needs time."

"Will time ease her grief?"

He shrugged. The memories of other funerals haunted him—his ma's, Sadie's ma. Then his pa. Grief didn't ease, but time dulled its sharpness. Made it possible to breathe again.

"We need to do something for her."

Marcy had said the same thing on the wagon ride from the lumber mill. She'd sat beside him while Mr. Whitt sat in the back with the newly formed cross. Joel didn't have a response then, and he didn't have one now.

The army had its orders. And the soldiers had guns and bayonets. Another storm darkened the horizon, and Jarrett had told Joel the captain had decided to delay the journey for one more day. But in the morning, the soldiers would force the Ponca to head south. Away from the land of their forefathers. Away from the only home they'd ever known.

The minister closed his eulogy with a word of prayer, and then Jarrett asked for everyone's attention. "Black Elk has a few words he'd like to say."

He stepped forward, his broad face stoic, his back straight. All the murmuring ceased in the pause before he spoke.

"I want the whites to respect the grave of my child," he said, his voice clear and strong, "just as they do the graves of their own dead. The Indians don't like to leave the graves of their dead, but we had to move and hope it will be for the best."

He halted and slightly bowed his head. Not a sound could be heard except for the lonely song of a distant bird.

"I leave the grave in your care. I may never see it again. Care for it for me."

Turning, he left the cemetery, trailed by Jarrett and the Poncas who had accompanied him.

Touched by the words, Joel twisted his hat in his hands. Beside him, Marcy shivered and sniffed. He pulled out his bandanna and handed it to her. She peered at him below her dark lashes and murmured a strangled thank-you.

Mr. Whitt touched Marcy's arm. "We should go home now."

"I'd like to go to the camp," she said.

"Why?"

"I brought food for Moon Hawk."

"You should have given it to Black Elk." Mr. Whitt shook his head, as if he knew it was useless to argue. But he wasn't ready to give in yet. "Marcy, she is grieving. Allow her to grieve in peace."

"Please, Pa. If I don't now, I may never—" Her voice caught again, and she turned away.

"I'll go with her," Joel heard himself volunteer. If only he knew his true motive—to be a helpful neighbor or because he wanted more time alone with her. He gazed into Marcy's hopeful expression. Maybe it was a little bit of both. "That is," he said, "if it's all right with you?"

"Please do." She turned expectantly to her pa, hope written across her face.

"Just don't be gone long," he said, resignedly. "I'm sure Benjamin will be waiting for you at the mill."

Marcy frowned slightly at the mention of Benjamin's name. "Why would he be?"

Mr. Whitt shrugged. "I imagine he wants to keep an eye on you."

"Then he should have been here."

Joel silently agreed, though he wasn't sorry Benjamin had stayed away.

"Don't worry if I'm not home before supper." Marcy lightly kissed her father's cheek. "I want to stay with Moon Hawk as long as possible."

Joel grinned at Mr. Whitt's pretense at grumbling. He hadn't realized how tightly Marcy had her pa wrapped around her little finger.

No real surprise. She had that effect on him, too.

◆　◆　◆

Marcy perched on the wagon seat and prayed the rain-filled clouds wouldn't let loose—at least not yet. The funeral lingered in her imagination, as if she were still there, watching herself mourn. Standing between her pa and a strong, thoughtful man who made her heart flutter.

Not her fiancé.

Joel.

As if he knew she was thinking of him, his elbow bumped hers and he smiled.

"Sadie took that fool rabbit to school with her today."

"How is Copper?"

"Seems to be fine."

"Do you need me to change the bandage?"

"Sadie's taking care of that. Probably more often than it's needed."

"She's such a sweet child."

"She admires you, too."

"Anyone could have cleaned out that cut."

"Maybe. But not everyone can do it the way you do," he said. "Not everyone has your gift."

"It's not a gift."

"What is it then?"

Marcy didn't know. She'd been tending injured animals for as long as she could remember. The compassion she felt, the need to do whatever she could to alleviate pain was central to her being. A fact. She sighed. "It didn't do me any good when it really mattered, did it?"

"There wasn't anything else you could have done. Not even Doc could have comforted that little girl the way you did."

She looked away from him, not wanting him to see the tears that had sprung to her eyes. Besides, she didn't want to talk about the child she couldn't save.

After they rode in silence for a few moments, Joel pulled a piece of paper from his shirt pocket.

"Thought you might want this."

"What is it?"

"What Black Elk said at the funeral. His very words."

Marcy unfolded the paper and read the plea written there. Not that she needed to—the words were already engraved on her heart.

"Thank you." She gazed at Joel's profile, her heart caught in the intensity of his focus as he maneuvered Toby around the worst of the mud-filled ruts. "We need to do this. In all the years to come, we need to do what Black Elk asked."

"The church has already started a fund. For a monument."

"I'm glad." She read the words again and sighed heavily. Inside one of the tents at the army camp, a grieving mother had been too stricken to attend her only child's funeral. The plea Black Elk had made to the people of Neligh would be kept. But would their promise soothe Moon Hawk's heart?

Toby rounded the grove of trees, and Joel's farm came into view.

"You've made this trip quite a few times in the past twenty-four hours," she said.

"I haven't minded."

"I'm grateful for it." She took a deep breath, gathering the courage she needed. If she didn't ask him now, before they rode past his place, it'd be too late. She gazed at him, taken with the scraggly appeal of his profile.

"Joel?"

"Hm?"

"I need a favor."

◆　◆　◆

Surprised and curious, Joel glanced at her. She averted her gaze, looking everywhere but at him.

"What kind of favor?"

"I need to borrow your horse."

More than curiosity twanged at him. "You want to borrow Toby? Why?"

"Actually I hoped you'd lend me Buttermilk. Could we stop at your farm? Please?"

"I thought you wanted to go to the camp."

"I do. But there's somewhere else I need to go first."

Flummoxed by her sudden change in plans, he hardly knew what to think. "Where?"

"If I tell you, you'll only try to stop me."

The scene at the lumber mill that morning flashed through his mind.

"I'm not Benjamin," he said, the words coming out harsher than he intended.

"No, you're not." She bent her head, the gesture fragile and sad. "But you probably won't approve."

A sudden flash of insight revealed her plan as surely as if she'd laid it out for him.

"You want to go to the Ponca village."

She nodded.

"To find White Buffalo Girl's doll?"

"If I can."

"Marcy—"

"It's the only thing I can think of that might bring Moon Hawk some comfort. That's worth something, isn't it?"

"Of course it is." He slowly shook his head. "But to ride to the village? In this weather?

It'll take two hours, maybe three, to get there and back."

He might as well have stayed quiet.

"I have a china doll that belonged to my ma," Marcy said. "It means the world to me, especially since I don't have her."

"I understand that."

"I was looking at it earlier. Couldn't seem to take my eyes off her painted face. That's when it came to me. I have to do this."

"But—"

She twisted on the bench. "Doesn't Sadie have a favorite toy?"

"You mean besides that silly old rabbit?"

"Doesn't she?"

"She sleeps with a doll." A raggedy one that'd been hugged so often its stuffing was almost flat. "Pa got it for her shortly after she was born."

"If—heaven forbid it—but if something happened to Sadie, you'd want to hold on to that doll forever. Wouldn't you?" The words tumbled toward him, quick and passionate. Another side of Marcy he hadn't known existed.

"Truth be told, I never thought about it." He couldn't think about it. They might not have the same ma, but Sadie was his little sister. The only family he had left.

"Wouldn't you?"

"Marcy. . ."

"I bet you'd even hold on to that 'silly old rabbit.'"

She had him there. He accepted his defeat with a heavy sigh. "I suppose I would."

"I need to do this, Joel. Please. May I take Buttermilk?"

"On one condition."

Her face lit up as if he'd promised her the moon. Something he wished he could do. "Anything," she gushed.

"I'm going with you."

Shyness touched her smile. "I'd appreciate that. Very much."

He allowed Toby to follow the road to the farm instead of going past it to the army camp.

"Does your pa know about this?" he asked.

"I left a note. I asked him to be sure Sadie was looked after, too."

Joel didn't know whether to be taken aback by her presumption or proud of her for thinking ahead. Pride won, but he pretended to glare at her. "How'd you know I'd agree to your crazy plan?"

"No harm done if you didn't. Pa would have just been surprised to see you, that's all." She picked at her skirt then met his gaze. "But somehow I knew you would. I prayed. . .so hard."

Joel covered her hand with his and gazed toward the skies. "Won't be long before those clouds open up again. Guess we better saddle up."

Chapter Eight

I'll open the door," Marcy said as Joel halted Toby in front of the barn. Before Joel could stop her, she climbed down from the wagon and pushed open the large door. Toby immediately pulled the wagon inside.

As soon as Joel set the brake, Marcy retrieved her bundle from beneath the wagon seat.

"I can put that in a saddle bag," Joel offered. "We can drop it off on the way."

"It's not just food." Suddenly embarrassed, she shifted from one foot to the other, willing him to read her mind. But he just stared at her, pulling her into the depths of his warm brown eyes. A place she wanted to go more than she cared to admit.

"I need to change clothes," she finally said. "You know. So I can ride."

The corners of his mouth curved slightly upward, and he tilted his head in the direction of the house. "Use Sadie's room. I'll be in soon."

"Thank you." She hitched up her skirt and scurried out the barn door.

Inside the house, she halted. In the main room, a few chairs surrounded a large stone fireplace. A table and cookstove stood opposite. A surprisingly tidy and masculine room. Through an open doorway, a colorful quilt covered a bed pushed against the window. Probably Sadie's.

Marcy glanced at the other door in the room—the closed one. It'd only take a second to peek inside.

But sure as shootin', if she snooped, Joel would catch her.

She entered Sadie's room, smiling at the rag doll propped on the pillow. A beloved toy no little girl should have to leave behind.

◆ ◆ ◆

Joel put together two bedrolls to tie behind the horses' saddles. Hopefully they wouldn't be needed, but he liked to be prepared. He'd already stashed food and a skillet in the saddlebags and scrounged up a slicker for Marcy to wear.

Sadie's door opened, and Marcy entered the room. She wore a flannel shirt—probably her pa's—over a pair of denim dungarees. Her hair was pulled back into one long braid.

"Aren't you a sight," he said.

"I wear these sometimes when Pa needs help at the mill. Not nearly as cumbersome as a dress." She seemed ill at ease, as if unsure what to do or to say.

He snorted to himself. No wonder. He could guess Benjamin Hollingsworth's response to Marcy's unladylike attire. She was probably thinking the same thing.

"You look fine," he said. "Just fine."

Gratefulness shone in her eyes. "You're a good man, Joel Ellison. I'm sorry it's taken me so long to realize it."

"It's not too late, is it?"

She gave a deliberate shrug, and a tiny dimple appeared in one cheek.

He picked up the slicker and handed it to her. "We need to get going or we'll never get back."

"I'm ready."

"Do you have a hat?"

"Just my bonnet."

"Hold on a minute." He entered his room and grabbed his good hat—the one he wore on Sundays. It wouldn't be his good hat after today, but that couldn't be helped. After returning to the main room, he playfully rested it on Marcy's head. "How's that?"

Her blue eyes sparkled beneath the brim. "I think it's 'just fine,'" she teased.

"Then we best get going."

He handed her the bedrolls, threw the saddlebag over his shoulder, and hefted his rifle. He didn't expect to need it, but only a fool rode out to the prairie without a weapon. Besides, they might cross paths with a deer. The Ponca could use the meat.

They finished readying the horses; then Joel led them from the barn. He cast another wary eye at the dark clouds.

"I don't like the look of that sky," he said.

Marcy held his hat in place while she looked upward. "We're going to make it, aren't we?"

For the first time, he heard a tremor of doubt in her voice.

"Come here," he said softly.

She joined him, and he gestured for her to put her foot in the stirrup. As soon as she was astride Buttermilk, he placed his hand over hers. "Are you ready?"

"Yes."

"We'll make it." He forced a reassuring smile and mounted Toby. *Help us make it, Lord.*

◆　◆　◆

Marcy trailed slightly behind Joel as he headed north toward the Niobrara River. She didn't want to think about how swollen the river might be, or how they would get to the other side where the Ponca village was located. They just had to—that's all. Somehow they had to.

For Moon Hawk's sake.

She glanced in the direction of the army camp and pulled up short. On this side of the camp stood a black buggy. Benjamin's buggy.

As she stared, Benjamin stood and waved his arms. Despite the distance, there was no mistaking his message. The men's clothing hadn't hidden her identity, and he wanted her to join him.

She wheeled Buttermilk back toward Joel, who stared at Benjamin.

"Hollingsworth?" he asked as she pulled beside him.

"I'm not going back with him."

"You don't have to."

"He said he'd ruin Pa. That no one would order anything from him again."

"I will."

A smile tugged at her lips, but she quivered inside.

"Other people will, too," Joel said. "Hollingsworth may think he and his family run the town, but they don't. That was pretty obvious when you look at who showed up for the funeral this morning."

"You're right." She glanced from him back to the buggy. Benjamin was driving it their way. "He's coming."

"What are you going to do?"

The verse she'd prayed this morning resounded in her heart. *He giveth power to the faint; and to them that have no might he increaseth strength.*

She needed strength now. Strength to do what she needed to do. Strength to be her own person instead of Benjamin's prize possession.

"I'm going to the village." She left the rest unsaid.

As long as you come with me.

◆　　◆　　◆

"What about him?" Joel asked, tilting his head toward the approaching buggy.

"I don't want to hear anything he has to say," Marcy replied. "Do you?"

"No, ma'am."

She wheeled Buttermilk around and urged her into a gallop.

Joel waited two heartbeats, long enough to see the buggy sway as it picked up speed. If Hollingsworth weren't careful, he'd capsize on the uneven ground. Something Joel wouldn't mind seeing some other time. He turned Toby's head and raced after Marcy.

They ran for a couple of miles; then Joel slowed to a walk and looked behind him. The buggy no longer followed them. Marcy drew up beside him.

"What do you think he's doing?" she asked.

"Regretting he's not on horseback."

Marcy patted Buttermilk's neck. "He still wouldn't have caught us."

Joel smiled at her faith in the mare's speed then frowned. Hollingsworth no longer pursued them, but that only delayed their confrontation. Once they returned, Joel had no doubt he'd have to defend his actions.

And not only to Benjamin.

"Your pa is liable to tan my hide when we get back. Can't say I'd blame him."

"I won't let him."

"You think he'll ban me from your presence?"

"Never."

"I hope you're right." If Marcy meant what she said about not wanting to be with Hollingsworth anymore, then Joel intended to court her.

They eased into a walk, directing the horses across the prairie in companionable silence. Joel soon realized they were riding parallel to the path the Ponca had made a couple of days before. The wet ground had been churned by feet and hooves, a rough and muddy testament to the forced march.

Every few moments, Joel glanced toward Marcy. She had the slicker buttoned up to her throat, and her face was barely visible beneath the too-large hat. Whatever her thoughts, she held them deep inside where no one could see.

Perhaps the hardship of this trip was more than she expected. She'd been so focused on Moon Hawk's grief she probably hadn't considered how miserable it'd be to ride all the way to the village in this weather.

For quite a while, rain had been spitting on them. Just enough to be bothersome. But he suspected the skies to open up any minute. They'd need to find shelter when it did.

He directed Toby across the trail created by the army and the Ponca, then headed slightly west. A few moments later, Marcy sidled closer to him.

"Shouldn't we be going this way?" She pointed toward the swath of muddied ruts.

"With all this rain, the crossing near the village will be too dangerous. I know a safer place a few miles from there."

"But it'll take us longer."

"We won't get there at all if we can't get across the Niobrara."

"Shouldn't we at least try?"

"What you want to do is a good thing, Marcy. I'm proud to help you do it. But I'm not risking your life for a toy."

"I can take care of myself."

"Then I'm not risking my horses."

The stubborn set of her jaw lessened. "I wouldn't want you to."

They rode in silence for several minutes. Suddenly lightning ripped apart the sky, and Buttermilk reared. Marcy held her seat and tightened her grip on the reins.

"Easy, girl," she said. "Easy."

Thunder rumbled, pushing heavy clouds their way. Buttermilk whinnied as she high-stepped and flung her head. Joel maneuvered Toby close to the mare and grabbed the reins near the bit.

"Whoa, there."

Buttermilk quickly settled at the sound of his voice, though her ears remained flattened.

"Are you all right?" he asked Marcy. She nodded, but anxiety showed in her eyes. "I can lead her."

Marcy flashed an uneasy smile. But before she could answer, the clouds descended upon them. Rain poured over the brim of his hat, momentarily obscuring his vision. Marcy bent her head against the drenching deluge. He tried to search through the downpour for cover, though the plains offered little shelter. They needed to get across the river.

"There's an old trapper's cabin not far from here," he shouted above the din.

"We can't stop."

"We don't have a choice." Lightning flashed, and Buttermilk reared again. Marcy gasped but managed to keep her balance.

Joel took Marcy's reins and maneuvered the horses alongside each other. He held out his arm. "Come here."

She hesitated then reached for him. He pulled her close, holding her tight as she slid from Buttermilk's back. Their eyes met, and the world seemed to fade away. The storm, the vast plains, the sodden ground—for one unforgettable moment, none of it mattered. Rain clung to her hair, to her thick lashes, and she had never looked more beautiful. He longed to kiss her, but he didn't dare. Like it or not, at least for now, Benjamin Hollingsworth was still her beau.

He settled her in front of him and touched his heels to Toby's flanks.

Chapter Nine

By the time they reached the river, the rain had lessened. Marcy silently prayed as Joel rode along the water's edge and scouted for the best place to cross. The Isaiah passage had become her mantra. *Give power to the faint, Lord. Increase my strength.*

"It's not as deep here," he said. "But it's wider because of all the rain."

"I'm not afraid." To her surprise, the words were true.

When Buttermilk reared, Marcy's insides had been as queasy as churned-up cream. But she'd been even more afraid Joel would head back to Neligh, and they'd come too far to return empty-handed.

But her fear had melted away as they rode together toward the river. Though the rain battered them, she felt secure with his strong arms around her. His closeness comforted her and kindled an unfamiliar warmth she found perturbing yet exciting.

The memory of him taking her from Buttermilk, of clasping her to his chest, made her breathless. She thought he might kiss her. She wanted to kiss him.

She still wanted to kiss him.

As if he'd read her mind, Joel leaned forward. "This looks like a good place."

She slightly turned toward him, and his breath warmed her ear.

"We might get wet," he said.

"Wetter than we already are?"

"River water's not the same as rainwater." He gave Buttermilk additional slack. "Hang on. Here we go."

Toby reluctantly waded into the water. Marcy focused on the opposite bank, squeezed her eyes shut then opened them again. The river soon lapped at her boots then her pant legs. But under Joel's firm-but-gentle guidance, Toby never floundered.

"You were right about a different kind of wet," Marcy said. The dungarees seemed to wick the river water straight to her waist.

"We'll be at the cabin in just a couple of minutes."

"Please don't stop because of me. I'm fine."

"I'm sure you are. But these horses need a rest."

She nodded agreement, but then a thought struck her. "This is the second time you've used the horses as an excuse to get your way."

He chuckled. "Not an excuse. A reason."

"I just wanted you to know I noticed."

" 'A righteous man regardeth the life of his beast.' "

"Is that scripture?"

"Proverbs 12:10."

"Why do you know that?"

"Pa used to say it when I was a boy and wanted to go fishing instead of tending the stock. I guess it stuck with me."

They neared the bank, and Toby picked up his pace.

"He also said to never trust a man who didn't take care of his horse before he took care of himself."

"My pa says the same." She idly wondered if Benjamin knew of that verse. Probably not. His family went to church every Sunday. Almost everyone in Neligh did. But she couldn't think of a time when he quoted scripture. Or anything his pa had taught him as a boy. In fact, their relationship sometimes seemed tense. She'd said something to him once about it, and he'd laughed at her. Told her she was imagining things.

She'd accepted his reassurance at the time. But now she wasn't so sure. It was as if she'd created her own set of blinders. Focused only on what was good about Benjamin—his gallant flirting, the way he spoiled her with gifts, the pride he took in having her beside him—she'd ignored his faults.

Her eyes closed. Not to shut out the river but to shut out her own shallow heart. Had she really convinced herself she loved a man because he gave her presents?

Toby scrambled up the bank, and Joel spoke into her ear. "Look. There's the cabin."

She opened her eyes and gazed upriver toward a clump of trees growing along the bank. Nestled among them was a cabin and lean-to. "I see it."

I see a lot of things.

Joel had taken the blinders from her eyes. Whether he meant to or not, he'd also taken her heart.

He might not have Benjamin's social status, but in every way that mattered, he was the better man. Everything that had happened since Joel walked into Doc's office had showed her what she really wanted. What she needed.

Not gifts and prestige, but a comforting shoulder for her grief. An understanding spirit for her outlandish schemes.

Someone who stayed beside her during a monstrous thunderstorm and a hazardous river crossing. During a long, sleepless night with a dying child.

Joel. She needed Joel.

◆　◆　◆

For about the tenth time in less than two minutes, Joel pulled his pa's gold watch from his pocket. The cabin provided shelter but little warmth. Marcy had managed to light a fire while he tended the horses, but she could only use the kindling in the fireplace. The few logs stacked by the hearth were damp. The incessant rain seemed to permeate everything.

Marcy sat beside the fire, feeding it sticks and scraps of paper she'd found. She didn't complain about the cold or the damp, but she was obviously chilled.

Joel peered through what passed for a window in this abandoned place—a chink between two logs. The rain had stopped, but the skies threatened more to come. Perhaps they should stay in the cabin. Perhaps they'd already stayed too long.

They'd be at the village in five or ten minutes, but they still had to find the doll and then make the long trek home. The day didn't hold many more hours.

"Rain's let up," he said.

Marcy rose and brushed dirt from her pants. Not that it did any good. "We should go then."

"We don't both need to go."

Her mouth gaped open, and he hurried to speak before she did.

"You can stay here. At least you'll be dry. The village isn't far, and I promise you, if the doll is there, I'll find it. I won't be gone long."

"You want to leave me?"

Her voice sounded surprised, which he expected. But also hurt. It lay in her eyes, too, and her questioning gaze told him the question went deeper than a temporary departure. He took a step toward her then stopped and clenched his fists. As much as he wanted to take her into his arms, to whisper that if she'd have him he'd never leave her, he wouldn't do it.

"I can go faster alone."

"This is something I have to do." She blinked then stared at the dying fire. "I thought you understood."

"It won't bring her back, Marcy."

"I know." Her voice cracked, and her shoulders sagged. "But at least I'd have succeeded at something."

His willpower broke. Next thing he knew, she was in his arms, her head buried in his shoulder. Right where she belonged. Right where he needed her. He held her tight, his jaw pressed against her temple, while he regained his composure.

"We'll go together," he finally said and pulled away. "I'll saddle the horses."

He grabbed his hat and walked out the door. The chilled air, scented with rain, enveloped him as he braced against the wind on his way to the lean-to.

No matter what, they had to find that doll.

◆　◆　◆

Marcy halted Buttermilk beside Joel and leaned forward in the saddle. The last time she'd seen the village, children had chased one another in the open area between the earth lodges and pine cabins. Women gossiped around communal cooking fires, and men encircled Pa's wagon to catch their first glimpse of the table he'd made for Chief Standing Bear.

The contrast between that sun-filled day and this dismal one pressed on her spirit. Debris blew between the dwellings, and a haunting emptiness filled the place.

Blankets, kettles, even a bow—things the Ponca needed for the arduous trek south—were scattered in the mud and muck. Useless and ruined.

The wastefulness, the heartlessness appalled her.

"I don't understand." she said. "Why did the army have to be so destructive?"

Joel shrugged, but the disgusted expression on his face spoke volumes.

Doors stood ajar on a few of the houses. The adjacent gardens, once thriving with vegetables and colorful flowers, were now crushed as if the army horses had deliberately trotted through them.

White Buffalo Girl's doll could be anywhere.

"Where do we start?" Marcy asked.

"Perhaps the lodge. They might have gathered everyone there before setting out."

"It's as good a place as any."

They walked their horses past an upended wagon. One back wheel had splintered, and its jagged spoke seemed to pierce Marcy's heart. She maneuvered Buttermilk around the debris then dismounted in front of the long structure.

Joel dismounted, too, and looped the horses' reins at a nearby railing.

Marcy entered the lodge but stopped in momentary confusion. A fire blazed in the central hearth, and two men emerged from the shadows.

"Hello, Marcy," Benjamin said. "What took you so long?"

Chapter Ten

Joel positioned himself slightly ahead of Marcy and kicked himself for leaving his rifle in its scabbard. Not that he planned to shoot anyone. But Hollingsworth and his pal both wore pistols strapped to their legs, and he didn't.

"What are you doing here?" he asked with more bravado than he felt.

"Came to get what's mine."

"What's that?"

"She's standing right beside you."

He swaggered toward Marcy, a self-confident smirk plastered on his face. A smirk Joel ached to punch.

Hollingsworth took Marcy's hand and stroked it between his. "We have an understanding, you and I. And this"—he eyed Joel and gave a haughty sniff—"farmer isn't going to interfere with that anymore."

"I haven't interfered with anything," Joel said, keeping his tone even. The best thing he could do to protect Marcy was to stay calm. "We're here to look for a child's toy. The sooner we find it, the sooner we can all go home."

"I don't care about no Injun toy," Hollingsworth said.

"But I do." Marcy insisted. "Since you're here, you can help me find it."

"Did you hear that, Cade?" Though he talked to his partner, Hollingsworth never took his eyes from Marcy. Zachariah Cade had been Benjamin's tagalong for years. He didn't say much to anyone, but his cold eyes and grim smile told the world not to mess with him. Cade took a few steps closer to Joel then stood, legs apart and arms crossed.

Hollingsworth continued, the polish of his voice giving way to a slow twang. "Marcy here wants us to help her find that Injun toy. Says then we can all go home. All friendly and companionable."

Cade grunted.

Marcy glanced around the lodge, an uneasy smile pasted on her face. Joel looked around, too. The furniture in the large room—white man's furniture introduced to the Ponca by hunters and trappers before Neligh was settled—had been pushed to the earthen walls. A variety of objects were scattered around the floor, items left behind by a people forced to leave in haste.

"Might as well start in here," he said.

"Good idea." Marcy tried to pull her hand from Hollingsworth's grasp, but he didn't let go.

"We're going back to town," he said. "Now."

"I'm not going without that doll."

"Ellison can stay behind and look for it." He glared at Joel. "Wouldn't bother me none if he stayed away for good. What do you think of that, Cade?"

"Fine plan." Cade's hand dropped to his side, threateningly close to his holster.

Fear sliced like a razor down Joel's spine. He didn't doubt he could best either man in a fair fight. He might even hold his own against the two of them as long as fists were the only weapon. But Hollingsworth, like most bullies, depended on Cade to do his dirty work. And Cade appeared itchy to use that gun.

He needed to get Marcy out of there, even if it meant sending her back to Neligh with Hollingsworth. She'd be safe. . .as long as she cooperated.

"I'll stay," he said. "Just take Marcy home."

"No," Marcy exclaimed. "I'm not leaving."

"Go with him, Marcy." Joel held her gaze, willing her to understand he only wanted to protect her. "I won't be far behind."

"Joel. . ."

"Go."

She bowed her head, and a triumphant smile creased Hollingsworth's gloating expression. "Told you they'd listen to reason, didn't I, Cade?" He released Marcy's hand and gripped her arm.

"Your horse out front?"

"Yes. Where's yours?"

"Not far from here. We hid them so as not to ruin the surprise. You were surprised to see me, weren't you, Marcy?"

"Very. I never expected you to travel in weather like this."

"I'd travel through Noah's flood to get back what's mine. So you can imagine what I'd do to someone who tried to *take* what was mine. That's why we've got to teach Ellison here a lesson. Don't we, Cade?"

Joel clenched and unclenched his fists, shifting his focus from Marcy to Cade and back again. Marcy's eyes were round with fear, and she turned to Hollingsworth.

"What are you going to do to him?"

"Teach him his place is all."

She stared at Joel, and he gave her an encouraging smile. "Just do what he says, and you'll be fine."

"What about you?"

"I'll be fine, too."

"Don't be so sure." Hollingsworth nodded to Cade. Marcy squirmed, trying to escape from his grasp, but he held her by both arms and pushed her from the lodge.

Joel focused on Cade, who slowly circled him. Pretending to back away, Joel shrugged off his slicker and maneuvered close to a broken chair near the central fire.

"Shooting an unarmed man is murder," he said. "That's a hanging offense in these parts."

"Not going to shoot you."

"Then why're you still wearing that gun?"

Cade smirked, slowly pulled the gun from the holster, and pointed it toward Joel. "Got rope back there." He waved the gun's barrel toward a far corner. "Going to tie you up."

"I don't think so."

Cade's cold eyes blinked, and he pointed the gun toward Joel's feet and fired. Joel leaped back, grabbed the chair, and flung it at Cade. When Cade raised his arm to block the blow, Joel rushed him. The men fell, tripping over each other and the chair. They grappled, and Joel managed to connect his fist with Cade's jaw. The gun fell to the dirt floor, and Joel wrestled Cade away from it.

◆　◆　◆

Marcy struggled to free herself from Benjamin's grasp, but he held her too tightly. When the door of the lodge closed behind them, he shoved her against the exterior wall.

"Enough of this nonsense," he said. "Do you have any idea what people are saying in town about you? What do you think you're doing riding off with that farmer? It's indecent."

"What about what you're doing? Treating me like a child. As if I didn't have a brain of my own."

"I'm not marrying you for your brain, Marcy."

"I'm not marrying you at all."

He stared at her, and all her bravado faded away under the chill of his glare. He leaned close and whispered. "You don't know me very well if you think that decision is yours to make. It's not too late for Cade to arrange a little accident for your friend in there. Do you understand me?"

Marcy's voice failed her. She had never before thought Benjamin capable of such cruelty. But there was no mistaking his threat. To protect Joel, she had to do what he said.

Taking her silence for acquiescence, Benjamin pushed her toward Buttermilk and boosted her into the saddle. Then he loosened Toby's reins from the railing and smacked him on the flanks with his hat.

"What are you doing?"

"Looks like Ellison's horse ran off. Guess he'll have to walk back to Neligh."

"In this weather?"

"He can hole up here in the village till the rain clears up." He took hold of Buttermilk's bridle. "Might be several days before he makes it back to town."

Marcy looked over her shoulder at the lodge as if her watchful eye could keep Joel safe. It was nonsense, of course. But what else could she do? When she turned around again, she realized Benjamin was leading Buttermilk toward the Niobrara.

"Aren't you going to wait for Cade?"

"He knows how to get home."

"What about the river? How did you get across?"

"Those Injuns keep boats on both sides of the shore. It wasn't easy to get across, but I'm a determined man. And I was determined to come after you."

"Your horses are on the other side?"

"That's right. We saw the tracks where you and Ellison went to the upper ford. Figured I'd get to the village before you did. Then all we had to do was wai—"

A shot exploded behind them, and both Marcy and Benjamin seemed momentarily paralyzed.

"Was that. . . ?" The words clogged in Marcy's throat.

Benjamin's eyes flicked toward the village. "I didn't mean. . . I told Cade not to shoot."

Marcy slid off Buttermilk, and Benjamin grasped her arm. "You have to believe me. No one was supposed to get hurt." He gave her a shaky smile. "Cade's probably just having some fun. To shake Ellison up a bit."

"Let go of me."

"You can't go back there, Marcy."

"Don't you tell me what I can and can't do." She shoved him, and he loosened his grip. "Ever again."

"I'm not." He blocked her path. For the first time that day, he sounded sincere. Almost apologetic even. "I'm, believe it or not, I'm trying to protect you. Cade can get mean when he's riled."

Tears burned Marcy's eyes, but she didn't cry. "I thought I loved you. But I don't even know you."

She pushed against him and ran toward the earth lodge. The slick mud caused her to fall, and her knee scraped against a partially buried rock. Dismissing the pain, she stumbled to her feet. Only one thing mattered. Getting to Joel.

◆　◆　◆

Joel and Cade rolled and punched, rose to their feet and punched again. Joel brushed blood from his chin as Cade slashed the air with a knife. The silver blade gleamed in the firelight. Joel instinctively raised his arm to block the attack. The blade gashed his forearm, and he cried out in anguish. Cade struck again, sinking the blade into Joel's shoulder.

The searing pain caused him to stagger. Starbursts momentarily blinded him. Sensing Cade closing in, Joel rammed him. The sudden attack pushed Cade to the edge of the fire. Flames licked his foot. He dropped the knife and hurriedly removed the burning boot. Joel used the distraction to retrieve the knife and the gun.

Ignoring the blood seeping from his shoulder and arm, he took several deep breaths to calm his racing heart. He directed the gun at Cade's chest.

The door burst open and a gust of rain-chilled air swept through the lodge. Marcy stood at the entrance, her eyes focused on him.

"We heard a gunshot." The words tumbled out in a rush. "I had to be sure. . . ."

He backed toward her, keeping a wary eye on Cade. "Are you hurt?" he asked, wincing in pain.

"I'm fine." Her expert fingers lightly touched the cuts and bruises on his face. Her eyes widened as the blood from his shoulder and forearm caught her attention. "Were you shot?"

"Knife."

She glared at Cade, who held his burnt boot at his side.

"I need to tie him up." Joel didn't know how much longer he could stay upright, let alone keep the gun pointed at Cade.

"I need to tend your wounds."

"Cade first." He thrust the gun toward him. "Take off your other boot."

Cade's stone-cold eyes flashed with resentment, but he sat on the earthen floor and removed his boot.

"Where's Hollingsworth?" Joel asked.

"I don't know. We were headed for the river when we heard the shots."

"He let you go?"

"He didn't stop me." She touched his injured arm. "We need to get you home."

"What about the doll?"

"You're more important."

"I'll be fine. Let's do what we came here to do."

She started to protest, but he cupped her face in his hand. Her blue eyes, tender and soft, gazed into his. Despite the agonizing pain, the oozing blood, and being chilled to the bone, there was no place he'd rather be.

Chapter Eleven

I t's no use," Marcy said after they returned to the earthen lodge. They had searched every house and walked the grounds but to no avail. "The doll isn't here."

"She may have dropped it on the way to the camp."

Hope flared inside Marcy, but one look at Joel and she let it die. She couldn't ask him to follow the trail from the village back to Neligh. Not in his condition.

His lower lip was swollen, and a purple bruise distorted his cheek and jaw. She had cleaned his stab wounds as best she could and fashioned a sling out of a discarded shirt. But he needed more care than she could provide in this deserted place.

"There's nowhere else to look," she said.

"You tried, Marcy." He sounded weary, and she knew he was in pain. He needed to be home, to have the knife wounds properly cleaned and bandaged. She lowered herself to the floor beside him and held her hands to the low-burning fire.

"I was so sure I'd find it. That God had led me here."

"Maybe he did. But for another purpose."

"What purpose?"

"You tell me."

The words from Isaiah, the words she'd been praying all day, echoed in her thoughts. "I asked God to increase my strength. To give me courage."

"I'd say he answered that prayer."

"I don't feel very courageous."

Joel put his uninjured arm around her shoulder and drew her close. "You did what you needed to do. Despite the weather. Despite being told no." He paused to take several deep breaths. "That kind of strength comes from your heart."

Drained by talking, he closed his eyes. She wished she could let him sleep, but it was more important for them to get back to town. If they stayed here and he became feverish in the night, she'd have no way to ease his discomfort.

She had no idea how to get him home. She'd been surprised to find Buttermilk tied to the railing, but Benjamin had disappeared and so had Toby. And as much as she'd like to, they couldn't leave Cade here alone. He sat on the other side of the fire, bootless, with hands and ankles tied in secure knots.

Lord, I need You to increase my strength again. How are we ever going to get home?

◆ ◆ ◆

Marcy raised her eyes to Cade's. "You have to help us."

"Why would I?"

"Because if you don't, we'll leave you here."

THE

"Heartless thing to do."

She resisted the urge to point out his heartlessness in stabbing Joel. "Benjamin ran off one of our horses, and now he's gone. You need our help as much as we need yours."

"Making a deal?"

"If Joel dies, you'll be wanted for murder. It's in your best interest to keep him alive."

He worked his jaw, as if chewing tobacco, then spat and looked at her expectantly.

"Get us to the other side of the river, along with our horse."

"Then what?"

"I'll let you have your boots."

"Need my boots to cross the river."

"Not really." She gestured meaningfully toward Joel. "At least you're not bleeding to death."

"Once we cross?"

"We go our separate ways."

"What if my horse ain't where I left her?"

"That's between you and Benjamin."

He chewed on his imaginary tobacco, his stare never wavering. Marcy stared back. "Won't be easy getting your horse across."

"But you'll try?"

"More than try." He snorted. "I'll do it."

"Thank you, Cade." She picked up his boots and headed for the door.

"Where you taking those?"

"I'm hiding them."

"You ain't serious."

She smiled sweetly then left the lodge. Once outside, she paused a moment to take a deep breath and settle her nerves. Her hope of finding comfort for Moon Hawk had endangered Joel's life, and now she had no choice but to trust Zachariah Cade to keep his word. It didn't help that she'd be going home empty-handed.

She carried the boots to a house on the edge of the village and tossed them inside the door. On her way back to the lodge, a spot of color by the upturned wagon caught her attention. A small clump of yellow daisies clung to life amid the mud and the debris.

Beauty among ashes.

Marcy couldn't remember where she'd heard the phrase before, but it gave her an idea. Using a stick as a makeshift trowel, she dug around the daisies and placed the root ball and flowers in an abandoned wooden bowl.

White Buffalo Girl's doll seemed lost forever, but Moon Hawk could travel south with a little bit of beauty from her home.

◆ ◆ ◆

Joel dreamed he was floating downriver in a canoe covered with buffalo skins. Water lapped the boat, and sometimes it fell on his skin. Refreshing, cool water that soothed his parched throat and eased the burning of the sun. He drifted in and out of the dream until an angel called his name.

He recognized the angel's voice. He listened for it every Sunday when they sang the hymns, and her clear soprano tugged at his heartstrings.

Marcy's voice.

Marcy's healing touch.

His eyes flickered open, but he didn't want to wake up. He didn't want to leave the dream.

"Joel," her voice whispered. "Can you hear me?"

He moved his hand and felt her fingers clasp his. She was with him. He could sleep.

◆　◆　◆

The sun neared the horizon to Marcy's right as they followed the broad rutted path the army and Ponca had created on their journey south. Mercifully, the rain had ceased shortly after they crossed the river.

Cade found his horse where he'd left her, though Benjamin's was gone. Apparently Cade could only hold a grudge against one person at a time. With his anger directed toward Benjamin for leaving him, he couldn't do enough for Marcy. They got Joel on Buttermilk with Marcy riding behind him. Even though he was bootless, Cade wouldn't leave her to ride across the prairie with an unconscious man.

When they were within a couple of miles of the army camp, Cade halted.

"Guess you won't be seein' me in town no more."

"Where will you go?"

He gave an elaborate shrug, chewed nothing, and spat. "Thinking about Mexico."

"Long way."

"First I gotta get my boots."

"I'm sorry I hid them."

"Sorry I fought Ellison." His jaw worked, and he opened and closed his mouth.

Tired as she was, and as much as she wanted to be home, Marcy patiently waited for him to say what was on his mind. Finally he cleared his throat.

"Never liked him much."

"Why not?"

He stared at her, but the coldness was gone from his eyes. "He works too hard."

Unexpected laughter bubbled inside Marcy. "That's a bad thing?"

Again, he took his time answering. "Not my philosophy."

Zachariah Cade had a philosophy? True, the cowboy appeared more at ease astride his horse than he did on his own two legs. That's where he belonged. Not working a steady job and definitely not doing Benjamin's bidding.

"I think I understand," Marcy said.

"You're fine now?"

"We are. Thank you, Zachariah."

He tipped his hat, wheeled his horse, and trotted north to the Niobrara.

◆　◆　◆

Joel awoke to the sound of voices, but he cared about only one. He didn't open his eyes, waiting, waiting to hear her speak.

"I'm ashamed of him." The deep voice was familiar, but Joel couldn't place it at first. "That a son of mine would behave in such a way."

Mr. Hollingsworth. Benjamin's father.

"I think the gunshot scared him."

Marcy.

Joel smiled, but his lips hurt too much. A damp cloth caressed his mouth, and his eyes flickered open.

"You're awake."

His angel.

"Where are we?"

"At the camp."

His head spun as he tried to fit together puzzle pieces that didn't match. They'd been in the lodge. Cade tied up by the fire. Marcy wrapping a cloth around his arm.

Blood, his blood, oozing from his wounds.

He forced his eyes to stay open, to gaze at Marcy's lovely smile while she dabbed his face with the cool cloth.

"How did we. . .?"

"I'll tell you all about it later. For now, you need to sleep. To get well."

"Cade?"

"He's gone."

Mr. Whitt appeared in Joel's line of vision. "No need to worry about him, son. He'd be a fool to show his face around here again."

Marcy bent over him and whispered, "We're home."

◆　◆　◆

Once Joel's even breathing assured Marcy he was sleeping peacefully, she joined her father outside the tent. The full moon cast its pale light, and a handful of stars twinkled in the cloudy sky. Pa stood with Mr. Jarrett, the Indian agent, and Black Elk.

"How is he?" Pa asked as he wrapped a blanket around her shoulders.

"Sleeping. Finally."

"We'll take him to his place in the morning. Get him settled."

"There's no one there to look after him. Only Sadie, and she's too young for that much responsibility."

"If it'll ease your mind, we'll take him to our place then."

"Thank you, Pa." She kissed his cheek and breathed in the familiar fragrance of sawdust and varnish.

"I do not understand," Black Elk said. "Why you rode to my village."

"I tried to explain," Mr. Jarrett said with a shrug. "But I have to say I don't quite understand it myself."

Marcy wasn't sure she did, either. At least not in a way that would make sense. "How is Moon Hawk?" she asked instead.

"She is not well."

"May I see her?"

"She has seen no one." Black Elk hesitated then bowed his head. "But I will take you to her. I do not know what she will say."

"Thank you. I'll be with you in a minute."

She returned to the tent where Joel was sleeping and retrieved the wooden bowl from Buttermilk's saddlebag. Cade had wrapped it in his bandanna. Another unexpected kindness from the strange cowboy.

Black Elk accompanied her to his tent then held up his hand. "Wait here."

"Of course."

He disappeared for a moment then opened the flap and motioned for Marcy to enter. Moon Hawk sat near the fire, her head bent in sorrow. Marcy knelt beside her and removed the bandanna. The clump of daisies, only a little ragged from being in a jostling saddlebag, seemed to glow in the light of the burning flame.

Perhaps her tired eyes were playing tricks. But Marcy didn't really think so.

She handed the bowl to Moon Hawk. "This is for you. From your home."

Black Elk translated, and Moon Hawk looked at Marcy with her tear-reddened eyes. She accepted the gift and cradled it in her lap. Her fingers traced the delicate leaves and petals. When she spoke, her words sounded almost musical.

"She says she will always remember you, especially in the spring when the yellow flowers bloom."

"I'll remember her, too." Tears slipped down Marcy's cheeks. "And your Beloved Child. Always."

Chapter Twelve

Marcy said a little prayer then laid the bouquet of wildflowers on White Buffalo Girl's grave. A month had passed since the Ponca camped near Neligh, since she spent a long, rain-drenched night desperately trying to save the life of the eighteen-month-old child.

The spring rains had finally ended, and today's June sun lit up a blue sky graced with white fluffy clouds.

Joel approached from the cemetery gate, carrying a bouquet of his own. "I don't mean to interrupt."

"You're not."

He placed his flowers beside hers then squeezed her hand. "We'll keep our promise to Black Elk."

"As long as we live."

They stood in silence for a few moments. Finally they followed the path to the gate. When they reached the wooden bridge, they paused and gazed at the flowing stream.

"I saw Mr. Hollingsworth in town a little while ago," Joel said. "He got a letter from Benjamin."

"Where is he?"

"Didn't say. But he's not coming back to Neligh."

"I guess that means I won't be marrying him."

Joel took both her hands in his. "Then perhaps you'd consider marrying me."

"Perhaps I will."

She gently touched his cheek then shivered with expectation as his mouth hovered above hers.

Within his arms, she was home.

Johnnie Alexander writes stories of heritage and hope while raccoons and foxes occasionally pass her window. *Where Treasure Hides*, her debut novel, has been translated into Dutch and Norwegian. Her Misty Willow contemporary romance series includes *Where She Belongs* and *When Love Arrives*. Johnnie treasures family memories, classic movies, road trips, and stacks of books. She lives near Memphis with a herd of alpacas and Rugby, the princely papillon who trees those pesky raccoons whenever he gets the chance.

The Doctor's
Woman

by Michelle Griep

Dedication:

As always and forever, to the lover of my soul.

Acknowledgments:

Mark Griep ~ for putting up with me for thirty-two years
Ane Mulligan & Elizabeth Ludwig ~ for your sweet slash-and-burn skills
Shannon McNear ~ for sharing your horse expertise and encouragement
Annie Tipton ~ for believing in me and my writing
Joe Whitson & Matthew Cassady ~ for your wealth of historical information

Chapter One

Mendota, Minnesota
1862

Emmy Nelson had lived with death for as long as she could remember. She'd watched it happen. Witnessed the devastating effects. Wept with and embraced those howling in grief. Even lost her betrothed—a man she respected, maybe even loved.

But she'd never tasted the true bitterness of it until now—and the acrid flavor drove her to her knees. Early-November leaves crackled like broken bones beneath her weight, but alone at last, she gave in.

"Oh, Papa."

Did that ragged voice really belong to her?

Her tears washed onto his grave like a benediction. How long she lay there, crying, she couldn't say; long enough, though, to warrant Aunt Rosamund's manservant, Jubal Warren, to put an end to it.

"Miss Emmaline." Jubal's footsteps padded across the backyard of the home she'd shared with her father, stopping well behind her. "Time we leave, child."

Swallowing back anguish, she forced sorrow deep and waited until it lodged behind her heart. She'd pull it out later, when there were no eyes to watch her grieve.

She flattened her palm on the freshly dug earth and whispered, "Neither of us wanted to say good-bye, did we, Papa?"

Overhead, tree branches groaned in the wind. Fitting, really. The death of a dream and a loved one ought to be blessed with a dirge.

"Miss Emmaline?" Jubal insisted.

This was it, then. Slowly, she rose, wiping the dirt from her hands and the pain from her soul. For now, anyway. She'd put off moving to Aunt Rosamund's in Minneapolis far too long. But walking away from a lifelong hope of settling in Mendota took more than courage.

It took time.

"Doc Nelson? Doctor!" Men's shouts carried from the front of the house. Clearly the news of her father's death hadn't spread as far as she'd imagined.

With a last sniffle, Emmy turned her back on her past and walked away, Jubal at her heels.

In front of the cottage, two lathered horses snorted on the road, distressing her own mare, hitched to a packed cart in front of them. Their riders—dressed in military blue—pounded on the office door. "Doc, open up! There's been an accident."

"I'm sorry, gentlemen, but you'll find no help here."

They pivoted at her voice. Sweat dotted the brow of the shorter man, confusion the other. "Excuse us, miss, but. . ." The taller of the two squinted. "Hey, yer the doc's daughter. Sorry to bother you, Miss Nelson, but where's he at? We need him."

"The doctor. . .my father. . ." She glanced at Jubal for help. How to explain when her chest cinched so tightly, she could hardly breathe?

Jubal stepped forward. "Doc Nelson passed away, going on two weeks ago, now."

One fellow slapped his hat against his leg with a curse. A curious reaction, one that pasted a scowl on Jubal's weathered face.

"What of the fort's doctor?" she asked. "Why didn't you seek him?"

"Doc Brandley left for the front at Antietam back in September. We been expectin' a replacement ever since, but he hasn't arrived yet."

The tall soldier stalked forward, jaw tight, shoulders stiff, torment clearly trapped inside his skin. He stopped in front of her, his Adam's apple bobbing. Whatever had happened at the fort couldn't be good.

"We need a doctor. Now. It's Sarge's leg. We tied it off as best we could, but the blood was still comin' when we left. It's beyond what any of us can fix. Next to your father— God rest him—yer the best we got." He peered at her, his voice frayed at the edges. "Will you come?"

Jubal stepped in front of her. "Miss Nelson is expected in Minneapolis."

Shoving his cap back onto his head, the shorter man darted around Jubal. "It'll take us too long to get help from the city, miss. Our sergeant could be dead by then." He stepped closer, smelling of horses and desperation. "Surely your father taught you some about healing."

Her throat closed. There was no way the solider could know how his words brought her papa back to life. . . .

"You have a healing gift, daughter. It's not for man to chide what God's given. Never be ashamed of what you are."

She nibbled her lip, turning over the memories and examining them in the weak November sunlight. Should she go? Papa would not only understand her wanting to help, he'd ordain it. Aunt Rosamund, however, would have the vapors.

"Please, miss. It was my bullet what tore him up. I never shoulda—" The tall man's voice cracked, and he wheeled about, head hanging like a whipped hound.

How could she refuse that?

"Very well." She tightened her bonnet strings as she walked to the back of the cart. Jubal protested her every step. Ignoring him, she snatched her father's worn leather bag then faced the men. "If one of you wouldn't mind riding along with Jubal here, I believe it will be faster if I take one of your mounts."

The tall man's eyebrows dove for cover beneath the brim of his cap. The shorter just strapped her bag to the side of his bay. Jubal prophesied the wrath of God and Aunt Rosamund.

And all gasped when she hauled herself astride and snapped the horse into motion.

It was a hard ride, dirt and rocks flying behind her and the soldier. The path to the fort wasn't well used from this direction, making it a challenge to stay in the saddle. By the time they charged through the wooden gates of Fort Snelling, her thighs ached from holding on and her fingers from gripping the reins. The soldier halted in front of the dispensary and hopped down. She followed suit, her feet barely touching the ground before he unstrapped the leather bag and shoved it into her hands. Had her father felt this unprepared, clutching his tools, dashing through a door into moaning and mortality?

Inside, a soldier lay on a table, soaked in blood and sweat. A woman hovered over him, wiping his head with a cloth.

Emmy darted into action with a "pardon me" to the woman and a visual assessment of the man's leg. Ruined flesh gaped below the poor cloth tourniquet, but at least the fabric held.

Straightening, she unbuttoned her coat and hung it on a peg then grabbed a stained apron off another, all the while spouting orders. "I'll need a bite stick for his mouth, plenty of brandy or whatever alcohol is on hand, and a poultice of milkweed and comfrey. Oh, and two strong men to hold him down."

"Are you mad?" A deep voice boomed behind her. "What you need is a bone saw and a tenaculum!"

She whirled.

Framed in the doorway, a broad-shouldered man shrugged out of a coat—a well-tailored blue woolen. His green eyes assessed her as though deciding which part of a cadaver to cut up first.

She stiffened. Who did this arrogant newcomer think he was? She flashed her own perturbed gaze at the soldier and the woman who had yet to carry out her orders. "I thought you said you required my help?"

The soldier shrugged. "Seems the new doc just arrived, Miss Nelson."

"That's Dr. Clark, if you don't mind." The man stalked past the soldier to a washbasin, rolling up his sleeves to the elbows. Dipping his hands in, he cast her a dark look over his shoulder. "And for God's sake, wash your hands. You look as if you've just ridden in from the backcountry."

Resisting the urge to hide her fingernails, she lifted her chin like a shield before battle. "*Doctor* Clark, if amputation is what you're about, you might as well sign the man's death warrant, for he'll have no livelihood out here with one leg."

"If that leg remains attached, I assure you I will be signing the man's death certificate, and you'll be the one to blame. Do really want that on your head?" His voice lowered. "Now are you going to assist me or not, Nurse?"

She sucked in a breath. Should she back down? Or worse. . .humiliate herself and admit she wasn't a trained nurse at all?

◆ ◆ ◆

James Clark hid his admiration for the feisty woman beneath a scowl. She was a confident one, he'd give her that, though a field nurse likely had to be strong to survive in these backwoods. Intelligence lived behind those blue eyes, flashing like a lightning strike. Strength pulled a jaunty line to her lips. Sweet heavens! Would that they'd met under different circumstances, for very likely, this was a woman who'd not be swayed by convention. A refreshing change from the ladies out East. Grabbing the brush at the side of the basin, he attempted to scrub away such a thought along with the travel grime from beneath his nails.

Miss Nelson's shoes clacked across the wooden floor, clipped and brisk. Water splashed into the porcelain bowl next to his. "I know it doesn't sound like much, Doctor"—she shot him a sideways glance—"but with a steady administration of laudanum to keep the patient still, I've seen milkweed and comfrey work miracles."

Bah! He snatched the towel off a hook, rattling the washstand with the force of it. This was just the sort of backward medicine he expected to encounter and further-more. . .furthermore. . .

His shoulders sank. Furthermore, this was the entire reason Dr. Stafford had sent him out here. If he didn't make it past this hurdle, he'd never get that fellowship at Harvard Medical School—the one his father had spent his life on pushing him toward.

Gritting his teeth, James crossed to the patient's side and examined the leg. The flesh beneath the knee was mangled, a hotbed for incubation should gangrene decide to grow. What to do? Dare he try the folkish cure suggested by the snip of a woman?

The fellow writhed, pumping out a fresh wave of blood—and making up James's mind. "Heat an iron, and I'll need those instruments. Now!"

Miss Nelson darted over from the basin. "But Dr. Clark—"

His gaze locked onto hers. "Either we are a team, Miss Nelson, or you can walk out that door." He angled his head toward the entrance. "What's it to be?"

Crimson bloomed up her neck and onto her cheeks. The sergeant groaned, and with a whirl of her skirts, she mumbled, "Fine."

It was a quick surgery. Miss Nelson's fingers were nimble, her instincts keen as she handed him tools before he even asked. She only bristled once, when he set saw to bone, but to her credit, she remained silent. The soldier who'd opted to stay, however, emptied his stomach into a nearby bedpan, and the other woman fled out the door. Just as well. The cold air it ushered in cooled the perspiration on his brow. Despite what Miss Nelson may think of him, removing a body part never came easy.

"There we have it." He tied a final suture, and she snipped the silk thread. Apparently when Miss Nelson committed to something, she did so wholeheartedly.

"While you didn't approve of my methods, your help was impeccable." He waited for her to set aside the tray of used instruments and meet his gaze. "Thank you."

She pressed her lips together for a moment then answered. "You're welcome."

They both washed their hands. Each removed their surgical aprons, their movements in unison. The woman may harbor archaic medical knowledge, but God and country, she acted with precision.

Retrieving her overcoat from a peg, she slipped it on. "Good-bye, Dr. Clark. I wish you the best."

He frowned. Oughtn't a nurse continue tending a patient post-op? "You're leaving?"

"Yes. I am expected in Minneapolis." She fumbled with her bonnet strings. "You see, I'm not—"

A woman's scream leached through the door, and Miss Nelson yanked it open. Worse sounds blasted in on a gust of wind. Children crying. Men cursing. Soldiers, horses, and guns. What in the world?

In four long strides, he drew up alongside Miss Nelson and blinked at the bloody chaos being prodded into the compound.

"Good Lord," he breathed. "What is this?"

Chapter Two

Alarm. Fear. Dread. Emotions rifled through Emmy so quickly, her stomach clenched. She stared, horrified, as a wretched group of Sioux spread over the parade ground like an open sore, mostly women and children, many elders, and several warriors—all sporting bruises. This close, face-to-face with the people responsible for her betrothed's death, she expected to feel some morsel of rage. Yet as she watched a soldier raise a horsewhip against a cringing woman, only one feeling pounded stronger with each heartbeat.

Compassion.

"No!" She jumped down the single stair and sprinted toward the man. "Stop!"

The private swung her way with a vow. "Back away, miss. This ain't no place for a lady. These savages—"

"The only savage I see, sir, is the one with a whip in his hand." She snipped out each word, sharp and pointed.

A scowl slashed across his face. "Oh? Injun lover, are you?" He hefted the whip once more. "Maybe you ought to join them, then."

"And maybe you ought to give me your name and rank, soldier." Dr. Clark shoved between them, his shoulders blocking her view of the man, his voice a steel edge. Though she couldn't see the soldier, she had no doubt the fellow probably froze slack-jawed. She'd read once that the growl of a tiger could paralyze its prey. Such was the bass tone of the doctor's command. A tremor shivered through her. She'd hate to be on the receiving end of Dr. Clark's anger.

A tug on her sleeve turned her around. Purple darkened a circle around the woman's left eye, and it had swollen nearly shut. Her split lower lip was crusted over with a scab, but even so, she offered a small smile. "Thank you, lady. You are kind."

Emmy blinked, astonished. "You speak English. . .and quite well."

A black-headed boy with eyes the color of a summer sky grabbed on to the woman's buckskin skirt, crying. She lifted the lad, letting him rest his head against her shoulder before she answered. "My husband is a white man. An agent. He will see you are rewarded when he comes for me."

"No need. I'm sure you would've done the same." The words flew from her tongue before she thought, leaving a bitter aftertaste. She sucked in a breath, stunned. How could she say such a thing to someone who may have supported killing innocents?

The woman's gaze stared straight into her soul. "Yes, I would have done the same."

Emmy breathed out, long and low, then startled when fingers gripped her elbow.

"Miss Nelson, shall we?" Dr. Clark tugged her away from the soldiers and their captives. "I've spoken with a lieutenant. These are the 'friendlies,' as he put it. Those not involved in some sort of uprising. Apparently these people are to winter here, down on the flats and, well, you can see for yourself they're mostly women and children, many sick, some beaten. Would you reconsider your stance on leaving? I. . ."

His jaw clenched, and a muscle corded on his neck. Though she'd known him for hardly two hours, she'd wager whatever he was about to say would cost him a dear price.

"I need you." He bent toward her, a rogue grin flashing across his face. "Though I won't admit to saying that in a court of law."

Over his shoulder, she searched the wreck of humanity. There must be more than a thousand souls to tend in this bunch. He'd need more than her help. He'd need a miracle.

And so would she. If she agreed to this, Aunt wouldn't simply have the vapors—she'd suffer an apoplexy. If Papa were here. . .her heart beat faster. She knew exactly what Papa would say.

Squaring her shoulders, she faced the doctor. "I suppose we'll have to clear this with the colonel."

He cocked his head. "Why?"

"I see by the cut of your clothing that you're not military. Nor am I."

His brow crumpled. "I have a six-month commission waiting for me once I walk through the colonel's door, but you? I thought—"

"I'll explain along the way." She set off with a confident step, fighting a sneeze from the dirt kicked up by her own shoes and those of the soldiers and Indians. Her father had brought her here a few times over the past years, and now the knowledge served her well. She waited until the doctor joined her side before she spoke again. "You might as well know I am no nurse, not officially, anyway."

Dr. Clark cut her a sideways glance. "I don't understand. Your work back there was—" He dodged a soldier who parted them like a rock in a stream. "Let's just say I've worked with many assistants, none as intuitive as you."

For the first time since her father's death, genuine warmth wrapped around her heart, as comforting as an embrace and far more effective than the weak afternoon sun. "I may not have a formal education, but I grew up at my father's side, shadowing his every case."

"He was an accomplished physician?"

"Quite." Despite the pain and misery mere paces to her left, a half smile curved her lips. "Some say the best west of the Mississippi."

"Really? What is your father's name? Perhaps I may have heard of him."

"Dr. Edrith Nelson." Her smile soured. Speaking his name was bittersweet.

Dr. Clark's step hitched, as if her wave of anguish moved him as well. "Did you say *Edrith* Nelson?"

"You've heard of him?"

He snorted. "I don't know if you know this, Miss Nelson, but your father's methods are published in many a forum in the East, and are a major factor why my sponsor sent me here. I look forward to meeting him."

"I am sorry that won't be possible." She trudged up the few steps to the colonel's front door and paused on the stoop. Clearing her throat, she fought to summon words she didn't want to say while battling an onslaught of tears. If she let one go, the floodgates would open. "My father passed on a fortnight ago."

Clenching her hands into fists, she braced against the sympathy that was sure to follow, for such would be her undoing.

But a gleam brightened the doctor's green gaze. "You are quite the enigma, Miss Nelson." He pushed open the door. "After you."

For a moment, she stood, mouth agape. Was everything about the man unpredictable?

Inside, a makeshift office transformed the foyer. The doctor stepped up to a soldier perched on a stool behind a desk. "Dr. James Clark and Miss Nelson to see Colonel Crooks."

The man didn't so much as look up from a stack of papers. "Can't you see the colonel's got a mess of murderers out there to deal with?"

"Do you think he'd rather deal with the dysentery and typhoid that are even now infecting every soldier in this fort?" The doctor's words fired out like a round of grapeshot.

Emmy lifted her hand to her mouth, hiding a smile.

The soldier jerked to attention. "Who'd you say you are?"

"Private!" A muttonchopped man wearing colonel stripes at his shoulder leaned out an open door down the hall. "Just send them in."

Emmy clenched her skirts. This was it. Meeting with the commanding officer would change the course of her life—and not in a direction Aunt would approve of.

Should she go through with this? Could she? How did one agree to care for a people who'd stolen Daniel from her so long ago?

◆ ◆ ◆

James strode through the colonel's door, directly behind Miss Nelson's swishing skirts. The colonel stood near a hearth, lifting the flaps of his dress coat so the heat warmed his backside. He eyed them upon entrance, yet said nothing, the pull of his sideburns accenting a glower. Except for a gilt-framed painting of the crossing at the Potomac, a clock ticking away on a facing wall, and a mirror opposite a window, the walls were as barren as the man's manners, for he had yet to acknowledge them personally. James expected a certain lack of etiquette out here in the wild, but was this what military life would be like?

Stretching himself to full height, James executed a salute he'd practiced to perfection back at Cambridge. "Dr. James Clark, reporting for service, sir."

The colonel dropped his flaps, his boots tapping out a cadence on the wooden floor as he crossed to the window. With one finger, he swept aside a curtain and studied the commotion on the grounds.

And still, the man said nothing.

Miss Nelson exchanged a glance with James, her brows lifting. Clearly she desired him to break the standoff, yet what more should he say? Dr. Stafford had prepared him for many things on this adventure that were "*for his own good*," but a taciturn officer wasn't one of them.

"I've been expecting you these past four weeks." The colonel's voice ricocheted off the glass. He and Miss Nelson flinched, but the colonel didn't seem to notice, for he continued, "Though I suppose the route here was a bit. . .disturbed."

That put it mildly. A steamship with an unsalvageable boiler. The coach with a broken axel. Dead oxen. Cholera at a wayside. Indeed. Fighting the urge to scratch the stubble on his jaw, he maintained his ramrod stance. "It was a piecemeal journey at that, sir."

The colonel allowed the curtain to fall then pivoted. His gaze slid from Miss Nelson to him. The clock ticked overloud. Angry voices pelted the building from outside. Yet the colonel held the deadlock of stares. What in the world went on behind those gunmetal eyes? If he intended a dressing-down, then why not have at it?

"I can see more information will not be forthcoming until you are released, so at ease. The both of you." The colonel swept his arm toward a few empty chairs as he moved behind his desk. "I expect doctors to be boorish at times, but oughtn't you introduce your wife instead of relegating her to anonymity?"

James choked, glad for the sturdy wooden ladder-back beneath him. Miss Nelson blanched to a fine shade of parchment.

"I am sorry for the misunderstanding, sir." He shifted in his seat. "But this woman is not my wife."

Across from him, the colonel's face darkened. "Then you are worse than boorish. We may be on the edge of civilization, Doctor, but we are neither lawless nor immoral."

In the chair next to him, Miss Nelson strangled a small cry.

"No! Nothing like that." Heat crept up his back, his neck, his ears. Sweet mercy, but it was hot in here. "Allow me to explain."

The colonel sat back in his chair, lacing his fingers behind his head. "Fire away."

James tugged on his collar, coercing words past the embarrassment tightening his throat. He could only imagine the discomfort Miss Nelson felt—for he refused to look at her. "When I arrived just a few hours past, I came upon Miss Nelson caring for a sergeant's wounded leg." The colonel pierced the woman with a gaze as sharp as a bayonet. "What the devil?"

Miss Nelson leaned forward. "Two of your soldiers retrieved me from Mendota, sir. I am Dr. Edrith Nelson's daughter. He's recently passed on, so I came in his stead, being your doctor had not yet arrived."

"I see." The colonel sucked in a breath so large, his chest expanded to the point that he might burst. At last, he stood and rounded the desk, offering his hand to the lady and helping her to her feet. "In that case, I thank you. Your willingness to rally to our aid is appreciated, especially at times such as these."

James rose, unwilling to have a lady stand while he sat. Whatever the manners might be out here, his would not falter.

Miss Nelson dipped her head. "I am happy to serve anyone in need, Colonel."

"You are a credit to your father, Miss Nelson. I shall have a lieutenant see you home."

James snapped to attention. "Sir, I request that Miss Nelson remain, and she's agreed."

Dropping the lady's hand, the colonel swooped over to him like a great bird of prey. "What's this?"

"I cannot tend both the military and native occupants of this fort single-handedly." He worked his jaw, for it galled him to have to repeat his earlier words. He'd been beholden to a lady once before. Never again. Still. . . He set his jaw. "I need Miss Nelson's help. She's proven to be a valuable assistant."

The colonel shook his head. "That may be true, but as I said, this is not a lawless garrison. Only married women or slaves may reside inside these walls."

Miss Nelson lifted a hand toward the window. "Yet you're allowing an entire population of females to stay the winter, many of which are neither married or slave."

James clenched his teeth, biting back a smirk. Intelligent and plucky? What other qualities did she hide behind those long lashes?

The colonel narrowed his eyes. "They are captives, Miss Nelson. They do not fall into the aforementioned categories."

James grasped the opening that might be the colonel's undoing—though insubordination might very well earn him a night's stay in the brig. "My understanding, sir, is those natives had nothing to do with an uprising, and in many cases, aided the settlers in escaping. You pride yourself on maintaining a lawful camp, yet I ask you, is justice served by locking up those that are as innocent as the victims of the massacre?"

"They will not be locked up, Doctor. They are free to come and go, though it is for their benefit to remain inside the encampment down on the flats."

"And it is to the fort's benefit if Miss Nelson remains as well."

The colonel's nostrils flared. A bullish snort followed. "It is for the safety of the lady that she be escorted to her home."

"Upon my word, Colonel, I will vouch for the lady's safety the entire time she's here." Immediately he stiffened. That had either been the most noble vow he'd ever given—or the most foolish.

"This is highly irregular!" The commander's voice bounced from wall to wall.

Quite the contrast to Miss Nelson's quiet gaze out the window. "So is that." She indicated with the tip of her head.

"My dear." Once again the colonel reached for her hand, patting it between his. "Life is hard here, and with winter coming on, it will only get worse."

She lifted her chin, and James couldn't help but marvel.

"I understand, sir, but is it not true that God doesn't always call us to the comfortable places?"

With a long sigh, the colonel released her and turned to James. "Keep your eye on this one, Doctor, for she knows her own mind, and quite possibly the mind of God as well. I will hold you fully accountable for her as long as she's here. Is that clear?"

He nodded, stiff and curt, unsure if he should shout a victory cry or hang his head in defeat. After the death of his parents, he'd been responsible for his hellion of a younger sister, and been glad of it when he finally handed her off to a husband.

Hopefully Miss Nelson would be easier to keep track of.

Chapter Three

A rap on the door startled Emmy awake. Rising, she rubbed a kink in her neck from a fitful first night at the fort then lit the lantern on the nightstand. Guilt had nipped her for displacing the dispensary's steward, but after sleeping on a mattress that hadn't been re-ticked in at least a year, she understood his eagerness to leave these quarters and move in with the smithy.

"Five minutes, Miss Nelson." Dr. Clark's deep voice seeped through the door. "I'll await you by the front gate."

Shivering, she dashed the few steps to her trunk, grudgingly left behind by Jubal. Good thing she'd fallen into bed exhausted last night, for if she'd taken the time to undress, she'd surely be frozen by now. The small hearth had given up its ghost of warmth hours ago. She donned a few more layers then with a quick snuff of the light, dashed off to meet the doctor.

Outside, a few resolute stars lingered in the predawn sky. The first brittle notes of "Reveille" marched across the compound from a bugle boy atop one of the lookout towers. Emmy drew alongside the doctor where he stood next to the massive fort gates. He snapped shut a pocket watch and tucked it away.

"I hope you won't make tardiness a practice, Miss Nelson."

His green eyes bore into hers, but there was a smile at the edges. Picking up his kit, he offered his free hand and aided her through a smaller opening cut into the wooden ingress.

The sentry's gaze followed their movement, and he shut the door behind them.

Her steps, two to the doctor's one, crunched on the frozen weeds, flattened by yesterday's procession. Gray light colored the world and her mood. The closer they drew to the encampment, the slower her pace. Forgiveness was one thing. Forgetting, quite another. It wasn't this tribe that had taken Daniel's life, but she still felt somewhat a traitor for tending to the "enemy."

Shoving down the feeling, she hurried ahead, surprised at how much ground the doctor had gained. "When you said you wanted an early start in the morning, you might've told me what time to expect. It will be a wonder if anyone's even stirring in the camp yet."

"Which is the best time to make our rounds unhindered, and after making diagnoses, we'll use the rest of the day to administer treatments."

The trail skirted the fort's rock walls, just like her mind circled the doctor's words, trying to make sense of them. Ahh. Of course. Understanding dawned as bright as the orange band rising on the eastern horizon. She peeked up at him. "I gather you're accustomed to a hospital setting."

"I am." He paused at the apex of a sudden sharp descent in the trail and once again offered her his hand. "It's a bit treacherous here. Hold on."

His fingers wrapped around hers, and as they picked their way down to the river flats, he righted her when a rock gave way or her shoe caught in a dip. Each time, the strength in his grasp warmed through her gloves and burned up her arm. A base reaction, surely. His attention couldn't mean anything, for had he not sworn to the colonel to see to her safety? Even so, she liked the way their fingers entwined so perfectly, the way his arm bumped against hers now and again, solid and reassuring.

La! She sucked in a lungful of frigid air, feeling a traitor to Daniel's memory twice over. Better to put her mind on other things than the feel of this man's grip.

"Why are you here, Dr. Clark?" she asked. "You don't seem the sort of man to—"

She clamped her mouth shut. What had gotten into her to speak so freely?

He glanced down at her. "What sort is that, I wonder?"

The first rays of sun stretched across his clean-shaven jaw. His hat rode neatly atop brown hair, brushed back and trimmed since yesterday. Morning light rode his shoulders like a mantle of power. His step was confident, his manners impeccable. She leaned a bit closer and sniffed. Mixing with the acrid scent of early-morning fires rising from the camp, the spicy fragrance of sandalwood tickled her nose, just as she'd expected.

She smiled up at him. "I should think you are better suited to ballrooms and dinner parties than to a rugged outpost in Minnesota."

He chuckled. "Indeed. You are perceptive, Miss Nelson, and very correct. My time here is a temporary yet necessary step if I'm to be considered for a fellowship at Harvard. Competition for the position is fierce. Most applicants have only book knowledge. I hope to gain an advantage by field experience."

The trail evened out, and he released her hand. Cold crept up her arm, and she shivered.

Dr. Clark stepped up to one of the armed guards blocking a crude log gate. Withdrawing a signed pass from the colonel, he handed it over.

The soldier leaned aside and spit then gave the paper back. "Don't know why you want to tend these animals. Ain't worth the time, you ask me."

"I didn't." The doctor's tone lowered. "So open the gate and save your commentary."

The soldier glowered, his skin pocked and ruddy at the cheeks. Red hair, far too long for regulation, shot out from beneath his cap. For a moment she wondered if he'd comply, but with a snap of his head, the other men set about removing the log.

The doctor turned to her with a boyish jaunt to his step. "And so the experience begins, hmm?"

She bit the inside of her cheek. He could have no idea of the apprehension churning in her stomach. Papa would want her to help, Daniel and Aunt Rosamund wouldn't.

Still, she'd given her word.

As she looked over the slipshod village of buffalo-hide teepees, her gaze followed the rise of smoke curling out the tops like pleading prayers—and she added one of her own.

Oh, Lord, please use this experience to benefit Dr. Clark and bring healing to the Indians— and to my heart.

◆ ◆ ◆

All the pleasantness of walking with Miss Nelson vanished the moment James stepped into the internment camp. Death was in the air, as tangible as the misty vapor snorted out from the horses they passed. Moaning, coughing, retching. . .the sounds of suffering nearly drove him to his knees.

Clusters of teepees formed a circle on the patch of cleared ground, bordered on two sides by the confluence of the Mississippi and Minnesota Rivers. Good for fresh water, bad for flooding.

Sharp groans from the tent on his right severed his speculations. He met the eyes of Miss Nelson. "You ready?"

She nodded.

For a moment, he paused at the flap of a door. How exactly did one enter such a shelter? There was no knocker or even something solid to rap against. Ought he call a greeting or—

Another cry of pain and he yanked the flap open and dove in.

The stench inside twisted his gut. Good thing he'd not eaten breakfast. A tiny fire burned at the center, adding fumes to the noxious stink of dysentery. Beside him, Miss Nelson pressed a hand to her stomach, yet did not gag. Two women and three small children huddled on woolen blankets on one side of the tent. A disheveled elder curled into a ball opposite them, releasing another wail.

Reaching into his greatcoat pocket, he retrieved a small pad of paper and a pencil.

Miss Nelson edged closer to him, lowering her voice to a whisper. "Is that all you're going to do, scratch a few notes? Will you not examine her first?"

"No need. The odor in here and the way she's clutching her abdomen says it all. The woman has dysentery. I'll order clean bedding and plenty of fresh water."

"You might want to add castor oil and ginger to that water."

He stifled a huff, anything to keep from breathing more than necessary. "Unconventional, but not dangerous. I suppose it's worth a try."

Though doubtful they understood, he mumbled a thank-you to the tent's inhabitants; then he and Miss Nelson retreated outside to the mercy of fresh air. By now, the sun cleared the horizon, washing the encampment in hope—but not for long. The pathetic bawl of a baby pulled Miss Nelson from his side and into the next tent.

He dashed after her and grabbed her sleeve, holding her back. "Stay next to me. Touch nothing." He didn't need to tell her to cover her nose, for she pressed her palm against her face.

The stench of death hung low and heavy, thick as the smoke suspended over the fire at the center. On one blanket, two skeletal girls clung to each other, locked forever in a perverse embrace. Sometime during the night, both had passed on. Across from them, a woman lay, staring up at their entrance, a baby crying in her arms. Both wore the first bloom of a spreading rash. Once again he drew out his notebook.

Miss Nelson wrenched from his grasp and darted ahead, grabbing a dipper of water on her way toward the babe.

His heart skipped a beat. "Miss Nelson! If that woman has smallpox, you've just exposed yourself."

She didn't so much as acknowledge him, just lifted the water to the woman's lips while she cooed to settle the baby. He watched, horrified and helpless.

"Look closer, Doctor," she called over her shoulder. "It's measles."

A growl rumbled in his chest. "Then you've exposed yourself to—"

"Nothing. I've already had it."

Ought he rejoice or admonish? He settled for a sigh. "I'll have an attendant remove these bodies. There's no more we can do for the woman and her babe but let time heal and set up a quarantine around this tent."

Miss Nelson rose, skirting the small fire. "Clearly this woman can't care for the babe. Maybe I ought stay and—"

"While your concern does you justice, truly, you will be of more help by coming with me." He pocketed his notes and held the flap aside. "After you."

She hesitated, her brow creasing a disagreement. After the space of a few breaths, she swept passed him. He ducked out after her, expecting a fight.

Instead, she huddled next to his side, pale-faced and silent. What the devil?

In front of them, one of the few native men strode by, neither addressing nor even looking at them. Why would a passing captive cause her skirts to quiver so?

He guided her aside, into the harbor between two tent walls. "Is there something I should know, Miss Nelson?"

She averted her gaze, focusing on tugging her coat sleeves well past her wrists. "It's nothing. I'm fine, Doctor."

He frowned. "Yet you tremble."

"It's cold."

"It's more than that." Setting down his bag, he lifted her chin with a finger, forcing her to quit fussing with her sleeves. "Tell me."

A sigh deflated her. Around them, the sounds of fires being stoked and waking children increased.

Lifting an eyebrow, he cocked his head, an effect that oft'times worked like a charm. "Either you tell me now, or I suspect we'll have an audience very soon."

Her eyes flashed. "Very well. If you must know, I was betrothed once. Daniel was a surveyor, the best, really. Which is why the government sought him out. He was on a project west of here. Pawnee country."

Her words slowed like the winding down of a clock, the last coming out on a ragged whisper. "He never came back."

Pain twisted her face, the kind of agony he witnessed when imparting the news of a loved one's death. But this time, a distinct urge settled deep in his bones, to gather her in his arms and hold her until the pain went away. He clenched his hands, once again feeling helpless—and dug his nails into his palms.

"Perhaps he will come back." He regretted the platitude as soon as it left his lips.

Her pain disappeared, replaced with a dark scowl. "You do not understand the Pawnee, Doctor."

Morning sun angled between the tents, lighting the complex woman in front of him. No wonder she took the suffering of others to heart, for it was a familiar companion.

He reached for her then lowered his hand, suddenly ashamed. "I am discovering, Miss Nelson, there is much I do not understand."

Chapter Four

Emmy paced at the front gate, working a rut into the dirt. Overhead, the late-November sun was lethargic, the entire world washed of autumn's brilliance. It was the brown time, the dead. . .as if color packed up its bags and fled before winter arrived.

Glancing over her shoulder, she squinted along the parade ground toward the colonel's quarters, past soldiers scrambling for inspection. The door that'd swallowed Dr. Clark an hour ago remained shut. She lifted her eyes higher, over the roof, where a cloud of smoke rose from the river flats below. She'd dallied too long already.

Despite the doctor's instructions to wait for him, she turned to the sentry. "Could you let Dr. Clark know I've gone ahead?"

Morning light caught the fuzz on his chin. The man-boy could hardly be more than sixteen. "Sure, miss. Not like him to be late, eh?"

Her lips quirked. "Over the past three weeks, I daresay we've both learned he's punctual to a fault."

"Truth is"—the sentry's gaze shifted side to side, then he stepped closer, lowering his voice for her ears only—"I'd rather take a whoopin' than live through another one of Dr. Clark's tongue-lashings. But don't tell him I said so."

"Your secret is safe with me." She mimicked his conspiratorial stance. "For I quite agree."

She strolled through the gate—already open for the day—accompanied by the soldier's laughter.

The trail didn't seem as long anymore. She might even wager on her ability to trek it in the dark. This was the first time, though, that no strong arm steadied her on the descent. She missed that. And, surprisingly, she also missed the doctor's banter, stimulating as the black coffee served for breakfast. A frown tugged her mouth as she sniffed. Neither was the air quite as sweet without the hint of his sandalwood shaving tonic. Yes, though this be the same path, this time, everything was different.

Her balance teetered on some loosened sandstone, as unsettling as her rogue thoughts. She threw out her hands, her father's bag nearly flying from her grasp. Pausing, she negotiated her next step and the curious attachment she felt to the doctor. Working long days, side by side, it was only natural to grow accustomed to a person's ways. Surely that's why she missed Dr. Clark's presence this morn.

That settled, she picked her way down the embankment, praying all the way that Private Grainger wouldn't be on sentry duty today, especially without the doctor at her side. The newly built walls of the encampment towered in front of her, and she smirked at the irony of the timbers. The very people group who attacked whites now needed to be protected from them.

She scurried ahead, her heart sinking to her stomach when she saw the shock of red hair shooting out from beneath a private's cap. A feral smile lit his face, one that would surely visit her nightmares. She held out her pass as a buffer.

Ignoring her paperwork, Grainger looked past her. "Where's Doc?"

"I'm sure he'll be along shortly. And I'm also sure you ought to address him as Doctor Clark, whether he's present or not."

"That so?" His gaze returned to her, touching her in places that ought not be touched. "Why don't you wait here? Not safe for a lone white woman in there."

Hah! As if remaining with the private was any safer. She bit the inside of her cheek, reminding herself to be charitable. "I've tended these people the past three weeks, Private Grainger. I know my way around by now."

"Snakes, the lot of 'em. Just waitin' for a chance to strike." Tobacco juice shot from his mouth and hit the ground. Swiping a hand across his mouth, he winked at her. "And yer mighty fine quarry."

She stiffened, taking courage in rigid posture. "Open the gate, or I shall report you."

"Your word against mine."

Heat crept up her neck. He'd never speak this way if the doctor were with her, and she couldn't decide what irked her more—that the presence of another man would stave off his remarks, or the way his tongue ran over his lips.

She gripped her father's bag so tightly, the strain might rip a seam in her gloves. "Who do you think the colonel will believe, Private? A lecherous good-for-nothing hiding behind a uniform, or a lady?"

His face darkened, and he lunged.

But she refused to budge. If he touched her, a court-martial would get him out of here faster than a scream.

A breath away, he pulled up short, a vulgar laugh rumbling in his chest. "Just playin' with ya, missy. Soldier's gotta have a little fun, don't he?"

He raised a fist and pounded on the gate. "Open up!"

She darted inside as soon as it opened far enough for her to pass through sideways.

Makawee's tent—the woman she'd saved from a whipping that first day—was the second on the right. The sound of retching broke Emmy's heart. She never should have waited so long to come.

Emmy tossed up the flap and stepped inside. This late in the morning, the rest of the tent's occupants were on their way to line up for roll. In front of her, a woman bent over a bucket, emptying her stomach.

"Oh, Makawee, I'm so sorry I didn't get here sooner." Emmy opened her father's bag and produced a small pouch, the scent of lemon balm and peppermint a welcome fragrance.

Makawee straightened, a weak smile belying the strain on her face. "It will pass, Miss Emmy. It is the way of nature."

"Even so, I've brought you some different herbs to try instead of ginger." She held out the pouch. "It's best for you and the babe if you can keep down food."

Across the tent, a little boy crawled out from a buffalo hide and launched himself at her.

Emmy grinned and swung the lad up in her arms. "Good morning, little Jack. How is this fine fellow today?"

"Growing as strong as his father." Makawee's eyes rested on her son; then she lifted her face to Emmy, pain tightening her jaw. "Have you any news?"

"Not yet. I'm sure your husband is doing all he can to get here."

Makawee's chest heaved, and then the moment passed like a fall tempest, her brown eyes clear and unblinking. "You speak truth, and I thank you."

Emmy reached out her free arm and rested it on the woman's shoulder. "I admire your strength, my friend."

She stifled a gasp. Had that sentiment really come from her lips? What was happening to her emotions? First missing a man she'd hardly known three weeks, and now such respect for a Sioux woman?

Makawee averted her gaze. "It is God's grace. Nothing other."

Emmy's admiration grew, for the woman had not only left behind tradition by marrying an Irishman, but her religion as well, turning to the "White Christ," as she called it. Both actions required strength.

Setting down the boy, Emmy patted his head. "I should check on Old Betts, poor thing. I'll stop in tomorrow to see how the new herbs work for you."

"Thank you, Miss Emmy. God smile on you."

"And you."

Outside, natives filtered back to their shelters, clogging the small roads between tents. Apparently roll was finished. She'd have to let the lieutenant know Makawee and her little boy were fine, but first, she ought to get laudanum to Old Betts.

Veering left, she squeezed onto the tight trail sometimes used by the doctor. The dirt path ran along the wall, skirting the teepees.

She raced ahead but then slowed when a warrior stepped into her path, arms folded, face hardened to flint. There'd be no easy way to pass him. Maybe this shortcut wasn't the best route after all. She turned.

And one tent down, another native blocked her route.

The first ember of fear flared to life in her chest. Surely they didn't mean to trap her. Perhaps they'd simply had a prearranged meeting here, that's all—one best not hindered.

Darting ahead, she veered left, onto the path between two teepees—and nearly collided with the chest of another man.

Panic burned the back of her throat. Even so, she lifted her chin. "Let me pass."

He advanced, forcing her back, until the wall clipped into her shoulder blades. A hare couldn't have been more cornered.

Stony faces searched hers. The man to her left pushed back her bonnet and reached for her hair. A flash of morning sun glinted off a knife at his side. *These are friendlies*, she reminded herself. Still. . .how had he gotten a knife in the first place? Worse—her mouth dried to ashes—had that blade taken any scalps?

A tear slid down her cheek. She never should have come here alone. And what would a scream accomplish? Private Grainger would only join in the game.

"Please." She trembled, and the tear dripped off her chin. "Let me go."

◆ ◆ ◆

"You let her go—alone?" James grabbed Grainger by the throat and shoved him against the timber wall, the smack of the private's head satisfying. "You were issued the same warning as I!"

The private's lips moved like a fish out of water. Just a little more pressure, and the esophagus would collapse, taking the trachea with it. James closed his eyes, praying for his anger to pass. Was this weasel of a man even worth this much passion? Stifling a growl, he threw Grainger to the ground and pounded on the gate. "Open up! Dr. Clark here!"

Grainger coughed and choked.

In the eternity it took for the gate to swing open, James flexed and released his fists, several times over, trying to calm the rage churning in his gut. Blast the colonel for wasting his time on a simple case of food poisoning. Double-blast sentries foolish enough to let a woman walk headlong into danger. And—*God, help her*—blast Miss Emmaline Nelson for her independent streak. Confidence would surely be the woman's undoing.

Clearing the gate, he sprinted to Makawee's tent first, dodging elders and children. She and Miss Nelson had developed quite a friendship, and hopefully the women yet chattered or played with little Jack.

He ducked through the tent flap. "Miss Nelson?"

Inside, the boy played with two sticks and some beads on a nearby fur. Makawee looked up from a pot she stirred over a small fire at the center. But no blond-haired, blue-eyed vixen—or anyone else—was inside.

Makawee stopped her stirring. "Miss Emmy is gone to Old Betts. Is there a problem, Doctor?"

"There'd better not be." He shot back outside, trying to erase the colonel's warning of unrest in the camp, that recent attacks against native women by imbecile soldiers like Grainger had angered the men.

That rumblings of revenge ran hot and thick.

With roll finished and nowhere else to go, women and children filled the camp roads—and Old Betts resided on the opposite side. It would take twice as long to navigate the main route, so he wove his way through tepees and dodged into the thin space between tents and wall.

Ahead, a few native men blocked the way, but that was the least of his worries. He dashed forward, sure that his heartbeat wouldn't resume a normal cadence until he found Miss Nelson. But as he drew closer, blond hair flashed at the center of the trio. His heart missed a beat. Emmaline stood ramrod straight, tears dripping off her jaw, her father's bag spilled open on the ground. To her left, a man held a handful of her hair to his nose. On her right, a tall warrior bent, burying his face against her neck. And in front, a shirtless brave reached out and trailed his fingers along her collarbone.

James dropped his bag and pulled out a gun.

"Touch her again, and you're dead where you stand." He fingered the trigger.

Three pairs of dark eyes locked onto his.

Only one spoke. "This woman yours?"

"She is." The words sank low in his gut. How dare he claim such a thing? Promising the colonel he'd look out for her was one thing, but this? The flare of the warriors' nostrils, the flash of white in their eyes, told him he'd just announced something far more.

Yet it accomplished his purpose. They filed away, one by one, disappearing between the tents.

Emmaline neither turned his way nor collapsed to the ground. She stood, face washed in tears, staring straight ahead.

Everything in him wanted to race to her side, cradle her close and never let go. But he forced one foot in front of the other, slowly, fluidly, until he stood a few breaths in front of her. "Miss Nelson?"

She didn't move. She hovered somewhere beyond his reach, trapped in the terror of the experience. He'd seen patients succumb to shock, and it was never pretty.

"Emmaline!"

Her chest fluttered with a shallow breath—then heaved. Great sobs poured out her mouth, and James wrapped his arms around her, praying God would use his embrace to bring peace.

"Shh. It's all over. I'm here. I've got you." He rubbed circles on her back, waiting for her weeping to subside. He'd let her go, then.

But as her tears soaked through his shirt and warmed his skin, he realized that was a lie. He might release her, but he'd never let her go.

And God help the man who tried to take her from him.

Chapter Five

Wind lashed like a bullwhip through the few inches of open window, slicing into Emmy's back. Setting down her pestle, she pivoted and crossed the few steps of the dispensary to wrench the glass closed. Despite the barrier, she shivered. The morning had dawned sunny and carefree, but now pewter clouds hung low, smothering the fort with a threat. They'd been fortunate thus far with no snow, but with December half spent, that blessing was stretched tight and ready to snap.

Behind her, the front door blew open, smacking into the wall with a crack. She couldn't help but jump, for since the awful encounter at the encampment, her nerves balanced on a fine wire.

She whirled, and her jaw dropped. A woman entered, her dark eyes burning like embers. Her face twisted by fear.

"Makawee?" Emmy ran to her. How strange it was to see the woman inside wooden walls instead of buffalo hide. "What are you doing here? How did you—"

"Little Jack is missing." Her voice was as raw as the chapped skin on her cheeks.

Emmy stiffened. "What do you mean, missing? How could he possibly get out of camp?"

"With snow coming, the soldiers led a group to collect wood. I brought Jack. When we were to leave, he was gone. The men would not search, nor let me. I slipped away but could not find him. Please." Makawee's fingers dug into Emmy's sleeve. "Will you and Dr. Clark come?"

Images of the blue-eyed rascal, alone in the woods, maybe crying—maybe hurt—horrified her. Emmy's hand shot to her chest A two-year-old wouldn't survive long out there.

"I'll find the doctor." She dashed to the sick ward's door. It was doubtful he'd be there, though, for only one private occupied a bed, having imbibed too much and fallen down some stairs. Served him right to break a leg. The man slept openmouthed on his cot, his snores filling the empty room.

Emmy darted past Makawee, who stood wringing her hands where she'd left her. Opposite the sick ward was a supply room, but that led to a door kept shut, one she beat with her fist. "Doctor Clark?"

She listened, willing herself to hear his strong steps on the other side. Nothing but panes of glass chattering like teeth answered her.

"Doctor!" She tried again.

Nothing.

Resting her fingers on the latch, she hesitated. Dare she? What would Aunt think of her entering a man's chambers?

She sucked in a breath and pushed open the door. "Dr. Clark, please. . ." Her words fell to the floor. No doctor sat at the tidy desk against the wall, or closed his eyes on the made bed, or sat lacing his shoes on the chair in the corner. The orderliness didn't surprise her. That he'd left the building without a word of his whereabouts did.

Retracing her steps, she grabbed her coat off the hook, ignoring Makawee's haunted look. "Maybe the doctor was called by the colonel. Wait here."

She flew out the door. If she couldn't find him, then what? No way would she venture out alone, not after what happened last time. She set her jaw. He had to be there, that's all.

A few soldiers scurried across the parade ground, all eager for the warmth of a fire instead of the wicked air. No one paid her any mind. Since word of the doctor's rage last month when he'd come to her aid, most men left her alone.

As she ascended the steps to the colonel's office, a soldier strode out the front door.

"Excuse me, but is Dr. Clark about?" She craned her neck, hoping to glimpse the doctor beyond his shoulder. "He is needed."

"No, ma'am. Haven't seen him."

The fellow whisked past her, and for a moment, she tried not to give in to panic. Where in the world had he gone? Ought she take a horse and try to find Jack on her own? The question hit her like a boulder fallen into still waters, jarring, disturbing, sending out ripples of fear and trepidation. Her throat closed. No. That was not an option.

The next gust of wind slapped her cheek with icy pellets, and she raced back to the dispensary, where Makawee greeted her with hopeful eyes.

Emmy shook her head. "It appears Dr. Clark is missing as well."

Makawee reached for the door. "Then you and I will go."

"No, Makawee." She tugged the woman back. "It's no more safe for you to be outside the camp walls than it is for me to be inside. Not to mention that you are with child."

Makawee spun, an angry slant on her lips. "I will not sit here—"

"But that's exactly what we must do. As soon as Dr. Clark returns, he will help. I am sure of it."

"No!" The woman flung out her hands, her voice rising like a fever. "My husband is gone, I will not lose my son, too. I will go. I will find him."

"Listen!" Emmy grabbed her friend's shoulders and shook, praying the action would jolt her to her senses. "Either God is in control or He is not. What do you believe?"

The question slammed into her own heart. If she really believed God was in control, would she not sacrifice her safety for the rescue of one of His little ones?

"You are right," Makawee finally breathed out. "The Creator governs all."

"Then let us hope and trust in Him with full confidence, hmm?" She spoke loudly, boldly, forcing the words to fill the frightened cracks in her soul.

Makawee's mouth wavered, not into a smile, not when her son was somewhere out in a land as cruel as the wind beating against the door. But Emmy took it as a smile, anyway.

"You are a gift, Miss Emmy."

She frowned and tightened her bonnet strings. "I doubt Dr. Clark will think so when he discovers I've gone ahead without him."

◆ ◆ ◆

Twice! Twice in the space of a month. James kicked his horse into a gallop, following the flattened path of grass that led to a stand of woods. Fool-headed, strong-willed woman. He'd excused the first time she'd ventured out alone, chalking it up to naivete, but after his stern warning to never leave the dispensary without him?

Sleet stung his face, as goading as Miss Nelson's disregard for his rule. This time he ought to take her over his knee when he found her. A cold worry lodged behind his heart as the sleet changed to snow. *If* he found her.

He reined the horse to a walk and entered the trees, leaning forward to study the ground. He should've thought to ask a scout to accompany him. What did he know of tracking anything other than the course of a disease? Already snow gathered in a thin but growing layer, covering leaves that might've been kicked up by hooves. And here in the wood, the last of day's light faded to a color as dark as his hope. Which way would she have gone?

Dismounting, he scanned the area for a better clue. Wind rattled the branches over-head, mocking his rash decision to search for her alone—and then it hit him. He lifted his face to the iron sky.

"I am as culpable as Miss Nelson, eh, Lord? Letting emotion get the better of me, running ahead of You time and again, wanting to help others but not waiting for Your lead. Oh, God"— he drew in a ragged breath—"forgive me, even as I forgive her."

The next gust of wind did more than shake tree limbs—it waved a small snatch of cloth tied to the end of a low-hanging branch. His breath eased. He knew that bit of calico, for he'd often admired the way it followed Miss Nelson's curves.

Launching himself into the saddle, he trotted the horse over to it then squinted in the whiteness to catch another glimpse of bright fabric. There. Not far off. He fought a rogue smile, wondering just how much of her skirt might be missing when he caught up to her.

He didn't wonder long. Ahead, a dark shape walked, a bedraggled swath of blond hair hanging down at the back.

"Emmaline!" He dug in his heels.

"Doctor?" She turned. "Thank God!"

He slid from the horse before it stopped and ran to her. The way she cradled her left arm, the sag of her shoulders, the stream-clear eyes now clouded to muddy waters—all of it screamed agony, and not just from want of a missing boy.

"You're hurt." He reached for her.

"I'm fine." She shrugged away, but not before he caught the slight groan she couldn't disguise.

"I know an injury when I see one. Now are you going to let me examine that arm, or are we going to stand here and waste time?"

Snow collected on her long lashes as she stared at him. It would do no good to prod her further. *Wait for it. Wait.* And there, the pursing of her lips, a standard signal she was about to give in.

She offered up her arm, her nose wrinkling with a poorly concealed wince.

He stepped closer, using one hand to brace her arm, the other to peel back layers of sleeves. "What happened?"

"A falling branch spooked my horse, and he threw me. I landed wrong, and—ah!" She grimaced.

Her pain sliced into his soul as he did what he must—probe for fractures or breaks. "Sorry. Won't be a moment more. You were saying?"

"By the time I stood, my mount was gone. Ow!" She gasped once more then scowled up at him. "That hurt."

"No doubt." Examination finished, he released her. "That's quite a sprain. It's not broken, though it will take some time to heal."

"Good." She sidestepped him and strode to his horse. "Then let's continue."

"Hold on." He pulled her back, taking care not to jostle her injury overmuch. "That arm needs to be wrapped first, and—"

"No, I'll ride with you and keep it as immobile as possible. Little Jack is still out here. His life is on the line, now more than ever." Fat, white flakes collected on her bonnet, adding emphasis to her words.

A sigh—or mayhap defeat—emptied his lungs of air. "Fine."

He hoisted her into the saddle then swung up behind her. She never cried out, but her muffled grunts belied her brave front.

She used her good arm to point. "That way."

He narrowed his eyes, trying to make sense of her confidence in the growing whirl of whiteness. "What makes you so sure?"

"My father was often called to tend settlers here, and—Oh!"

The horse lurched sideways and she slipped. Shifting the reins to one hand, he wrapped his other arm around her, settling her against his chest.

She peeked up at him, an accusing arch to her brow.

He winked. "In situations such as this, Miss Nelson, propriety be hanged."

She nestled back, allowing his hold. As much as he wanted to find the boy and get them all to safety, he gave in to the sweet feel of the woman snuggled against his coat.

"There's a ravine not far from here with a maze of fallen trunks," she continued. "A haven for a young boy in search of adventure."

"How do you know little Jack is in this wood?"

"It's near to where Makawee gathered kindling earlier this afternoon. That and, before the snow started falling, I followed a trail in the dirt from a dragged stick. Wild animals don't play with sticks, but little boys do."

"Except for when it comes to your own safety, Miss Nelson"—he bent his head so she'd hear not only the words but the admiration in his voice—"you are a very wise woman."

She stilled in his arms, and slowly her face lifted to his—but then she leaned forward, pointing, a cry of pain accompanying the movement. "There!"

"Wait here." He missed her warmth the moment he dismounted. Picking his way down the ravine, he alternated between calling for Jack and straining to listen.

Halfway down, he stopped. Then turned.

"Jack?"

Beneath a fallen trunk, in a world of white and cold, a dark little head peeked out, wailing for his mama.

"Thank you, God," James whispered as he scooped up the lad and hefted him to his shoulder. The boy's tears burned onto his neck.

No. Wait.

Holding the boy in one arm, he yanked his glove off the other with his teeth then pressed the back of his hand to the lad's forehead.

Fire met his touch. And as he looked in the boy's throat, a blaze raged there as well.

He worked his way back to Miss Nelson, thanking God for her injured arm. There was no way she could hold the boy, exposing her to—no. He wouldn't think it. He couldn't be sure of the lad's diagnosis yet, but even so, he would buffer Emmaline by putting the boy in front of him and her behind. She may have survived measles, but he was pretty sure she'd not yet experienced the reason why he'd been absent from the fort in the first place—

Setting up quarantine for those with smallpox.

Chapter Six

Emmy retrieved the last cloth from a bucket of cold water and wrung it out as well as she could with a tender wrist. How many times had she done this the past week? She frowned at the cracked, red skin on her hands. Clearly, too many.

Coughs and a few moans followed her across the sick ward. Winter winds raged against the windows, but the blankets she'd nailed up blockaded drafts from attacking those too helpless to parry. No sense adding more misery to the men suffering from the spate of severe measles.

Major Clem occupied the bed nearest the door. When she bent to lay the cloth on his brow, his eyes popped open, glassy and shot through with red.

His lips worked a moment before any sound came out. "Thirsty."

"Good, I've just the thing for you." She smiled, taking care to mimic the soothing tone her father used to employ. Papa always said healing was more than medicine. *Oh, Papa.*

She straightened, once again shoving grief to a cellar in her heart. "I'll be back in a thrice with some licorice-root tea, Major."

Crossing to the dispensary door, she eased it open, glad she'd stood her ground for the extra bear grease. The men slept fitfully enough without ill-mannered hinges scraping against their ears.

Sweet tanginess rode the crest of the smoky scent in the room, and she inhaled deeply as she drew nearer the hearth. Some said licorice smelled of wildness, the untamed spoor kicked up by one's feet when tromping through loamy earth, but not her. Why, she'd pour herself a large mug just for the sheer enjoyment of it if they weren't so low on stock.

"Afternoon, Miss Nelson." Dr. Clark's voice entered on an icy gust from the front door. "How goes it?"

She felt the touch of his eyes upon her, and irrationally wished she'd chosen her green serge instead of her drab gray. La! What a thought. She was worse than a moonstruck schoolgirl. Even so, after she returned the kettle to the grate, she smoothed her skirts before she faced him.

The doctor shrugged out of his coat, waistcoat fabric taut across the muscles of his back as he reached to hang it on a peg. Ahh, but she could look at that fine sight all day and never tire of the long lines, of the suggestion of strength and protection. And when her thoughts strayed to what lay beneath that fabric, heat flared up her neck.

"Quite dashing," she murmured.

"Sorry?" He pivoted, head cocked.

She grabbed handfuls of her apron to keep from slapping a hand over her mouth, for surely that would be even more indicting. "Oh, er, the day is quite dashing away from me, I'm afraid. How goes it down at the camp?" She rushed on. "How is little Jack faring?"

One of his brows quirked as he crossed to the counter and set down a package. "Makawee won't let me near him. Swears by the 'old medicine,' as she calls it."

"Good. It is enough you tend the smallpox victims on your own. You needn't add another disease to your repertoire."

A muscle jumped in his jaw. "I am no novice, Miss Nelson. I assure you, I take every precaution."

"Of course." She bit her lip as warmth bloomed over her cheeks. Sweet heavens! What was wrong with her tongue today? Or any day, for that matter. Whenever the man entered the room, her words flew out before she could think. "I am sorry. I never meant to imply such."

Little crinkles highlighted the sides of his mouth as he grinned. "Apology accepted. And you'll be glad to know Jack's rash has stopped spreading."

"Then he's on the mend, unlike a few of the men in there." She nodded toward the ward, though she needn't have—wretched coughing crept from under the closed door. "Truthfully, I fear for Major Clem, which reminds me. . ." She reached for the mug of tea.

But the doctor stayed her arm with a light touch. "Then I've come just in time. I've brought something."

There was almost a bounce to his step as he retrieved the package from the counter and ripped it open, revealing a small, wooden box. He held it out to her like a crown of jewels to be admired. "A new shipment of fresh leeches, which was quite the feat in this weather."

She suppressed a groan but couldn't stop the censure in the shake of her head. "You know my feelings on the matter."

He drew back his box, taking the warmth in his voice with it. "The siphoning out of bad blood is proven science, Miss Nelson."

"Maybe so, yet my experience proves it weakens the patient. My father said—"

His hand shot up, and what was left of his grin faded into a straight line. "Not another lecture. If your methods are not working with the major, then it's time you use scholarship."

The implication smacked her. Hard. *Scholarship?* As if what she'd been using was nothing but folderol and superstition? For a moment, she clenched her teeth so tightly, crackling sounded in her ears. Perhaps she should give in to Aunt's entreaties, go where she was wanted, find an orphanage in the city and tend to their needs instead.

She met his stare dead-on, not wanting to leave, but not wanting to stay, either. "Maybe, Doctor, it's time I leave. You barely consider my medical advice, nor do you use me at the encampment anymore. Give me one reason why I should stay."

◆　◆　◆

Because your beautiful smile will no longer brighten this barracks.

Because you are life and breath and air.

James staggered, pushed back by a rush of emotions and the real reason lodging low in his gut.

Because I fear my heart will stop beating without you.

He raked his fingers through his hair, a desperate attempt to push back the wild thoughts and fatigue that ailed him. This couldn't be. When had this snip of a wilderness woman worked her way so deeply into his soul? A relationship with her would change his plans, his future. . .his everything. Everything he'd worked so hard to gain. Years of study. Of jockeying for position on Harvard's wobbly ladder of success. His goal to achieve all his father had dreamed for him. He should just stride to the door, hold it open, and thank the lady for her service.

And while he was at it, he might just as well grab a knife and stab it into his chest.

For a moment, he searched her eyes, desperately trying to judge if leaving was what she really wanted. Did she?

Sweet mercy! The woman ought to be a card shark the way she hid every emotion behind those long lashes. There was no reading her desire—and there was no discounting his.

He forced words past an ache in his throat. "You should stay because I ask it of you."

"But why do you ask?"

The question gaped like the sharp jaws of a bear trap. If he answered too personally, he'd frighten her away. Too detached, and she'd not feel needed. Either would set her and her bags on the next possible wagon out of the fort.

He caught both her hands in his, hoping the added touch might sway her. "Despite our differences on manner of care, the fact is, Miss Nelson, that you do care. I would be hard pressed to replace you and, in fact, could not. Truth is, I am in over my head at the encampment with this foul weather. I cannot possibly tend to both the men here and the people down below. Would you force me to choose, knowing what the colonel would have me do?"

A sigh deflated her shoulders. "No. Of course not. I will stay, leastwise until you can manage both."

"Thank you." He squeezed her fingers then released his hold. "If it's any consolation, the colonel is holding a Christmas dinner day after tomorrow. Would you do me the honor of attending with me?"

A small smile lifted her lips. "I suppose it would please my aunt to know I am owning some measure of society out here."

"Good." He returned her grin. Though the festivity might pacify her relative, it would please him even more to have her at his side.

Chapter Seven

Emmy scowled into the small looking glass nailed to her chamber wall, her lips a flawless shade of red, her brows arched to perfection—and a rogue curl dangling front and center on her forehead. Stifling a growl, she eased out one more hairpin from the chignon at the back, praying the silly thing wouldn't fall down her neck, then skewered the curl and stabbed it into the puff of hair on top. Oh, to be a princess and command a lady's maid.

"Miss Nelson?" Knuckles rapped on her door. "Are you ready?"

With a final tap on the pin and a whispered, "Behave!" she whirled from the mirror. "Coming."

She lifted the latch, and her heart skipped a beat. Lamplight brushed over Dr. Clark in a golden glow. Did she not know him to be a man, she'd wonder at his supernatural appearance. His hair was slicked back. His jaw, clean-shaven. An indigo frock coat contrasted richly with his white shirt, all tailored to ride the long lines of his body. Her glance slid to lighter-blue trousers and Hessians that shone with a polish. She tried to catch her breath, but it eluded her, like a milkweed pod blown open, scattering seeds into a thousand directions.

"I fear I shall have my hands full tonight." His deep voice murmured.

She angled her face to his, looking for a clue. Full of what? Had her hair fallen again? His shiny eyes gave no hint.

"Whatever do you mean, sir?"

"Once we walk out that door, I may have to stave off an entire battalion to defend your honor, for I guarantee"—he winked—"you will turn the head of every officer."

"La, sir!" She swatted his arm. He was a charmer, she'd give him that. "How you exaggerate."

He laughed and retreated a step.

Then, shaking his head, his smile faded. His gaze smoldered. "You have no idea how beautiful you are, do you?"

Heat burned a trail to her belly. She swallowed, trying hard to remember Daniel's face, but all she could see were the green eyes of the man in front of her, the strong cut of his forehead, his cheeks. Oh, she'd loved Daniel, but that was long ago, and truthfully. . .she searched memories, shaking them out like a laundered sheet. No, she'd never felt the kind of sweet ache that gripped her when the doctor's gaze wrapped around her and held her in place.

She swallowed, coaxing out a voice that wouldn't crack. "We ought be going. I've made us late enough as is."

But he didn't move. He stood there, fumbling his hand inside his dress coat. "Wait. I've brought you something."

He held out a small box, nested atop his palm. A young lad offering flowers to his girl couldn't have been more proud.

Emmy bit her lip. Why had she not thought to get him something? "I. . .I have no gift for you."

He pressed the box toward her, so that she had no choice but to take it. "Ah, ah, ah. Doctor's orders."

It was a poor jest, nevertheless a dear one. She lifted the lid and gasped. "Oh!"

Inside, a silk flower brooch, no larger than her thumb, lay on white satin bedding. She pulled it out and examined the tiny rose, one way then another, letting the light set fire to the deep red.

"How lovely." She peered up at him with a smile. "Thank you."

"May I pin it on for you?"

She handed it over, and his fingers brushed against hers, gentle as a fairy's kiss. He stepped closer, so near she inhaled his scent of sandalwood and masculinity. For a moment, she wobbled on her feet, dizzy from the heat of his body.

"There. All done." But his stance contradicted his words, for he didn't step back, nor did his hand lower. His fingers trailed upward from her collar, slowly, as if asking for permission, then slid across her cheek and rested just behind her ear. His eyes flashed with questions, promises. . .desire.

"James?" she whispered.

He dipped his head, and his lips skimmed over hers like a summer breeze. Closing her eyes, she leaned in to his embrace, his arms as strong as a beam that could carry her world. Her heart pounded hard in her ears. This—*this*—was where she wanted to be, wanted to live.

For always.

"Emmy." He breathed her name against her mouth, her jaw, her neck.

She shivered—and pressed closer.

With a gasp, the doctor stumbled back a step. The world stopped. Air and life and hope hovered somewhere overhead, beyond reach. Only the rattle of the night air against her window anchored her to the real world.

He drew his hand across his mouth, and it shook—as did his voice. "I am so sorry."

"Are you?" Despite what Aunt would have to say, a wicked half smile tingled on the very lips that had just been so finely kissed, and Emmy lifted her chin. "I am not so sure I am."

◆ ◆ ◆

Miss Emmaline Nelson would be the death of him. Carve it on his gravestone, killed by a woman—a beautiful bit of a woman, all fire and passion. And that is exactly what he loved most about her, the unreserved way she gave herself to that which she cared about.

Beads of perspiration lined up like little soldiers at the nape of his neck. One broke rank and trickled down his spine as he stared at her, her eyes full of the knowledge of what lay in his heart. One fingertip ran across her lower lip. Was she remembering?

Or lamenting?

Ah, yes, but such a kiss. One he wouldn't mind repeating—and one that never should've happened in the first place. Working with her from now on would be awkward at best.

He exhaled a shaky breath. "You are right, Miss Nelson."

Her brows shot up, and a delightful curl fell down to meet them. "I am?"

"Yes." He pivoted and held out his arm, eager for a face full of cold night air. "We ought to be going."

The short walk to the colonel's quarters cooled his feverish skin, so much that he shook beneath his greatcoat.

She shot him a sideways glance. "You tremble as if you have the chills. Are you well?"

He kicked at some snow with the tip of his boot. "Need I remind you I am born and bred a Boston man? I am not used to such a severe climate."

"Well, I think it suits you."

He frowned. "Why?"

She blinked up at him. "Is your temperament not as extreme?"

The pixie! He grinned in full as he led her up the stairs to the colonel's door. "I fear you're coming to know me too well."

The colonel's wife rushed over to them as they entered the foyer. "There you are! And about time, too. We are just going in to dinner."

Beyond her, the last blue tail of an officer's jacket disappeared through a door.

"My apologies, Mrs. Crooks." He spoke as he helped Emmy—Miss Nelson, out of her coat. Giving himself a mental thrashing for his lapse, he removed his coat as well, handing both off to the servant standing nearby. It would not do to think of Emmy too intimately, or her Christian name would fall unguarded from his lips.

Miss Nelson stepped nearer the colonel's wife, mischief in the tap of her shoes. "The doctor was working overtime."

The woman's hands fluttered to her chest. "Nothing serious, I hope."

"Very serious, I'm afraid." Laughter danced a jig in Emmy's gaze as she looked at him.

Blast the woman, and hang the effort of ever thinking of her as anything other than Emmy—*his* Emmy. He tugged at his collar. Gads, but it was hot in here.

"Oh, dear! It's going to be a very long winter, I suppose." Mrs. Crooks ushered them to the dining-room door.

Besides the empty chair reserved for the colonel's wife at the foot of the table, only two other seats remained. A servant held out Emmy's seat. James sat opposite, a lieutenant's wife at his right—one very large with child—and a major to his left—one with a sizable interest in Emmy, judging by the way his gaze traveled over her.

The man leaned forward, ogling her as if she were the appetizer now being served. "Major Darnwood at your service, madam. I've only recently arrived. And you are?"

Emmy answered with a small smile—one that did not reach her eyes. "Miss Nelson, Dr. Clark's assistant."

"Oh, *miss*, is it?" He leaned back, elbowing James. "Your assistant, eh? Wonder if I could get her to assist me."

Anger curled his hand into a fist, yet he flexed it and rested his palm on the man's shoulder. "Did you know, Major, that if I apply a little pressure to your carotid artery, which is just a twitch away from my index finger, you'll land in your soup before the next spoonful reaches your mouth?"

The man glowered and shifted in his seat, putting as much space between them as politely possible.

A smirk lifted James's lips, but the victory didn't last long. The lieutenant next to Emmy closed in on her, serving her a slice of roast goose and a whisper, his shoulder brushing flush against hers. Her jaw tightened, and scarlet spread across her cheeks.

James bristled. Enough was quite enough.

He pushed back his chair and stood. Throbbing pounded in his temples. The world tipped. He reached out a hand to grasp the table's edge. Why were there suddenly two colonels sitting where there should be only one?

"My apologies, sir, for interrupting this festivity." His voice rasped, and the duo-colonels melded into one.

No, this could not be happening. Not to him.

He quickly slugged back some wine from his goblet before continuing. "Miss Nelson and I must return to the ward."

"Such a sorry business, Doctor." Mrs. Crooks shook her head. "But your commitment to the men is admirable."

"Indeed. Well then, you are excused." The colonel and all the men stood as Emmy rose. "Happy Christmas to you both."

Emmy's steps clipped next to his, but she held her tongue until they cleared the foyer. "I was enjoying that dinner, despite the few rogues in attendance. You're taking this guardianship thing too far. What is wrong with you?"

Shoring his shoulder against the wall, he shuddered. Heat poured off him in waves.

And his next words barely made it past the raw flesh in his throat. "I am ill."

Chapter Eight

Emmy shoved aside her plate of cold beans on the dispensary counter, having managed only a few more bites of leftover dinner. Her appetite was gone, taking with it the remnants of her optimism. How much longer could James hold on?

The front door opened on a whoosh of cold air. Major Clem entered with a tug at his hat, a dusting of snow stark against his blue overcoat. "Afternoon, Miss Nelson. On my way to file a report with the colonel and thought I'd check in on the doctor. How's he doing?"

The question slapped her hard. She'd been trying all day not to answer it, to ignore the symptoms, the way his life was packing its bags for a long, long journey—one from which he wouldn't return.

"Not good." The words tasted like milk gone bad, sour and rancid.

"Sorry to hear that." He rubbed the back of his neck, sending a sprinkling of white falling from his coat. "But if anyone can pull him through, it'd be you."

She snorted, and though vulgar, it could not be helped. "Your confidence, while appreciated, is misplaced, Major. I fear I've done all I can."

His boots thudded on the wooden planks. He stopped in front of her like a bulwark, immovable and stony. "I don't know much about medicine and such, but here's what I've learned of war. Find out where your enemy is then strike hard as you can, and for God's sake, keep on moving. To stop is to die."

She wanted to grasp on to the strength he offered, but her hope hung as lifeless as her limp hands at her sides. A simple "Thank you" was the best she could manage.

"I trust you're taking great care of the doctor, but give a thought to yourself as well." He nodded at her half-eaten beans before he wheeled about and strode from the dispensary, out into January's brittle arms.

The last light of day colored the room in a lifeless pallor. She shivered and lit the oil lamp. Taking the major's words to heart, she once again hauled out the fat medical book she'd taken from James's shelf. It flopped open from the crease she'd made in the binding, having pored over the same section one too many times.

Rubbing her heavy eyes, she tried to focus on the words. Ink blurred into fuzzy lines. No need though, really, for she could recite the diagnosis and procedures in this chapter without error. The measles had hit James hard, and his body had fought valiantly. But once pneumonia set in, what little strength he'd rallied bled out in rib-breaking coughs that produced nothing other than thick green mucus and weakness.

She slammed the book shut, the noise of it a satisfying *thwack*. This wasn't fair. None of it. She'd tried it all. Papa's treatments. Medical journal advice. Textbook treatises on the proper care of lung inflammations. She'd tended patients like this before, but none of them drained her of every possible cure—or wrenched her heart in quite the same way.

Fatigue pressed in on her, sagging her shoulders. Despite the major's admonition, she considered giving up. Simply march right into James's chambers, lie down by his side, and close her eyes to life along with him.

Wretched hacking hurtled out from his room down the corridor. She jerked up her head, listening with her whole body. This was new. Gurgly. Choking.

Ugly.

She raced from the dispensary and flew into his chamber. "James!"

He writhed on the bed, chest heaving—and a small trickle of blood leaked out the side of his blue lips. Sweat darkened the chest and armpits of his nightshirt. The doctor who'd saved so many lives now fought for his own.

Snatching a cloth from a basin on the stand, she knelt next to him. "Shh. Be at peace, love," she cooed as she wiped his face. "Be at peace."

He stilled.

So did she. Not that she hadn't known the truth for weeks now, but speaking the words aloud made it real. She loved him—the man who at any moment might stop breathing altogether.

Tears burned down her cheeks and hit her lips, tasting like loss. She brushed back his hair, wishing, praying his green eyes would open, that he'd berate her manner of healing. . .and tell her what to do.

"Don't leave me. Do not!" Her cry circled the room, but James neither woke nor stirred.

Defeated, she rested her cheek against his chest, now fluttering with quick breaths. At least the thrashing had stopped. "Oh, God." Her voice soaked into his nightshirt along with her tears. "Please don't take him, not yet. Not now. Show me what to do."

All the anguish of the past three weeks closed her eyes. How long she lay there, she couldn't say, long enough, though, that when she lifted her head, darkness crept into the room from every corner.

James's breaths still wheezed on the inhale, rattled around, and gurgled back out. Nothing had changed. Nothing.

Or had it?

She shot to her feet, listening beyond his labored breathing. In the distance, a steady beat pounded on the night air. Drums.

Of course! Why had she not thought of this before?

Darting from the room, she raced to her chamber and grabbed her woolen cloak then snatched the lantern off the counter. She flung open the dispensary door as easily as she flung aside any care for her own safety or caution. What did it matter anymore?

She took off at a run toward the gate, already shut for the night. She might have exhausted every resource known to white man, but Makawee was a master of the "old medicine."

◆　◆　◆

Scorching heat. Frigid cold. James swam from one extreme to the other, all the while gasping for breath beneath the dark waters of pain. He'd give anything to emerge from this ocean of hurt—even his own life.

Occasionally blessed relief allowed him to float...a gentle touch on his brow or water pressed against his lips. But those were not enough to pull him out of the deeps.

And so he sank.

Until the whisper came. No, something stronger. He strained to listen. A mourning dove cooed. The haunting sound reached out like a rope, tethering him to a faraway edge of land.

"Be at peace, love. Be at peace."

He clung to those words, holding fast when his chest burned and his ribs crashed and air was nearly a memory.

Peace.

Love.

His eyes shot open. Maybe not. Hard to tell. So he stared, waiting for shapes to form out of the darkness. Was God's face the next thing he would see?

He blinked. Slowly, his gaze traced silhouettes. Color, though muted, seeped in and spread. Smoky sweetness wafted overhead, altogether foreign and pleasing.

"James?" Fabric swished. Troubled blue eyes bent near to his. "James!"

Ahh, dear one. His heart beat loud in his ears. Could Emmy hear it, too?

He struggled to lift his hand, wipe the single tear marring her sweet cheek, erase the fear shadowing the hollows beneath her eyes.

But it took all he had in him to simply open his mouth. "Emmy."

The effort cost more than he could spare. Blackness covered him like a blanket pulled over his head.

When his eyes opened again, morning light streamed in, kissing the top of Emmy's blond hair. She sat in a chair next to his bed, her face bowed over the pages of a book.

"Em—" he croaked. Clearing his throat, he tried again. "Emmy?"

The book hit the floor.

"James?" She slid from the chair and knelt, face-to-face. "Stay with me this time."

"I'd...like...to." He inhaled strength, or was it her trembling smile that bolstered him so? "Water? So thirsty."

She retrieved a mug from the nightstand then propped him up with her arm behind his shoulders. More liquid than not trickled down his chin, but it was enough to simply have her embrace sustain him—so satisfying that he drifted away once again.

Next time he woke, the room was empty, save for the ticking of the New Haven clock he'd brought with him from Cambridge. The last light of day peeked into his chamber window—but which day? How long had he lain on this bed?

He pushed himself up, propping the pillow behind his back. The room spun, but his lungs didn't burn, nor did he feel the need to hack until his ribs fractured.

"Well!" Emmy swished into the room with a smile that would shame a summer day. "Good to see you are on the mend, Dr. Clark."

"Oh? It's back to that now?" His voice, while raspy, at least worked this time. "I rather liked it when you called me James."

Fire blazed across her cheeks. She turned from him and poured liquid into a mug. "Yes, well, I tried anything and everything to pull you through."

"Whatever you did apparently worked."

She held the cup to his mouth, and as water dampened his lips, his thirst roared. He grabbed the mug from her and—though she warned against it—drained it. His stomach revolted, and he pressed the back of his hand to his lips.

"When will you listen to me?" She removed the mug then settled the chair so that she faced him.

Slowly, the nausea passed, and he lowered his hand. "I did listen—especially when you called me James."

She smirked. "I see your wit is quite recovered as well. Tell me"—she leaned closer, her worried gaze searching his—"how are you feeling?"

He studied her for a moment. Her cheekbones stood out. Her dress hung loose at the shoulders—and the brooch he'd given her for Christmas was pinned at the top of her bodice. Dare he hope she entertained a place in her heart for him? And if she did, then what? How could a wife fit into his life at a time when he needed to focus on scholarship?

He sank into the pillow. The questions exhausted him. He'd think on them later. For now, better to get her to do the talking. "I might ask the same of you. How do you fare?"

She nibbled her lower lip, one of her stalling tactics. Her chest rose and fell with a deep breath. "I am better, now that I know you are well. You gave me quite a scare, you know. I thought I'd lost you. I tried everything, but nothing worked."

He scrubbed a hand over his chin, where whiskers scratched. He could only imagine the days—weeks maybe—of hard work she'd endured for him. She should be attending dinners and dances, not slogging away in a sick man's chamber. How many other women would willingly suffer through such?

"Yet I live, thanks be to you." His words came out more husky than he intended.

She laughed. "More like thanks be to God and to Makawee."

"What do you mean?"

"I employed every manner of care I knew for pneumonia. I read through all your books and applied those treatments also. But I believe it was Makawee's methods, the rabbit tobacco, the pleurisy root, that helped you turn the corner."

Roots? Tobacco? How could he even begin to understand that? He frowned. "Preposterous."

"Yet as you've said, you live." She leaned toward him. "Think on that."

He sank farther into the pillow. Had he been wrong? Was there more to healing than the sterile procedures of academia? Maybe knowledge and all he held most dear were not to be found in the East, but rather here, in the middle of a wilderness he'd scorned not long ago.

He fastened on her clear blue gaze a moment more before closing his eyes. "I believe there is much I should think on."

Chapter Nine

With a last shudder, winter turned its back on March and shuffled off, taking along with it the icy chill and the worst of the measles and smallpox outbreaks. By April, spring ran wild with flowers and green and promise, reviving the dead, and spurring Emmy into a sprint down the path from the encampment.

"Hold up," James called from behind.

She waited, content to simply watch him as he strode toward her, his long legs eating up the ground. After having witnessed him near death, she'd never tire of seeing the flush of health on his cheeks or the bounce in his step. The past few months had flown by, working at his side, living for his smile, but mostly drinking in his companionship like cool water from a stream.

"I've got something for you. Hold still." He produced a spray of tiny flowers, each petal brushed with a faint swath of violet. His strong fingers could crush them without trying, but he used his surgeon's skill to work them into her hair like a crown. She'd wished to be a princess once—and now she was.

It took every bit of willpower she owned not to wrap her arms around him and nestle her head against his shirt. Though they never spoke of it, that kiss on a wintry evening had changed everything.

He crooked his finger and lifted her chin. "Beautiful flowers for a beautiful lady."

Her lips ached, her whole body yearned to rise up on her tiptoes, lean a little closer, and—what was she thinking?

Judging by the gleam in his eye and the way he bent just a breath away, he thought the same.

She smiled up into his face. "Do you like nature, James?"

"I do."

She ran her hands up his arms and lightly rested them on his chest. His heart beat strong against her fingers.

"Would you like to be closer to it?" she whispered.

"I would." He leaned in.

Laughing, she shoved him backward, so that he stumbled into a tangle of sumac.

"Pixie!" he roared.

She giggled and fled down the path toward the road—then pulled up short before running headlong into an oncoming carriage.

"Whoa!" A familiar voice, wooly and gruff, rumbled from the driver's seat.

"Jubal? Aunt Rosamund?" Skirting the prancing horses, Emmy strode to the window of Aunt's lacquered carriage.

"Emmaline?" A gunmetal-gray head peeked out the window, a single peacock feather wagging from her sateen bonnet.

Emmy choked back a sob. The Nelson family high cheekbones and long nose reminded her of her father. "Oh, Aunt! How lovely to see you."

"This is exactly what I feared." Aunt's lips pinched, as did her tone. "Look at you! Running about in the wild. What would your father have to say?"

Emmy bowed her head, feeling as small as the time her aunt had caught her splashing in a puddle as a young girl.

"I think he'd say, 'Job well done.'" James caught up to her side, his presence as solid and strong as the poplars taking leaf around them. "Thanks to Miss Nelson," he said, "there are two new souls in the camp, for she just delivered twins, and breech at that."

Aunt peered at him then rummaged for a moment and produced a set of spectacles, eyeing him as if he were an insect to be dissected. "And you are?"

Emmy stepped forward, filling the gap between the doctor and the carriage. "Aunt Rosamund, allow me to introduce Dr. Clark. Doctor, my aunt, Miss Rosamund Nelson."

"Pleased to meet you, Miss Nelson." He dipped his head in a bow, ever the charmer. "I've heard so many good things about you."

"Have you?" She lowered her glasses and speared Emmy with a frown. "I wonder."

Hooves pounded up the road, heading straight toward them. Jubal's arms strained to keep the carriage horses under control.

A corporal on a bay reined in next to them. "Colonel's looking for you, Dr. Clark. Says you're to come at once."

"Oh? Is someone hurt?"

"Nah. Nothing like that." The corporal's horse pawed the ground, scraping up gravel. "First mail of the season arrived upriver, and along with it, the new doc."

James's brows rose.

Emmy's heart sank. She knew he'd be leaving sometime this spring, but were these halcyon days to end so soon?

James nodded then turned back to her and Aunt. "Forgive me, but I need bid you ladies adieu. Pleased to meet you, ma'am."

He swung up behind the corporal, leaving Emmy to face her aunt alone. Her throat tightened, fearing the purpose for Rosamund's visit. She swept an arm toward the fort's front gate. "Will you come in for tea, Aunt?"

"I didn't come for tea, child." Grooves carved into the sides of Aunt's mouth, forged by a magnificent scowl. "I came to take you home. Get in the carriage."

◆　◆　◆

James slid off the horse with a "thanks" to the corporal, feeling a little uneasy for leaving Emmy alone with her aunt. The woman could intimidate a battalion of dragoons. No wonder Emmy had learned to fend for herself.

A makeshift post office—nothing more than a table with a bag of letters dumped onto it—sat in front of the colonel's quarters. For the first mail of the season, the usual protocol—and discipline—stretched as thin as the cook's gruel. A swarm of soldiers buzzed around, some with stony faces as they read of bad news from home, others letting out whoops of happiness. The worst, though, were those walking away with a drag to their step from receiving no letters at all.

Bypassing the ruckus, James climbed the front stairs then halted when he heard his name called.

"Letter for you, Doctor. Looks all official-like." A private who might better serve as a scarecrow held out a thick-papered document.

"Thanks, Private." Grasping the letter, he retired to a corner of the front porch and leaned against the wall.

His name was scrawled across the front in black ink. Burgundy wax bled into a circle on the back, a single word embossed in the center—*veritas*. He sucked in a breath. Truth, indeed. He didn't need to read the signature inside to know that Dr. Stafford was either opening the door for his advancement or slamming it shut in his face. . .but which did he really want?

He swallowed then broke the seal.

Greetings James,

Word of your stellar performance this past winter season at Fort Snelling has reached my ear. I trust by now that from your experience, you've learned there is more to medicine than textbooks. I know you weren't happy about this arrangement initially, but I hope you've come to see the benefit and necessity. The position for director of surgical instruction is recently opened up. I can think of no better candidate than yourself. It will be a fight, but one I am sure we can win. Catch the next available steamship back to Boston, where we may begin your campaign strategy.

~ William Stafford, MD, MS

Stunned, James tucked the letter inside his waistcoat then ran both hands through his hair. Director? So soon? Could he really bypass being an instructor first? This was unheard of—but so was attaining the sponsorship of Dr. Stafford, one of the most influential men walking the hallowed halls of Harvard Medical. And if Stafford thought he had a chance, then, well. . .*veritas*. There was no doubt about it.

"Dr. Clark?" A major held open the front door. "Colonel Crooks is asking for you."

He pushed away from the wall, shoving aside further speculation—for now, anyway.

"Pardon me, but you're the doc?" A tall man, tawny-headed and with eyes bluer than cornflowers, stepped into his path.

James angled his head. Something about the fellow was familiar.

"I'm Dr. Clark," he said.

The man reset his cap, likely fresh off the steamship and eager for some movement. "I just came from a meeting with the colonel. He said you'd know the layout of the encampment, having tended the inhabitants all winter, particularly who lived in what tent."

"Ahh." He nodded. "So you're looking for someone."

"I am." His hand dropped, and a starved look haunted his blue gaze. "My wife and son."

James took a step closer, studying the man. Like the combining of symptoms to diagnose an ailment, he added up the information and what his own eyes told him. "Let me guess. . .Makawee and little Jack?"

The fellow's mouth dropped. "How did you know?"

James grinned. "Because except for the hair color, your son is a miniature of you."

"How are they?" The fellow leaned toward him, as if by sheer proximity he might learn the answer.

"They are well, and you will find them very conveniently in the second tent to the right as you enter the camp."

The fellow reached out and pumped his hand. "Thank you."

Then he flew down the steps and sprinted across the parade ground before James could answer.

With a chuckle, he headed for the colonel's office, imagining what a homecoming that would be.

The colonel stood near his desk, nodding at his entrance. "High time you show up, Doctor. I've other matters to attend." He motioned James into the room. "Dr. Griffin, meet Dr. Clark. And Clark, meet Dr. Griffin."

At the mention of his name, a short man pushed himself up from a chair and crossed the room. A few memories of hair tufted near his ears. His handshake matched with a wispy grip.

"Pleased to meet you, Doctor." The man pumped his hand, or tried to, anyway. "Colonel Crooks has been telling me of the hardships you've endured this past winter."

He schooled his face, trying hard not to smirk. This slight fellow wouldn't last the summer. "What doesn't kill us makes us stronger, eh? I'm sure you'll have an easier go of it, though."

The colonel skirted his desk. "Dr. Clark, would you see that Dr. Griffin is familiar with the dispensary and ward before you leave? Oh, and there's a bit of paperwork I'd like to have you take care of as well."

Leave? His breath hitched at the colonel's words. It was so final. So jarring. Like the slamming of a door in an empty house, the implications reverberated in his chest. His work here was done. Finished. It was time to leave the natives he'd come to admire—and the woman he'd come to love.

"Dr. Clark?"

"Hmm? Oh, yes. Of course." He turned to Dr. Griffin and swept a hand toward the door. "Shall we?"

Griffin exited. He followed but stopped at the threshold at the colonel's command.

"Oh, one more thing, Dr. Clark."

"Sir?"

Crooks tapped a letter against one palm. "I've received word the Sioux are to be shipped out West, away from those with long memories and longer arms of vengeance. They'll be under the management of Fort Randall—a garrison without a doctor. You've done a fine job here. Lives were saved because of you. On my word, the position is yours, if you want it."

Him? The one who barely survived a Minnesota winter? He let out a breath, long and low. "I shall think on it, Colonel."

"I couldn't ask for more. Dismissed."

James strode out into the sunlight. How dare the day be so bright when dark and heavy decisions weighed on his shoulders? What to do? Hop a steamship east to his former dream of power and prestige—one that would eclipse any thought of love or family?

Or mount up and ride farther west, to a land more rugged than the one he now claimed?

His steps stalled. So did his heart. How could Emmy possibly fit into any of this, especially with an aunt determined to drag her into society?

Well, Lord?

He stood waiting a long time, praying, ignoring the soldiers around him. Waiting for what? A lightning bolt to write an answer in the sky? *Show me, God. Clearly.*

And. . .nothing.

With a sigh, he lowered his gaze—then jerked his face back overhead. Two sparrows, flying in tandem, swooped gracefully toward the west.

Moving as one.

He smiled. It was a small answer, but answer enough. *Thank You, God.*

Setting his hat tight, he set off at a run, straight toward the dispensary.

Chapter Ten

Emmy sat on the edge of her bed, her trunk by her chamber door ready for Jubal to fetch. Her father's medical bag lay in her lap. She ran a finger along the top, smearing tears into the worn leather. Once she moved to Aunt Rosamund's fine Minneapolis home, this bag would be relegated to the attic. Aunt would never allow her to degrade herself by caring for the sick. No more tending to births or coughs or fevers. No more sweet friendship with Makawee and little Jack.

And no more working long days next to James, shadowing his every move, inhaling his scent of sandalwood and strength. She pressed her fingers to her mouth, stifling a sob.

She might as well box up her heart and store that in the rafters, too.

"What's this?" James skirted the trunk as he entered the room, the pull of him drawing her to her feet.

Oh, how she'd love to run into his arms, rest her head against his chest, and forget about Aunt and the new life she didn't want. Yet she stood there, as straight as one of the soldiers at attention.

His gaze slid from the empty nightstand, to the bare pegs on the wall, and finally rested on her. He cocked a brow. "Are you leaving?"

She shrugged, stalling for the right words. How to tell him that in mere minutes she'd be walking out that door forever? Her throat closed, and it took several swallows before she could manage a simple, "I am."

"Oh? What a coincidence." He grinned. "So am I."

She grabbed handfuls of her skirt to keep from slapping the silly smile off his face. Did the man not care their friendship would be ending? That he'd never see her again? Had she been wrong about his feelings?

She drew in a sharp breath. "Evidently your meeting with the colonel went well."

"Better than that." He rocked onto his toes, the movement stoking her anger. "My dream is nearly within reach."

Coldhearted, selfish man! She knotted the fabric tighter, choking the life from her skirt. Had the past six months meant nothing to him that he could ball up all their tender moments and cast them aside like a wadded bit of paper?

So be it. If he could let her go that easily, neither would she hold on. She splayed her fingers, letting her skirt drop.

"Well, then, Dr. Clark, I am happy for you. It's good to know some of us get what we desire. You will no doubt rise quickly to the top at Harvard Medical." She hurled the words like a porcelain teacup against a wall, wishing the impact would break his heart into as many piece as hers. How could she have been so wrong?

"But I—"

"Good-bye." She swished past him. She didn't need justifications or explanations. Her eyes filled, turning the room into a watery mess.

"Emmy!"

A tug on her shoulder pulled her back.

His breath came out in a huff. "You jump to conclusions faster than a raging bout of chicken pox, woman. Hear me out."

She scowled at his hand on her arm, then up into his face. "What more is there to say? Aunt is waiting for me. I'm bound for Minneapolis, and you're headed east."

"What?" His brows shot skyward. "I never said I was going east. Quite the opposite, actually. I'm traveling west."

His declaration rattled around like rocks in a can, making noise but no sense whatsoever. She stared into his eyes, yet no hint of meaning surfaced in those green pools.

She shook her head. "I don't understand."

"Clearly." He drew closer, entwining his fingers with hers. "Colonel Crooks received orders that the encampment is to be struck and moved to Dakota Territory. The fort there is in need of a doctor, and he's offered me the position."

"But. . .but that's even more wild than here, and it's a far cry from teaching at a medical institution. That's not your dream."

"You're right. Not quite. But this is." He slid to one knee. Slowly, he lifted one of her hands to his lips, pressing a kiss from one knuckle to the next then repeated the action with the other.

Her knees weakened. His warm breath caressed all the way up her arm. What on earth was he doing?

He lowered her hands and lifted his face. His eyes glowed—no, his whole face, from the cut of his square jaw up to his fine, strong brow.

"My dream, Miss Emmaline Nelson"—his voice deepened, laced with an urgency she'd never before heard—"is that you would not only be my assistant but my wife."

The world stopped. Sound receded. All she could hear was her breath rushing in, rushing out. It took all her concentration to keep her lungs pumping. Had she heard correctly, or was she imagining things? Was this real?

He squeezed her hands. "What do you say?"

◆　◆　◆

James stood on a cliff's edge, holding his breath. One word from the woman in front of him and he'd fall into her arms—or plummet to his death. She blinked at him, yet said nothing. Not even a murmur. Oughtn't a woman in love say something?

An ember of doubt flared in his gut. As a lad, on the cusp of adolescence, he'd mustered his courage to ask a girl to dance once. He'd often wished she'd snubbed him with a loud rejection, but she'd simply turned her back and walked away, leaving him standing alone, abandoned like an old shoe, pity shining in the eyes of the dancing master—and snickers assaulting him from the other boys attending the lessons. It was mortifying, humiliating.

And that same feeling seized his heart now.

Would Emmy do the same?

Slowly, he rose, his legs as weak as if the winter sickness revisited him. Emmy's eyes did not follow the movement. Her gaze remained fixed on the hands he'd so recently kissed.

"Emmy?" He cupped her face, lifting it to his. This might be it, the last time he held her. The thought lodged bitter at the back of his throat.

He gulped for air, prayed for wisdom, but mostly memorized every freckle and curve on her face. If she declined. . .his heart skipped a beat. *God, help me.*

"I love you, Emmy, with everything that's in me." He choked then cleared his throat and tried again. "I know you dreamed of a home in Mendota, the one you shared with your father, but dreams can change, can't they? Is it possible, in some small way, that I could be your new dream?"

Her eyes filled, shiny and luminous. A tremble quivered across her lower lip. Beneath his fingers, her skin warmed, flushing her cheeks like the first blush on a spring rose.

"Yes," she whispered, barely discernable.

But it was enough.

Sweet mercy! It was enough.

He pulled her against him, and when her mouth touched his, a tremor shook him. Hard. She breathed out his name, again and again. Ahh, but he'd never tire of hearing her say it.

"Yes, yes, yes!" She emphasized each word with a kiss, running her fingers up his back and twisting them into the hair at the nape of his neck. She leaned into him, hungry, searching—

"Emmaline Abigail Nelson!" Thunder boomed from the open door. "Get in the carriage. Now!"

He froze.

Emmy whirled. "Aunt! This isn't what you think—"

"What I think is that it was a mistake to have allowed you to stay here in the first place." Rosamund Nelson eyed him like a buck to be shot through the heart then gutted, leaving his innards to dry in the sun. "And you, sir, are responsible."

With a light touch, he drew Emmy to his side, facing the dragon. In spite of the situation, he grinned. How could he not, when the woman he loved had just agreed to share her life with him? "You are one-hundred percent correct, Miss Nelson. I have been—and will continue to be—responsible for this woman, for she is soon to become Mrs. James Clark."

Aunt Rosamund threw her hands wide, chasing after words as if she gathered an overturned crate of mice. "Well. . .I. . .Emmaline? Is this what you want? You would give up dinners, dances, society for the hard life of a doctor's wife?"

She turned to him, and this time, there was no hesitation, just a brilliant smile. "Yes, Aunt. There is nothing I want more than to be the doctor's wife. This doctor."

"Well!" Aunt Rosamund sputtered. "I never!"

Tucking Emmy under his arm, James smiled over the top of her head at the woman. "Then I pray that God will bring to you a special someone. As long as you're still breathing, there's always hope."

Hope, indeed. With Emmy nestled against him, it was time to start planning a new hope, a new direction, and together, a new dream.

A dream that would last a lifetime.

Michelle Griep's been writing since she first discovered blank wall space and Cray-olas. She resides in the frozen tundra of Minnesota, where she teaches history and writing classes for a local high school co-op. Historical romance is her usual haunt. *Brentwood's Ward* is her latest release. Follow her escapades at www.michellegriep.com or www.writeroftheleash.blogspot.com

An Everlasting Promise

by Eileen Key

For the mountains shall depart, and the hills be removed;
but my kindness shall not depart from thee,
neither shall the covenant of my peace be removed,
saith the LORD *that hath mercy on thee.*
ISAIAH 54:10

Chapter One

Texas
1890

Aunt Susan?" Veronica Fergus leaned over the bed and tucked wispy strands of gray hair behind her aunt's ear. So tiny. The tough prairie woman with the booming voice now lay clutching a threadbare quilt, her blue-veined eyelids fluttering. "Aunt Susan?"

A smile tilted one side of Susan's dry cracked lips. "Go home."

Veronica leaned in closer, her brow furrowed. "I can't—"

"Go. . ." Susan coughed a stale breath. Veronica lifted her aunt's head. Susan's rheumy blue eyes darted about the room. "Home." She closed them and sighed, nestling back into the pillow.

Veronica tucked the quilt in tighter against the bedroom's chill and propped her elbow on the headboard. *Go home.* What lovely words. But maybe her aunt meant she was going home—heaven home. Veronica stroked the soft hair, a sob strangling in her throat. Her father had deposited her with Aunt Susan over a year ago with the promise to return within a month, two at the most. But he'd not come back. And now Aunt Susan was leaving. A tear tipped over her eyelashes and trailed down her right cheek. Veronica swiped it with the back of her hand. She straightened and smoothed her skirt.

With a glance at the rise and fall of Aunt Susan's chest, Veronica pushed away from the bed and stepped into the small kitchen. The smell of coffee too long in the pot stung her nose. She poked at the dying embers in the fireplace and dropped in more wood. By morning she'd need to split a few more logs. She placed her hand in the small of her back and pressed hard. After three weeks sitting, watching her aunt wither away, her body cried out for rest, but there was none to be had. No one else to call upon. Her family did for themselves. That's how she and her dad had built their ranch—her home.

A pitiful wail mewed from the bedroom. Veronica dashed to the bedside and grasped Aunt Susan's hand, wincing when the old woman's nails dug into her palm. Her aunt struggled to raise up. "Ronnie, go home." Susan lay back, a raspy rattle deep in her throat. She looked at Veronica and closed her eyes. One more crackling breath, and she was gone.

Gone. . .home.

Tears streamed down Veronica's cheeks. She tugged the quilt over the small frame and shuffled to the kitchen table, her chest tight as she struggled for breath. It was as though her aunt's gasps now filled her body. *Ronnie.* The nickname clapped on her by her daddy had finally escaped her aunt's lips. She had longed to hear the word for the last few lonely months, but Aunt Susan wasn't one for terms of endearment or nicknames.

Veronica folded her arms atop the table and laid her head down. "I need a few minutes." She sighed, tears trickling, and her nose running. *Just a few moments.*

"Then I'm going home."

◆　◆　◆

Dust swirled around the bawling cattle, and Seth McKenzie pulled the kerchief tighter against his face. He blinked furiously and swiveled in the saddle. Despite the heat of the day, the dust, and the long road ahead, he smiled. He'd give McCrosky Ranch credit. Fort Worth stockyards would receive some of the finest beef he'd worked in a long time. He settled back into the saddle and nudged Ranger into a trot. Once they got the count in Alvin, stocked up on provisions, and hired a cook—a good cook—they'd head out.

Some three hundred miles north, he'd be done. Maybe for a long time. Seth sighed. He reined up beside Ernie, his head drover.

"Tighten up." He pointed east. "Drive them into the third corral."

The wizened cowboy raised a hand and circled his horse, lariat flying high and slapping his saddle. "Hiyah! Hiyah."

Bawling and tossing their heads, the cows surged forward into the corral. Seth pulled up short at the gate, removed the kerchief, and watched the herd. Mamas and babies pushed through the opening and bawled their displeasure at the fence line. With the three corrals filled, Mr. Miller would count and give Seth a report. He sighed and prayed the tally in Fort Worth would be near about the same.

"Stick with 'em, Ernie. I'm heading in." Seth pointed toward the general store, the site for information and supplies.

Ernie nodded, and Seth turned Ranger in the direction of the store at a slow pace. He took in the clapboard buildings, store, small hotel where he'd bunk for the night, barbershop, and a church at the end of the street. "Wonder if there's a service this Sunday, boy. Might have to get some preaching and singing in before we head to the wilderness." He patted his favorite companion's sweaty neck. He'd had the roan for six years and spilled most of his tales while in the saddle. No one to yell at him or tell him to stop talking back. He'd had enough of that.

Seth lifted his hat and wiped his brow with his forearm. Setting the hat back on, he nudged the horse to the hitching post and dismounted. He loosened the girth a bit then pulled off his saddlebag and slung it over his shoulder. Three steps led him to the wide boardwalk. He paused and scratched his cheek. Maybe a shave would be in order, too.

He stepped inside the mercantile and surveyed the room. The smell of peanuts brought up an instant memory: reaching in the barrel for a handful and being popped on the back of the head. He'd never had much taste for them after that. Cheese and crackers. Peppermint and licorice sticks. Every time he came in this building, his mind wandered.

"Seth." A stout Mrs. Goodman waved at him. "You got a list for me?" She swung around the corner of the counter and stood before him. "Of course you do. You're the most prepared cowboy this side of the Mississippi River."

Seth leaned forward and pecked her cheek. "You haven't been to the Mississippi River, Mrs. G. You're telling a tale." He grinned. "But I do have a list." He pulled a notebook from his back pocket and jerked a piece of paper out. "Reckon y'all have all I need, too."

He handed the list to her, and she scanned the page, nodding. "Think you're right."

She squinted back up at Seth. "When you heading out? How much time before you need this packed?"

Poking his fingers into his pockets, Seth studied the floor. "Before we go, I need us a cook." He raised a hand. "A good cook." He grinned broader. "You wouldn't want to go to Fort Worth, would you? I've tasted your apple pie."

Mrs. Goodman's cheeks flushed, and she chuckled. "Get out of here, boy. The only cook I know of is sitting at the café down the street. Rusty Mills can stir up a pan of beans, but he don't hold up next to my pies." She stepped back to the counter. "Go tell him I said he needed work, so get to it." Her eyes gleamed mischievously. "And don't take no for an answer. My brother has been sitting on his fanny far too long."

Seth laughed. "Thanks for the recommendation. Hang on to the order 'til I get our count and a cook." He tipped his hat. "You're the best, Mrs. G." He turned toward the door then paused. "Hey, are there services tomorrow?"

She nodded. "Same time, same place. And if you want to sit next to us, I'll feed you roast after." A sly grin crossed her face. "And possibly some pie."

Seth patted his stomach. "Now how can I *possibly* refuse that invitation? Thank you." He tipped his hat once again and wandered out the door. He scanned the street and noted the café. Best find Mills and see if he'd hire on. Seth's mouth watered. "Could he *possibly* make something worth eating on this trail?"

Clomping down the steps, he untied Ranger and led him down the street. "Lord, I'm hungry right now, so help me find food, and give me a real cook. Amen." Prayer in place, he tied the horse up again and headed on his cook quest.

Journal
March 29, 1890, Saturday

Contracted McCrosky with regular pay, hired Ernie Stillman and charged with drovers, herd bedded for count, possible cook, last real bed for a spell.

Chapter Two

Ronnie tied bonnet strings under her chin and surveyed her face in the wavy mirror. Not too bad—other than the crater of dark circles under her eyes. Eight days since the funeral and she was still worn out. Didn't seem to be much rest in the future she could see. Aunt Susan had sold off most of her furniture to pay doctor bills, and what was left wasn't worth trucking home. If she had a way home. No wagon, no mule, only an old mare and a worn-out saddle. It would be a long, lonely ride back to Fort Worth. She had enough money to stop over at the hotel there and then ride out to their homestead, but little else.

A sob threatened. She put her fingers over her lips in an effort to hold it back. "It's going to be all right. I can do this." She shivered and plucked her shawl from the nail by the door. "Hot as blazes outside and cold in here." She arranged the shawl, picked up her reticule, and gave one last glance in the mirror. "I'll sit with Mrs. Goodman, Aunt Susan's friend." She opened the door and stepped into the morning breeze. "Then I won't feel so alone."

The dust stirred about her skirts as she made her way down the street toward church. Last time she'd been inside was for the funeral. Only seven in attendance. Aunt Susan's crusty side had kept most people away. Except for the Goodman family. Susan smiled. "Good. Man. Yes, that's what they are." She stopped in front of the church steps, grasped her skirt, and shook it a bit to freshen it up before trekking inside. Someone collided into her back, and she lurched forward, catching herself on the banister with two hands. She straightened, swiveled, and glared at a man.

He held out his hands. "Ma'am, I am so sorry. Wasn't watching where I was going. Hope you aren't hurt."

Nothing but my pride. Ronnie ducked her head and brushed the skirt again, ignoring her stinging palms. "I'm quite all right, sir. But you might pay attention to where you're going." She looked at the man. The hat shaded his face. "Excuse me, service is about to begin." Ronnie jerked about, held her head high, and walked up the stairs. The shadows in the foyer helped cool her cheeks.

Mrs. Goodman and her family sat on the third pew, left side. Ronnie moved toward them and tapped her on the shoulder. "May I?"

"Of course, dear." Mrs. Goodman shuffled over, and Ronnie sat down. Her hands probably held a splinter or two from the fall, but there was no blood. She'd deal with them later.

A warm breeze blew through the windows and stirred the hair at the edges of her bonnet. Ronnie sighed and felt her shoulders droop, releasing some tension. For the next bit, she would focus on church, not on traveling home. The small, stained-glass window above the cross caught her attention. It painted the pulpit in rainbow colors.

Someone coughed, and Ronnie looked up. The stranger who had knocked her down stood beside the pew. Mrs. Goodman reached across Ronnie, a broad smile on her face. "Seth, you made it." She scooted down a bit more and patted the seat. "Come sit between us, young man. I love to hear your deep voice when we sing."

The man hung his hat on the end of the pew and stepped across Ronnie's legs, barely catching her toes. "Excuse me, again, ma'am. Seems we keep bumping into each other." A lopsided white smile crossed his tanned face. He settled himself in the seat.

Ronnie could feel the heat crawl into her cheeks. Relax? Focus? With. . .beside a cowboy? Her heart pounded so loudly she was certain it could be heard throughout the church. The sharp smell of a fresh shave tickled her nose. Her daddy smelled like that after he visited town. Tears stung. She cleared her throat and glanced at the man out of the corner of her eye.

Broad shoulders had made her scoot to the end of the pew. Fresh britches and a pressed shirt. He seemed clean. She darted a look at his face. And met piercing hazel eyes.

◆　◆　◆

Seth shifted uncomfortably and looked away from the girl. He leaned closer to Mrs. Goodman. The girl beside him seemed positioned to run out the door once he sat down. He'd not make the mistake of spooking her with a touch of his shoulder—that was for sure. Maybe he should move. He leaned forward, ready to leave.

Mrs. Goodman slipped her hand in the crook of his elbow and tugged him back. She whispered in his ear. "You are a fine example to the men in this town, Seth McKenzie. If only more of you boys would show up and hear God's Word." She tsked, tsked.

Seth grunted, his attempt to flee thwarted. "Few of my men are on the back row." He wished he were sitting with them. The lure of pie had brought him forward.

"Glad of that because I have a pretty good lunch spread waiting." She squeezed his arm. "Might be a surprise, too." She took her arm away. "Rusty said he signed on, so now's you have a cook, guess you're leaving."

"Yes, ma'am." He shoved hair from his forehead. "By Tuesday we will be Fort Worth bound."

The girl jolted into his side. He turned his head and smiled. Tiny freckles dotted her brow and nose, and bright green eyes looked as though tears might begin. His mouth grew dry. He sure hoped not.

She lifted a shapely brow. "Fort Worth?"

Seth nodded and stared at her. "Taking a herd to the stockyards."

The girl sighed and gripped her reticule tighter. She drew her legs together and seemed as though she shrunk into herself. Was his presence upsetting her?

"Ma'am?" Her bonnet hid her face, so Seth leaned forward a bit to catch her attention. "I sure hope you're okay after that tumble."

"I'm fine." She shifted again and looked out the window away from him.

Well, fine. He drew his arm across his chest in an effort to pull away lest he touch the skittish girl. How would he focus on a sermon with her by his side? When they stood for singing, he'd slip away and join Ernie and the boys. Seemed a kind thing to do.

An elder stepped into the pulpit and announced the opening hymn. As they stood, Seth patted Mrs. Goodman's arm. "Think I'll join my men so I can guide them to your house." He turned toward the girl. "Ma'am, reckon I can get by without stepping on your toes this time?" He worked his lips into a passable friendly smile in the hopes she wouldn't wilt. She nodded, drew back, and he sidled around her. Seth grabbed his hat and trekked to the back row.

Whew. Think my shoulder's out of place with all that effort.

He drew in a deep breath and belted out the words "How great Thou art," knowing within himself how true those words rang.

Despite the stirring words and a rousing sermon, his eyes returned time and again to a shapely neck and a lovely bonnet.

Chapter Three

Sunday dinner at the Goodmans' was proving uncomfortable for Ronnie. The tall cowboy, Seth McKenzie, and several of his hands had joined them. The food tasted wonderful—succulent roast beef and fresh vegetables. No one could fault Mrs. Goodman's kitchen handiwork. Even so, swallowing proved difficult when Mr. McKenzie looked her way. Ronnie kept her eyes on her plate.

"Wouldn't you agree, Miss Fergus?" He squinted in her direction.

She blinked and looked at the man, her cheeks flushing. "I'm sorry?"

"The pleasant weather we are experiencing. It's been refreshing after the cold." Seth seemed to study her face.

Heat crept up her neck. "Yes, yes. Quite pleasant." She dabbed her lips with a napkin and nodded at Mrs. Goodman. "Your meal is delicious."

"Just wait till dessert." Seth chuckled and leaned forward to whisper, "The real reason I came."

Mr. Goodman popped the table with a meaty hand. "If you folks will excuse me, I have a couple of chores to finish." He stood and smiled at his wife. "I'll take my dessert tonight." He touched his brow in a farewell and trundled out the door.

"That man." Mrs. Goodman's lips drew in a tight smile. "He's just not comfortable with company. Never understood that." She rose and plucked the roast platter from the tabletop. "Pie coming up." She gave a halfhearted laugh. "Glad someone appreciates my cooking."

"More than appreciates, Mrs. G." Seth licked his fork and held it at the ready.

Ronnie giggled then caught herself, pressing her fingertips to her lips. Seth tipped his head and watched her. Her heartbeat sped up, and she tucked her hands into her lap.

True to her word, Mrs. Goodman brought out her apple pie and served Seth and Ronnie. She nodded at the other young men seated at a table in the corner. "Boys, got another one just for you." The thank-yous reverberated. Soon clinking of forks and murmurs of approval filled the room.

Ronnie sighed in delight. She'd not been this relaxed since—she frowned. Since when?

Mrs. Goodman held out the pie plate with one last slice and gave it a shake. "Come on, sweetheart, this is just for you. I know how you love sweets."

Ronnie readied her fork and tipped her plate—at exactly the same time the cowboy did. The ceramic dishes collided and hers cracked across the edge. Ronnie looked at Mrs. Goodman's rounded eyes, her face aflame. "Oh, my." Ronnie jerked back as though burned. "I'm so sorry, Mrs. Goodman. I'm so sorry."

The cowboy chuckled. "What makes you think she was talking to you, *sweetheart?*" His hazel eyes appeared grayer in the lighting of the dining room. He had a strong chin and really nice teeth. He could use a haircut, since the blond-red locks tumbled over his forehead when he looked down. Ronnie had watched him finger-comb them back time and again.

"Never you mind about that old dish, Veronica. And Seth. Don't go making the girl feel bad." Mrs. Goodman bustled to the kitchen and returned with another piece of pie. "I'd put this back to tuck in your give-away bag, so it already belongs to you. Veronica, you scoop up the piece on the plate. A little crack isn't going to mar the set, I promise." Mrs. Goodman fussed over Seth's pie.

Ronnie's throat had closed up at Seth's words. She'd never been anyone's sweetheart—certainly not to her hardworking dad or her crusty old aunt. Pretty much the sum total of her social life. The tone of his words stung. She shoveled the pie onto the cracked plate and choked each bite down. After the confusion, she ate every morsel. And it was amazingly good.

Mrs. Goodman topped off coffee cups then plopped in the chair at the end of the table. "You said you'd be heading out on Tuesday?" She raised a brow in Seth's direction.

Seth chewed another bite and nodded. "Yes, ma'am." He patted his lips with a napkin. "Tomorrow morning we load up, and I get the count. Have to move before fourteen waddies and a passel of cows get too restless."

"Waddies?" Ronnie glanced his way.

"Trail hands, cowboys. Youngsters, most of 'em." Seth sipped his coffee then smiled. "With a new cook on hand, thanks to you, Mrs. G., at least they'll eat good."

Ronnie toyed with the napkin in her lap. He was leaving for Fort Worth. What if—

"Mr. McKenzie, your cook could use a hand, and I need passage to Fort Worth. If I rode with you—for free, of course—I'd work alongside him and be of no trouble." She shifted in her chair to face him and found the hazel eyes flashed more green than gray this time. A bit disconcerting. Still she pressed on. "I can hold my own." She twisted the napkin tighter and held her breath. "Promise."

◆　◆　◆

Seth watched the rangy gal broach the topic of traveling with him and choked back a laugh. Her wide green eyes begged, but he was not stupid. A woman traveling for days on the trail? Someone else to look after?

"Miss Fergus, I am sorry, but that will not work." He dropped his napkin on the table and stood. "Mrs. G., I'm sorry you turned down the chance to ride north, because this pie would make fine eatin' as we ride—"

"I can cook. Fried apples, vinegar lemonade, johnnycakes, biscuits fluffier than a cloud." She counted off each item on a finger and beamed at him, eyes pleading.

He lowered his gaze and toyed with a crumb on the tablecloth. "I'm sure that's true, Miss Fer—"

"My daddy loved my cooking, and when we were on the range, he showed me many a trick." She pushed her chair back and stood, almost eye to eye, she was that tall. She gripped his forearm. "I can ride and rope and shoot. I am not a town girl—I was ranch bred." She drew her shoulders back. "And I want to go home."

The last words were delivered in a whisper. She tucked her hands back into her waist and did that draw-into-herself thing. She might be ranch bred, but at the moment she looked like a drooping flower. He had the desire to tuck a stray dark curl behind her ear. She had one of those widow's peaks, where her hair grew into a point, and mighty fine skin in spite of those freckles. He tipped his head. Or maybe the freckles just painted a pretty picture.

She cleared her throat, and the tips of Seth's ears burned. He'd been staring. She'd quit talking, and he'd kept gawking.

"Miss, I hope you do get home." He shoved his chair under the table. "But it won't be with me." Ernie and two of his riders stood by the door. He nodded and Ernie stepped outside. "Mrs. Goodman, the boys and I thank you for a great meal. Probably the best we'll see for a long time." He nodded in the girl's direction, "Nice to meet you." He proceeded outside.

Trey laughed. "Thought we was getting us a tagalong, Boss." He slapped Seth on the shoulder.

Seth's shoulder stung. But no more than his conscience.

Journal
March 30, Sunday

Rested. Good food in belly from Mrs. G. Funny lunch conversing with lady from church.

Chapter Four

Ronnie shook off Sunday's memories and stomped across the kitchen to finish chores. She washed up breakfast dishes and grabbed the dishpan. The water would help the remainder of her aunt's garden to flourish. Maybe she'd get an early vegetable or two. She used her elbow to lift the back-door latch and flung the dirty water out the door—smack into a youngster's face. He sputtered and backed up, indiscernible words flowing from his mouth.

"Oh my." Ronnie bit her bottom lip to keep from laughing. The young man's hat drooped at the brim and water streamed from the brow. She stifled a chuckle, until he looked at her with big brown eyes. She could contain it no longer. A fit of giggles overcame her, and she dropped the dishpan to grab a towel. "I'm so sorry." She tried to stop laughing but couldn't seem to catch her breath.

And it felt so good to let go.

The lanky boy swiped water from his face and drew in a breath. "Mighty fine bath, Miss Fergus. I'm thanking you." He swatted his hat against his leg and tugged his wet shirt from a skinny chest. "I'm Trey Walker. We met yesterday." His eyes searched her face.

"Yes, I remember." She hiccupped. Ronnie pressed fingertips to her chest. *Oh no. Not this.* A bout of laughter often produced hiccups.

Trey grinned and ducked his head. "Wonder if I might trouble you for a cup of coffee?"

A hiccup escaped, Ronnie nodded and ushered the boy indoors. She poured them both a cup and sat at the table. "What might I do—*hic*—for you?"

Trey blushed and ran a finger around the edge of the cup. "Nothing much." The rosy cheeks turned scarlet. "Before we hit the trail, I thought we might could visit." His brown eyes darted to look at her then back into the cup. "Gets lonesome out there. I grew up with sisters and my mom, and miss fellowship. Cowboys never talk." He sighed. "They don't even sing much, 'cept to calm those cows."

Ronnie watched the boy spill out his misery. She placed a hand on his. "How old are you, Trey?"

He drew back his shoulders. "Be sixteen my next birthday come June. Only two-and-a-half months." He straightened. "Plan on finishing the drive and taking my earnings home. My mama and sisters can bake me a real cake." His glassy eyes were full of unshed tears. "Wish you were coming with us, Miss Fergus. Would make it much funner."

A hiccup escaped. She smiled. "Don't think Mr. McKenzie agrees."

Trey sunk lower in his seat. "Yeah. I heard him at dinner yesterday." He gazed at her face for a moment, chewing on his bottom lip. "Want to know how I hired on?" He leaned forward, his voice dropping. "I hid away."

Ronnie stared at the boy. "A stowaway?" She swiped at a crumb on the table. "And he kept you on? Didn't send you back?"

Trey shook his head. "Nope." A slow grin spread across his face. "I can tell you where I hid, too, if getting to Fort Worth is that important."

Ronnie leaned back in her chair. What an interesting idea. She surveyed the kitchen and sparsely furnished front room. She could send for anything she couldn't carry. Didn't need much just to get home. Had all she needed on the homestead. Would that crazy idea work? She searched the boy's face then stared out the window.

And what if it didn't? Mr. Seth McKenzie couldn't hurt her. He'd send her home and be done with her. A stab of loneliness pricked at that thought. He seemed educated as well as ranch smart. He'd carried the conversation at the dinner table, and she'd followed with rapt attention, her day feeling brighter than any she'd had in recent months. If she were sent back, if he rejected her on the trail, that brightness would fade. A lump formed in her throat. She scanned the kitchen once more. And she'd be right back here in Aunt Susan's home. Not hers.

"Would you like a biscuit to go with your coffee, Trey?" She would press the boy for details and decide. Maybe the plan was foolhardy, or maybe it would work.

What did she have to lose other than a cowboy she'd just met?

◆ ◆ ◆

At daylight on Tuesday, Ranger side-stepped, eager to get moving. Seth tugged at the reins. "Whoa. We aren't ready yet." Pulling the paper from his shirt pocket, he read the numbers once again. Almost a thousand cows to move and seventeen horses. And fourteen men. Well, some of them boys. He stuck the paper into his pocket, drooped the reins over the saddle horn, and lifted his hat to comb through his hair. He scratched his head and surveyed the scene.

Loaded supply wagon, herd, cowboys. Why did he feel he was missing something? Rusty was gone. He had pulled the chuck wagon ahead to scout a spot for a rest.

The image of a lovely, freckle-faced lady drifted through his mind. "Ha. Not her." He clapped his hat back on. "McKenzie, this is not the time to daydream." He tapped Ranger on the side and loped toward his crew.

"Y'all ready?" he hollered. He was answered with yips and shouts. "Ernie, set 'em up." He was blessed to have this experienced cowhand along on the drive and didn't mind letting him pass out assignments. Seth rubbed his thigh. Truth be told, trailing cattle had lost its luster, and sitting in the saddle was tiring. Time to set aside his daydreams from a pretty face and focus on a small corner of the earth to call his own. He'd pull down close to two hundred on this contract and had a fair amount saved up. He shook his head. "Time for thinking later." Time to begin droving.

Ranger snorted. "Let's ride, boy." He circled the horse and whistled at Ernie. They'd meet up with Rusty for beans and corn bread by sunset. He would ride drag for now to see how each waddie worked. "Lord, let them be ambitious and conscientious. Keep us safe. Thank You. Amen." He jerked a kerchief over his nose and rode.

Hours later he rolled his head to get the cricks out of his neck. He'd done that so often it was surprising it was still attached. Seth's back ached the first few days of a ride nowadays. He'd been soft on himself, staying at that hotel in town. Getting old in the saddle was proving hard. So when he spotted the chuck wagon and a fire, he whistled softly. "Good sight to see."

He trotted into camp, dismounted, and tied Ranger onto one of the wagon wheels. He noted the wagon's tongue was pointed north, ready for the following day. "Arbuckle's axle grease, Rusty. Fast." He shoved his hat back on his head, slipped off his thick work gloves, and tucked them in his back pocket, flexing his fingers.

Rusty laughed and lifted the coffee can. "What other coffee besides Arbuckle? Hot, strong, and black coming up, Boss." He lifted the pot and poured a cup. "How was the ride?"

Seth sipped the hot brew carefully, his parched throat welcoming the strong liquid. "Hot. Dusty." He pursed his lips against the coffee cup. "Successful so far."

"Only seven hours in and no trouble. Pretty good." Rusty pointed at Seth's back pocket. "Might need to jot those words down in your journal."

"Man at the pot." Ernie's voice split the air.

Seth nodded at the familiar greeting. When a cowboy spotted a fire, coffee, and someone to pour, he hollered.

Rusty held a cup high in the air then leaned to fill it. "Ready when you ride in. First day out, pot's filled and vittles ready." He poked the fire. "Know we'll feast on bacon and beans pretty much, so when my sister offered up some of her fried chicken, I didn't turn it down. She must like you, Boss, because there's a heap." He grinned. "And bless her heart if she didn't include a few pies."

Seth sighed. "If your sister wasn't already married, I think I'd turn back to grab her up, even though it's a far piece to ride and would slow the drive." He nodded at Ernie, who crouched beside him. "Whatcha think, pal? Think we need a lady on the trail?" His thoughts flickered to freckles.

"Boss, if she can cook like Mrs. G, I'd say haul her in."

Rusty laughed. "My sister or that gal she spoke of?"

Seth leveled a stare at the cook. Rusty turned back to the chuck wagon and dinner preparations, the grin never leaving his face.

Lovely Veronica Fergus said she could cook. Seth shook his head and settled on the ground, dropping his hat in his lap. He rolled his head to the side again, blew on the coffee, and sipped, eyes closed.

Best think on buying property, not on a pretty face.

Chapter Five

Ronnie wasn't sure she'd ever been this miserable. No, come to think of it, she was sure. Coiled in a ball, jostling over rough terrain with a measly saddle blanket for cover, her teeth rattling, and straining to stifle the urge to find the nearest bush was becoming unbearable. And now the smell of coffee teased her nose.

Trey had hollowed out a spot late in the night in the supply wagon, tucked in her saddle and a carpet bag, then given her a leg up just before sunrise. "Don't get up for as long as you can, Miss Ronnie." The boy smiled. "You get down the road, and he ain't coming back. You'll be home to Fort Worth before long." His encouragement had given Ronnie confidence.

By daylight, she'd slipped into her spot, adding Pa's holster and pistol to the stash. And now, hours later, she'd sipped the last of her water, chewed on jerky, and defied stretching her legs by curling her toes for exercise. But the call of nature—

Voices drifted in and out. The supply wagon had pulled in behind the chuck wagon and she could hear Rusty set up the campfire in front, on the far side from her. If she were to slip out the back and the drovers were busy with eating or cattle prodding, she could relieve herself and slip back in. The water supply. . .well, she'd think on that in a bit.

She raised up and lifted the canvas covering the wagon. Spotting no one, she looped the small canteen about her neck and began to slide toward the end of the wagon. Getting over the tailgate wouldn't be easy, but she'd managed so far. Twisting and turning, she drew the back of her skirt in between her legs and tucked it in her waistband so it wouldn't catch on the wooden slats when she climbed. She threw her left leg over the edge, her toes gaining purchase on a slat, then began her ascent. Up, over—she collapsed on the ground with a groan. "Oh my." Pain shot up her sleeping legs, prickling and stinging. She slid into the wagon's shadows, clapped her hand over her mouth, and swayed back and forth, attempting to restore circulation. A minute or two later, she scrambled out and into nearby bushes. Relief came and brought tears to her eyes. How many days would she be able play out this scenario? And how would she fill her canteen?

Despair trickled in. What a foolish thing she'd done. Once more, she'd jumped before she thought things through, before she'd even thought to ask God His plan.

Here you are, Ronnie. Nothing to do now but make the best of things.

She rose, arranged her skirts to make movement easier, and scuttled toward the wagon and a dinner of beef jerky. She yanked the canvas away from the wagon, scrambled up the side. Drawing her left leg over, she ducked under the canopy and—

"What is going on?"

Ronnie closed her eyes, and her heart raced. A hand clamped on her right ankle and pulled. She shivered. Blinking away tears, she backed out from under the canvas. Arms grabbed her waist and swung her around to face Mr. McKenzie. "Hello."

He dropped his hold on her and stepped back, his mouth forming a perfect O. "Miss Fergus." His dark eyes studied her, his jaw working back and forth.

Ronnie smoothed her skirts. "Good evening." Words wouldn't form in her brain. How could she justify this scheme? Blame it on Trey? She held out a hand. "Let me explain—"

Mr. McKenzie drew in a deep breath. "I'm sure there is a logical explanation why you, an uninvited guest, are in our supply wagon." He jerked off his hat and slapped it against his leg. "Do you have a ticket? Is that it?" His eyes blazed, and his voice rose with each word. "Maybe an invitation issued by the ranch I contract with?" He turned around, muffled words spilling from his mouth.

Ronnie clutched her hands and pressed against her stomach. She was tired, achy, and hungry. Not in the mood to be railed at. Yet she knew she deserved his ire.

"Sir." She stepped closer to Mr. McKenzie and touched his elbow.

Mr. McKenzie swung around so fast her hand slapped his arm. She stumbled. He reached out and grabbed her shoulder. "Steady." He clapped his hat on and propped his hands on his hips. His eyes bore a hole in her. "Miss Fergus, would you please explain your presence at this time?"

◆　◆　◆

Seth couldn't believe his eyes. Veronica Fergus stood before him, her calico dress rumpled, her dark hair trailing over one shoulder, and eyes filled with tears. He'd turned away to keep from hugging her close. She could've been injured jostling around in a wagon beside the crates. He drew in a ragged breath and tipped his head. "I'm listening."

"Sir." She drew her shoulders back, soldier style. Seth almost laughed. Whatever she was, she had spunk.

She cleared her throat. "I want to return to my own ranch outside Fort Worth. I do not have enough funds to travel any other way. My aunt's horse didn't seem sturdy enough—"

Yeah, she'd lost her aunt. Maybe bereavement had made her crazy. Great. I have one thousand cattle and a lunatic on hand.

Veronica leaned toward him. "Sir, I know I've taken great liberties here—"

Seth barked a laugh. "You can say that again, lady." He noticed they had an audience. "You men get back to work. We will settle this." The cowboys slunk away, tossing looks over their shoulders and muttering.

"Yes, I'm imposing." She gulped. "I'm asking for your mercy, sir." She posed her clasped hands under her chin childlike, as though in prayer. "I will not be a burden. I will cook and help in any way possible if you will allow me to continue. I will not complain. I will eat a small amount to keep your supplies fresh." She sniffled, shook her head, and a tear spilled over where she hastily brushed it away. She glanced up at him and whispered, "Please let me go home."

"Lady, do you know what kind of danger lies ahead?" He stomped a boot, his voice hard. He'd have to send her back. No telling—

Veronica stiffened. "Mr. McKenzie, you don't know anything about me. I helped my pa build our ranch. I've battled a lot more than a bunch of cows meandering through the meadows on their way—"

"Meandering?" Seth drew in a breath. "Meandering?" Words failed him. He rubbed the back of his neck. "Miss Fergus, we do not meander. We do not wander. We have a fixed destination and have the job of moving this herd"—he motioned toward the cows—"to Fort Worth. The trail is often full of danger." He leaned in closer. A hint of lavender tickled his nose. He choked out words. "And I can't promise you'll be safe."

"No one but God can do that, Mr. McKenzie." The girl's eyes flashed.

That statement took the wind out of him. Logic began to give way to emotion. Seth gritted his teeth, yet he could feel the fissure begin in his heart. He stared beyond her into the twilight and watched the herd begin to settle in for the night. Seth didn't have much to offer someone, but this he could do. He could allow her to travel with them. He shook his head, inhaled sharply, and pinched the bridge of his nose.

"All right, Miss Fergus—"

"Ronnie," she whispered.

"Ronnie?"

She nodded. "I'm Veronica Fergus, but my pa called me Ronnie when we were working. And I plan to work." She gestured toward the chuck wagon. "I'll work for room and board."

Seth surveyed the scene. "Not much in the way of room."

Ronnie's lips tilted up. "Don't ask for much. I've got my bedding in the back." She sighed. "But I would be grateful for a cup of coffee."

"Axle grease coming up," Rusty called out.

Ronnie lifted a brow and looked toward the cook then back at Seth.

"On the trail, it's hot, black, and strong. A lot like axle grease."

She nodded. "Sounds heavenly."

Seth barked a laugh. "Not sure about that, but it's wet." He sighed. Logic or emotion? With one hand he motioned toward the campfire. "After you, Ronnie." She stepped around him, and he watched her walk away, silhouetted against the sky. This was a first. "Well, Lord." He looked heavenward. "Going to trust in Your plans, Your timing. This is *not* of my doing."

No, sir, not of my doing. I'll be shed of her as soon as possible.

Ronnie stood beside the campfire, shadows playing across her face as she smiled and talked with Rusty, her hair trailing along her cheek.

Longing stirred in Seth. He sucked in a deep breath.

Fort Worth looked farther and farther away.

Journal
April 1, Tuesday

Insanity to let a woman travel with us. Rusty will work her. Drove as far as creek. Good grazing, herd trailed fine.

Chapter Six

The wagon's jolt yanked Ronnie from sleep in her new spot. Rusty had shoved crates to one side and placed a couple in the other wagon, giving Ronnie a space in the center of the chuck wagon as they moved on. He'd pulled on the trail not long after she'd cleared supper dishes from the dishwater in the wreck pan. She'd moved her bedroll and saddle blanket into her tiny room and had a few hours of sleep.

She yawned, leaned on an elbow, and peeked from under the canvas cover. Stars sprinkled across the inky black sky, creating a beautiful picture. She inhaled the fragrance of early morning, enjoying the prairie's fragrance with less dust. Riding with the cook would have her moving before the herd. She closed her eyes. With Seth McKenzie trailing behind.

Ronnie slumped against her bedroll, one arm over her forehead, a picture of Seth playing through her mind—his broad shoulders, which she'd bumped during church, and those changing hazel-gray eyes. His red-blond hair brushing his collar, skin tanned from the weather. She heaved a sigh. In her twenty years, she'd not come across a man who'd interested her like Seth McKenzie.

And he held her in little regard.

"You up, missy?" Rusty banged on the tailgate. "Got to get them beans started." He'd dumped red beans in the pot before they pulled out hours before. Life on the trail kept Cookie Rusty busy.

Ronnie rose on a knee and folded her blankets. "I'm up." She shoved the pot of beans toward the tailgate with one foot. "Tell me what you need me to do."

Rusty flipped the latch, and the tailgate dropped. "Let's get started."

With those words, Ronnie's day began. By daylight, the bacon was frying and the fragrance of coffee drifted through the air. Ronnie rolled out biscuit dough and cut pieces big enough for a rider to tuck in bacon and hit the saddle. Her hair strayed over her forehead, the day already getting sticky.

"Arbuckle." Ernie rode in and swung down from his saddle. Rusty handed him a cup of coffee. Ernie blew on the brew and sipped. He surveyed the area. "Good pickings. Grass, creek over yonder." He chucked Rusty on the shoulder. "Done good, Cookie. Cows will be happy here for a spell, and Boss will be happier." He nodded at Ronnie. "Morning, Miss Fergus."

Ronnie smiled at the older man. Wiry and brown as a nut, Ernie was a proven cowboy. He rode and roped as fast as her daddy. He'd make a fine ranch foreman. She bit her lip. When she got to her ranch, would there be enough to build up again? To even need a foreman?

"Herd's 'bout a mile back." Ernie snagged a tiny piece of dough and popped it in his mouth.

"Hey there." Ronnie reared back in mock indignation.

"Mama used to clap my fingers when I done that." He laughed full out. "Couldn't resist." He tossed his cup to Rusty and mounted. "Boys will be in shortly, and they're mighty hungry."

"When are they not?" Rusty chuckled and waved with a ladle. "Breakfast will be ready. Stirring gravy now."

Ernie turned his horse and trotted off. Ronnie looked at Rusty. Despite the early hour and hard work ahead, this trip was proving to be an adventure. She cut another biscuit. Soon Seth would appear. A tiny shiver ran down her back. What a foreman he would make.

"Don't let dreams die, girl. Life's hard work, but the good Lord will provide."

Her daddy's words reverberated through her. Seth McKenzie was a dream. Her waiting ranch was not.

◆　◆　◆

Ronnie stood beside the chuck wagon, flour dotting her face and her black hair stringing down her cheek. Seth covered his mouth to hold back a laugh. She'd signed on for this trip, so she would get the full measure of work. He reined in Ranger and watched her. She and Cookie had a system it seemed: he barking orders and she jumping to task.

Seth nodded. That would work. She would soon discover her desire to travel with the herd would prove an arduous task. He dismounted and looped the reins over the rope strung between trees. He lifted his hat, ran his fingers through his hair, set it back on his head, and strode into camp.

"Boss." Rusty held out a cup.

"Thanks." Seth slipped a glove off and took the cup. He tipped his hat at Ronnie. "Ma'am." Spotting a large rock, he shoved it over with his boot and parked on it. "Chose a good spot for a stop." He watched Ronnie.

"Seems like it." Rusty spilled more water into the bean pot. "We'll get on ahead and have these ready for supper." He grinned. "Miss Ronnie's got another secret recipe for us. She's gonna add—"

"Shhh." Ronnie held a finger to her lips. "Don't spoil the surprise."

Seth chuckled. "Surprises are fine—just don't spoil the beans."

Her forehead wrinkled. "I'm not prone to ruining beans, Mr. McKenzie. If my daddy taught me one thing, it was how to ranch cook." She turned her back to him with a sniff.

"Well, your daddy isn't here now, and Cookie is in charge." Seth bit out the words.

Ronnie swung back around, her skirts flapping against her long legs. She could almost meet him eye to eye, Seth had noted. "Mr. McKenzie, I would appreciate it if you'd give me the benefit of the doubt. I'm quite capable of following his orders"—she jerked a thumb in Rusty's direction—"and using my memory to aid him. So drop it." She turned around again.

Seth's eyebrows rose. He swallowed hard and sipped more coffee. The girl had spirit. He liked that. A lot. Her attitude stung, though. Seth pushed up from the ground, tossed his cup into the pan, and paused beside her. "Just be sure you do follow his directions. We don't have supplies to waste." He stomped off to Ranger. Let her be like that. He didn't need to think about Veronica Fergus while he was working. Dangerous to let his mind wander.

Especially to beautiful women.

He jerked the reins, and Ranger pulled back. "Sorry, old boy. Didn't mean to take it out on you." With a nudge to the horse's sides, Seth headed back to the herd. Where he was needed. Not where he was ignored.

Journal
April 2, Wednesday

Moved about seven miles, no hard weather, cows settling in to trail. Only bad-temper is woman.

Chapter Seven

Nine days and hundreds of hours and cups of coffee and beans and cowboys and cattle calling left Ronnie weary. She puffed a breath to blow away a stray greasy curl, longing for a bath. Every bit of her was caked in dirt. No telling what her hair looked like under her bonnet.

She stirred a hunk of lard into the dutch oven. More beans awaited the drovers, but she'd mix up these fried cakes and sprinkle a pinch of sugar on for a treat. She had tried to provide things that her papa had taught her would spark up meals and show Mr. McKenzie her worth. Rusty let her use slivers of butter and canned peaches last night for a cobbler. Wasn't even anything left to scrape off the pan when the last man finished. He'd licked up the syrupy remains with a finger and a grin.

Ronnie wiped sweat from her brow with her forearm, her bonnet tipping off. The sun broke through the clouds and warmed her clear through. She stood, braced her back with one hand, and pulled the bonnet back on. She'd freckle and burn. Aunt Susan's scolding rang in her ears. *"Total ruination of yourself, Veronica. All leathered up."* Her aunt would've pulled the bonnet strings tighter under Ronnie's chin and frowned. *"Total ruination."*

"Guess I'm totally ruined by now, Auntie." Ronnie lifted her arms and stretched.

Just beyond a small rise was a creek where the herd drifted, water and fresh grass calling to them. At least the dust cleared as they settled in.

" 'Bout finished over that fire, missy?" Rusty sidled up closer.

Ronnie nodded. "Almost have this melted. Then I'll stir in the rest and fry up batter." She lifted the coffeepot and shook it. "Probably need more."

"Let me." A cowboy stepped around her and reached for the pot with a crooked smile.

"Thank you. . . ." Ronnie wrinkled her brow.

The boy's eyes widened. "Wally, ma'am."

"Yes, of course. Thank you, Wally." Ronnie stifled a chuckle. The eager boys tumbled over themselves at the campfire trying to please her. Like puppies. "I'd appreciate it. Mr. McKenzie said a creek was just behind—"

"Those trees." Wally lumbered away.

"Can't do enough for you, but let me ask 'em for something, and they run." Rusty shouted at the retreating boy then laughed. "Course I ain't near as pretty and sweet smelling."

Ronnie swatted at the rotund cook's arm. "Stop it. They're just homesick boys. Doesn't mean a thing." At the sound of a horse approaching camp, she swung around. Seth McKenzie dismounted, looped the reins over the rope strung between two cottonwoods, and strode toward her. He didn't look homesick. With a tight jaw and eyes blazing, he just looked—mad.

◆ ◆ ◆

Fury burned in Seth's belly. "Wally!" he shouted. His gaze roved across the camp, past Rusty, past Ronnie, and landed on the youngster, coffeepot in hand, standing stock-still on the rise.

"Get over here."

The boy scampered to Ronnie, handed her the pot and tipped his head, then rushed to stand in front of Seth, his gloved hands fidgeting with his belt buckle.

Seth bit his lip against harsh words ready to lash the boy to ribbons. He'd had enough of those in his lifetime. He needed to get control—

"Boss." The boy quivered, his face pale. "Boss?"

Heaving a sigh, Seth gripped the boy's shoulder with one hand and measured out words. "Wally. Where are you to be right now? In camp?"

Wally's head drooped. "No, sir."

"Then why are you here?" Seth resisted the urge to swat the kid on the head, a move he was oh so familiar with.

"Canteen was empty, Boss, and I rode toward the creek. Then I smelled the fire and saw Miss Ronnie needed to make coffee—" Words tumbled from the boy's mouth, his eyes darting to and fro.

"Miss Ronnie asked you to help?" Seth glared at the cook's helper, who placed the coffeepot on the wagon. She glared back, hands propped on her hips. Shapely hips, he noted. That thought caused his anger to rise. "You're not here to help Miss Ronnie." His words sounded sarcastic to his own ears. "You're here to ride herd. And you're on drag." He gave the boy a shake. "Now get to it."

"Yes, sir." Wally raced to his horse, slapped the reins over his head, and leaped into the saddle. Dust swirled as the horse and rider headed toward the rear of the herd.

Seth stomped toward the cooks. "In the future, please ask Rusty for help, Miss Fergus. Our drovers don't need their attention drawn from their duties."

Flashing eyes bored into his. "I assure you, Mr. McKenzie"—she stiffened and spat the words—"I asked for no help from Wally. Rusty and I have all well in hand." She turned away.

Her skirts swayed, and her bonnet couldn't hold a curl trickling down her back. Seth rubbed his chin whiskers, wishing he hadn't shaved days ago. By now a full beard would be a good thing to pull on and keep his thoughts from wandering. Rusty held out a cup, and Seth accepted the cold water.

"Everything all right out there?" Rusty said.

"All right." He gulped the remaining water and dropped the cup in the wreck pan to wash. "Just seems a few white-faced are missing. Ernie's riding through to spot 'em. But they'd been hanging back the whole time." He frowned and pinched the bridge of his nose. "Doesn't figure."

"They's just mixed up in the bunch, Boss." Rusty swished the cup through the murky dishwater and slapped it against his apron to dry. "No rustling Indians out this way." He tossed the cup into a box. "Thank God."

"Thank God is right." Seth nodded to the man and eyed Ronnie's back, her shoulders rigid. He drew in a deep breath and let it out in slow measure. "Sorry I jumped to conclusions, Ronnie."

She swung around and fixed him with a level stare. "Apology accepted."

Words froze in his throat, and he realized he was waiting for a sparring comment. He'd come to enjoy the frenzy of words passing back and forth between them as they debated everything from grass to glory.

She tipped her head. "Anything else, Boss?"

The last word was laced with acid, and Seth knew he deserved it. "No." He turned on a heel and made for Ranger. He'd be late to supper tonight, might even keep company with cows instead of drawing near the lady by the fire.

Journal
April 10, Thursday

Moved cattle as far as creek, drag cows on one side, lead on other. Water a bit muddy. Plenty of grass to graze. Staying night to spell boys. Ernie can't spot heifers. Lady keeps kids jumping to look at her. Can't say I blame them.

Chapter Eight

A rumble awakened Ronnie, and she lay still, ears attuned to the prairie sounds. Thunder. A trace of fear ran its fingers up her spine. Thunder and lightning. A rancher's enemies. She slung the saddle blanket from her legs, hitched her skirts, and climbed from the wagon. Raindrops the size of nickels began to pelt the ground. She felt the sting on her shoulders. She reached back, grabbed her shawl and bonnet, and covered up. The rain began in earnest.

Rusty scrambled toward the fire and motioned her way. "Grab this oven. Get it into the bed." He slung pots and pans into the wagon and jerked the tripod from over the fire. "Going to hitch up." He slapped water from his hat and face. "Drover's getting other wagon ready to roll, too. With this storm, we might have to move."

Ronnie glanced back at the store wagon. Two mules stood in their traces, ready to be harnessed. She stumbled to follow Rusty's commands then headed to the back of the wagon.

A flash of lightning illuminated the scene. Seth had bunched the herd out from the creek, and she could see them rise, a huge mound of beef drawing up like the ground, rising with a roar, rattling horns, bellowing their fear as the thunder increased. Riders circled the herd, lariats flapping and voices hollering to keep the cattle in a tight circle. Ernie signaled directions to other riders, his hat waving in the wind gusts. Piercing whistles. Total cacophony. Ronnie wanted to drop into the wagon and cover her ears.

"Miss Ronnie." A cry echoed from the night. She came around the tailgate, and Trey barreled into her. He clutched his right arm against his belly, his hand dangling. "Got throwed." His eyes were wide, and his mouth drew in a tight line.

Ronnie wiped water from his cheeks. "What can I do?"

"Need a sling." His eyes dropped toward her skirt. "My mama used her skirts for ties. Reckon you can?" His eyes shone with unshed tears. "I gotta get back to the herd but can't ride with my arm hanging down."

Ronnie carefully removed his coat. She tugged the canvas back on the wagon's end and reached for her carpetbag. She drew out a chemise, bit one end in her teeth and pulled. The fabric tore, along with a tiny piece of her heart. She had precious few things of her aunt's. Creating long strips, Ronnie fashioned a sling and strung it around Trey's neck.

He stumbled against her and sniffled. "Thank you, ma'am." He closed his eyes and swayed. "Gotta ride—"

Ronnie pushed the boy against the tailgate. "You're not riding."

He shoved against her hand. "You see this storm?"

The absurd question almost made Ronnie laugh. Instead she ushered him to the wagon wheel. "Trey, you can be thrown and trampled. I won't let you ride. I can take up your position." She pointed at the wagon. "Get in back."

"You can't," he wailed. "Mr. McKenzie will have my hide." Trey turned toward her and clacked his elbow against the wagon. He quivered, a shock of pain crossing his face.

"See what I mean?" Ronnie bent low and shouted at him. "Now get in there." She tossed her shawl and bonnet inside, grabbed his hat and pushed him gently.

A sob tore from the boy's chest. "Gonna mean my job." He threw one leg over the edge of the wagon. "Mr. McKenzie's going to kill me."

Ronnie pulled the canvas cover tight and tied it on the side. "Better yelled at than being trampled." She bent over and grabbed the back of her skirts, drew them between her legs and tucked them into her waistband. "Might need me some britches before long." She pulled on Trey's coat and hat. Her stockings and shoes were caked with mud, and she slipped as she stomped toward the string of horses. Trey's brown horse look tired, his head drooped.

"Sorry to rouse you, boy, but we need to ride." Ronnie mounted, tugged the hat down on her head, and swung toward the herd, watching for Ernie and his hand signals when the sky lit.

It felt good to be in the saddle.

◆ ◆ ◆

The rain let up, and Seth hoped the worst of the storm was over. His thighs tightened against Ranger's sides as he trotted from side to side, trailing cattle back into the circle. Ernie directed the waddies and kept cows from straying. They stumbled and walked about, but none had struck out in a run. If he could keep them milling, things would be fine. Like stirring soup. He watched for strays and the front-runners. Would they follow the lead and settle in?

Ranger snorted and lifted his head. Trey headed in their direction, his coat pulled tight and his hat drawn low. "Whoa." He leaned forward in the saddle and watched the boy.

A split of lightning flashed and Seth jolted, causing Ranger to jump.

What—that was not Trey in the saddle. Mouth agape, Seth watched Ronnie urge a cow to turn, leaning low in the saddle and talking. Talking. Not hollering. Just talking. His breath caught in his throat at the sight.

"Probably singing some lullaby." Ranger stepped forward, and Seth gave him his head. He surely didn't seem to have his on. He surely was seeing things. Veronica Fergus could not possibly be herding cattle in the middle of a storm. Where was Trey?

With that thought, fear stabbed Seth's middle. Where was Trey? He angled toward the rider. She was astride Trey's horse. He breathed a sigh of relief then drew in one of exasperation. Crazy woman.

"Miss Fergus?" he bellowed over the roll of thunder. A cow grazed his leg. He ducked his head to look at the animal, grateful it didn't have horns to catch him or his horse while he was not paying attention. Crazy woman causing trouble.

Trey's horse drew alongside Ranger, and both animals paused. Another lightning flicker allowed Seth to see her clearly. Ronnie smiled and tipped her head, rain drizzling down the back brim of her hat. Her wet hair strung down her back like a thick black cord.

"Mr. McKenzie." She patted the horse's neck, a splatter of mud from the dirty horse dotting her nose. "Nice night for a ride."

"Trey?" Concern tinged his words, and she drew up.

"Broke his arm." She sighed and wiped the mud from her face. "I put him in the wagon. He can't ride until it's splinted. I'm taking his place." She reached out a hand and shook a finger in Seth's face. "Do not tell me to go back, because I'm not. I know you need help in a storm." She met his gaze for a moment then tapped her heels against the horse's sides.

When they moved away, Seth watched in wonder as she continued around the edge of the milling herd, a calm, steady voice calling out low. Heat rushed to his face.

He only hoped the cattle didn't experience the rush of emotions he felt as he heard her drone.

Journal
April 11, Friday

Storm last night, not much loss. Rider down. And woman up. Must say she pulled her weight.

Chapter Nine

Mud seemed the word for the day. Ronnie poked a toe into the dark rushing water of the creek, rinsed the caked dirt from her shoe, and stomped her foot. She turned to watch the sun rise. Leaves sparkled after the drenching rain, the grass greener having been washed free from dirt. If only she could bathe, too. She filled a bucket and set it on a rock beside a towel and bar of soap. She'd do the best she could. She plopped on the rock and scrubbed her face and hands. When the rain had begun to let up, she had removed her hat and let the water flow through her hair. She wrung it out and coiled it into a bun before replacing Trey's battered hat.

The boy hunkered into the wagon, sleeping, his face etched with pain. Ronnie didn't envy the person who would set the child's arm. She smiled and shook her head. Not a child now. A fifteen-year-old man.

Ronnie leaned back on her elbows, face to the sun. Her backside ached from the saddle, but she'd had such—fun. She chuckled. When was the last time she'd used that word? Riding a horse had always been pure pleasure, and working cattle a chore she knew well. Her daddy had put her in the saddle by the time she could walk. Her roping skills might need brushing up, but—

"Miss Fergus?"

Ronnie jerked around. "Mr. McKenzie." She straightened.

Seth side-stepped down the slope and squatted in front of her, sliding his hat to one knee. "Haven't had a chance to speak to you this morning." He tugged a blade of grass from the ground and put it between his teeth. Worry wrinkled his brow. "Gave me a scare last night."

"I didn't mean to." Ronnie settled her damp skirt over her knees, ignoring the butterflies in her chest and the flush creeping up her neck.

"Appreciate your help, but I don't plan for you—"

Ronnie clasped her arms about her knees to still her hands. If only she could reach over and brush his hair from his forehead. She cleared her throat. "Trey won't be able to ride for a few days. When the weather is dry and my chores are done, I'd enjoy trailing." She tipped her head. "If you don't mind, Boss."

His mouth pinched in a line. "Boss?" In the bright morning light, his ever-changing eyes scrutinized her. "Cookie will keep you plenty busy." He grew quiet and stared just over her shoulder.

A bird call broke the silence. Ronnie gave a little shake and stood. "Yes. He probably will." She tossed out the wash water, dropped her soap and towel in the bucket, and turned on one heel.

"Wait."

Ronnie spun around. "Yes?"

Seth rose, slapped his hat on, and dusted his britches. "Going to need some help splinting the boy's arm. Reckon you're up to it?" He reached for the bucket, his fingers brushing her hand.

A tingle ran up Ronnie's arm, and she released the handle. "I've never—" She bit her lip and thought of the sleeping boy. "Of course." Queasiness assaulted her stomach. "You tell me what to do, and I'll help."

◆　◆　◆

Trey leaned against the bedroll in the storage wagon, his face white, sweat covering his brow. Rusty had poured him a strong dose of whiskey against the pain. Seth wished he'd had some, too. Nothing ever prepared him for the task of physically hurting anyone. He'd had more than one broken bone in his life and knew the misery.

"Just rest." Ronnie wiped a damp cloth over the boy's forehead, her low croon soothing and relaxing the muscles in Trey's face.

Seth realized his shoulders had drooped in tune with her voice. Her very presence washed peace over him. He gave the boy a reassuring smile. "Miss Ronnie's right, boy. You will need to rest up."

"But I gotta ride—"

"We've got it covered, Trey." Seth patted the boy's knee. "Don't worry yourself. Why, your nurse rode so well through the storm, we might put her in the rotation." And he wouldn't mind riding alongside her at all. Seth poked his fingers in his pockets and mentally nudged that feeling to one side. He didn't have time for sentimentality. And he certainly didn't need to concentrate on anything besides cattle.

Ronnie walked in step beside him to the chuck wagon, stood on tiptoe to reach inside for her bonnet, and lost her balance. Seth grabbed her by the shoulders. "Steady, cowgirl." He resisted the urge to give her a squeeze, instead lifting the canvas and handing bonnet to her. "Need the wrap?"

She shook her head, the black ponytail that had snaked from under the hat still damp and slapping her shoulders. Curls had worked their way loose from the band and framed her face. *A few more freckles.* Seth cleared his throat. "I'm grateful for your help, Ronnie. Both with the herd during the storm and Trey just now."

"You did a fine job splinting that arm." She slid the bonnet on and tied the strings under her chin, squinting at him against the brightening day. "Must've had practice."

"Had my fair share, that's right." Seth rubbed his shoulder. "And been fixed up a time or two myself. Part of ranch life."

"True, true." Ronnie sighed. "Lost my mama after her bad break."

"What?" Seth stared at her. "How could she—"

"Broke her leg in two places and was stove up for a long while." Ronnie shuddered. "She caught pneumonia, and even though I tended to her, she died."

Seth's heart swelled. "I'm so sorry." He touched her elbow and turned her a bit toward him. "How old were you?"

Eyes bright with unshed tears, she stared at him. "Eight." She pressed fingers to her lips for a moment. "And yes, I know I was young, but that doesn't make the hurt go away."

She held up one hand. "Prayed and prayed, but no answer came. Daddy was gone." She sniffled. "Long time ago. But it still brings bad memories." She stiffened. "Bet Cookie is looking for me. Thanks for your help." She tugged a bonnet string.

Seth smiled. "Thank you for yours." He lowered the canvas flap and watched her retreating form. What an unusual woman.

Journal

Set in for the day today. Plenty of grass and water. Moving out in morning. Cookie will leave at dawn. And take her. Might let her ride. Might be nice.

Chapter Ten

The early morning mist began to clear by the time Rusty and Ronnie had camp set up. "How far back is the herd, do you suppose?"

Rusty groaned and lifted the pot of beans, settling it into a circle of coals. "Reckon we've moved six, seven miles this morning. Maybe more." He lifted the lid, stirred the contents, and slapped the lid back on. "They'll catch up by about dark thirty." He grinned. "And be powerful hungry. The jerky ain't going to hold 'em too long."

Ronnie tucked a towel in her waistband and pulled a gallon of apple cider vinegar from the wagon bed. She'd start work on vinegar lemonade and store it to one side for thirsty throats. Then she'd chop pecans and dried apples to add to the cinnamon and other spices for a special treat. Mixed together and set aside, she could divide the mixture into strips of cloth. Each rider would have a sweet to toss in his saddlebag. She smiled. *Bet they eat it before they hit the saddle.* She always did when Mama passed it out.

A heavy cloak settled on her shoulders as it usually did when thoughts of her mother danced through her mind. Mentioning Mama to Seth stirred up memories of a lonely little girl standing by a grave. Her daddy was kind but never loving and tender like her mother. Her throat grew tight. No use thinking on the past. Maybe she could find some wildflowers in the pasture and take them to Mama's grave when she got home.

Home. Excitement stirred her middle. Home. She was really going home. Her lips tipped up then immediately dropped. She wrinkled her brow. To what? Had Mr. Adamson kept watch on the place, or had he left it? What awaited her?

Ronnie stirred the sweets and plopped the mixture in a flour sack to set. Worry would get her nowhere. She had faced hardships with her daddy, and nothing would keep her from moving on with her plan for home.

If only Seth could come with me. She flushed and straightened her shoulders as though the action would toss aside the thought. "Don't be ridiculous." She swung toward Rusty. "What's next?"

Rusty held out a cup of coffee. "Axle grease?" His rotund belly shook a tad as he chuckled. "You talking to a flour sack? Or dreaming out loud?"

"Talking out loud?" Ronnie grasped the cup and bit her lip. Had she spoken Seth's name?

"Just joshing. But you were heavy in thought." The cook propped his hand on the wagon bed and watched her over the rim of his cup. "What you planning to do once you go home?"

Ronnie sipped coffee, hiding behind the cup. Rusty the mind reader? "Settle in. Raise some cows. What else do I do?"

"Marry. Get some kiddos." Rusty's eyes twinkled, and he tossed his cup in the wreck pan. "Need some water for dishes." He tipped his head in her direction. "Best haul some from the barrel." He stepped away and poked at the fire.

Ronnie lifted the water jug and filled it. She dumped some into the pan, washed the dirty items, and dried them with the towel on her waistband.

Married. Kids. She sighed. A dream.

A picture of Seth swam before her. She could see him in Daddy's big rocker by the fire with a boy on his knee. "And I suppose a hundred head of cows out back, Veronica Fergus?" She snorted. "Keep dreaming, girl. Keep dreaming."

◆　◆　◆

Seth's head bobbed, and he jerked upright, causing Ranger to dance a step or two. Falling asleep in the saddle wasn't a smart idea. He rolled his aching shoulders. Sleep eluded him the night before, and he was weary.

Ernie sidled up beside him. "Boss, can't spot about thirteen more."

"What?" Seth swiveled about and pulled his horse to a halt. "How many does that make?"

Creases formed across Ernie's forehead as he gazed at the ground, making a count. "'Bout forty from what I can tell. The white-faced count I know. I watched them through the chute myself. By riding through, I can't spot some of the others. I just rode drag and ain't spotted any behind. Mike's got the tail, and he said nothing strayed." Ernie lifted his hat and scratched his head. He stood in the stirrups for a stretch. "No Indians." He set his hat back on. "Got to figure rustlers."

Unease stabbed Seth's middle. "Rustlers? Have you seen other riders?"

"No, sir. Not yet." Ernie gazed over Seth's shoulder as though he could spot a band of outlaws. "Don't mean they ain't out there."

Seth nodded. "Keep watch. Spread the word." He looked at the cows as they plodded by. "I will take drag for now and bring Mike up."

"Sure could use another rider." Ernie lifted a hand at the store wagon. "Reckon Trey will ride soon?"

Seth shook his head. "Not for a day or two. We can handle it." He turned Ranger's head toward the end of the trail. "Spread the word, and keep watch. Let me know every couple of hours." He spurred the horse and rode.

Rustlers? Danger? Is Ronnie safe? The thought nearly jolted him from Ranger's back, and he had a desire to gallop to find the chuck wagon. He wheeled around and began a slow walk, tension stringing out his muscles. Ranger minced his obvious displeasure at Seth's demeanor. "Sorry, fella. Can't help but worry." He patted the horse's neck. "She's a treasure that one is. I just know it."

A treasure he'd found. He chuckled. Found hidden in a wagon. So did the finders-keepers rule apply?

Did he want to keep her?

He watched cows. That's what he needed to do. Watch over cows. No other thoughts for now. Just. Watch. Cows. He yawned. *And stay awake.*

Chapter Eleven

E rnie rode in to camp first, his grin widening as he spotted Ronnie. She lifted a hand and waved. "Good to see you made it."

Evening stars had begun to spring out before the lead cows wandered on the open ground to graze. They lowed their pleasure at the place Rusty had selected. Cowboys began to filter in, and Rusty passed out plates of beans and bacon. The smell teased Ronnie's nose. She'd not eaten yet. She toed the ground with her shoe. *Waiting for someone special to join me?* Her ears tingled. Yes, she admitted to herself. She was.

Wally straggled in and smiled at her. "Evening, Miss Ronnie." He grabbed a cup of coffee and slurped it down. "Smells good."

Ronnie laughed. "Smells about the same every evening, doesn't it, Wally?" She glanced over her shoulder. "Others coming now or later?"

A grin crept across his tired face. "Boss is riding drag. He's bound to be in later." Wally nodded at the string of horses. "Course you wanna take an evening ride, Trey's horse is saddled. We worked him today."

Ronnie brightened. "Yes. I'd love to do that." She stepped forward, jolted to a stop, and whirled around. "Suppose it's okay with the boss?"

Wally nodded. "Bet he'd like the company, ma'am." He rubbed the bridge of his nose. "I'll get someone to ride out with you." He looked around to spot a cowboy.

"I'll be fine." She shook her skirts free, grasped them in one hand, and stepped toward the end of the wagon. "Let me ready myself for a saddle."

"No, ma'am. You can meet up with the boss, but you ain't riding out alone. Ain't safe." His brow furrowed. "Get fixed, and I'll help you mount."

Ronnie watched the boy for a moment then shook her head. She slipped around the corner, tucked her skirts in her waistband, and walked toward Trey's horse. Wally stood ready to give her a leg up. Mike slumped in his saddle—he'd ridden drag. She felt sorry for the tired boy, but surely it wasn't a far ride out to meet Seth. A flurry of excitement dashed through her.

"Let's go." She nudged the brown horse away from the others and turned toward the back of the herd.

The stars popped out in clusters as the evening descended. Sweet smells of grass mixed with the odors of dust and manure. *Ranch smells.* The familiar routine stirred up a sense of pleasure, of blessing. *Blessing?* Ronnie smiled. At this moment, a sense of blessing described her mood. "Lord, let this feeling of well-being stick with me for a long time. Don't know when I've felt such contentment." She trotted beside straggling cows headed in the opposite direction. The brown horse twitched his desire to return to camp.

She kept the reins tight and wouldn't give him his head. "Mike, I've got it from here. Go on and eat."

The boy shrugged. "Straight out to Mr. McKenzie."

Ronnie saluted. "Straight out." A giggle burst from her lips. The boy rolled his eyes and turned toward camp.

She rode a bit farther, and Seth's silhouette showed through the dust on the horizon. Ronnie fought the urge to spur her mount and reach him faster. His head jerked up when he caught sight of her.

"What in the world?" His voice was tinged in anger.

A sinking feeling began in Ronnie's middle. She cleared her throat. "Fine night for a short ride, Boss." She gave a half-hearted smile.

Seth turned to walk Ranger beside her. "Why are you out here?" His words were clipped. Short. Tense.

Ronnie eyed him. His mouth set in a grim line and creases lined his forehead. "Wanted to get out of camp for a bit." She settled her shaking hands on the saddle horn. "Wally told me you were on drag—"

"Wally." Seth spit out the boy's name. "He's a never-ceasing source of trouble."

"Now don't go getting on to him. I was eager to come, and he sent Mike with me...well, most of the way."

Seth pinched the bridge of his nose then gazed at her. Moonlight filtered through the copse of trees. Cows lumbered by, an occasional grunt or moo answered by another. Ronnie turned to watch the herd.

"I thought maybe we could visit." She sighed. "Should've known you'd be too tired to talk." She almost added too stubborn but bit her lip before the words escaped.

Ranger began to walk, and the brown horse set in beside him. Ronnie's knee grazed Seth's. She tugged the reins to the right. Seth continued to frown.

Minutes later he said, "I am glad to see you." His voice softened, and he tugged his hat lower.

A flood of emotions rose inside Ronnie. Her cheeks flamed. She fussed with the edge of her skirt, smiling at the ground.

◆ ◆ ◆

Seth's heartbeat slowed as they rode. This woman's unpredictable actions could cause any manner of trouble. If she'd just cook and ride in a wagon and be a plain, ordinary—

He paused. Nothing about the woman beside him was plain or ordinary. She wasn't a striking beauty, but she was pretty. Tall, big eyes, a mane of hair. He shivered. Riding alongside him. Veronica Fergus had chosen to ride out to see him. He stifled a chuckle.

"Seems you're making good time today."

"Uh-huh." Seth watched a white-face pass. He'd need to tell Ernie he'd spotted one.

"Supper is ready. Bet you'll be glad for the last of these to straggle in." She pointed to the campfire glowing in the distance. "Almost there."

"Yep." Wally had best be riding when he arrived or he might shake the boy. Allowing Ronnie to ride alone.

"I made a special sweet treat for everyone."

"How nice."

Ronnie leaned toward him and waved a hand. "Never mind. I thought we might have a discussion of some kind. Talk about—I don't know. Cows or water or grass or sky. But all you have to say is *uh-huh*." She kicked the brown horse in the side and began to lope. "I can get that from Rusty."

The ever-present coil of hair bounced across her shoulders as she rode away, and emptiness descended. Ronnie's presence had filled a void Seth hadn't known existed. What would he do with these feelings?

Get rid of them, McKenzie. No good can come of thinking on her. Stick to cows. He sighed and shrugged. "Least I know about them. Can't ever figure a woman." Especially the beauty who dismounted by the chuck wagon, jerking her skirts free and sashaying fireside, greeting each cowboy. "Lord, keep her safe till I can get her home."

Seth loped to the last straggler and angled Ranger behind him. "Let's go, buddy. I'm tired and hungry."

And ready to talk.

Journal

Seven or eight miles. Water scarce, grass thin. Won't stay long. Could push through tonight, but staying put. Loss report worrisome. Will tighten watch.
And watch over her closer.

Chapter Twelve

Bone-weary, Ronnie clambered from the chuck wagon to help Rusty. She'd kept to herself the last few days, aggravated with Seth and too tired to bandy with the boys. They'd enjoyed their sweet treat and watched every night to see what else she might dish out. For the moment, her creativity was exhausted.

She'd changed to her second dress the day before yesterday, just in time to spill molasses on the hem. Despite scrubbing, she continued to be a dust magnet. But then dust and dirt were constant companions. Trail driving certainly wasn't an easy way to travel.

"But it's a free trip, girl." She shook her skirt.

Rusty glanced at her. "Watch for ants. They'd love to latch on and slurp molasses." He chuckled.

Ronnie shot him a sharp look. "Thanks for the advice." She surveyed the nearby grass. "Think I'll change." She clambered up the side of the wagon and plopped on her pallet. With much squirming and ducking beneath the canvas, she changed dresses. She would soak the ruined one all day. Coiling her braid under her bonnet, she flung a leg over the side of the wagon and searched for a slat with her toe.

"Good morning."

Ronnie jerked upright and grabbed for the canvas cover. Her fingers grazed the fabric, but she didn't catch a grip. She felt the momentum as she toppled and closed her eyes to wait for the earth to meet her backside once again. Instead, strong arms encircled her waist and lowered her to the ground. Seth. Of course, it was Seth witnessing her graceless movements. A flash of Aunt Susan's pinched mouth flickered through Ronnie's memory. She laughed. "Thank you, Mr. McKenzie." She settled her skirts and straightened her bonnet.

"What's funny?" He leaned in a bit closer and peered under the edge of her bonnet, one hand on her elbow.

Ronnie surveyed his eyes. What color would they be in this morning light? Hazel. She nodded. She liked them best that color. His chin whiskers had grown during the ride but didn't quite cover the dimples that only showed when he grinned. . .like now. She shrugged.

"I'm a source of amusement to many as clumsy as I am." His touch caused her heart to race and her hands to tremble. She shrugged away. She tipped her head and looked at him, determined to still her mind enough to focus on a conversation. "I appreciate your kindness. Thank you." She waited a moment. The silence stretched as they stared at each other. She cleared her throat. "Did you need me for any reason?"

"No, no." He poked fingers into his pockets. "Just happened to be in the right place at the right time." He nodded toward the end of the wagon. "Reckon I'll get me some coffee." He toed the dirt with his right boot. "Want to join me?"

Ronnie was sure the whole camp could hear her heart hammer against her ribs. Blood surged into her cheeks and ears, and her fingers twitched against her skirt. She stared at Seth. Dirt had filled the tiny creases by his eyes. Like her, he could use a dip in a river.

"Will we make it to water soon?" She placed a hand on the wagon to steady herself. Staring at him was making her dizzy.

"Uh-huh." His mouth split into a wide grin. "By morning, you and Rusty will set up camp by the river. It's low where we will cross," he rubbed his cheek, "but deep enough to wash up if you so desire."

"Oh, I so desire." She laughed. "This frock is the only one not spoiled by something to draw ants." She ran her hand over the braid hanging from her bonnet. "And let's not discuss hair." She sighed. "I'm quite a mess, I'm sure. Just glad Rusty didn't include a mirror in my accommodations, lest I never leave the wagon."

Seth tweaked her nose, and she gasped. Her eyes widened, and her stomach coiled in a knot.

"Veronica Fergus"—he leaned forward, his voice husky—"you are a vision on this drive."

Surely a blood vessel would burst in her head. Nothing could contain this heat and confusion without splitting open. A shiver ran up her spine. Tears sprang into her eyes. The first sincere compliment she'd ever received and she was a dirt-encased mess. "Thank you," she whispered. With a tug on her bonnet, she reached out and strung her arm through the crook of his elbow. "Shall we have coffee?"

◆　◆　◆

Whatever possessed him to ask her to join him for coffee? There was no café in sight, no wrought-iron chair to pull out for her. Only a ring of rocks around a blazing campfire. And lounging dirty men alongside. Men who watched his every move. They'd notice Ronnie and Seth with their heads together. And laugh.

A muscle worked in his jaw. Well, let them laugh. For the first time he'd met a woman who understood his job. Shoot. She'd even shared in the ride. He tugged her arm a bit tighter to his side as they walked the fifteen or so feet to a boulder. He bent and brushed away some dirt and leaves. "Sit here. I'll grab us a cup."

He turned but could see from the corner of his eye she primped, fluffing her skirt, brushing hair under her bonnet, wiping her face with a hanky. A smile crept up his cheek. Ronnie seemed nervous.

"Boss, you wantin' coffee for her, too?" Rusty lifted a brow and held up the coffeepot.

Seth wondered how long he'd been rooted to the spot watching her. And how many boys noticed. "If it's not too much trouble." Rusty's eyes widened at his sharp tone. Seth sighed as coffee filled the cups. "Thank you, Cookie. Miss Ronnie and I appreciate the axle grease."

"No problem, Boss." Rusty wheeled on a boot heel and stomped to the wagon.

Great. Now he'd aggravated the cook. Over her. That's why he should only focus on the cows. On the drive. Not pay attention to a dark-haired vision of loveliness. He snorted. Where had that thought come from? Vision? A chuckle worked its way up his chest. He reached Ronnie and handed her a cup. "Seems you've got a break from work. Me, too." He dropped to the ground beside her feet.

"Yes. Only dishes waiting for me." She sipped the brew. "You're taking it easy. That's a change."

"Resting before the river tomorrow. It's not much to cross, but it takes concentration." *Which I desperately lack right now.* "You could ride in the supply wagon and cross with us, if you'd rather. Rusty will be all right on his own."

Ronnie shoved her bonnet off, and curls trickled across her cheeks. "I'd love that. It's been a long while since I've watched a herd cross." She leaned forward, elbows on her knees, and her eyes widened. "Would you mind if I cow punched?" She tipped her head. "Please?"

Seth closed his eyes against the appeal. But having her horseback beside him would keep her close, and he could assure her safety more so than in a wagon.

"I suppose." He shoved a leg out straight, his boot heel digging a furrow in the dirt. "But you're following Ernie's signals and riding the horse I choose." He swallowed bitter brew. "Trey is mounted again, so the brown is out." He paused and considered the string of horses. "Appaloosa is strong should there be the least bit of current. Don't expect any, but don't know what rains have been upstream."

Her delighted laugh stirred his insides. "Thank you, thank you." She patted his shoulder. "I will follow directions to the letter. Promise." She giggled. "I can't wait till morning."

"What's waiting for you when you get to your homestead?" Seth's question was out before he could catch it.

Ronnie's face fell. "I don't know."

Seth drew a hand across his mouth. He'd stolen her joy with one sentence. He could kick himself. He'd given her a chance to ride then ripped a hole in her heart. He watched her face.

Ronnie sighed. "Had a neighbor helping Daddy work our place, and I hope he's still around." She dumped the remainder of her drink. "Expect I will have a lot of work ahead of me. But it's what I love." She smiled down at him, a curl tickling the edge of her lip. "Ranching is in my blood." She trailed a finger up and grasped the curl, winding it around and around her finger. "I do thank you kindly for letting me ride along with you. I'm ever so grateful." She lowered her eyes, the lashes fluttering. "I'm not sure how I would've gotten home—" Her voice grew tight.

"Glad to be of service, ma'am." Seth almost laughed at his formal words. How could he explain to her that her very presence had taken the monotony out of this trip. "Look forward to settling you in Fort Worth."

"Hello in the camp." A strong voice broke the moment. "Friendly riders approaching."

Rusty lifted the coffeepot. "Arbuckle waiting."

Seth shot to his feet, one hand extended. "Seth McKenzie." The oldest man gripped his hand.

"Sheriff Henley. Looking for three outlaws." His eyes roved the area. "Seen any strangers?"

Ernie coughed, and Seth caught his worried look. *The rustlers.* His voice caught in his throat. "Not yet." He motioned toward the chuck-wagon tailgate. "Join us, and tell me more."

Chapter Thirteen

Ronnie watched the three other riders dismount and stride into camp. The older man and Seth had their heads together, and Seth's serious countenance gave her pause. Worry creased his brow. She trailed in their direction, an ear attuned to the conversation.

"Been searching for this group nigh on to a week now. Three riders." He spit out a stream of tobacco. Ronnie wrinkled her nose.

"We've lost some cows. Reckon they're responsible?" Seth looped his fingers in his belt.

"Could be. Stole horses from one ranch and robbed a wagon full of travelers last week. They're the ones reported it." The sheriff sighed. "And it's my county." He grabbed the plate Rusty handed him and nodded his thanks. "Been in the saddle long enough."

"We plan on crossing the river tomorrow. You going our way?"

Ronnie's heart thudded against her chest. Bandits and outlaws going in the same direction they were traveling? A ripple of fear raced through her. Danger came in all forms out here.

The sheriff and his three men settled on the ground, shoveling in beans and slurping coffee. Ronnie reached for the dishpan and slid it to the edge of the wagon platform, still listening. A sweaty rider lifted his eyes and grinned at her. Ronnie flushed and turned back to her work. Wouldn't be seemly to look at the man. *Sorry, Aunt Susan. Not a lady yet.*

"Suppose we best head out now before we lose daylight completely and before your herd stomps out any prints." The sheriff leaned back on one elbow and his eyes drifted toward her. "Don't take these men lightly, McKenzie. Especially with your wife along."

Ronnie bit her tongue to keep from blurting out her identity. Wife, indeed. She sprinkled the shaved soap flakes in the water. Would be nice, though. Heat burned her cheeks. In a few days she'd be out of this world and at home. Alone. Again. Sadness stabbed her middle. No Seth in sight. Just alone.

"Miss Fergus?"

Ronnie jolted from her reverie at the sound of Seth's voice.

"Would you join us for a moment?" Seth tipped his head as she drew closer. "This is Sheriff Henley." His eyes twinkled. "Though I expect you know that by now." His lips twitched. "There's reports of rough men in the area."

"Ma'am." The sheriff ducked his head in greeting. "I reckon you better stick close to camp. Close to riders at all times. I'm not sure what these men are capable of." His brow furrowed. "And we don't want to find out."

"I understand completely, sir." Ronnie gave a half curtsy. "Thank you for the warning."

She slipped away and rounded the back of the wagon close to the string of horses and whoever was on guard.

Trey leaned against the wheel, his bandaged arm tight against his chest. "Miss Ronnie, I ain't letting you out of my sight after what you done for me." The boy's mouth drew in a grim line. "Don't you worry. Nothing happening to you on my watch."

Ronnie gripped his good elbow and gave a little shake. "I'm not worried." She glanced at Wally guarding the horses. "I've never felt safer in my life with my friends nearby."

Trey blushed. "Glad you're still thinking me a friend." He shrugged and stared at the ground. "Best you know, with a ma and sisters, I understand your need to creep away a time or two every day. But you call one of us to stand watch even then."

Ronnie's eyes widened, and she stifled a laugh. This young man did understand a woman's needs. She drew him in a one-sided hug. "Trey, your thoughtfulness and kindness will make you a fine husband one day. Thank you." She shoved him gently aside. "Right now I need flour from the store wagon."

She took two steps and realized the boy shadowed her. Trey was proving true to his word.

◆　◆　◆

Seth watched the posse lope away from camp. He gnawed on the inside of his cheek. Just what he needed as tired as he was. Something else to guard against. He glanced back and nodded at Ernie.

"Boss." The wiry cowboy tipped his hat back. "I'll talk to the boys. We'll draw the herd in tighter. River crossing might be dicey, but we can watch." He scratched his chin. "You thinking we need to arm the waddies?"

Seth drew in a deep breath and let it out slowly. Cowboys and guns. How many accidents had he seen with that combination? Stampedes, wounded legs, downed horses. He seldom let anyone carry, but in this situation. . .

He nodded. "Choose carefully."

Ernie chuckled. "I understand." He pointed his chin at Rusty. "He's tucked his shotgun under the seat. I'll get him to pull it out. Don't want to scare Miss Ronnie, though."

"She won't be scared. She's ranch tough." He smiled at the thought. "She's riding with us, too. Grab her gear and saddle the Appaloosa."

Ernie strode away. Seth looked around for Ronnie and spied her skirts at the edge of the wagon out of sight of camp. Fury rose in his chest. Had she not heard the warning? He stomped toward her.

"Thank you, Trey." Her laughter floated in the air. "I appreciate your kindness." He saw her wave at Wally. "And you, too, big guy."

His shoulders drooped in relief. The boys kept watch. He stopped in his tracks. But they weren't armed. Should they be? He lifted his hat and ran his fingers through his hair. Ernie's decision, he remembered. Ernie knew the boys best.

"Seth?" Ronnie touched his arm.

He swung to face her, an overwhelming desire to scoop her to his chest burning inside him. *Lord, help keep her safe. I can't lose her.* He grasped her shoulders and bent his knees so they were eye level.

"Ronnie, I want you by my side tomorrow at all times. Understand?" He could get lost in those green eyes.

She nodded. "I understand." She looked over her shoulder. "And I have my own personal watchdog." Her lips tipped up. "Thank you for caring."

"I do care." His heart tripped in his throat. "I want to deliver you safely. Let's move your blanket and gear to the other wagon, and Ernie will saddle up for you in the morning. Cookie can move out without you at daylight."

A tiny wrinkle crossed her nose. "I hate for him to travel alone."

"He won't be." For the first time, Seth thought about the chuck wagon. "I'll have Mike ride with him." He gave a tight smile. "Bet he'd be glad to be out of the saddle for a spell."

Ronnie's shoulder muscles tightened, and a flush painted her cheeks. Seth realized he still clung to her. If he bent right now, he could taste those pink lips. He released his grip like he'd been stung and stumbled backward.

Focus on cows. And rustlers. And riders.

Not on Veronica Fergus.

Journal

Travels fine. Weather holding. Ford Brazos in morning. Sheriff report concerns me. Ernie updating count. Must keep sharp eye out. Watch over her. Especially her.

Chapter Fourteen

Excitement bubbled in Ronnie's throat. She held the reins while Mike tightened the cinch on the Appaloosa.

"He's strong, Miss Ronnie." The cowboy reached up and shook the saddle. "Buster can get you across right fine." He turned his head and spit out tobacco juice. "Just give him his head in the water."

Ronnie nodded. "Buster and I will do all right. Thanks." She tightened the rope belt she'd fashioned through the loops of an old pair of Trey's britches. Seth had suggested she rid herself of cumbersome skirts, and she was glad for the freedom. Mike gave her a leg up. Buster pranced to one side. "Whoa." She steadied herself in the saddle and made him stand still. *Wonder if he feels the butterflies dancing in my stomach?* She giggled.

Mike's eyebrows rose. "You okay?"

She touched a finger to her lips. "Feeling my oats, is all. Thank you." She reined the horse around and walked toward the herd and Seth. Ranger stood with his head down while Seth stared out over the parade of beef passing by. Horse and rider were attuned to one another.

Ronnie wiped the sweaty palm of her hand across her thigh and drew in a deep breath. "Lord, I pray for this drive and this day. Please watch over every cow, horse, rider... and me. I must admit to a bit of jitters." She batted her eyelashes against tears. Sitting astride a horse reminded her of home. A home she would soon see. "But first I have to cross a river." She tapped her heels against the horse and trotted to meet Seth.

Both he and Ranger looked up at her approach. He tugged the reins and wheeled toward her, his lips tipped up. "Morning. See you're ready." His gaze roved her face then across the horse and back. "Mike fixed you up with a better saddle, I see."

Ronnie lifted herself in the stirrups and patted the cantle behind her. "Right sharp one, too. Thank you."

Seth nodded. He settled Ranger beside her. "Let's talk about the crossing. Ernie scouted our spot, and the river's running higher than we thought. Must've had heavy rain upstream." He frowned. "But it's passable. Lead cows will show 'em how it's done." He leaned forward and patted Buster's neck then eyed her. "Like I said, this is a strong horse. You hang on to him, no matter what." He tipped his head. "Understood?"

"Yes." Ronnie inhaled and held her breath for a moment, her adventurous nature taking a momentary lashing. "I'm ready."

Seth pointed to her leg. "Nice britches, too." He smiled, and her stomach fluttered. She could follow Seth into the river—and beyond, if need be.

◆　◆　◆

Clad in denim, those long legs stirred Seth's middle. Veronica Fergus cut a fine figure no matter her appearance. He watched her nudge the horse forward and sidle up to a stray. She had no idea how beautiful she was.

Seth sighed. "Focus, man." He reined his horse about and moved to the front of the herd. Ernie rode beside him. "News?"

Ernie nodded. "It's fine. We go in easy and those"—he pointed to several cows—"will take a natural lead. Kept my eye on 'em trailing, and the others been following 'em." He wiped his mouth. "Sent Wally in, and it's just past his stirrups in the deep. Shouldn't be too hard." He grinned. "Even for our new cowgirl."

Seth glanced at him. "She's earned the right to ride. But keep a sharp eye."

"Yep. Let's take 'em in, Boss." Ernie prodded his horse into a trot and began to signal other riders to bring the stragglers in closer.

Seth rode alongside the lead cows. The riverbank sloped down at the beach head so they would be able to walk in. Wouldn't take much encouragement, even when they had to swim. He spotted Ronnie close to his flank and smiled. *Following directions. What a relief.*

The lead cattle plunged into the water with no hesitation, heading up the north riverbank and shaking off the water. Waddies bunched them as they came out. Shrill whistles and sharp shouts filled the air. Seth waved his hat at a couple of strays to move them forward. Ranger cut and moved, dancing the way he'd been taught. For the most part, Seth gave him his head. When he reached the center of the river, he swiveled in the saddle to watch for Ronnie. Someone had passed on a lariat, and she flapped it against her saddle like a fly swatter, joining in the mayhem. Dust swirled and covered her, yet she didn't miss a beat.

Seth's heart swelled. *Ranch girl, indeed.*

Chapter Fifteen

Sweat trickled down Ronnie's back and dirt caked on her eyelids, but there were cows to move, and she'd been given the chance to prove her mettle. Two mamas bawled their displeasure at losing babies in the crowd. "Move on. You'll find 'em. Move on." She flapped the rope across their backsides. "Hiyah. Move on." Her raw throat ached for a drink of water. "Move on."

Her ever-present shadow, Trey, nudged one with his boot. "Let's go, let's go." He rode ahead of her.

She caught movement from the corner of her eye. Several strays rambled the wrong direction. "Come on, Buster, let's round them up." He trotted into the small grove of trees and bushes. Ronnie tried to flatten herself against his neck to avoid branches and brambles. The horse jerked to a stop and quivered. Ronnie raised her head.

Three men sat stock-still watching her. They'd rounded up the cows she chased. Ronnie felt bile rise in her throat. Her eyes darted from the cattle to the men and back again. Rustlers. Her heart hammered and her fingers dug into Buster's mane. Time to move.

Giving a tug on the reins and a hard kick, she wheeled Buster around and set off at a gallop along the river's edge. Branches slapped at them, but Ronnie stretched out and gave the horse his head. He plunged down the slope toward the river.

A crack split the air. Tree bark flew into her face. *Gunshot.* Fear ran its icy fingers up her spine, and tears welled in her eyes. She rose a bit in the stirrups to get her bearings. She didn't want to scatter the herd as they forded the river, yet she had to find Seth.

Seth. A fierce longing and desire to protect him filled her. She had to warn him of the dangers skirting the herd. She spotted him across the river, on the bank, his back to her. She felt Buster's strong legs begin to swim against the swollen river. She'd entered at a deeper spot. No matter, the horse could get her to Seth. She stretched as low as she could and hung on.

Another crack but no pain. She glanced over her shoulder at the young rider who wielded a gun. Probably no older than Trey. Tears blinded her. Panic stabbed her middle. Seth.

Oh, Lord, keep us safe.

Looking up, she saw Seth turn her way and spur Ranger into the water. She raised a hand and another shot rang out. She slumped in the saddle but felt no pain. Seth.

"Ronnie." He yelled.

Terror licked at her. "Seth! Move out! Get help! Rustlers." She waved the lariat in an effort to gain Ernie's attention.

Seth and Ranger swam closer.

The next shot caught him. He slumped, grasped for Ranger's mane, and rolled into the water.

Ronnie screamed and lunged for him. She caught his shirt collar and tugged his face up. His eyelids fluttered. "Seth. Oh, Seth."

The current pulled her downstream, toward the men shooting. She kicked, pulling at the water with one hand and trailing Seth behind her. Ranger's reins floated by and she grabbed them. Using the horse as leverage, she yanked Seth higher and up against the saddle. The horse swam between them and the rustlers. The growing blood spot on Seth's shoulder frightened her. Ronnie drew him closer as Ranger swam toward shore. Soon her toes touched the ground, and she stood, mindful to keep the horse in place.

"Ernie, Wally, Mike! Help!" Glass shards of pain sliced her raw throat, but she continued to scream.

"Miss Ronnie, Boss!" Horror filled Ernie's voice. Dirt from his horse's hooves slapped her in the face, but she held Seth to her chest. The cowboy slid to her side and dragged them from the water.

Ronnie collapsed in a heap, her chest heaving. "Rustlers." She pointed downstream. "Shot."

She laid her face against the sweet-smelling grass and let tears trickle down her face. When she caught her breath, she rose on an elbow. "Will he be all right?"

Ernie ripped Seth's shirt open. The blood trickled from a wound in his shoulder. "He's not gut shot. For that be thankful." His mouth drew in a grim line. "We got to move him." He glanced at Ronnie then searched the riverbank. "No sight of 'em now, and ain't no never mind. We got to tend to the boss."

Ronnie nodded. "Tell me what to do."

◆　◆　◆

Fire. He was on fire. Seth jerked his body to one side, but arms clamped him down. He had to move out of the fire. He tried again.

"Lie still." Ronnie leaned over and pressed her cheek to his. "You have to lie still," she whispered into his ear.

A hint of lavender tickled his nose. She usually smelled of firewood or dust. Lavender. He smiled. He would like to wake to that smell every day.

"Seth." Ernie's voice prodded him from reverie. "Seth."

He didn't want to open his eyes. He only wanted to think on lavender. Soft, sweet-smelling hands rubbed his cheek. Fire wasn't so bad when you weren't alone. He shifted, and Ronnie pressed him down again. But he had to move. Couldn't she see the flames licking him? He drew in a sharp breath. Was she about to burn, too? Dread filled his chest. He would lose her. Biting his lower lip, he raised an arm from the fire. Ronnie grabbed it and pulled it against her chest.

"Boss?"

The smell of tobacco filtered into his nose, drowning out the lavender. Ernie. He opened his eyes.

A sob burst from Ronnie. "Oh, Seth. You're awake. Thank goodness." She pressed her lips to his hand.

"Ronnie," he croaked. He licked his lips. So thirsty. Fire did that. Burned a thirst into you.

She reached back and poured water into a cup. Ernie lifted his head, and he took a sip. She pulled the cup away before he could take a long draw.

"Enough for now."

She was using that settle-the-cows tone. Crooning. He closed his eyes.

"Seth, open your eyes. Now." The croon changed to determination.

He did as he was told. A bolt of fear ran through him. He saw no flames, only prairie grass. He could hear cows lowing and the ranch smell filled his nostrils. What was he doing sprawled out on the trail? He stared the question into Ronnie's eyes.

She tipped her head. "You were shot."

His eyes widened. "Shot?" He swallowed hard. Memories of fire then muddy water filtering into his eyes and nose. He'd crumpled into the river. "How—"

"Rustlers." Ernie's gruff voice spat out the word. "Shot at Miss Ronnie and then hit you." He slapped a hand against his thigh. "But as luck-of-the-draw would have it, that sheriff didn't ride far. He reckoned they'd be back. So he's rounding them up." Ernie tugged his hat low and rose. "We got to get you tended, though." He frowned. "Gonna get you to Cookie."

"I patched you up for now." Ronnie gripped his hand. "Wally rode out and stopped the chuck wagon, so it won't be a far piece to ride in the store wagon." Her smile didn't reach her eyes. "I'll ride with you." Worry tinged her tone.

"Thanks." He lifted the free arm and wiped his forehead. "The others?"

"Boss, we've got everything across." A shadow pressed against Ernie's back. "Mike and Wally here are going to load you. Then we'll go." The boys leaned into his line of sight. He tried for an encouraging smile. "Don't you worry none." Ernie nodded.

The waddies took corners of the blanket spread beneath him and carefully slid him into the nearby wagon. Fire burned his body once again. He gritted his teeth until his jaw ached. Ronnie arranged herself above him, and he placed his head in her lap. Her upside-down grin made him chuckle, and fire filled him.

"Ranch girl, you're something else." He closed his eyes against the pain.

Chapter Sixteen

Rusty handed her soap and the wreck pan. "Wash up, then wash the wound some." He stared at Seth lying so still. "He's tough. He'll be fine." He eyed Ronnie. "Not so sure about you, though."

Ronnie glanced down at her filthy shirt. Dirt and blood caked her. She shivered and trudged to the water barrel. She scrubbed her hands and arms raw then returned to Rusty's side.

"How do we take the bullet out?" The very question made her stomach roll.

"We don't." Rusty reached for the petticoat, which once again would prove itself as a bandage, and ripped strips. "Town ain't far. The doctor can take care of him. All we gotta do is try and stop the bleeding." He pressed a bandage against Seth's shoulder. Seth grunted.

"But I thought—"

"Wrong doctoring can bring too much infection." Rusty held the bandage in place with one hand and bit another piece and ripped. He nodded his head. "Little help here?"

Ronnie ripped more of the petticoat and handed it to Rusty. He made a compress, tied it down, and splinted the shoulder with a blanket.

"Don't want him moving around." He stepped back and eyed Seth. "Think he's all right for now. You haul in and hold on to him. Mike's taking this wagon on ahead." He lifted a brow. "It ain't but a few hours till Fort Worth, anyhow. Reckon you can stand it." His lips tipped up. "Don't think you mind just you and the boss."

She clambered into the wagon and settled in to cradle Seth's head. His wan face concerned her. She longed for the strong cowboy with the ever-changing eyes to sit up and order them to move out. But he remained still.

The wagon jerked, and the slow journey to help began. Tears clouded her vision. She swiped at the lock of hair on his forehead then bent low and pressed her lips to his cheek. "I think I love you, Boss." He didn't stir. Ronnie stifled a sob and checked his shoulder. Nothing had moved. If only they could gallop to town. She closed her eyes, drained, and leaned against a crate. The sharp corner jabbed her back. Maybe that would keep her awake. She had to keep watch over Seth. For just a while longer.

For just a while longer. She wouldn't see him after they got to town. The realization stung. Tears tipped over and trailed down her cheeks. Yes, she'd go home. Her very mission accomplished.

But she would once again be alone.

◆ ◆ ◆

Lavender again. Seth smiled. He hoped she would always wear lavender when they were together. He opened his eyes and stared into an unfamiliar face. The lady patted his cheek.

153

"There, there, dear boy." She stepped back and said, "Dr. Mery, he's awake."

Dr. Mery? Only one he knew was in Fort Worth. He struggled to sit up, but the woman pressed him against the bed. Bed. Soft. He was no longer on the trail. How long had he been out? He swallowed hard, his throat scratchy.

The doctor appeared at his side and nodded. "Looking good, McKenzie. Sight better than when they brought you in last night." He pushed his spectacles on his nose. "How you feel?"

"Like I got shot." Then run over by a flaming stampede. Fire no longer ran up his arm, so he knew he was in better shape. "Where's everybody?" He only cared about one, but he dare not mention her name.

"Gone. Lady settled into the hotel, and your hand said he had to bring in the herd." Dr. Mery quirked a brow. "Nice girl you had riding with you. Reminded me of my Lorena when we first came west." He smiled. "Now you rest up. Another day here and you'll be ready to move on."

Seth rolled his head against the pillow. Ranch girl disappeared. She hadn't stayed. Well, what did he expect? She wanted transport to Fort Worth and she got it. He sighed. "Well, Lord, You got part of us here safe, please bring the herd the rest of the way." He stifled a yawn. "Watch over her, please. And let her know I'm grateful—"

"Grateful? For what? All I did was cook and feed a bunch of cowboys. Then save you from drowning." Ronnie sidled up to the bed. "What do you have to thank me for?" Her eyes twinkled. She patted his hand. "I'm grateful, Seth. To you. Your generosity allowed me to get closer to home." She hitched her skirt and perched on the edge of the bed. "Soon I'll find me a way out to see what shape my ranch is in." She toyed with the hem of her shirt. "Reckon it will take me some time to get it in shape again." She glanced up at him. "But I'm the one grateful."

She leaned over, and a sweet fragrance enveloped Seth's senses. Wasn't lavender, sweeter. Ronnie pressed a kiss on his forehead. "Thanks, Boss, for everything. I'll check in before I leave town tomorrow." With a swish, she left the room before he opened his mouth. He ran a finger over his forehead. He closed his eyes and let sleep overtake him. Her soft lips and sweet smell filled his dreams.

Chapter Seventeen

Ronnie pulled the strings on her reticule tighter, giddiness trickling through her middle as she trekked toward a general store. Seth McKenzie had paid her almost a cook's wages. Certainly enough to get supplies for the trip to the ranch. He'd even let her purchase the Appaloosa at a ridiculously low price. "Least I can do for saving my life," he'd said.

By twilight she'd be on her own property. "Home." The very word conjured images of her daddy and mama. She brushed away a tear. "I'll get it up and running. Just you and me, Lord."

The livery owner handed her the reins and helped her mount, not even frowning when she tucked her skirts between her legs. Reckon he'd heard stories about the McKenzie drive already. She knew they circulated around town, fresh from the doctor's office. She sat atop her horse and watched two coaches pass. No, town life wasn't for her. She was ready to be ranch girl. She tapped her heels against Buster's sides, and they began the ride. Each milestone swelled excitement then trepidation within her chest. What awaited her at the end of the dusty trail?

"Home. No matter what we find, it's home." And she was alone. An ache stabbed under her breastbone. Seth had paid her, thanked her, and wished her well. No kiss or hug. She'd been another trail rider. "Well, that's as it should be." She rounded a bend and pulled Buster to a halt.

Before her sat her house. All looked well. She chewed her lower lip then nodded. "Let's see the rest." Buster trotted the rest of the way in.

Ronnie dismounted, looped the reins in a ring on a porch post, and opened the front door. Dust mites floated through the air, stirred by her skirts. She flung back a curtain. Windows still intact. With each step, her apprehension drained away. The furniture she'd left behind, the stove, a few books—the room sat as though time had stood still.

Ronnie threw back her head and let out a whoop. Relief sagged her into the rocking chair by the fireplace. She clutched her stomach. The cloud of worry dissipated in the cool breeze from the front door. She had arrived, and nothing had changed.

Nothing except her. Longing rose up until she could taste it. Longing for someone she'd never have. Seth McKenzie. A dream. Evaporated.

"In all things be thankful, Veronica Fergus." Aunt Susan's voice drifted through her mind.

"Yes, ma'am. I am thankful." She shoved from the rocker and strode out to unload the supplies she'd purchased. Thankful ranch girl. That was who she was now.

◆ ◆ ◆

Seth sat in the café and sipped cold coffee. He stared out the window at the hustle and crowds along the street. He needed to get out of town. He rubbed the back of his neck and felt a stab of pain in his shoulder. A reminder of the dangers on the trail. Hadn't he told Miss Fergus she'd experience danger? She had most definitely done that.

"And done it well," he whispered into his cup. Ronnie had ridden away a week ago and the loneliness he felt overwhelmed him. He missed her laugh, her walk, the sauciness she exhibited when she wanted her way. He thought of those long legs astride the Appaloosa. A fetching sight indeed.

He tossed coins on the table and pushed to his feet. Ernie and the boys waited at the livery to say their good-byes. Some were headed back south to Alvin and others scattering to wherever they could get a job. Ernie had signed on with another drover to move cattle to Kansas.

Seth placed a hand on his back and stretched. He was tired of the saddle. Contracting didn't seem to suit him anymore. But which way was best?

A bell rang. Church. He frowned. Must be a Wednesday night service. He turned around and ambled toward the sound. He had free time. Maybe God would speak to his heart in a church service. Sure couldn't hurt. And he was ready to listen.

Two hours later, Seth mounted Ranger and turned the horse west. The strong words of the itinerant preacher had stirred a desire inside Seth like never before. He dug in his heels, and the horse shot into a gallop. He'd gotten the directions from the general store. Not far to go. Not far to the ranch.

Girl.

◆ ◆ ◆

Ronnie flung open the door at the sound of hoofbeats. A rider's silhouette loomed down the road in the twilight. She shaded her eyes and stepped back inside to grab her daddy's gun. She stood on the porch, the pistol hidden by her skirt. The horse and man rode closer. Her mouth grew dry. Her heart hammered against her ribs. She slid the pistol inside the door and walked toward Seth. Ranger pranced in front of her and slid to a stop. Seth dropped to the ground, his boots stirring dust with each step.

"Miss Fergus."

"Mr. McKenzie." She licked her lips.

"Heard tell you might need a foreman." Seth removed his hat and forked his fingers through his hair.

"Heard tell right." Ronnie cleared her throat. "Pay's not much, but food is good." She smiled.

Seth nodded. "I know that for a fact." His eyes roved across her face, and he held out a hand. She slid her hand into his. "Reckon I can serve two jobs around here?" He squeezed her fingers.

Ronnie cocked her head. "Two?"

Seth drew her into an embrace and lowered his head. His lips almost touched hers. Ronnie closed her eyes. "Two," he whispered. "Husband and foreman." He kissed her.

Ranch girl kissed him back.

Eileen Key retired after teaching school for thirty years. She is a freelance writer and editor, with two mysteries and seven novellas published. Mother of three, grandmother of five, Eileen resides in San Antonio, Texas.

Love on the Run

by Debby Lee

Acknowledgments:

Thank you to my fabulous Inklings critique group, Barbara, Carolyn, Joyce, Kristie, Kyle, and Robert. Your passion for truly exceptional fiction motivates me to keep writing. Thank you to my wonderful agent, Tamela Hancock Murray. Your patience with me, your dedication to the publishing industry, and your unwavering faith inspires me to put forth my best work. Many, many thanks to my amazing family: my husband Steve and my children, Michelle, Devon, Toni, David, and Steffen, you have stuck with me and encouraged me when I felt like I couldn't write another word. You teach me the meaning of love. I will love and cherish you all forever.

I will lift up mine eyes unto the hills, from whence cometh my help.
My help cometh from the LORD, which made heaven and earth.
PSALM 121:1–2

Chapter One

Daisy Hollister's gaze fell on the slicked-up man in army blue stepping down from the stagecoach. The polished medals and shiny buttons on the officer's uniform glistened in the summer sun like the thirty pieces of silver once held by Judas Iscariot. From a distance the man appeared to be Randall "Butch" Butchovick, the snake who had haunted her nightmares for a year.

A slight breeze blew through the branches of a nearby tree, causing the late-afternoon shadows to dance around the horse-drawn conveyance so Daisy couldn't recognize the man for sure. For a closer inspection, she snuck forward a few steps. A small barrel of sugar sat atop a larger barrel of dried beans. They provided a measure of obscurity as she stepped behind them. Her gloved hands clutched her reticule so hard her fingers ached.

"See to it my trunks are delivered to the hotel," the man called to the stagecoach driver.

Air flew from Daisy's lungs in a whoosh. That voice! This was Butch, all right. Her knees went weak with fear and rebelled at the thought of holding her upright. Thank the Lord the barrel provided support. She leaned against the rough wooden container. What now? She couldn't spend the rest of her days running from the goon, yet confronting him could mean a trip to the pearly gates.

Heavy boots clomping along the boardwalk jerked Daisy's attention to the approaching person.

The stagecoach driver carried a mail sack. "Afternoon, ma'am." He tipped his hat as he passed by.

Daisy nodded but was too frightened to manage a reply. Two young boys lugging a large trunk followed the driver. Farther down the boardwalk she spied Butch. He puffed on a cigar and leered at a saloon girl who had just stepped through the establishment's batwing doors.

Daisy had to find a way out of town, fast. An alley between the general store and the hotel offered a means of escape. She dashed between the buildings, the path littered with broken crates and empty rain barrels.

The boardinghouse she called home sat at the far end of town. If she could reach the sanctuary of her room, she could throw her meager belongings into her trunk and leave. Daisy chided herself. Hadn't she just vowed to never run again? She had grown weary of hiding and running like a coward. Something had to be done about this wolf stalking around in a woolen, army-issued uniform.

The hem of Daisy's skirt caught on a tangle of briars, but she yanked it loose and kept going. The large white clapboard house with red trim came into view. Then she spotted her horse. The brown mustang she'd named Clancy drank from the trough in the corral. Clancy had been a gift from the man who had helped her escape from Butch that terrible night, and the trusted animal had carried her through the most heartbreaking moments of her life.

A plan formed in her mind. She could ride out to see her friend Green Grass at the Cottonwood Springs Pony Express way station.

Green Grass represented everything Daisy hoped to be someday. The girl from the Kiowa tribe braved the elements, warring tribes, and thieves, to ride wild mustangs and deliver mail. Green Grass would not only provide refuge at her home for a few days, she would speak with the elders of her tribe. Daisy thought highly of her Indian friends and hoped they would provide some sanctuary and with luck, share some wisdom. She hoped, prayed they would have ideas on what to do about Butch.

After slipping into a pair of trousers, Daisy rode north. With luck Green Grass would be at the station and not out on a run. She asked the Lord to guide her and protect her while Clancy trotted along to their destination.

The station was two miles away when screams for help pierced the air, followed by three gunshots. Daisy clenched the reins of her horse. Pony Express riders faced dangers of all sorts. Had one of them come into trouble? The situation could be hazardous for Daisy as well. Sweat tickled her forehead and her hands trembled, but she was tired of running from danger. She kicked the sides of her horse to nudge him into a gallop.

A half mile later Daisy came upon a Pony Express horse tied to a tree. The poor animal bucked and neighed as she approached. She leaped off her own horse and looped the reins around a nearby branch.

A body slumped against a large boulder. Deep red stained the person's shirtfront, but she couldn't determine the rider's identity. She took a moment to reach into her saddle-bag and pulled out an old shirt that she immediately tore into strips for bandages.

"Don't worry. I'm here to help you," Daisy called out. "Lord Jesus, if he's still alive, please, don't let him die." The Pony Express owners, Russell, Majors, and Waddell, could ill-afford to lose a rider, but that was beside the point. This was still a human life, precious in the eyes of God.

After yanking the canteen of water from the pommel of her saddle, Daisy raced to the rider. She turned the wounded soul around to face her and dropped both canteen and bandages. Waves of horror coursed through Daisy.

"Green Grass," Daisy cried. "Green Grass, what happened?"

Her friend slit her eyes open, and for a brief moment relief swept through Daisy. "You're gonna be okay, Green Grass. Hang on, I'm gonna get you to the way station and Billy will fix you right up."

A feeble moan slipped past her friend's blue lips. "Forget me. Get the *mochilla*, the mail pouch, to Billy."

Blood seeped from the ragged gunshot wounds in her friend's chest. She pressed the makeshift bandages, along with her handkerchief to the wounds, but they were soon soaked through. Daisy held Green Grass in her arms as the tension eased from her friend's body. Pain clawed at Daisy's heart. It was only a matter of time before she passed into eternity. Tears slipped from her eyes and slid down her cheeks. First she lost her dear ma and pa to the likes of Butch Butchovick, and now she could be losing her best friend.

◆ ◆ ◆

Billy Cook perched on a battered chair at the way station's only table and read the disturbing letter from the New York orphanage, again. His nephew, Luke, suffered from yet another bout of sickness. If the lad ailed this often in the summer, how much worse would he be during the long cold winter? Billy didn't want to imagine.

As soon as he had enough money saved, he planned on purchasing a farm and sending for his late sister's only child, but a lot could happen between now and then. He was tempted to send for the child right away, but the dangers surrounding the Pony Express station kept him from doing so. Way stations were raided, burned, and had horses stolen so often he could hardly keep track of them all.

But what could he do in the meantime? Maybe he could send a package, some crackers and a toy, if it didn't cost too much. He paused to remember the tow-headed boy who had followed him around when they came to visit last Christmas. Billy had purchased a stick horse and given it to him. Luke had been so excited. He warmed at the memory of watching him ride it around outside, even in the cold weather.

Screams and pounding hooves yanked Billy's thoughts to the present. He stuffed the letter in his shirt pocket and bolted outside. In the distance, across the Wyoming landscape, he spotted two horses with riders galloping toward him.

The animals reached the corral and jerked to a stop. His friend Daisy Hollister leaped down from her horse. On the other horse a bloody, slouched-over form was tied to the saddle. He recognized the fringed buckskin trousers. Dread swept through him.

"Billy, Green Grass is hurt! Bad! Come help me."

Billy sprinted toward the pair and helped Daisy pull his best rider from the saddle.

"You've got to help her. Please!" Daisy cried.

How he hated the sound of a woman crying. Wait a minute. Did Daisy say the rider was a she? Billy inspected the chest wounds and discovered Green Grass was indeed a she. Worse yet, no pulse thrummed against his fingers. The Indian girl was dead.

"Can we help her? I hope we can dig those bullets out of her. Shall I ride and fetch the doc—"

"There's nothing we can do for her, Daisy, she's gone."

A pitiful whimper, along with a sniffle, were the only sounds from the woman. Billy hated to be so gruff with the distraught woman, but it was the truth. He touched the pocket of his shirt and remembered his nephew. His job depended on getting the mail through.

Billy cleared his throat. "Where's the mochilla?"

"The mail pouch? It's right here on the saddle."

With Luke's well-being at stake, Billy swung into action. "Jack," he hollered at the bunkhouse. "Get out here. I need you to take a run."

Billy stepped around Daisy and ran to the barn. He hurried to saddle the freshest pinto and then trotted her outside. He tossed the mochilla on the pony and yelled again for his rider. "Jack."

The teenager ambled from the bunkhouse, in his nightshirt, and rubbed his eyes. "What do you want, Billy? I just finished a run this morning. I'd rather not take another one just now."

"Everyone else is out on a run, and Green Grass is dead. I need you to take the pouch as far as Fort Laramie. Send it on with a fresh horse and rider, then you can rest for a spell."

Jack grumbled. "I've been riding for hours, Billy. I'm tired."

Billy was determined to take it himself if it meant keeping his job. He needed the money to provide for Luke, and he couldn't let the child down.

"Let me take it. I can ride, and I need to get out of town anyway."

Billy whirled around, and there stood Daisy. He'd forgotten about her. She looked up at him. Her big green eyes were puffy and the edges were red from crying.

"Woman, you're more than a few pickles shy of a quart jar if you think I'd let you ride the Pony Express." Billy rubbed the sweat from his forehead with a red bandanna. "Hurry up and get dressed, Jack. You're up."

Jack yelped and disappeared into the bunkhouse.

"Give me a chance, Billy," Daisy said. "Green Grass did a good job getting the pouch through, and she is—was—a woman."

"Need I remind you how that turned out?" Billy asked. He was in no mood to debate the subject, especially with a lady as pretty as this one. He watched her as she leaned against the posts of the corral for support. Fresh tears brimmed in her eyes, and her bangs ruffled when she blew out a sigh. His heart softened.

"If you're that desperate for a job, I can see about finding you some work around here, but I'm not letting you ride."

"Very well," Daisy lifted her chin and walked toward the main house.

As he watched her go he admired her spunk. She was one of the few woman he knew who could ride astride. Maybe if he got in a pinch he could let her take a run. Um, no. What was he thinking? The superintendent of this region was as prickly as a porcupine about the company's rules, rules that forbid women to ride for the Pony Express. If he got caught allowing Daisy to ride, he'd lose his job. If he didn't have money enough to care for Luke, the boy would have to spend the winter in the orphanage. Billy wouldn't let that happen.

Jack emerged from the bunkhouse and ran toward the pinto. He leaped onto the horse in one fluid motion.

"Ride hard, Jack, this pouch is behind schedule enough as it is," Billy said. "When you're done resting, find the superintendent and tell him we're down a rider and need a replacement."

"Will do," Jack called as he galloped for the horizon, stirring up a cloud of dust.

Billy turned and plodded to the main house. He hoped Daisy had let go of any notion to ride for the Pony Express.

He wasn't about to risk his job, but what could she need money for? She already worked as a cook at the hotel in town, and from what he'd heard she was a good one and got along with everybody. So why did she need to get out of town right away? Was the same person who had killed Green Grass after Daisy as well?

Something wasn't right, and Billy suspected she was in some kind of trouble. He didn't know what kind of fix she was in, but he was determined to find out.

Chapter Two

"You want to explain to me why Green Grass rode for the Pony Express?" Billy asked.

Daisy swallowed the lump in her throat and shifted in her chair. Memories of her friend danced in her mind and brought a fresh onslaught of tears to her eyes. Green Grass's family would soon learn of her demise. The loss of income would be difficult for them, but even more devastating would be the loss of Green Grass herself.

"Well?" Billy stood in the doorway, his muscular arms folded across his chest.

In her grief-stricken state, she struggled for the proper words. Would Billy understand the hardships her friend faced? She hoped he would not only understand, but sympathize, too.

"Green Grass and her family are very poor. They live in a tiny shack, and their tribe is too poor themselves to be of much help."

Billy nodded.

Daisy drew a deep breath and continued. "Her father was killed some time ago leaving her mother and grandmother to care for the younger children. The two women can only do so much farming and the younger children are too small to find jobs. They need money to buy food and extra blankets so they can live through the winter."

Billy's eyes seemed to peer into the depths of her soul. Daisy choked back a cry that crept up her throat and continued.

"Besides the need for food and blankets, her youngest brother is very sick and needs medicine. You don't have children, and you're a man, so I can't expect you to understand, but she loved her family very much and would have done anything to help Little Bear." Thinking of the tyke wrenched her heart. A mournful sob escaped from her lungs. Her shoulders sagged as she wiped tears from her eyes.

Billy crossed the room with a sure stride and pulled her into his arms. Daisy laid her head against his chest and listened to his heartbeat. Comfort washed over her as she listened to the steady cadence.

"Don't worry about Green Grass's family. I'll see what I can do about getting her ma a job in town. I heard the laundry lady was looking for some help. I'll even talk to the doc and see if we can get that little boy the medicine he needs."

Judging by the kind words and the offer of assistance, Daisy surmised that Billy cared about the predicament of her friend's family. She relaxed considerably and eased herself onto a chair. Although she couldn't figure out why he cared so much, she was grateful for his compassion. She sat a bit straighter and fished around in her pocket for her handkerchief. Then she remembered she'd used it to stem the bleeding from Green Grass's wounds.

Billy must have sensed her need; he produced a red bandanna. She used it to dab at her eyes. The musky smell lingering in the cloth brought a strange sense of comfort.

"Thank you," she murmured, overwhelmed with gratitude. Now her heart thumped against her rib cage, causing heat to flow through her.

"Now that we've settled the matter of your friend, do you mind telling me why you're busting to get out of town?"

Daisy didn't particularly want to tell him about the evil man who had hunted her like prey, but figured she'd better. The thought of confiding in Billy frightened her. If someone else knew her secret, she would be placing them both in danger. But she needed help and she was weary of harboring the secret, so after a moment of hesitation, she began.

"A little over a year ago, I overheard Pa and Ma talking when they thought I was asleep. Pa worked for the railroad, and some army men came along to see how tracks were laid. There must have been some kind of trouble because Pa told Ma he knew something real bad about one of the men." Daisy closed her eyes. She could still hear the frightful tone in her mother's words, and her pa cleaning his Kentucky rifle.

"Go on," Billy said.

"A few nights later, when I was sleeping in my room, Ma burst in and dragged me from my bed and shoved me into the closet. She told me to keep quiet, no matter what I heard. It was dark, but I could see a little because Pa had lit a lantern. Then a man crashed into our house. Pa called him Mr. Butchovick, and they argued."

The man's raucous growling could've jolted a grizzly bear from the depths of hibernation. She cringed but forced herself to continue.

"Now he's following me. I didn't think he knew I was hiding in the closet, but now I think he must have."

"Wait a minute," Billy interjected. "If Mr. Butcho-whatever has a beef with your pa, why is he following you?"

"You don't understand." Daisy shook her head. The desire to evade Butch turned strong and steady within her like the wheels of a locomotive, but determination to help her friend's family was equally as powerful. Riding for the Pony Express would solve both problems. She jumped from her chair, ready to take the oath and ride east, with or without Billy's approval.

"What don't I understand?" Billy placed his hands on her shoulders.

To Daisy's chagrin, he held tight and refused to let her loose.

"Butch," Daisy finally stammered. "I saw him kill my pa and ma."

◆ ◆ ◆

Billy sighed with resignation and then hooked his thumbs into his belt loops. This girl was in a fix all right. Her eyes pleaded with him to let her go.

"Why don't we ride into town and make some inquiries. I need supplies anyhow."

Daisy shook her head. "When Butch got off the stage, he said he'd be staying at the hotel. I can't go back there. He'll see me and probably kill me like he did my folks."

"Fine, I'll go right now, and I'll let the hotel manager know you can't work for a while. I should be back before dark, but if I'm not, can you cook up something for the crew here? There's only two hired hands out mucking stalls, plus a couple of riders."

Daisy nodded. "Thank you."

Billy plopped his hat on his head, hurried to the barn, and hitched up the wagon. From there he rode to the town of Cottonwood Springs. First he stopped at the boardinghouse and asked the proprietor to send some of Daisy's things out to the way station. Then he went to the hotel and let Daisy's employer, Mrs. Adrianne Larson, know she'd be gone for a while. The flushed-faced woman hustled around the sweltering kitchen, preparing a plate for a mangy vagrant and his equally mangy pooch. Adrianne communicated her displeasure with the circumstances but seemed to understand.

Exiting the kitchen, Billy walked around to the front of the hotel. The clerk had stepped out for a moment so he leaned against the counter and waited. He tried to appear nonchalant as he glanced around the lobby, looking for anyone wearing an army uniform.

Neither the clerk nor anyone in army blue appeared, and it was getting dark. With a sigh of resignation, he stuck his hat back on his head, crossed the lobby, and was clomping down the steps, lost in his thoughts when someone bumped against his arm.

Startled, Billy looked over and noticed a man sporting a blue army sergeant's uniform.

"Excuse me," he said, hoping not to arouse suspicion. "The name's Billy Cook. Welcome to Cottonwood Springs."

The sergeant smiled. "Pleased to meet you. I'm Jake Hunter. Say, my horse threw a shoe. Would you by chance know of a good smithy in town?"

"Sure, Barker's is just down the street, on the left." Billy pointed west, past the saloon.

"Much obliged." The sergeant nodded and continued up the hotel steps.

"If you wouldn't mind, I'd like to speak with you a bit. I've heard some things about a certain officer. I'm not sure what to make of it."

"What's the officer's name?"

"Randall Butchovick."

A dark cloud settled over Jake's face. He descended a few steps to look Billy in the eyes. Billy didn't want to risk Daisy's hide by divulging too much information, but this guy didn't seem to think much of Butch, anyhow.

Jake glanced up one side of the street and down the other. "Meet me around back in fifteen minutes." He cast another look around and then disappeared into the hotel lobby.

Fifteen minutes later Billy paced behind the hotel. A mild uproar engulfed the kitchen, probably due to Daisy's absence. He paid them no mind and paced faster. What if this Jake Hunter character was in cahoots with Butch? Did he have ulterior motives for the clandestine meeting? He could be walking into a trap.

Sweat broke out on Billy's forehead, and he reached for his bandanna. He peered down the alley. Darkness obscured most everything. An uneasy moment passed as he wiped a fresh onslaught of sweat from his brow and stuffed his bandanna in his trouser pocket.

There wasn't much time to contemplate disastrous possibilities. Sergeant Hunter rounded the hotel corner, alone. "We have to make this fast, and keep it quiet."

"All right, Sergeant Hunter," Billy said.

"Call me Jake."

Billy noticed the man gripping the handle of his revolver as he spoke. He stepped closer. Billy dug his boot heel into the dirt and wished he had brought his own weapon.

"I hope you're not a friend of that skunk." Jake shot a stream of tobacco juice onto the ground near Billy's foot.

Billy whistled between his teeth. This Butch character must be as dangerous as Daisy said. With the lady's well-being at stake, he pushed his anxiety aside and glanced sideways to make sure no one was within earshot. "Hey, look, I've never met the guy, okay. Just tell me what you know about him." Billy asked, getting down to business.

Jake rolled a wad of tobacco around in his mouth and glared at Billy. Caution and fear mixed in the man's face. He was probably wondering if Billy could be trusted.

"Look, Jake, I'm not associated with Mr. Butchovick. You can trust me."

A slow moment elapsed before Jake spoke. "Butch killed my best friend, and a few others, I suspect. I just can't prove it."

Chapter Three

S am, I need your help," Daisy said.

"What for?" The hired hand looked up from mending a harness.

"I need you to help me get Green Grass's body back to her home. It's a cabin not far from here. We'll be back before it gets too late." Anger simmered in her heart at the one who had taken her friend's life. She would dig deep into her soul and scrape up the courage to find the criminal. Then she would take down the monster who had killed her parents. She vowed to bring them to justice, just how she wasn't sure, but she'd think of a way.

"All right," Sam replied. He pulled a saddle from the stand and strapped it onto one of the work horses not used for making Express runs.

Daisy placed her own saddle on Clancy's back and cinched the straps down. Then, with Sam's assistance, she lifted Green Grass's body from the ground onto a litter. Swiping tears from her eyes, she pulled a ribbon from her own hair and tied it to one of her friend's long black braids. More tears streamed down her cheeks as she covered the body with an old sheet.

"I promise you, Green Grass, I'll find whoever did this to you, and I'll send the law after them." With resolve, Daisy stood and mounted her horse.

For thirty minutes they rode through a thick section of trees until they reached a gurgling stream. A small log cabin with walls in desperate need of chinking offered a gap-toothed welcome. Thin wisps of smoke rose from the chimney. Green Grass's mother emerged from the structure.

Daisy bit her lip and nudged her horse slowly forward. She pulled on the reins a moment later and urged the animal to stop. Through tear-clouded eyes she watched her friend's mother take in the scene.

A scream flew from the woman's mouth. Daisy cringed at the anguish-filled sound. Her friend's mother rushed to the litter and sobbed over her slain daughter's body.

Daisy's heart constricted painfully as her friend's grandmother and her siblings raced from the cabin. They wailed in an anguished chorus. Witnessing their heartbreak strengthened Daisy's resolve. She would find the killer and see to it he paid for his crimes.

"My courageous daughter braved the wild frontier to earn money for Little Bear's medicine. Now look what has happened," Green Grass's mother cried. Daisy's middle ached as she watched the woman hold the spindly child close. The woman's body shook as her sobbing increased.

"My friend Billy said he'd speak with the doctor in town about getting Little Bear's medicine. If that doesn't work, I'll find the money somewhere and get it myself. I promise." Daisy slid down from her horse, and Sam was there to help her undo the litter. They placed the body next to the cabin.

"Thank you," the woman said. "We must begin the burial preparations for Green Grass."

The family began to sing songs of mourning. Their voices rose in a crescendo of grief. The women's feet pounded against the ground as they danced in remembrance of their fallen loved one. A wave of misery crashed into Daisy as she watched Little Bear lay his head on his dead sister's chest and run his tiny fingers through her hair.

Daisy watched for a few moments before deciding to give the family some privacy. With a heavy heart, she and Sam headed back to the way station. It was a quiet trip that gave her time to reflect on the day's events. Embers of anger slowly smoldered away the dull aching sadness and gave way to a fiery desperate hunger to right this terrible wrong.

It was late when she unbridled Clancy and led him to the corral. She dumped grain into his bucket and fed him a chopped apple. Then she went in to start dinner for the crew.

As Daisy pulled biscuits from the oven, succulent aromas filled the kitchen of the main house. She stirred the beef stew and finished setting the table but didn't feel like eating. Her stomach convulsed at the thought of facing Butch, and finding another murderer, but the hired hands had to be hungry so she pushed the troubling thoughts aside and hurried outside to ring the triangle.

"Supper's ready," she hollered to the small crew at the station.

Two cowboys strolled from the barn and a rider stumbled from the bunkhouse. They joined Sam and came into the main house, said grace, and ate their meal.

When the men had consumed their fill they ambled back outside. Daisy pumped water into the kettle and set it on the cookstove to heat so she could scrub the dinner dishes.

Daisy nearly dropped a stack of plates when Billy stepped into the house and kicked the door shut. "What on earth?"

"I need to talk to you, Daisy. It's about the man who killed your folks."

◆ ◆ ◆

Billy dropped into a chair and combed shaky fingers through his sweat-streaked hair. "Can you get me a cup of coffee, please?" He had hurried back from town so fast his throat was parched.

Daisy poured the steaming brown liquid into a tin cup and set it before him. "What did you learn about Butch?" she asked with wide eyes.

"He's under investigation for killing someone else, some private in the United States Army. Several officers questioned him at length, but they just don't have enough evidence to convict him." Billy took a big gulp of his drink.

"Do you think it has anything to do with why he killed my folks?"

"I don't know, but you're right about one thing. The man is dangerous. You can hide here for as long as you need to." Billy didn't mind her taking on a share of the cooking, but he still hadn't resigned himself to letting her ride for the Pony Express.

"What do you know about the army private?"

"Butch and the guy were sent to a railroad camp to make inquiries for transporting military goods. Probably the same camp your pa worked at."

"Go on," Daisy said.

"Rumor has it, while at the railroad camp, Butch raped an Indian girl. When the private, Daniel Tully, threatened to turn him in and have him court-martialed, Butch killed him. Or so the rumors go."

"Pa must have found out—and it got him and Ma killed." Daisy paled and swayed to the left before she plopped down in a chair.

"Apparently so." Billy downed the last of his coffee. "Are you all right?" He leaned toward Daisy and reached for her hand. Jake Hunter, the man he'd met behind the hotel, overheard Butch bragging that he'd hurt an Indian girl. Green Grass was probably that girl.

Billy wondered if Butch would eventually connect Green Grass to Daisy. He hoped the sneaky sidewinder wouldn't get any crazy ideas and come out to the way station looking for her. They didn't need a heap of trouble like that.

Chapter Four

Several hired hands sat around the dining-room table waiting on the meal. By the way their huge eyes followed her every move, Daisy guessed they were a famished lot. She sang another stanza of "Amazing Grace" as she finished making dinner. She noticed the way young Johnny smiled at her. She'd have to talk to him later and see if he knew the story of Jesus on the cross.

The roast she pulled from the oven smelled succulent and filled the room with a rich aroma. She set it on the counter to cool and then spooned the potatoes from the pan into a bowl and placed them on the table.

A rider was due soon, which meant another was heading out, and she wanted to make sure his belly was full before he rode off into the starry night. She poured a round of coffee for the crew, set the pot back on the stove, and carved the meat. If only Billy wasn't so put off by the hymns she sang while she worked. His company would provide some welcome conversation in the kitchen. Not that she wasn't entertained by the teen-age riders, but they hadn't been in the kitchen while she cooked.

"You boys wait until we say the blessing, all right?" Daisy said when she set the roast on the table.

A moment later, she dropped into her chair, and the boys bowed their heads. "Lord we thank You for the bounty that we are about to receive." After they all cho-rused a hearty "Amen," she watched them dig into the meal. It stunned her how fast they could devour the food she prepared. Most of them were young orphans and had never had anyone to cook for them. Their gratitude convinced her that she was right where God wanted her to be.

Billy stomped through the front door. Daisy jumped when he threw it shut with a bang.

"Are you through with your prayers and all that hymn singing?"

Daisy squirmed in her seat but kept the tartness from her reply. "Yes, Billy. We're glad to see you. Supper is ready. Your place is set at the end of the table." Daisy hoped her kindness would someday tenderize the toughness she detected around his heart. She tried to smile at him, but the scowl he aimed at her sent shivers down her spine. Ducking her head, she scrutinized the food on her plate and dug her fork into her potatoes.

"Best be careful on these night runs," Billy said. "I hear a band of Indians chased a rider from one station all the way to the next. They didn't do him any harm, but you never know."

Billy's words of warning caused Daisy's stomach to roil. Several moments of awk-ward silence followed. The riders exchanged wide-eyed glances and shifted in their seats.

"You boys don't mind if I sing while I cook, and pray over the meals, do you?" she finally asked. When the men shook their heads, she blew out a sigh of relief. "And I'm gonna double my prayers for you all while you're out on runs."

"My ma used to sing and tell me Bible stories, so I don't mind you praying one bit, Miss Hollister," Johnny, the youngest one, said.

Billy huffed and clanged his coffee cup on the table. Daisy felt tiny cracks ripple through her heart. She couldn't bury her feelings about God, but she couldn't continue to upset Billy with her expressions of faith, either. If she displeased Billy, he might fire her. Then where would she be?

Pounding hooves snagged Daisy's attention before she had time to reply to Johnny's comment. The lad jumped from his seat and bolted out the door. Billy followed suit, muttering something about making sure the pony was ready to run.

Daisy bowed her head and prayed for Johnny's protection. It warmed her clear through when the others joined in. She wanted to make a difference in the lives of those around her, especially Billy. It bothered her that he didn't put much stock in things of a spiritual nature.

She wouldn't cease to pray for the riders' safety no matter how much it might upset her boss. This was a dangerous profession, and it would break her heart if anything happened to one of these kids.

◆　◆　◆

The moon shining overhead would provide Johnny with plenty of light to ride by. Billy tried to soothe himself with the thought. Still, he worried. He hadn't mentioned at dinner that the Indians who chased the last rider had shot arrows at him. Thankfully, he'd reached the next way station before any real harm could be done. For a brief second he considered praying and then stopped himself short.

Where had God been when his parents died? What was God thinking when He let his sister die, and leave behind a small helpless child? Images of little Luke in the orphanage flooded his mind. How was the youngster faring? Had he received the last package Billy had sent him?

Even though he hadn't finished dinner, he shuddered at the thought of eating. His stomach twisted into a mess of knots. First thing tomorrow he'd ride into town and send another letter to the orphanage, asking for news about his nephew. As soon as he completed that task, he'd head over to the hotel to see Jake. Several days had passed, and the man had to know something by now regarding the investigation of Butch.

"Excuse me, sir, is supper ready?" the young boy who had just completed his run asked, drawing Billy from his thoughts.

"Yep, head on in and get something to eat."

"Much obliged," the weary-looking rider replied as he traipsed into the main house.

Billy led the pony to the barn. The animal's coat glistened with a layer of sweat, and the poor creature panted as if he hadn't drank water for ages.

The moment Billy stepped into the warm stables, his muscles relaxed and his heart rate slowed to a gentle rhythm. Growing up in an orphanage, his only friends were the stray dogs that came along. He had developed a love for animals. They didn't seem to possess the betraying qualities some humans possessed. Like Randall Butchovick.

The exhausted pony whinnied, drawing Billy to the present. He fed and watered the creature. He also gave him a good brushing and laid down some fresh hay for him to rest in. After checking on the other horses, he went for a walk.

The night air held a slight chill in spite of it being midsummer. Crickets chirped, and bullfrogs replied with a series of croaks and groans. Billy delighted in nature's symphony as he strolled along the fence line. It provided a welcome relief from Daisy Hollister's unceasing singing and praying.

Why did she have to be so pretty? And so sweet-natured? For the most part, she was fine to get along with, but then she'd open her mouth and say something about that faith of hers. If she were a man, Billy would just tell him to move along and find work elsewhere. At least she limited her preaching to the riders and the hired hands. If she dared make a crack to him about this God she loved, well, he didn't want to think about what he'd do.

Perhaps he could let her take a few runs after all. If Indians managed to capture her, she'd probably drive them crazy with all her Jesus talk, and they'd be only too happy to dump her off at the nearest way station. If she didn't get captured by Indians, she should have no problem making it to the next way station. Let the folks there deal with her.

Either way, at least she'd be out of his hair.

Chapter Five

The wind whipped Daisy's hair as she rode east to the Scott's Bluff way station in Nebraska Territory, her next stop on the Pony Express route. She hadn't spotted any sign of Indians, but her heart pounded in her chest nonetheless. Thankfully, no rustlers or bandits made their presence known. Daisy gripped the revolver in her loose-fitting holster. If she did see some varmint on the road, animal or human, she wouldn't hesitate to defend herself.

"Rider coming!" Daisy hollered as the station house came into view.

In the distance she watched as the hired hands raced toward the barn. Daisy rode to the entrance and slid down from her mount just as a young man led a fresh horse out. In a swift, fluid motion, Daisy swept the mochilla from the tired horse and placed it on the saddle of her fresh mount.

"A rider just came from the east," the hired hand said. "They're expecting some government documents in this pouch, and it needs to get to them as soon as possible. Ride hard!"

"Sure thing." Daisy jumped onto the horse, one named Buttercup, and kicked the animal's flanks. They bolted from the yard.

Riding for Russell, Majors, and Waddell was exciting. She was making money while Billy investigated the death of her parents back at Cottonwood Springs. She was grateful to him for that. He had shown such kindness, with the exception of growling at her for being too preachy. A sense of well-being flooded through her. If they could prove what Butch did, and put him away for life, she wouldn't have to run anymore.

She could stick around and help Green Grass's family through the winter. She could also keep in touch with her new friends working for the Pony Express.

Riding at a full gallop, Daisy passed a stagecoach. The occupants leaned out the windows and waved. She waved back as she rode by.

The rock and sagebrush landscape passed by her with a blur. Every so often she spotted the soft pink blossoms of the bitterroot plants. Green Grass had dug some up one afternoon and made a pleasant meal out of them. Daisy thought they had tasted well enough. Fresh tears brimmed in her eyes. She missed her friend.

The next station, Chimney Rock, should come into view in a short time. She had to remember to tell the next rider about the government documents they carried. She wondered if she'd be taking a mochilla back the other direction right away, or if she'd have a chance to rest for a spell before heading back to Cottonwood Springs.

Without warning, her horse whinnied and bucked hard. Daisy tried to hang on but lost her grip on the reins. She slammed onto the unforgiving ground with a painful thud.

Her ears caught the horrifying sound of rattling nearby. When she reached for the pistol in her holster, it wasn't there.

"Where is it?" Daisy asked aloud.

It must have slipped free of her holster when she fell. She twisted to her left and then her right, searching the ground for her weapon. She spotted it a few yards from where she sat. Her heart sank when she realized it was way out of her reach. She couldn't take a chance and lunge for it without angering the slithery creature into a strike. Panic bubbled in her heart, and her breath caught in her throat. She wasn't afraid of much in this world, but snakes were the creatures of her nightmares.

After steadying her breathing, she forced herself to focus on how to get out of the mess she was in. Where was her horse?

"Buttercup?" She called out, quietly. She didn't care to further spook the animal. If he ran off with the mail pouch she'd be in trouble. A whinny sounded from behind some bushes several yards from where she lay sprawled on the ground.

The air gusted from her lungs. She needed Buttercup to get the mochilla to Chimney Rock, but she couldn't risk either her or the horse getting snakebit. Sitting still and waiting for the rattler to slink away seemed like the best option, but that could take hours. Time Daisy didn't have to spare.

Off in the distance Daisy spotted a cloud of dust rolling toward her. The stagecoach she had passed earlier now approached. The stage would be rolling past soon, which left Daisy with mere seconds to calculate her options. With any luck the noise and movement would scare the snake away and she could continue on her ride. With bad luck, it would frighten the wretched thing bad enough to sink it's fangs into her.

◆　◆　◆

Billy snuck a quick glance around the army camp before ducking into Jake Hunter's cabin.

"So, what have you been able to find out?" Billy asked the whiskered young soldier.

"Shhh, I don't want Butch to know we're on to him. He's likely roaming around here, and I don't want him to overhear us."

"Fine." Billy lowered his voice. "What do you know?"

"I spoke with Daniel Tully's family about his death. Mr. Tully told me his son confided in him about something terrible. Apparently, the young soldier was forced to watch Butch rape an Indian girl at some railroad camp. Daniel had even spoken with the railroad worker who somehow knew about it. The two men collaborated and wrote out statements testifying to what they knew. Then they filed the documents with Butch's superior officer."

"So why didn't the army do something about it?"

"When I went to check on the paperwork, I couldn't find it."

"What do you mean you couldn't find it?" Billy huffed and clenched his hands. Logic told him Green Grass was the girl Butch had raped, but without those statements he couldn't know for sure. Butch had more than likely killed her, and the soldier, to shut them up. He didn't want to think a cover-up had taken place. Butch had discovered the coconspirators had filed complaints against him. Given his rank and slick mannerisms it wouldn't have taken much to trace the paperwork and make it disappear.

"I think Butch intercepted Daniel's statement and destroyed it to hide his criminal actions," Jake growled.

Billy nodded his head in agreement. "I was thinking the same thing."

A tall man threw open the cabin door and loomed in the entryway. "Did I hear somebody say my name?" He glared at Billy with dark menacing eyes and spat tobacco juice on the cabin steps.

Several medals on the soldier's uniform gleamed, even in the dim light of the cabin. Billy would bet money the man hadn't come by them in the most honorable fashion.

"I was just showing this civilian around and telling him about our camp here," Jake stammered.

A cold sweat trickled down Billy's forehead. Butch was an imposing man, and rude. No wonder Daisy was afraid of him.

"If you'll excuse me, I have to get back to the way station." Billy eyed Jake and pushed past Butch to exit the cabin. The dots began to connect in his mind. Butch raped Green Grass and to save his hide, he killed everyone who knew about it. Green Grass, Daniel, and the railroad worker. That worker was more than likely Daisy's father.

Butch was a cold-blooded killer. One way or another, Billy would haul his sorry hide before the proper authorities. Perhaps he could talk Daisy into testifying against him. Granted, the man terrified her, but she wanted justice for her parents.

His thoughts swirled as he strode past two soldiers using their bayonet spikes to roast meat over a campfire, and another who sat polishing his trumpet. Billy unhitched his horse and rode back to the way station. As he led the animal into the barn he heard a distinct voice behind him.

"I've heard some disturbing rumors, Mr. Cook. Have you let a woman ride for the Pony Express?"

Billy turned and stood eye to eye with Mr. Andrews, the regional superintendent.

Chapter Six

The noise of the approaching stagecoach grew louder. The snake swung its body toward the clatter long enough for Daisy to reach for her six-shooter and fire two rounds. The second one took the rattler's head clean off.

After shoving the weapon back into her holster, she sprinted toward her horse. Buttercup hadn't run off in the melee, and for that she uttered a prayer of thanks. Once the animal's reins were firmly in her hand, she marched over to where the snake lay dead.

"The only good snake is a dead snake," she muttered to herself. She grabbed its corpse by the tail and wrapped it around the saddle horn. The creature would make for some fine eating come suppertime.

Daisy shoved her foot into the stirrup and swung up onto the saddle. Then she dug in her heels, and Buttercup jumped into a gallop. She just might make the next way station before dark. That is, if she didn't run into any Indians or robbers. The last thing she needed was more trouble.

Her thoughts churned as fast as her horse's hooves as she flashed by towering ponderosa's and sagebrush. Billy's image floated to the surface. His blond hair and blue eyes cut a dashing figure. Daisy respected and admired him for the way he'd taken charge and investigated the death of her parents. But respect and admiration could take her only so far. Faith didn't settle well with the man. Handsome or not, she could never allow herself to fall in love with someone who didn't share her beliefs in Christ. So why did her heart rate sputter like a tired steam engine every time she spoke with him?

Daisy shifted her weight and peered at the horizon. The sun had dipped below a stand of trees, casting shadows across the rugged landscape. Her thoughts turned toward the scriptures she had studied the other day. She prayed for Billy, that God would keep him safe as he dug into Butch's past. She hoped Billy would realize how much God cared for him. A heavy sigh rolled out of her mouth, but it didn't ease the weightiness in her heart.

Even if Billy developed an interest in church, attended regularly, and decided to settle down, she imagined he'd want to find some pretty girl in hoops and fancy laces. It was highly unlikely he'd consider a trouser-wearing, rattlesnake-shooting, tomboy like her. Oh well. At least God loved her the way she was.

"Rider coming!" Daisy hollered as the barn and other buildings of the Chimney Rock station grew larger on the horizon. When she reached the barn, she pulled hard on the reins and Buttercup lurched to a stop. She jumped off the horse and grabbed the dead snake from her saddle.

The next rider yanked the mochilla off Buttercup and placed it on his fresh horse.

"There're important government documents in the pouch, so ride hard," Daisy said.

The rider nodded his head in acknowledgement. Daisy watched as he mounted the animal and galloped away, leaving a cloud of dust in his wake. She yawned and stretched her aching muscles.

"I'm starving. You got anything to eat?" she asked the station manager.

"The cook is taking care of that now. I'll tell her to set an extra place for you."

"I've got a snake here." Daisy held up the nasty creature for the man to see. "If you don't mind cleaning it, I'm willing to share."

"That would be fine. We have company, and any extra would be greatly appreciated."

Daisy handed her contribution to the man and went to wash up. So company was visiting the station. She wondered who it might be, and if they had an aversion to rattlesnake. Some folks from the East didn't easily take to the wild ways of things out West.

The water pump squeaked as she worked the rusty handle until cool water flowed. She wet her handkerchief and wiped her sweaty face. She glanced around with as much nonchalance as possible to see if anyone was looking at her.

Coast was clear. She pulled her hat from her head, yanked the pins from her hair, and let it tumble down her back. It felt good to free her long mop from what had constrained it.

"Evening, ma'am."

Daisy gasped. Her hat and handkerchief slipped from her fingers. She turned to stare at two soldiers in uniform.

◆　◆　◆

"I need a word with you, Mr. Cook."

Billy gazed into his supervisor's hard, prying eyes. Mr. Andrews, a tall man with graying muttonchops, raised an eyebrow. Billy squirmed. He might not be a man filled with enough religious zeal to rival Miss Daisy-Hymn-Singing-Hollister, but he wasn't about to lie to the man, either.

"How can I help you?" Billy asked. Hoping to avoid looking into his boss's eyes, he looked up at the sky to see if any birds were overhead. Then he studied the ground to see if any snakes slithered nearby, finally he checked the barn to see if any hired hands needed help with their chores.

"We've had two riders, and the manager from Chimney Rock Station, say there was an Indian girl who got killed riding for the company."

Billy shifted from one foot to the other. Again he scanned the rocky terrain around him to check for rattlesnakes. He almost preferred facing a rattler to enduring any more questions from his boss.

"An Indian rider got killed a few weeks ago, but I didn't exactly do a full examination of the body." At least that much was the truth. Billy's insides flipped. He hated keeping secrets from the man, but if the guy knew Daisy was out on a run, he'd be fired for letting her do so. When Billy mustered the courage to look his boss in the face, he noticed his gray whiskers twitching, as if the man tried to stifle a chuckle.

A lopsided grin stretched the corners of Billy's mouth. He wanted to steer the conversation anywhere but toward Daisy Hollister.

"Dinner!"

Billy jumped at Johnny's ear-piercing announcement. "Won't you join us?" He hoped his boss would oblige and then leave.

"Sure thing," Mr. Andrews said.

"Good." Billy smiled. "There's a pump by the bunkhouse. You can get washed up and then head inside."

Turning to the main house where they ate their meals, Billy drew in a deep breath. The hired hands were in the kitchen cooking dinner in Daisy's absence. He scuttled across the yard. Upon entering the kitchen he explained the situation to Sam and the rest of them.

Several minutes later Billy finished pleading with the other workers. They had agreed to keep quiet. He almost dropped the pan of burnt biscuits from his sweating palms. He coughed, and told himself it was probably from the smoldering contents of the pan in his hands.

Amid the smoke still pouring from the cookstove, he muttered something about hiring Adrianne Larson. He'd heard she quit cooking at the hotel after the owners scolded her for giving away too many free meals to every ruffian who happened along, human and otherwise.

"Supper's on," Billy mumbled and cleared his throat as his boss entered the room.

Dinner was a silent affair with the exception of his boss announcing that he planned to stay the night at the station. Billy suddenly lost his appetite, and not just because the biscuits were charred crispy.

The next morning, Billy woke to pounding on his door.

"What in tarnation?" He rolled from his bed, staggered to the door, and opened it. He rubbed the sleep from his eyes and tried to focus on Jake Hunter's face before him. The blinding rays of the rising sun didn't make it easy.

"We found some information about Butch, evidence of his wrongdoing," Jake said.

Billy was fully awake now. "What evidence?"

"My superior's received a letter from Mr. Hollister, Daisy's father. The man must have mailed it before he was killed. It gave details of Butch's involvement in the rape of that Indian girl. The letter described a piece of jewelry that belonged to her, and it was found in Butch's possession."

"So they caught him?"

"He snuck out of camp through an unpatrolled section in the back. We're looking for him now. That's partly what I'm doing here, to ask if you or Miss Hollister have seen him."

"Rider coming," someone yelled as Johnny burst from the bunkhouse and hurried to saddle a fresh horse. Mr. Andrews ambled from the dwelling and over to where Billy and Jake stood. Mr. Andrews stood on his toes and peered down the road. Billy shielded his own eyes with the flat of his hand.

As the rider arrived in a cloud of dust, Billy's heartbeat stumbled as if it had tripped over a rock and couldn't quite regain its balance.

Daisy jumped down from the saddle.

Chapter Seven

The mochilla slipped from Daisy's trembling fingers and fell to the ground. She hastily picked it up and tossed it over the saddle of her fresh mount, averting her face from the soldier standing next to Billy. The bewhiskered man didn't seem a threat, but after receiving such a start at the last way station, she vowed to be more careful of men in army blue. She never knew which soldiers might be in alliance with Butch or when he might catch up to her.

"Ride hard, Daisy, and try to stay gone for a while." Johnny leaned close and whispered in her ear. "That's Mr. Andrews over there. He's the local superintendent."

"Oh." Daisy adjusted the hat on her head to make sure her hair was covered.

"Thanks for the warning, Johnny," she said and shot up into the saddle and kicked the flanks of the wild mustang.

The horse reared. Daisy gripped the reins as the animal took off at a gallop. She couldn't get far enough away from that army man and the superintendent. Who was the soldier, and what was he doing at the way station? And why was the superintendent at the way station? She hoped his visit wouldn't culminate in the loss of her job. As soon as she rode back that way, she'd be sure and ask Billy all about it. For now, she focused on the task at hand.

Several rugged miles passed while Daisy admired the landscape. Rocky buttes jutted from the earth like hands reaching toward heaven. She thanked God for protecting her on the job, and from Butch.

The next way station snuck up on her. She had ridden back and forth so much she didn't remember which station she was at and hardly knew what direction she was headed. She climbed down from the horse and greeted the station manager.

"Can I get some breakfast before I go back out?" she asked.

Before the man had a chance to reply, another rider came in. The young lad slid from the saddle in a near faint.

"I've been going for almost two days. I can't go on anymore."

"Very well." The station manager pointed to Daisy. "I need you to take the pouch and go back the way you came."

"Okay, boss." Daisy ignored her rumbling stomach, climbed onto a fresh horse, and cantered back the way she had come. She lifted her canteen to her lips and drank the last of her water. It hardly wetted her parched throat and dry lips, but the next station was only a few miles away. Exhaustion made her muscles ache. Lack of sleep left grit in her eyes, but she was grateful to be out from under the watchful gaze of the superintendent, Mr. Andrews.

A multitude of bright yellow, prickly pear blossoms dotted the side of the trail. They were edible and high in water content. If only she had the time to stop, pick a few, and savor the natural juices. Over and over she muttered to herself, "Just a little bit farther."

A relief-filled chuckle rolled out of her mouth when the next station popped up on the horizon. Weariness crept over her, and she longed for something to eat and a warm bed when she arrived.

The station manager and a rider named Gabe Jackson emerged from the house. Daisy pulled her horse to a stop in front of the barn and helped them ready the tan-colored mustang for the next run. When Gabe hefted the mochilla on the saddle Daisy stepped back. She watched him mount the horse and ride off before stumbling to the house.

The cook set a plate of cold biscuits and jerked buffalo meat before her. It wasn't a savory meal, but Daisy didn't care. It was palatable, and that was all that mattered. When she finished eating she traipsed out to the barn and collapsed onto a pile of hay. The comforting smells of leather and the warm straw beneath her filled her nostrils as she drifted into slumber.

The next afternoon, after a good meal and some much-needed shut-eye, Daisy jumped astride the mustang and pointed him back toward Cottonwood Springs. If she was lucky, she'd have some pay waiting for her. On her next day off, she would ride out to see Green Grass's family and take some food and medicine with her. As demanding as the job was, she was grateful for the money.

Daisy's heart soared at the thought of seeing Billy again. Her feelings for the man were growing stronger, and she didn't know just how to handle the situation. A part of her was afraid to admit she might be falling in love.

The sun hung high overhead, and Daisy felt its heat seep through her clothes. Perhaps a dunk in the swimming hole would be beneficial after lunch. She was sure Clancy would love to get out of the paddock for a while and roam the countryside.

The miles passed in a blur, and before she could blink twice she arrived at the way station she called home. Daisy didn't see any sign of the soldier and breathed deep with relief. She did notice the gray-whiskered man conversing with Billy over by the bunkhouse.

"Can you take this run from here?" Daisy asked Johnny, who had just exited the barn with a fresh horse.

"You bet." Johnny placed the mochilla on the saddle, leaped onto the horse, and was off with a loud holler.

Daisy watched him go and walked toward the main house in search of some food. Billy jogged over and grabbed her arm.

"You need to lay low for a while Daisy. That's the Pony Express superintendent, Mr. Andrews, over there. If he finds out you're a girl, we're both fired."

◆　◆　◆

Billy escorted the superintendent to town to catch the stage. The stagecoach arrived in a cloud of dust, carrying a sack teeming with new mail, and several patrons for the hotel. Mr. Andrews would be on it when it left and Billy stood to the side, eager to see it happen.

"Nice to see you again, sir." Billy tipped his hat to Mr. Andrews. "Be sure and tell the company owners that everything is right as rain here." He stepped back as Mr. Andrews climbed into the stage and the driver prepared to leave. The superintendent nodded and held up a hand in farewell. With the rattling of traces and the squeak of leather, the coach pulled away from the crowded and busy boardwalk. The air hissed from Billy's lungs, and he wiped the sweat from his brow with his bandanna. Nothing pleased his soul more than to say good-bye to the man who could have cost him so much.

Billy pushed the troublesome thoughts to the back recesses of his mind and strode into the mercantile. The way station needed more supplies, and Johnny could handle things for only so long. After placing his order for additional beans, flour, and lamp oil, he moved on to the feed store. Horses that ran for an average of ten miles at a time sure went through fodder.

"Mr. Cook, Mr. Cook."

Billy pivoted on his heel to see a lad approaching him, waving an envelope. He took the envelope and handed the boy a penny. The child beamed and skipped down the boardwalk swinging his arms the way Billy's nephew always did.

Billy noticed the address on the letter. It was from the orphanage. Although tempted to read the news right there on the boardwalk, Billy decided against it. What if something terrible had happened to his nephew? He didn't want to express any unmanly emotion on a public street in front of a gaggle of onlookers.

He stuffed the paper into his shirt pocket. He hurried to the feed store and placed an order for grain. With his Pony Express business in town completed, he drove the wagon out to the way station and brought it to a stop when he reached the barn.

Johnny emerged from the bunkhouse when Billy arrived.

"Can you get somebody to help unload this feed and put it in the back of the barn?" Billy asked.

Johnny nodded and proceeded to the back of the wagon.

In the privacy of the bunkhouse, Billy tore open the letter from the orphanage and hastily read through it. He kicked one of the wooden bed frames. The medicine he had sent to little Luke hadn't helped him one lick. The youngster was getting sicker. For all he knew, the people at the orphanage had pocketed the money he sent and kept the medicine for themselves. Perhaps the letter was a ruse to get him to send more money. Maybe Luke wasn't sick after all, and maybe Billy should just send for him.

After considering his options he decided to go ahead and bring the lad to Cottonwood Springs. He hated to send for the tyke and have him fall smack into the danger involving Butch, and all the other perils associated with the West, but what else could he do? At least around the way station Billy could keep an eye on him.

He stomped to the main house and penned a letter. If only he could afford to send it via Pony Express, but at five dollars an ounce he could ill afford it. In his short note he demanded that Luke be sent by train to Cottonwood Springs immediately. If he had to go to New York to personally retrieve the child, he would.

After sealing the envelope, Billy grabbed his hat and reached for his riding gloves. He had to get to the post office and send the letter. He hated making another trip into town the same day and shoving the responsibility of the station onto Johnny. The kid was reliable but still fairly young. If Indians or robbers decided to raid the way station, Johnny would be at great risk.

Billy shook his head as he stepped outside. If his nephew's safety wasn't so precarious, he wouldn't take such a gamble, he reasoned with himself. He'd take the fastest horse available, gallop into town, and be back in no time, before anything awful could happen at the way station.

"Johnny." Billy jogged to the barn.

"Me and Jack got all the feed put away, sir," Johnny replied.

"Thank you, son. Look, I have to make another quick trip into town. I hate to ask, but I need you to keep an eye on things around here for just a spell, okay?" Billy slung a saddle onto the back of an energetic mustang and cinched it down. Then he climbed on and hoped the beast would cooperate and get him to town unscathed. One never knew with the wild horses from the plains.

"Will do, Mr. Cook." Johnny puffed out his chest, and Billy felt a twinge of fatherly pride surge through him. He liked to think he was a good role model for the youth. Something told him Daisy Hollister was just as good a role model as he was. Just where she happened to be at the moment he couldn't fathom, nor could he take the time to sit around and worry. A small child demanded his attention. He led his horse outside.

Darkness encroached. Billy drank in the beauty of the sun languishing in the distant horizon, coloring the sky with ribbons of magenta and bright gold. Another rider wasn't due for another few hours. Billy would return by then. Perhaps he could complete his errand without having the misfortune of running into Butch.

Circumstances appeared bleak for his nephew, but Billy wouldn't give up hope that things would get better. He scoffed at himself. Daisy Hollister's praying ways must be getting to him. He wasn't sure if he was ready to commit to the Gospel like she had, but what could it hurt to ask God for a favor? In a moment of sheer desperation, he uttered a prayer for the safety of little Luke.

Chapter Eight

A sliver of sun peeked over the rocky buttes in the distance. A stand of pines poked up from the ground, the branches waved in the breeze along with the tall green prairie grasses. Daisy wished she could pause and admire God's handiwork. Instead, she rode hard. She had to get to Cottonwood Springs soon, before those Indians came after her again, and before she dropped from exhaustion.

"I know you're tired, but c'mon boy, you can make it." Daisy urged the pinto named Little Joe onward, hoping she could somehow infuse her own strength into the weary animal.

Ten minutes later Daisy reined the beast to a stop in front of the barn. Johnny emerged with a mustang that looked anxious to gallop. No sooner had she slid from her horse when Johnny grabbed the mochilla and slapped the mail pouch onto the back of his own mount.

Once Johnny rode off she blew out a weary sigh. Sam led a worn-out Little Joe to the barn. Daisy traipsed into the main house for breakfast. The new cook greeted her with a smile, and she returned the heartwarming gesture.

"Morning, Adrianne, would you like some help?" Daisy asked. The quicker the meal was cooked, the quicker she could eat, and get some sleep.

"Sure." Adrianne turned the bacon sizzling in a cast-iron skillet.

The savory aroma wafted through the room, and Daisy's mouth watered in anticipation. Adrianne was great at concocting fabulous meals and had always been a great friend. Daisy was glad Billy had hired her on at the way station.

"Morning, ladies." Billy nodded as he strolled into the room.

He yawned and poured himself a cup of coffee as Daisy slid the biscuits into the oven. Tension had run high while Mr. Andrews lurked around the corners of the way station, but now that he was gone, she could relax.

When the meal was ready, they sat down to eat. Daisy prayed, hoping Billy wouldn't mind too much. He didn't seem to. Lately she had noticed him looking at her with a strange expression on his face whenever she prayed.

"That was kind of you to visit Green Grass's family last week, Daisy. How are they getting on?" Adrianne asked.

"Much better now that Little Bear has his medicine. Thank you for asking."

"Glad to hear they're doing all right," Billy said.

Daisy glanced up from her plate and stared into Billy's enchanting blue eyes. Why was she so befuddled whenever he talked to her? She must be really tired. She shoved a biscuit into her mouth to keep from saying something stupid.

"Well, let me know next time you head out there, and I'll make up a basket of food for you to give them." Adrianne smiled so warmly Daisy couldn't help but smile at this kindhearted woman.

When finished with the meal, she walked to the bunkhouse for some shut-eye. There weren't any men around, and for that she was thankful. The riders and hired hands who did know she rode for the Pony Express were good to steer clear of her.

The empty cot against the back wall beckoned her. Without taking the time to undress, she dropped into it and snuggled the pillow close to her heart. She mumbled a prayer for her Indian friend's family as sleep wafted in to claim her.

In the afternoon, after a long, peaceful nap, she sat up in bed and stretched her achy muscles. Straddling a horse all day and riding at breakneck speed sure did wear on a body.

Daisy rose from her bunk and quickly brushed her hair. Rather than pin it up, as she did when she was out on a run or working in the kitchen, she let her long tresses flow down her back. It was a welcome change.

Once she recinched her trousers tight, she moseyed to the barn. The comforting smells of fresh hay and horses met her as she strolled through the door. Clancy needed a brushing, some feed, and lots of attention. She had been neglecting him while she worked and wanted to make it up to him by taking him out on a walk.

"Here you go, boy." Daisy chopped an apple and held it out for Clancy. The animal's warm soft neck made a cozy resting place for her to lay her head. She combed her fingers through his long dark mane. Money was no longer an issue, as long as she could keep riding for the company. She had food to eat and a safe place to sleep at night, that is, when she wasn't out on a run. A combination of contentment and angst filled her life at the moment; the only burr under her saddle was Randall Butchovick. "How much longer must I wait, Lord, before he's arrested for killing Pa and Ma?"

Billy burst in through the side door and sidled up to her. He thrust a hat at her. "Put this on, quick."

"What? Why? This isn't even my own hat, Billy," Daisy protested.

"You need to, there's no time for explanations. Now, will you hush and do as I say? The superintendent is back and he's snooping around the bunkhouse, asking Johnny all sorts of questions." Billy's eyes widened in distress.

Daisy gasped. She yanked the cap from Billy's hands and stuffed her hair up into it.

"Billy, this hat is way too small," Daisy stammered.

"I got it for my nephew and haven't sent it yet."

Daisy didn't have the time to pin her hair up, but she didn't have any other options at the moment. Their boss tramped through the barn entrance.

"Good afternoon, Mr. Cook. I know it's only been a few days, but I've decided to pay you another visit," Mr. Andrews declared.

Daisy turned to see the superintendent fold his arms across his chest. She kept silent, afraid her feminine voice would give her away. She kept busy grooming her horse and prayed Mr. Andrews would leave. Instead, he followed her everywhere. For more than an hour he trailed behind her like an orphaned puppy in desperate need of some love and attention.

Hoofbeats announced the arrival of a rider coming. Daisy was all too anxious to get out of there. She saddled Little Joe and prepared to lead him outside when she felt someone tap her shoulder.

"Pardon me," Mr. Andrews said, "but would you mind putting your hand on this Bible and swearing that you're a boy? We can't have ladies riding for the company, you know."

"Oh," Daisy yelped. Her eyes scanned the vast confines of the barn but saw only Billy standing at the entrance, his eyes wide and his mouth agape. Her mind whirled. She silently beseeched God for help. Where was He when she needed Him?

Before she could comply, the horse whinnied and bucked, yanking the reins from Daisy's hands. Her hat fell off her head and her long hair tumbled down her back.

◆ ◆ ◆

Horrified, Billy watched Daisy scramble to pull her hair into a knot and tuck it back under the ill-fitting cap. If only he'd had the opportunity to run to the bunkhouse and get her own hat for her. It might have contained her tresses a little better.

"Mr. Cook?"

Billy clenched his fists when Mr. Andrews snapped at him. "Yes, boss." It wouldn't do any good to argue with the man.

"Get another rider for this run," Mr. Andrews continued. "I have a few things to discuss with the lady, and then I want to see you."

"Yes, sir." Billy bolted toward the stalls and hitched a saddle to a fresh mount.

"Young lady." The superintendent addressed Daisy. "If you don't want trouble with Russell, Majors, and Waddell, you'll tell me everything."

Billy tried to ignore Mr. Andrews conversing with a blubbering Daisy, but how could he? Swallowing the lump in his throat, he led Little Joe from the barn to the waiting Gabe Jackson. Gabe tapped his foot and drummed his fingers against the mochilla.

"Here you go," Billy said.

Gabe placed the mail pouch over the saddle and climbed on the horse. "Hiyah!" he shouted and kicked the animal's flanks. They raced toward the horizon.

Swiveling to his left, Billy caught sight of Daisy as she fled the barn and sprinted to the bunkhouse. No doubt she had confessed to their boss. Billy couldn't imagine her telling a lie, or even skirting the truth, given her devotion to her faith.

Mr. Andrews stepped from the barn and marched toward Billy. The man's face and neck were as red as a ripe tomato.

"Mr. Cook." Mr. Andrews's chest heaved as he spoke.

In desperation Billy sent another prayer heavenward. He thought of his nephew. If God was merciful, he wouldn't lose his job and he'd still be able to provide for the lad.

"Yes, sir." Billy gulped, but the lump in his throat wouldn't budge.

"This company doesn't abide by liars and rule breakers. You've done both. Don't try to deny it. That girl told me everything."

"But, sir," Billy pleaded. He hated sounding desperate, but he was desperate to provide for his nephew.

"Don't give me any excuses, young man."

Sweat beaded on Billy's forehead as his boss continued.

"You and that girl are fired."

Chapter Nine

The rough wool blanket Daisy wiped her tears with scratched at the tender skin around her eyes, but she didn't care. She was fired. So was Billy. How would she pay for food for Green Grass's family and medicine for Little Bear?

"Where are you, God?" she whispered. "You said You'd be our provider; now look at the mess we're in."

Without a job, she'd be out in the streets. To make matters worse, if she moved back into town, Butch would have a greater opportunity to find her and kill her. By now he had to be aware that she and Billy were on to him. Considering the things he'd done, Daisy didn't think Butch would hesitate to murder her and hide her body where nobody would find it.

Shivers swirled in her gut at the thought of his calloused hands on her body, and her skin crawled as if a thousand bugs marched over her. She'd rather die by rattlesnake venom than fall prey to the likes of Randall Butchovick.

Daisy dried the remnants of her tears, vowing they would be the last she'd shed because of that odious toad. She had to think of others, too. Billy was also without a job. How would this affect his sickly nephew in that run-down orphanage? Oh what a mess, and all because she had to provide for herself and her friend's family. Yes, she craved a life of adventure, too, but things like adventure sure didn't matter now.

"Lord, please help me, and please help Billy. He only let me ride because I pestered him. Please don't let him suffer on my account."

Daisy flinched when the door to the bunkhouse flew open. Billy stood in the doorway, the lines of his jaw cold and hard.

"Didn't I tell you this was a bad idea?" he growled.

He folded his arms over his chest and glared at her with eyes as icy as a glacier in January. She squared her shoulders and stood straighter. Determined to find a way out of the financial sinkhole that threatened to swallow her, she drew from her deep well of faith.

"I know this looks bad, but I trust that God will find a way to get us out of this dilemma."

"There you go with that God stuff again. I tell you, I'm sick of hearing about God. If He's as compassionate as you claim, then where was He when my folks died, when my sister and I nearly starved and froze to death in a cold, damp orphanage? Why did He let my sister die without a soul in the world to comfort her except my nephew? How could He condemn my nephew to the same horrible fate?"

Daisy took in Billy's blond ruffled hair and pale blue eyes. Only a moment ago, those sky-blue eyes were filled with anger. The emotion was still there, but now she noted a measure of sadness in them also. She knew all too well, the pain of losing one's parents. Her heart ached for Billy and his nephew.

"I'm sorry I haven't been more understanding about your past, Billy. I should have taken the time to listen more. I'm sorry. Please forgive me."

"That's all fine and dandy, but your fancy words don't do a thing to help save my nephew."

"You're right. I'll speak with the boss and see what I can do to get your job back. With all you've done for me, it's the least I can do."

By the way the man rolled his eyes at the sky and shook his head, her promise didn't placate him. He leaned against the door frame, arms still crossed over his chest. "Just what are you aiming to say to make him change his mind?"

"I don't know, Billy. I'll think of something." She'd decided not to run anymore, and she had vowed to end Butch's criminal activities. She and Billy had come so far in their investigation. She couldn't allow herself to stop now. Did she dare go back to town and confront Butch?

Feeling a wave of inner strength and courage sweep through her, she pulled her trunk from under her bunk. She undid the buckle, opened it, and commenced the task of packing her meager belongings.

"What are you doing?" Billy asked.

"I'm packing my belongings. If I'm not employed by Russell, Majors, and Waddell anymore, there's no sense in me staying."

"Where will you go?" Billy huffed and threw his hands in the air.

He pushed away from the door frame and stepped into the bunkhouse, but still kept his distance.

Tears brimmed in Daisy's eyes at the indifference in his tone. She choked them back and turned to face him. "I'm headed into town to face Butch and put an end to his insane behavior."

"On your own? Yeah, good luck," he scoffed. His chuckle reverberated off the interior of the structure. He obviously didn't take much stock in her ability to stop Butch. Did he even care?

No, Billy didn't seem to care what happened to her, and that knowledge stung. Her chest constricted like a dozen belts circled her. Had she lost his friendship? She gasped as if they'd cinched tight. With moving from one town to the next over the past year she'd said good-bye to a number of folks. It hadn't bothered her until now. Why did the possibility of losing the affections of this tall, rugged cowboy matter so much?

"Eh-hem."

Daisy's thoughts were unceremoniously interrupted as the superintendent cleared his throat. Daisy's former boss stood in the doorway, his gaze bore into her. What could that man possibly want now? Hadn't he done enough damage already? Daisy's heart constricted.

"Excuse me, Mr. Cook," Mr. Andrews continued. "I need to take Miss Hollister into town. I have instructions from the owners to bring in any females caught riding for the company."

◆　◆　◆

The words punched into Billy's gut. He had been mad enough at Daisy to let her think he'd allow her to ride away and face a killer. He wouldn't have really permitted her to go alone, but he was too angry to let her think otherwise.

Now their former boss wanted to take her into town where Butch was *and* face the owners of the company? He couldn't let that happen.

"Look here, sir," Billy said. He glanced at Daisy, her ashen face the color of the sheets Adrianne had hung on the line yesterday. "You don't need to take her. Why don't I ride into town with you and we can get this whole thing straightened out?"

"No, it's imperative that I take Miss Hollister, alone."

Billy's suspicions stirred. Something didn't feel right. Daisy gasped. Granted they had broken the rules of the company, but that was no excuse to frighten the lady and take her away unchaperoned.

"Oh." Daisy gasped again.

Billy's pulse quickened. "I'm sorry, but I can't let you ride off with her alone." He clenched his fists to his sides. He might be hopping mad at Daisy, but he was still a gentleman, and in no way would he allow this man to compromise her.

"Two of my men have just arrived. They will be accompanying us, so you can rest assured we won't be alone." Mr. Andrews puffed out his chest as he spoke. The man lunged toward Daisy and grabbed her by the arm.

Billy jumped between them. "You can't take her." The words rumbled out of his mouth, the raw harshness startling him.

"Billy, please," Daisy yelped.

"Don't make this any more difficult, Mr. Cook." The stark bunkhouse walls amplified his bellow. He yanked Daisy from the dwelling. Billy followed close behind. In front of the main house he spotted two men standing beside a surrey. One was lanky but had been blessed with height. The other wasn't as tall but appeared stocky enough to wrestle bulls. Billy didn't consider himself a coward, but these two wouldn't be an easy duo to reckon with.

In the seconds that it took Billy to realize the seriousness of the situation, the tall man pulled a gun and leaped to assist Mr. Andrews. Horrified, Billy saw Daisy struggle against the man's grip.

"Now hold on just a doggone minute!" Billy's stomach curdled at the way the tall man handled Daisy. He'd never shot a man in cold blood, but he wished he had his pistol with him at that moment.

The shorter man took two steps forward.

Billy raised his fists, ready for a fight, but the man flipped his revolver and hammered him over the head with the butt end.

Billy's sight blurred. He dropped to his knees and sucked in air, pain reverberating through his temple. Stars danced in his field of vision. He heard the muddled voice of Mr. Andrews as he loaded a frightened-sounding Daisy into the buggy. With one last measure of chivalry he lunged toward Daisy.

His fingers grasped the hem of Daisy's clothing, but it did no good. Something heavy and metallic snapped his head back. Darkness swallowed him.

Chapter Ten

I demand to know the meaning of this!" Daisy squirmed in her seat in a desperate effort to wrench free from the man who'd assaulted Billy. She prayed that he was okay.

"All in due time, missy," the shorter man said.

A taller, darker man drove the buggy, and her former boss followed them on his horse.

"Do take gentler care of the lady," Mr. Andrews said to the two surly men. "Miss Hollister, I apologize for these measures, but all will be explained in due time, when we get back to the hotel."

Daisy refrained from struggling further. The worst thing she could do was upset them more than they already were. But they were taking her back to the hotel, where Butch was staying. She didn't relish the idea of facing the outlaw, but figured she could somehow handle him if she had to. A part of her wanted to square off with him and get justice for her ma and pa. Would the company owners detain her in some way and thwart her hope of doing that?

Daisy sent silent prayers toward heaven and clamped her mouth shut as they rode along in silence.

Soon the tall clapboard front of the hotel appeared in the distance. When they arrived, the men jumped down from the buggy and tied the reins to the hitching post. Daisy alighted and managed to stand on shaking legs.

The three men pushed her through the batwing doors to her former place of employment. The aroma of roast beef wafted from the kitchen to the lobby and made Daisy's mouth water. She remembered her carefree days of cooking in the kitchen and wondered how things could have gotten so bad. If only she hadn't been caught riding for the Pony Express.

Mr. Andrews escorted her to a corner where they met up with an older couple. Daisy noted the three exchanging glances. Were these people in cahoots with Butch? No, that couldn't be, but the uneasiness twisting in her middle told her something was up.

"Excuse me, where are the company owners?" Daisy asked as they moved from the corner to the stairs. This older couple didn't look like the tintype she'd seen of Russell, Majors, and Waddell.

"Please be quiet, Miss Hollister. I'll explain in a moment," Mr. Andrews whispered. He shoved her up the staircase.

Thus far, her protests hadn't been so desperate, but when the boss dragged her into a room she grew more desperate. The couple followed them inside and closed the door behind them.

Daisy searched the room for some means of escape. She spotted a man in army blue. This wasn't a meeting with the owners of the Pony Express. This was a setup. No matter how many hounds of fear nipped at her heels, she had to keep her wits about her.

A scream for help erupted from her mouth. She tried to push past Mr. Andrews and escape from the room, but he blocked her path. The soldier clamped his hand over her mouth.

"Please Miss Hollister, allow me to explain. This is all for your protection," Mr. Andrews said. He moved to the window.

Daisy watched and struggled to breathe as he looked down to the streets below. Mr. Andrews nodded to the soldier, who released her. She sucked in a few gasps of air and found her voice. "Protection? From what?" She planted fists on her hips. "And who's to protect me from the likes of you?" she demanded.

"Miss Hollister, this is Mr. and Mrs. Tully. The parents of Private Daniel Tully who was killed a year ago near a railroad camp, under suspicious circumstances. That man over there is Jake Hunter, dearest friend of the deceased Private Tully."

Daisy's stomach roiled in confusion. "What does that have to do with me?"

"We've been investigating the death of Private Tully and suspect Mr. Randall Butchovick is responsible. The man has discovered how close we are to arresting him, that you can identify him as the murderer of your parents, and that we'll tie this whole case together. Thus, he's threatened your life."

"Why couldn't you just tell me that at the way station? Why couldn't you have explained that to Billy?" Daisy demanded.

"Randall Butchovick is on the loose, possibly headed to the way station as we speak, and will no doubt pressure Mr. Cook into divulging information about you. The less he knows about your whereabouts, the safer you are."

"But that puts Billy at risk!"

"You are a witness to a crime, Miss Hollister. The United States government needs your testimony to convict a ruthless killer. We can't risk Mr. Butchovick getting his hands on you."

Daisy's thoughts swam with all the added information. "How do you know all this, sir?" she finally managed to ask.

A sardonic grin crept across the face of her former boss. "Why, Miss Hollister, one doesn't become a Pinkerton detective without knowing a great many things."

◆　◆　◆

Billy winced as Adrianne applied a wet cloth to his aching head. As soon as the bleeding stopped and a bandage was applied, he'd ride into town and find out what was going on with Daisy and their former boss.

He didn't know Russell, Majors, and Waddell very well, but they had a spotless reputation for moral behavior. He couldn't fathom them doing anything unscrupulous with Daisy.

"Here you go, Mr. Cook." Adrianne patted her handiwork. Billy's head ached more at her gesture, but he said nothing and stood up.

The kitchen spun a few times before righting itself. He reached for the table, inhaled deeply, exhaled, and blinked a few times. When a measure of strength returned to his legs, he staggered from the room.

Once outside, he took another minute to steady himself. The summer sun beat down hot and heavy, causing sweat to break out on his brow. He wiped it with the sleeve of his shirt and shuffled to the barn.

Before he had the chance to grab a saddle from the shelf, a horse galloped to the barn doors and lurched to a stop. Johnny jumped down from his mount and sprinted toward him before thrusting a letter into Billy's hands.

"What is this?"

"A man from the army, said his name was Jake Hunter, asked me to deliver this to you." Johnny leaned over and puffed a moment. "Mr. Hunter said not to ask how he got his hands on it. The fellow paid me handsomely to give the message to you, and only you."

Billy tore open the missive. He paid Johnny no mind as he read through the pages. His heart convulsed in spasms of fear. In the letter Jake explained how he'd come across a contract, penned by Butch. The contract said he would kill Daisy, gave details on how he would carry out the plan and how much he'd paid his cohorts.

Were the men who had taken Daisy earlier part of Butch's evil intentions? He hoped not, but what if? He had to save her, and hopefully not get himself killed in the process.

Billy shoved his meandering thoughts aside and focused on the task at hand. "When you're done putting Little Joe in a stall, head on in to the main house and get yourself something to eat. Lay low if you can, but go ahead and take a run if one comes in."

Johnny nodded and jogged toward the house. Billy wasn't officially the station manager anymore, but he'd see to it things got taken care of anyway.

After saddling his horse and cinching the straps down, Billy climbed on and headed toward town. He didn't know what he'd find when he got there, but he wasn't about to let that deter him.

While riding along, he said a prayer for Daisy. "Lord, if anything happens to her I'll never forgive myself." Perhaps there was something to this religion after all. Funny how he thought of God when he had nothing left. He'd lost his job, the means to help his nephew, and now it looked like he'd lose Daisy, too.

Gripping the reins tighter, Billy kept the horse at a full gallop. He had to get to Daisy before any harm came to her.

The town appeared on the horizon. Billy kicked the flanks of his horse and urged him to go faster. He detested being hard on an animal, but someone's life was at stake. The woman he loved, Daisy. Yes, he loved her and would do anything to save her.

What if he was too late and the men took advantage of Daisy? No, he wouldn't think that. The men who took her could in all likelihood be with the Pony Express. Surely they would protect her from Butch and his ilk. Billy prayed again for Daisy's safety. As he did, a sense of warmth enveloped him. Peace, so deep he couldn't comprehend it, settled into the depths of his heart.

His horse shrieked. The weary animal reared and twisted as it fell onto its side. Billy berated himself for pushing the poor beast too hard. He pulled his bandanna from his pocket and wiped the sweat from the horse's head. He poured some water from his canteen into his cupped hand and allowed the animal to lap it up. After ensuring the horse would survive, he focused on getting to town.

In the distance he could see the buildings, but he was still a good half mile away, and he was on foot now. It would take him longer to get there, but get there he must.

Billy double-checked to make sure his pistols were loaded, and after a few deep breaths and another prayer, he sprinted toward town.

Chapter Eleven

Daisy couldn't believe her good fortune in running into a Pinkerton detective. Granted, the man hadn't been honest about bringing her to town to meet the Pony Express owners, but at least he'd protect her from Butch and his band of no-account crooks. But who would protect Billy? She uttered a prayer on his behalf and beseeched God's aid.

Daisy introduced herself to Mrs. Tully. The woman spoke kindly of her deceased son. She said he died because he threatened to turn Butch in for raping an Indian girl. Mrs. Tully related the news of how the investigators found Green Grass's jewelry in Butch's belongings. After hearing the story, Daisy knew that Butch had raped her friend. Butch killed her, too, in an effort to cover his crime and to keep her from testifying against him.

Anxiety twisted so hard in her middle it caused a spasm of pain. Daisy winced and clutched her stomach. How could one person be so evil as to wreak such anguish and misery on humankind? She almost felt sorry for Butch, that his mind could be so warped he'd resort to such treachery. Her thoughts could have rattled around in her head and driven her mad, but she chose to silently surrender them to the Lord and let them go.

"Your son was an honorable man, Mrs. Tully. You must be very proud of him," Daisy said. She patted the woman's hand. Mrs. Tully dabbed at her eyes with a handkerchief. Tears swam in Daisy's eyes, as well.

"I'm going to the sheriff's office. I want to ask when the circuit judge will be in town next. You folks stay put," Mr. Andrews said. He placed his hat on his head and strolled out of the hotel room door.

Daisy crossed to the open window and leaned out to watch him. She saw Butch sneaking behind Mr. Andrews. Butch had a gun, and if she knew anything about Butch, he was about to waylay the detective. She wasn't about to let that happen.

Daisy yelled to warn Mr. Andrews, but her cries were swallowed up by the noise of a stagecoach rolling through town and the vulgar shouts flowing from the saloon.

"Butch is following Mr. Andrews. He's going to shoot the man. We've got to stop him." Daisy pleaded with Jake to go help.

"I can't leave you here unprotected. I'm following orders and staying put. They'll have to handle Randall Butchovick."

Daisy fumed as she formed a plan with Mrs. Tully.

"You pretend to fall into a faint, and when Mr. Hunter is distracted, I'll knock him over the head with this lamp," she whispered. She didn't know if the harebrained scheme would work, but she had to try, and judging by the grin spreading across Mrs. Tully's face, the woman liked the idea.

A gasp flew from Mrs. Tully's lips and her eyes rolled back in her head as she slid to the floor. For a second, Daisy almost believed the fainting spell was for real. Mr. Tully and Jake Hunter dashed to the woman's side.

"Let me get some water," Mr. Tully said as he hurried across the room to the pitcher sitting in the stand.

Daisy's fingers latched on to the glass lamp. She was ready to strike. Jake was leaning over the matronly body of Mrs. Tully when Daisy let him have it. Shards of glass flew in every direction as Jake dropped to the floor. She considered it a wonder that her hands weren't cut in the process. She grabbed the pistol from Jake's holster.

"Run and get the sheriff, Miss Hollister," Mr. Tully ordered. "We'll stay here with Mr. Hunter."

Daisy nodded her head at Mrs. Tully who had made a speedy and miraculous recovery from her faint. Jake moaned from his spot on the floor, and she was grateful that he hadn't been harmed too badly. She asked God to forgive her for what she'd done to Jake, and for strength to deal with Butch as she ran outside to face him for what she hoped would be the last time.

The steel revolver was cold and smooth in Daisy's trembling fingers. Heavy, too, so she used both hands to steady the weapon. While hiding behind a rain barrel at the corner of the hotel, she checked to make sure the gun was fully loaded. A shiny bullet sat ready in each of the six chambers. She rolled the gun's barrel back into place until she heard it click.

Mustering courage, she peered around the corner and spotted Butch pushing Mr. Andrews into a back alley.

They exchanged harsh words, but she wasn't close enough to hear exactly what they said. Judging by the way they pushed and shoved each other, Daisy sensed their disdain. Neither Mr. Andrews nor Butch had spotted her, so she would have the element of surprise.

"Lord, give me strength," she prayed as she inched along behind the building toward the alley. Verses from Psalm 121 seeped into her mind.

My help comes from the Lord.

Power and courage surged through her. With God's assistance she would set things right. Keeping her back to the side of the clapboard structure she inched along, hoping to avoid detection.

A cat screeched and darted off in pursuit of a rat scampering toward a pile of wooden boxes. Daisy bit her lower lip to keep from screaming. She hated rats. Especially the one who killed her parents, raped her friend, and was about to kill a man who stood for justice.

Daisy knew the Bible said, "Thou shalt not kill," but she felt duly responsible to protect others from this crooked skunk. She pushed the scriptures from her mind and crept nearer.

She had sneaked close enough to hear their voices more distinctly.

"If you shoot me, Mr. Butchovick, you'll just go down for another murder. The army already knows all about what you've done. If you give yourself up, you can get a fair trial, and at least you'll have a chance to live."

Daisy cringed. The fine hairs on her body tingled and her stomach churned.

"How about I just kill you, and then ride down to Mexico and avoid a trial, and a probable hanging," Butch said.

"Personally, I think hanging is too good for you," Mr. Andrews muttered.

The sinister chuckle that rolled out of Butch's mouth seared Daisy's ears. So the varmint planned on killing yet again and heading for Mexico to avoid facing his consequences? What a coward! Did this insufferable weasel really think he could get away with what he'd done to Green Grass, her pa and her ma, and Private Daniel Tully? That was the last straw for Daisy.

The gun clicked softly when she pulled the hammer back to cock it. Squaring her shoulders, she stepped from her hiding spot to face the cruel and heartless murderer.

◆ ◆ ◆

Billy gasped and sucked in air as he sprinted the last few yards into town. Sweat dripped down his brow and neck. He knelt before a water trough and plunged his head into the cool refreshing water.

When he came up for air he slicked his hair back and took another deep breath. Now that he was cooled off, somewhat, he scanned the town in search of Daisy. He had to find her before Butch did. He could only hope and pray that the men who had taken her were not in cahoots with the creep.

Movement along the side of the hotel snagged his attention. He narrowed his eyes to make out the dim alley. The blood in his veins nearly congealed. It was Daisy.

Billy stood and spotted Butch holding a gun on Mr. Andrews. Daisy lurked close by. What on earth did she think she was doing? He didn't know what was going on, but he knew it had to be something bad. He sprinted toward her.

When he reached the hotel he saw Daisy with a gun in her hands, and his heart rate stuttered. He had to get to the woman he loved before she got herself shot and killed.

With a mighty shout he raced into the alley just as Daisy jumped in front of Butch and aimed the gun at him.

◆ ◆ ◆

Daisy stared at her parents' murderer. He didn't seem so tall now that she faced him in daylight, with a revolver in her hands.

"Hello, Mr. Butchovick. I'm the woman who's going to take you down, if not here in the streets then later on at a trial." Daisy took two steps toward him. Judging by the hard glint in his eyes, he wasn't afraid of her, but then again she wasn't scared of him, either.

"Drop your gun," she ordered.

"You drop yours, missy, or we'll all be dead."

"Mr. Butchovick, please, there's no sense in making a bad situation worse," Mr. Andrews pleaded.

His appeal didn't do any good. Butch kept his gun aimed at the man's heart.

Daisy kept her gun pointed at Butch, but a noise distracted her. She turned her head and saw Billy. He skidded to a stop next to her.

"What's going on here?" Billy asked.

"Don't try to stop me," she said. "I'll be hauling this snake to the sheriff's office; that is, if I don't kill him first."

"The only way you're taking me in is if I'm dead." Butch sneered and shot a wad of tobacco at her feet.

Not about to give Butch an inch, Daisy clenched her jaw in disgust but held her ground.

"Daisy, don't shoot him. That would be murder, and it would go against what you believe. You'd never forgive yourself. I understand now that God knows and wants what's best for us, and killing Butch isn't it."

Daisy could not believe the words that came from Billy's mouth. She never thought she'd hear him speak so highly of her faith. Her heart jerked and then resumed beating in a rapid-fire rhythm that warmed her clear through.

"I care a great deal about you," Billy continued. "Please don't murder Butch. What about the law?"

"I can tell the sheriff that it was self-defense." Even as she said the words, she knew her logic was flawed.

"Not with me and Mr. Cook as witnesses," Mr. Andrews said.

"You don't really want to kill him, do you?" Billy asked.

A huge chunk of Daisy's heart told her Billy was right.

His words rolled around in her head like a tumbleweed, eager to take root in spite of the thorns that might cause pain. Her stomach churned at the memory of her dead pa and ma, soaked in blood on their bedroom floor. For a moment she wanted to forget about being a follower of Christ and render her own measure of justice.

"Daisy, please." Billy's soft words caressed her ears.

He was right. "Lord Jesus, help me," she whispered.

She was about to escort him to the sheriff when a loud commotion reverberated in the distance, followed by a gunshot from the saloon. The noise startled her. The gun in her own hands fired.

◆　◆　◆

Blood poured from the gunshot wound in Butch's left leg. Mr. Andrews helped Billy wrestle Butch's gun away from him before he could shoot anyone. Billy thanked the Lord nobody had been killed. He wrapped his bandanna around the wound, but the small cloth did little to stop the gush of blood.

"Look what you just did. You stupid woman. You haven't seen or heard the last of me yet," Butch hollered.

"You hush up. You're under arrest," Mr. Andrews said.

He joined Billy in treating the injury. When they had stopped most of the bleeding, Billy hoisted Butch from the ground. Each took one of the criminal's arms. Together they hauled him in the direction of the sheriff's office.

Billy silently thanked God for protecting Daisy in the midst of danger. He glanced behind him and noticed her following them.

They staggered down the boardwalk with Butch cussing every step. He vowed to escape and run to Mexico and ranted until Mr. Andrews told him to shut up or he'd gag him.

Billy chuckled, happy that Butch couldn't hurt anyone else.

"Here you go, Sheriff," Billy said when they pushed through the door to the lawman's office. The sheriff promptly sent one deputy for the army officials and another for the doctor.

The jail doors clanked as the sheriff opened them and dragged Butch to the cot. The doctor rushed in a moment later. Billy watched as the doctor cleaned and dressed the wound in the crook's leg. When Butch screamed in pain, he felt a twinge of sympathy. Butch was a human being after all, and God didn't want him relishing in another's pain.

The army officials, along with Jake Hunter and Mr. and Mrs. Tully, finally arrived. Billy stood back and listened as they informed the sheriff that they would testify at the trial.

"Mr. Butchovick," Jake said. "You'll get a fair trial and will most likely be found guilty and court-martialed. After that, you'll be sent to prison for the rest of your days."

Billy dropped into a chair by the sheriff's desk and let relief flow through him. It was over. He rose from his seat and left the office with Daisy and the detective.

At a water pump he washed Butch's blood from his hands. He splashed some water on his face. The cool liquid refreshed him.

Daisy sidled up to Billy. His heart rate accelerated at the sight of the loose curls bobbing around her face and the serene look in her eyes. Once he ditched the detective he would get Daisy alone and profess his love for her. He wanted to ask her to marry him, but he needed a job first.

Mr. Andrews and the Tullys marched down the boardwalk, toward him and Daisy.

"What do you suppose they want?" Billy asked.

"I don't know," Daisy replied.

"So, Mr. Cook, you and Miss Hollister will be rich now," Mr. Andrews said. A grin lit up his face.

"What do you mean?" Billy's curiosity piqued.

"Why, the reward money, of course," Mr. Andrews continued. "The Tullys are very wealthy people and have put up a reward for the capture and conviction of the man who killed their son."

Billy let out a whoop that could have echoed all over Wyoming Territory.

"There's more," Mr. Andrews continued. "Mr. Hunter has informed us that Butch is wanted in five states. There will be reward money coming from them, as well."

Billy pulled Daisy into his arms and kissed her.

Epilogue

D aisy's heart flipped when the Pinkerton detective explained the details of the reward money. God really did provide for them after all. Now Billy could get his nephew from the orphanage, and Green Grass's family wouldn't have to fret over food or medicine this coming winter. Overcome with contentment, she laid her head on Billy's chest and cried tears of joy.

Later that evening, after a candlelight dinner at the hotel, Daisy accepted Billy's offer to go for a walk in the moonlight.

She gazed into his sky-blue eyes, and her insides turn to mush. Her heart rate raced like the pony rider who was behind on a run. A small gasp escaped from her lips as Billy took her into his arms.

"I realize now how much I need God, and you. Daisy, I love you. Will you marry me?" Billy asked.

Daisy's skin heated with emotion. She loved Billy and had realized just how much while he'd been in danger. She needed him and wanted to be with him forever.

"I love you, too, Billy, and yes, I will marry you." She gasped again as he pulled her closer and laid a tender kiss upon her lips.

The next morning they made a trip to the telegraph office and wired a train ticket to the orphanage. Billy's nephew should be home in another week.

That afternoon Daisy and Billy rode to the outskirts of town to look at a farm he planned to purchase. The beauty of the place took her breath away.

The big white house had plenty of rooms. One was for Billy's nephew when he arrived, as well as the bunch of children Daisy hoped to have someday. A large garden plot sat ready for planting the following spring, and Daisy would have a good time sowing corn, peas, and a large assortment of vegetables. She loved to cook, and the large modern kitchen held a big cookstove and a shiny new water pump.

Billy said the barn was big enough for a whole slew of animals, and the chicken coop would hold dozens of hens. The large paddock would serve their horses well. Daisy smiled when she envisioned Clancy prancing around in it.

Peace settled over Daisy. She wouldn't have to run anymore.

When they finished looking at the farm, Billy dropped Daisy off at the hotel.

"I'm headed to the bank to make sure the Tully's reward money arrived. If it has, I'll sign the paperwork and get the deed," Billy said before riding away. Soon they would all be settled in their new home, but he and Daisy had to get married first.

Daisy spent the better part of three days making the preparations. Adrianne baked a wedding cake. Daisy sewed a nice wedding dress, and this Sunday the circuit preacher was coming to town.

Billy and Daisy planned to marry right after the service. Daisy had already drawn her last paycheck from the Pony Express, and she rode her horse out to see Green Grass's family.

Upon her arrival the family tumbled out of their home and embraced her. The children, especially Little Bear, clung to her legs and smothered her with hugs. Her friend's mother and grandmother embraced her as well. Daisy gave them the money they needed to get through the winter. Green Grass's mother happily told Daisy that she had gotten a job at the hotel.

"I'm going to be the new cook." The woman beamed. "We will no longer need money from you to get by."

Daisy was pleased to hear that the oldest daughter now worked in the laundry in town. She wiped a tear thinking how proud Green Grass would be to see her family now. They invited her to stay for dinner, but Daisy had to get back. She had a wedding to plan, but before leaving she invited the family to her and Billy's ceremony.

In the span of a single breath, it was Sunday afternoon, or so it seemed to Daisy. Her wedding day. Johnny and several of the Pony Express riders sat in the church pews. Johnny, Gabe, Jack, and Sam took up a whole row. Daisy chuckled and wondered who'd be riding in their absence.

Green Grass's family sat in the back. Much to Daisy's delight, little Luke, Billy's nephew, had arrived on the train just the day before. He seemed to be a happy youngster, in spite of the trauma's he'd faced, and she looked forward to getting to know him. Even the Tullys had decided to attend the nuptials.

Summer flowers, native to the region, decorated the altar. Billy stood at the front of the church with the preacher. Little Luke served as the ring bearer. The youngster jerked a frog from his pocket and announced to everyone that it was his present to the couple. Daisy laughed so hard her stomach hurt.

A silent moment passed, and the situation grew serious. When the music began Daisy proceeded up the aisle. A twinge of sadness ached in her middle. She missed her papa and would have loved for him to give her away. Her mama would have taken great joy in helping her sew the lace on her dress. Green Grass would have made a beautiful maid of honor. Daisy had to forgive Butch for what he'd done, but that would take time.

One thought didn't escape her. Would she have ever met Billy if this had never happened? She had to trust that God would return what the locusts and cankerworm had stolen. God would always be there with her, like He had protected her even from the time she had hidden in her parents' closet.

Daisy reached the front of the church and Billy took her hand in his.

"Dearly beloved," the preacher began.

Billy and Daisy exchanged their vows. Life would throw some hitches in their get-a-long, but she anticipated many happy moments, too. God's grace would see them through.

Debby Lee was raised in the cozy little town of Toledo, Washington. She has been writing since she was a small child and has written several novels but never forgets home.

The Northwest Christian Writers Association and Romance Writers of America are two organizations that Debby enjoys being a part of. She is represented by Tamela Hancock Murray of the Steven Laube Literary Agency.

As a self-professed nature lover, and an avid listener to 1960s folk music, Debby can't help but feel like a hippie child who wasn't born soon enough to attend Woodstock. She wishes she could run barefoot all year long but often does anyway in grass and on beaches in her hamlet that is the cold and rainy southwest Washington.

During the football season, Debby cheers on the Seattle Seahawks along with legions of other devoted fans. She's also filled with wanderlust and dreams of visiting Denmark, Italy, and Morocco someday.

Debby Lee loves connecting with her readers through her website at www.booksbydebbylee.com.

Hidden Courage

by Rose Allen McCauley

Dedication:

This book is dedicated to my youngest granddaughter, Elinor, whom the heroine in my story is named after. Our Elinor actually lives in a pre–Civil War home in Kentucky where a hidden cellar room was discovered during remodeling, which spurred the idea for this story. I pray Elinor and all our grandchildren will live lives of courage even when times are tough.

It is also dedicated to my aunt Hilda Allen Mullins who recently went to her heavenly reward. She was like an older sister to me and taught me to read and to ride a bike. I was proud to be her niece and friend.

Acknowledgments:

Special thanks to:

My husband who reads my stories aloud with me to help make them the best they can be.

Tamela Hancock Murray for always believing in me and guiding my writing career.

Cecelia Dowdy, who encouraged me to write a story for this collection.

My wonderful brainstorming group of Loretta Gibbons, Jennifer Johnson, Jackie Layton, and Christina Miller.

My faithful critiquers who made the story better and helped to delete the unnecessary words—Joy Liddy and Loretta Gibbons.

The other authors in this collection who formed a close bond through our private loop of encouragement and help.

Great research help from great friends—Lynn Coleman and Martha Barnes. (Any mistakes are my own!)

The many friends who have told me they pray for my writing, especially the Unity Christian Church Book Club ladies—Ellen W., Ellen K., Jean F., Chris H., and Betty J.

ACFW for all the writing instruction I've received over the years and especially for the friendships that will last throughout eternity.

Most of all to my Heavenly Father for giving me the privilege of writing stories for Him. I pray my words may always bring Him the glory and draw all readers closer to Him.

Chapter One

Be of good courage, and he shall strengthen your heart,
all ye that hope in the LORD.
PSALM 31:24

Cynthiana, Kentucky
1833

Elinor Peck slipped into the cellar kitchen of her home, hoping to avoid her mother until she could make herself presentable. Her eyes met Dottie's.

The slave shook her head. "Look at you now, missy. You done gone and got your new dress all muddy. No way I can get it clean before dinner tonight. You gon' have to change, and make it quick now. I already sent Shug up to your room to help with your hair, so skedaddle on up there."

Elinor tiptoed up the stone steps to the first floor then searched both ways before scurrying to the wooden staircase in the middle of the hallway. Just a few more steps and—

Someone cleared their throat.

Elinor turned to see the one person she was trying to avoid.

"How did you manage to get this filthy so close to dinner? What am I going to do with you, Elinor?"

Which question to answer first? "I'm sorry, Mother. I went to check on Pansy's sick baby and fell into a mud puddle."

"Always rescuing someone. Hurry, or you'll make dinner late. You know we're having guests tonight."

Elinor flew up the stairs into the solace of her room. Shug had a clean dress laid out and water in her bowl. After stripping off her dress, Elinor cleaned off as much of the mud as possible.

Shug dumped the filthy water into the slop jar, poured clean water into the bowl, then lifted the cloth from Elinor's hands. "Let me get the rest of the mud off the back of your legs." She looked Elinor over. "It'll have to do until you take a proper bath tonight. Now sit down and let me work on that hair."

What would she do without Shug? Elinor hated slavery but couldn't imagine life without her best friend since childhood. She also hated that Shug was her personal slave, a gift from her father last year when she turned eighteen. She'd vowed to one day set Shug free.

"Missy Elinor, you gots to help me get this dress over your head now without mussing up those curls."

Elinor gave Shug a quick hug. "I don't know what I would do without you."

Shug's eyes lit with affection. "Hold still now, and let me look you over front and back."

Elinor obeyed while Shug circled her. *Life isn't fair.*

"Nobody'd ever know you wore a mud puddle a few minutes ago. Now get down those steps afore your mama come up and fuss at both of us."

With a curtsy, Elinor lifted her skirts and left the mess to Shug.

"There you are, my dear." At the foot of the staircase, her father offered his arm and escorted her into the dining room.

Her uncle and a handsome younger man stood while her father seated her next to her mother.

The men took their seats across from them, and her uncle nodded. "Elinor, I'd like you to meet my new apprentice, Mr. William Chandler, from Ripley, Ohio."

"Pleased to meet you." She smiled then dropped her gaze to the table, so her mother wouldn't censure her later for staring too long. His longish hair was brown. What color were his eyes?

Dottie and Shug passed plates filled with roast and vegetables to each person. Then Dottie returned to the kitchen while Shug stood in the doorway, ready to fetch anything needed.

Elinor's father set down his fork and turned to William. "My brother wanted to be a doctor for as long as I can remember, son. What made you decide to study medicine?"

William swallowed, as Elinor sneaked another glance. "Since I was sixteen, sir. My younger brother died of a ruptured appendix because there was no doctor near where we lived. I vowed then to get the training to save as many lives as I could."

"Very noble." Her mother nodded then turned to Shug. "Clear the table, then go tell your mother we're ready for dessert."

Shug obeyed then left, her eyes on the floor.

The two slaves soon returned with heaping bowls of peach cobbler for the men and smaller ones for the women.

Her mother scowled. "I thought we were serving whipped cream with the fruit."

"Yes'm, but the cow only gave enough milk to mix in the taters and make the gravy. None left to make cream."

Mother turned toward Father. "Nicholas, you must see to that tomorrow. I'm ashamed to serve fruit pie without any cream."

"Now, Clarissa, the cobbler Dottie makes is the best in town, even without cream."

Uncle John nodded. "I've heard many people say so. Why do you think I never turn down an invitation here?" He grinned.

Her mother straightened. "I still don't want it to happen again."

Her father stood. "Gentlemen, shall we retire to the study to smoke our local burley?"

The other men pushed in their chairs. William glanced at her father then at Elinor. "I'd rather take a stroll through your lovely gardens we saw when we parked the buggy. Could Miss Peck join me?"

Surprised, Elinor looked at her father, who gave a short nod of assent. She glanced at William and smiled. "That would be nice."

Mother looked at Shug. "Grab Elinor's shawl, then chaperone them as they walk."

"Yes'm." Shug left then returned with the shawl and placed it around Elinor's shoulders.

William crooked his elbow. Elinor linked her arm with his, amazed at the warmth. Flustered, she gazed into his eyes—light green like spring leaves.

William stared down at the beauty on his arm. Her blue eyes mesmerized him, so he looked away before he got lost in them. "Shall we begin our walk in the front yard then go to the back?"

"Certainly."

After reaching the bottom of the steps, she stepped to the right, her hand lightly touching his arm.

"What a tall pine tree." He tilted his head back to see the top.

"Father planted it the day I was born, to shade my room." Her eyes shone.

"The tree grew faster than you."

Laughter bubbled from her lips. "You're right."

They turned at the front corner of the yard, and he glimpsed the slave girl following them several yards behind. How could Southerners stand to enslave a fellow human being?

The stone pathway wound its way beside some boxwood bordered with taller arborvitae.

Elinor sniffed the air. "I love the scent of the 'tree of life,' don't you?"

He drew in a breath. "Yes, what else do you like?"

"I like to read, and I love to help the slaves feel better when they're sick."

"I love to read and to help sick people, too. What kind of medicines do you use?"

"Mostly herbs from my garden." She waved her hand toward a fenced-in area at the corner of the backyard. "Would you like to see it?"

"Of course." How wonderful God had led him to meet someone in his new town who liked some of the same things he did, especially the healing arts.

They approached the narrow gate into the garden, and he let his arm fall away to allow her and her hoop skirt to enter. His arm ached to hold hers again, but from this view he could observe her lovely blond curls and petite form.

She pointed to sticks with little pieces of paper tied to them. "I grind these peppers to make a salve for Dottie's achy knees, and I have several plants to make poultices—mullein, mustard, goldenseal, and onions."

"I'm impressed. How did you learn so much about herbal medicines?"

"From Dottie and some of the other slaves who visit her. Once when I was little I had a bad earache the doctor couldn't heal, and Dottie made me an onion poultice, and the pain disappeared overnight." Her eyes misted. "Of course, her love and prayers helped a lot, too."

His heart swelled with admiration for this sweet woman. "You seem very close to your slaves."

"Shug has always been like a sister to me. We're only a few weeks apart in age and played together on the floor while Dottie cooked."

"You're a special woman, Elinor. I hope we can get to know each other better."

"That would be nice." She grinned, and a dimple appeared on each cheek. "Do you want to see my willow tree?"

"You have a willow tree?"

"Yes, it's outside my other window. I begged Father for it so I could use the bark for pain relief." She walked through the gate. "Follow me."

He'd never been so enchanted with a woman—a book, maybe, but never a female. Medicine had been his whole focus for the past five years. Wait. He would need to remain focused for the next three years to reach his dream to save lives. He had to. In his brother's memory.

◆　◆　◆

Saturday afternoon Elinor couldn't concentrate on her book. The image of her uncle's apprentice flitted into her mind. She'd dreamed about him last night, although she couldn't remember the details.

Her mother entered the library, carrying a package. "I need you to take this to your uncle John. I had the slaves rip up some old sheets into bandages for him."

Excitement mounting, Elinor put down her book and lifted the package. "Certainly."

"And take Shug with you."

Her heart sang with joy. "Yes, ma'am." Shug would be glad to get out of the hot kitchen, and Elinor would love extra time to visit with her, a rarity nowadays.

She went downstairs to seek Dottie. "Mother has a package for me to deliver and told me to take Shug."

Dottie wagged a finger. "Remember to walk behind Elinor, Shug."

Her friend's dark eyes danced. "I will, Mama."

Elinor and Shug giggled and hugged as soon as they went out the back door.

They strolled down Pike Street, Shug keeping a step or two behind Elinor but close enough so they could chat.

"What did you think of the new doctor, NorNor?"

Elinor smiled. Shug had given her that nickname when they were tiny. Just like she had called her Shug instead of Shirley.

Shug whispered. "He had eyes only for you."

Elinor blushed as they passed the mercantile owner with a nod. After he went into his store, she admonished Shug. "We have to watch what we say. If that got back to Mother, we would both be in big trouble."

"I know, but it's true. And you sure liked talking to him, too."

"He was easy to converse with. He loves herbal cures and books, like I do." She waited while a couple of women passed them. "What did you think of him?"

"Mama would say he's pretty easy on the eyes." Shug giggled.

He was handsome, but she enjoyed his personality even more. "I agree."

Even strolling, they soon reached her uncle's office, a mere two blocks from their house.

Shug stood outside the gate while Elinor walked up to the door and knocked.

"Come in," a deep male voice called out. Not her uncle's voice. Her heart raced as she waited.

The man from her dream opened the door. "Oh, it's you."

"Yes, I'm me."

Their laughter mingled in a pleasant way.

He cleared his throat. "I'm sorry I can't invite you in. Your uncle isn't here."

"I might sit on the porch if he won't be long. My mother said to give these bandages to him."

"I could sit outside with you. Dr. Peck walked to his patient's house, so it must not be far. And we do have a chaperone." He nodded toward Shug.

Elinor called to her friend, "We're going to wait for Uncle John, so why don't you come sit in the shade under his chestnut tree."

"Yes, please do."

Besides being good-looking, the apprentice was also kind and respectful.

"Could I get you both a drink of water?"

Shug shook her head.

Elinor smiled. "No, thank you. It's not a long walk." How could she explain the ruckus it might cause if a slave drank from a white person's cup? She sat down in a porch chair.

"What kind of books do you like most, Elinor?"

She edged forward on her seat. "I love to read all kinds and have read most of the books in our library at least twice, some even a dozen times. Especially the poetry."

"A fellow poet lover." William cocked his head. "Have you heard of a poet named Phillis Wheatley?"

"No, and I wonder why. My father has an extensive poetry collection."

His eyes bore into hers as though he searched her soul. "Phillis was a slave who lived in the eighteenth century."

"No, what did she write?"

"Various subjects, mostly religious and moral themes."

"A slave who wrote poetry? Slaves around here can't read or write." She couldn't tell him she'd taught Shug how to write the alphabet and her name for fear it would bring the wrath of others down on them both.

"Phillis came from a country in Africa called Senegal and was raised by a family in Massachusetts. Some of her poetry is quite extraordinary."

"I'd love to read some of her work."

He stood. "I have a book I'll loan you." When he returned with the slim volume, he handed it to her wrapped in brown paper and whispered, "For your eyes only."

She nodded and placed it in the folds of her skirt.

Uncle John approached the gate. "My favorite niece come to visit me."

"I'm your only niece, Uncle John." She laughed at the familiar game.

He grinned. "That's why you're my favorite."

She pointed to the package she'd brought. "Mother sent you some bandages from old sheets."

"Tell her I surely appreciate them."

"I will. We'd better be going." She walked to the tree where Shug joined her. "Goodbye, Uncle John, and you, too, Mr. Chandler." With a wave, she departed.

◆　◆　◆

When she left, the gaiety and laughter departed with her. William had never been affected like that before. What was going on?

He followed Dr. Peck into the cabin that served as their living quarters and office. "How is your patient?"

"I had to give him three stitches behind his ear." He pulled a scrawny chicken out of a feed sack. "He gave me this chicken and some potatoes, so we'll eat well tonight. A successful visit."

William grinned at the vision in his mind of Elinor. "Yes, a successful visit." When could he see her again? "Are we going to church in the morning?"

"Yes, you're welcome to attend the Methodist Church on the next corner with me if you like." He winked at William. "It's where all the Peck family worship."

William's face warmed. "What time do services begin?"

"Eleven o'clock for church, and some people go to the new Sunday school my niece and some of the ladies started for the children."

"Yes, we had Sunday school at my church in Ohio. What do you need me to do now?"

Dr. Peck held up the bird. "How are you at cutting up a chicken?"

"Pretty good, if I do say so. My mom used to let me use them to practice surgery as long as I didn't take too long."

Doc chuckled. "Your mom sounds like a special lady. Hope you can find a helpmeet like the Bible called Eve. I never found one who would put up with chickens and turnips as pay for my services."

William had never thought of a wife before today, but now it struck him as a grand idea. "Where's your butcher knife? The sooner I operate, the sooner we eat."

Chapter Two

After supper, Elinor begged off their usual family hour in the parlor by saying she was tired and wanted to read for a while.

Her mother touched her forehead. "You don't seem to have a fever, so a good night's rest is probably all you need."

"I agree." The book Mr. Chandler had loaned her was calling her. She knew her parents loved her, but sometimes all the love and attention suffocated her.

As she walked past the chest in the hallway, she grabbed a couple of candles from its top drawer for her light supply. She wouldn't stop until she finished the book from William. She whispered his name. It wasn't proper to call an acquaintance of the opposite sex by his first name, but his seemed so right on her tongue, even though she wouldn't dare do it in front of him or anyone else.

As the last glimmers of dusk peeked through the tall bedroom windows, Elinor slipped into her nightgown then removed the slim volume from under her mattress. The anticipation of reading a slave girl's words in a book given to her by William sent tingles up her arm. He'd trusted her with this treasure.

She traced the gold embossed words on the brown leather cover—*Poems on Various Subjects, Religious and Moral by Phillis Wheatley*. Slipping under the covers, her mind took her back to the last century as she read the words penned by a girl about her age, words of beauty, courage, strength, and insight beyond her years.

Funeral poems and one even written to the king of England. How could this young girl who'd learned English as her second language write such moving, stirring words?

After she finished the whole book in a couple of hours, she reread some of her favorites—"An Hymn to the Morning" and "An Hymn to the Evening." She fell asleep while committing to memory the words that seeped into her soul:

The morn awakes, and wide extends her rays,
On every leaf the gentle zephyr plays;
Harmonious lays the feathered race resume,
Dart the bright eye and shake the painted plume.
Ye shady groves, your verdant glooms display
To shield your poet from the burning day.

◆ ◆ ◆

Someone tapped her arm. Her eyes flew open in a bright, sun-filled room and peered into the chocolate-brown eyes of Shug.

"Wake up, missy. Your mother says she's coming up to check on you if you aren't down to breakfast in ten minutes."

Elinor threw back the covers. The small volume hit the floor.

Her friend picked it up and studied it. "What's this about?"

"A book William, I mean Mr. Chandler, loaned me. You can't tell anyone about it."

"I won't."

"You know I trust you. Help me dress before Mother comes up."

In a few minutes, she walked down the stairs under the watchful eyes of her mother.

"How are you feeling, dear? Do you need to stay home from church today?"

Elinor loved church and couldn't wait to talk with William and ask him more about Phillis Wheatley. "No, I'm fine."

"Sunday breakfast is out on the buffet. Hurry. We need to leave in under an hour."

"Yes, Mother." Her heart skipped a beat in anticipation of soon seeing William.

◆　◆　◆

William arrived at the Methodist Church, hoping to spend every possible minute with Elinor. He sat on the back pew to see all the parishioners as they entered.

To his frustration, most mothers, their daughters in tow, stopped by to meet him and have the minister introduce them. The only one he was interested in hadn't arrived yet.

After the opening prayer, the Peck family came in, and Elinor and her mother walked straight past him to a room in the back.

So much for his plans. He turned his thoughts to the scripture reading and lesson.

Later Dr. Peck came in and sat down in one of the front rows. When the class ended, he beckoned to William to join him. "This is the Peck pew, my boy. I want you to feel like part of the family while you're here."

William smiled. Perhaps Elinor would sit by him.

The Pecks entered the row with their daughter ensconced between them. Mrs. Peck sat next to William, then Elinor, then her father. He nodded at them all, but Elinor only nodded once then kept her eyes averted. Was this the same vibrant girl who'd entranced him on the stroll at her house and who showed such interest in the book he loaned her last night?

Father, help me keep my mind on You during this worship service, and help me speak to Elinor again today.

Calm settled over him. God had answered the first part of his prayer. He prayed and trusted Him to answer the second part.

At the last "Amen," Doc tugged at his sleeve and nodded toward a mother and daughter standing in the aisle next to the doctor.

"Dr. Peck, I cooked plenty this morning. Would you and the young doc come to our home for Sunday dinner?"

The doctor looked at him and quirked a brow. "I didn't fix anything, so do you want to join me for lunch with Mrs. Obed and her family?"

Following Doc's lead, William nodded. "I'd be obliged. A woman's cooking is always better than a man's."

Mrs. Obed smiled as she pushed her daughter toward William. "This here's my Miranda. She helped me do the cooking."

Miranda fluttered her eyes at him. He wanted to run the other way but couldn't embarrass his host. "How nice of you both."

"Come along then, so the roast won't dry out." Mrs. Obed linked arms with Miranda and marched up the aisle. He followed them.

Even the promise of a good home-cooked meal couldn't brighten his mood. When would he see Elinor again?

◆　◆　◆

After their noon meal, Elinor sat in the parlor, embroidering a sampler for a wedding gift for a friend. She'd never thought much about weddings until a couple of months ago when two of the girls she'd attended school with had announced their engagements. The weddings would take place later this summer.

Her mother laid down her stitching to wipe her brow with a handkerchief. "June is already unbearable. I'm going to lie down in hopes a breeze will blow through the windows. How about you?"

"I'm not sleepy. I think I'll take a walk."

"Shug will have to accompany you. It's not proper for a young woman to walk about alone." She stopped on the bottom step. "Be sure to wear your bonnet."

"Yes, ma'am." Anything to get out of the house and maybe run into William.

She checked her hair in the hall mirror then went down the steps to the cellar. Cooler air met her, making her happy for the slaves' sake. They had such hard jobs.

Shug and Dottie sat peeling apples.

"Dottie, Mother says I have to take Shug if I go for a walk."

"We just finished up the dishes, so she can go for a bit."

"Thank you."

Dottie's stern face melted into a smile. "Go on with you now."

Shug joined hands with Elinor. Outside the house, she turned, a twinkle in her eye. "Where do you want to walk this afternoon—maybe down the hill to the doctor's office?"

"It might be cooler, but then we'd have to climb the hill on the way back."

"We could walk to the Licking River and dip our toes in like we used to."

"I'd love to, but Mother would think it very unladylike."

Shug's eyes dared her. "Let's mosey on down to the river to see if any air is stirring. Then we can stop by your uncle's house to rest on our way back."

They started down the street, assuming the position her mother always insisted on— Elinor in front, followed by Shug.

Reaching the riverbank, Elinor sent Shug down to the stream to dip her handkerchief in the cool water to wet her neck on the trip back.

Shug handed the wet cloth to Elinor, who placed it on her cheeks then rolled it inside the back of her bonnet.

The coolness afforded some relief. "I think I can make it back now."

"Without stopping?"

"We'll see." Elinor grinned.

They paused when they reached the gate in her uncle's white picket fence. Elinor turned to see if Shug still followed. As she spun back around, a blur rushed by, almost knocking her off her feet. She stumbled.

Strong arms wrapped around her.

Elinor looked up into the greenest eyes she'd ever seen. William.

He released her. "I'm sorry. I need to slow down and look both ways when I come out of the yard. Are you all right?"

"Yes. Thank you for catching me." Heat burned her cheeks, and she stepped back.

A couple of her mother's friends stopped in the middle of the street. Their chilled glares pinned her in place. What would they tell Mother?

◆ ◆ ◆

William offered his arm to her. "I'm on my way to see Mrs. Stephens. Your uncle said she lives near you. May I accompany you home?"

"Certainly." She took his arm.

"What did you think about Phillis Wheatley's book?"

The beauty beside him shot him an excited glance. "I loved it so much I tried to memorize some of it."

His heart beat faster at the news. "I'm happy to hear you liked it."

"It's hard to believe she was a slave."

The earnestness in her tone warmed his heart. "Yes, but the Wheatley family loved her more like a daughter than a slave."

She tilted her head to one side. "I wonder if more slaves could write poetry if they were treated better."

"Your slaves seem to be well treated."

"Father would never let them be ill-treated, but they work hard every day."

"You're a compassionate woman, Miss Peck."

"You're the one who plans to be a doctor and save lives."

"I want to save all lives, people of all races."

"I agree."

He needed to know more about her. Her thoughts. Her hopes. Her dreams. Everything. "What was your favorite part of the book?"

"I loved the hymns to both morning and evening, and the story of how Phillis Wheatley traveled to America moved me to tears. I wish she were still alive so we could sit down and talk."

His steps slowed as they approached her house, wanting to savor this time with her. "I wish we had time to talk more, but duty calls. I hope to see you again soon."

She stared up at him with those gorgeous blue eyes. "Me, too."

His face heated. " Could I. . .would it be all right if I called you Elinor in private?"

She nodded. "We'll keep it our secret. . .William."

He watched as she climbed the steps to her home. *Parting is such sweet sorrow.*

◆ ◆ ◆

As soon as she entered the hallway, her father's voice boomed from the parlor. "Elinor, come in here, please."

She swallowed as she entered the room. "Yes, Father." Her eyes roamed from him to Mother.

Her mother squeezed a handkerchief. "How could you let that man hold you in broad daylight in front of the whole town? Mrs. Bishop and Mrs. Florence told us of your shameful behavior."

Stunned, she tried to defend their actions. "Nothing happened. I fell, and—"

"Go to your room," her mother pointed toward the stairs.

Elinor glanced at Father, who nodded.

With a clear conscience, Elinor left. She would reason with Father later. She climbed the steps, stroking the inlaid parquets he'd let her design and carve, up and down the length of the staircase. Happy memories.

Inside her room, she dropped to the side of her bed and poured out her prayers to the only One who would listen.

After dark, a soft tap at her door warned her someone was there. "Come in."

Her weary-looking father set down a tray of food. "I hope you'll eat something. Your mother insists we send you to Aunt Charlotte's house in Washington tomorrow morning. Joseph will drive you in my carriage. You should arrive by noon."

Alarm brought a protest to her lips. "I love Aunt Charlotte, but I don't see why I have to go away, since I did nothing wrong." She blinked back tears.

"If you were a boy, I'd bring you to work with me. You'd make a fine lawyer." Handing her a bag of coins, he smiled. "This should help you pass the time in Washington while your mother cools off. Remember to pick her up something, too. She always likes something from the shops there." He bent over and hugged her then left.

Shug entered, her sad face mirroring Elinor's. "I wish I could go with you, but the missus insists I stay here."

Elinor threw her arms around her best friend, her heart aching for both of them. "I'll miss you. But they surely won't expect me to stay long."

Shug pulled the trunk from the corner of the room toward the closet. "While I pack your undergarments, do you wish to choose your dresses?"

"No, you pack it all, please. I have something else I must do." Elinor sat at the desk in front of the side window. She had to let William know this sorry state of affairs.

Thankful for her new metal-tipped fountain pen, she dipped it into her inkwell then wrote to William. She told of the misunderstanding and included her aunt's name with the address of Washington, Kentucky. After folding it, she sealed it with wax then handed it to Shug. "Please take this to William early tomorrow."

Her friend stuck it into her apron pocket with a nod.

The young women embraced, tears streaming down both faces. They'd never been apart more than a day or two. *God, give me the strength to bear this trip and to trust Your good to come from it.*

Chapter Three

A loud noise startled William awake.

Hurrying to the back door, he opened it, and found Shug. "Come in." She handed him a folded piece of paper before running away.

He unfolded the letter and glanced at the bottom. *Why would Elinor write me?*

Dear William,

By the time you read this I will be on my way to Washington, Kentucky, to visit Mother's sister. Some neighbor women witnessed you catching me yesterday and told my parents we were embracing in public. I'm not sure how long I will be banished, hopefully not for long. Please do not go to my house or try to speak with my parents, as that might make things worse. Do write me if you can, and I will try to write back to you, so we can continue to converse about books and other similar interests.

Your new friend, Elinor

P.S. My aunt's full name is Charlotte Bratcher, Post Office, Washington, KY

He couldn't believe someone would take a gossip's word over that of their own daughter. Might this be an excuse to keep them apart? He pulled out his quill and wrote a letter to Elinor then marched to the post office to mail it, taking his anger out on the wooden boards.

While making visits to his patients' homes, his mood worsened. By suppertime, his distress bubbled to the surface, and he stabbed his ham hard enough to bend the fork.

"Something bothering you, my lad?" The doctor cocked an eyebrow.

How should he frame his reply since the object of his wrath was the doctor's brother and sister-in-law? The words poured out in a rush. "Did you know Miss Peck's parents sent her away to Washington, Kentucky?"

Doc's eyes widened. "No, when did that take place?"

"This morning." He related the details of what happened then asked, "Do you think this is a ploy to keep us separated?"

"I couldn't say since I haven't spoken to them about—"

William shook his head. "Please don't mention it to them. She warned me not to."

"When did you speak to her?"

"What I tell you must be kept private."

"Of course."

"She sent me a letter by her slave. But if her parents find out, they may punish her longer."

"I'll wait to see what reason they give for Elinor's departure."

"Thank you. It's good to have someone I can trust. Right now it feels like some people are conspiring against me."

"All my patients sing your praises. But you'll find busybodies in every town, so don't take it personally. Just continue to do your job, and you'll be fine."

"I hope so." If only he could be certain. If only he would hear from Elinor soon. If only this hadn't happened.

◆　◆　◆

After soaking in the metal tub her aunt's servant had prepared, Elinor dressed in a simple gown, glad only the two of them would be sharing dinner this evening. The jolting ride had taken hours longer than Father had predicted due to a broken carriage wheel, and she ached from toes to head.

She wished to eat then go to bed, and hoped Aunt Charlotte wouldn't be too disappointed to wait until tomorrow to catch up on all the news.

Elinor walked down the plain wooden staircase so different from the one in her home. Aunt Charlotte's kind and jovial manner always made visits here fun.

Her aunt drew her into her arms for the third time since she'd arrived. "My dear, I am delighted to have you here. The letter from your mother said you might have an extended stay—one or two weeks or more." She clapped her hands. "We can shop and catch up and—" She stopped mid-sentence and fanned herself. "I'm so excited, I'm babbling. I know you're tired and hungry, so let's eat then get you to bed. We have days and days ahead of us."

Two week or more? Unthinkable. They sat at the plank dining-room table. Aunt Charlotte reached across to take Elinor's hand. "Dear heavenly Father, I thank You for this great surprise of a long visit with my niece. Thank You for this food, and help her to rest well tonight and every night she is under my roof. In Jesus' Name. Amen." Elinor placed her napkin in her lap and smiled but inwardly groaned at the thought of a long visit. She loved her aunt, but there was only so much to do in this small town. And she needed to be in Cynthiana with a certain doctor's apprentice she wanted to know better. She spooned potatoes from the bowl in the middle of the table then placed it closer to her aunt, who passed her the platter of fried chicken.

The servant girl rushed in with a bowl of green beans. "Sorry, Miss Charlotte. These just finished cooking."

Her aunt patted the girl's hand. "That's fine, Betsy." She passed the dish to Elinor. "Betsy's a wonderful cook, just like her mother."

Surprised at the closeness between her aunt and servant, Elinor wished it could be so at her house. Mother didn't want her and Shug to do anything together like they used to. At least her mother often sent Shug to chaperone her since she'd turned eighteen, giving them more chances to talk.

"Are you still reading a lot of books, dear?"

"Yes, I've read all those in our library, some several times. I hope you have more I can read while I'm here."

"Of course. We'll check out my small library before we retire. I have a new novel I finished last week by James Fenimore Cooper—*The Bravo.*"

"I love Cooper's Leatherstocking Tales. Is it another of those?"

"No. I wish he would write more in that series. This is set in Venice, Italy, and leans more toward political issues, but it's still great writing."

"I shall plan to read it while I'm here."

They finished their supper then visited the library where Aunt Charlotte placed the book in Elinor's hands. "Don't stay up too late reading. I hope we can shop and do some visiting tomorrow."

"Of course." She gave her aunt a peck. "Thank you for always understanding me." *If only Mother could.*

◆ ◆ ◆

Elinor awoke to full sunlight. *How long did I sleep?* She tiptoed out of bed and pulled her robe around her gown, since her aunt had said they would be alone this morning.

As she descended the stairs, Aunt Charlotte appeared in the hallway. "It's only eight o'clock. I hoped you would sleep later. But now you're up, come into the dining room and I'll bring in your breakfast. I cook it myself nowadays since it's only me. Betsy comes in and fixes my lunch around noon, then cleans for a few hours, and goes home after dinner."

Contentment filled Elinor's heart at the familiar prattle of her dear aunt. She wouldn't have to say much, which was a good thing. Too much conversation about her parents and her predicament might worry Aunt Charlotte.

Her aunt placed a plate of scrambled eggs and toast in front of her then added a jar of strawberry jam.

Elinor smiled. "You remembered."

"Of course, and since strawberries are in season now, I hope we can make more while you're here, like we did when you were younger."

"I'd love that. Sweet memories and sweet jam."

Aunt Charlotte's tinkling laugh filled the room. "And I have a ladies' meeting to attend this afternoon I think you'll love. Have you heard of the abolitionists?"

"A little."

"The women in Washington are small in number but interested in women's rights and slaves' rights. Of course, we can't vote yet, but our day will come. Even if I don't live to see it, I hope you will, my dear. This world would be a much better place if women had a say in how things are run.

Elinor nodded. She had never heard a woman express these ideas. What other surprises awaited her in Washington?

◆ ◆ ◆

William awoke before the doctor and penned another letter to Elinor by candlelight. Not sure how long it might be before they would see each other again, he wanted her to know he missed her.

Sounds of the doctor moving around the kitchen forced William to sign and seal the letter. He stuck it in his pocket. Rain hit the roof, the foul weather matching his mood, but doctors had to go out in all elements, so he was sure he'd get to mail the letter sometime today. He opened his door into the kitchen. "'Morning, Doc."

"Good morning, William, even if it is a mite wet outside." The man chuckled.

"What's on the agenda for today?" Another thing he liked about doctoring—no two days were ever the same.

"I need to go check on Mrs. Wells. Her baby is overdue, so I'm taking some castor oil. It works for some, but oftentimes things go pretty fast. I'll stop by her house first, then go check on Mr. Mullen's broken leg, then back to the Wells' home. I may be gone most of the day."

"What can I do?"

"Stay here, unless someone comes who needs you to go with them. If you do leave, put a note on the door saying where you'll be so they can track you down." Doc carried an iron skillet to the table and slid heaping portions of scrambled eggs onto the two plates. "Better eat up. We may not get to eat again for several hours."

William forked a bite into his mouth. "You're right."

Doc cleared his plate then stood and grabbed his bag. "I'll try to send word if I need to stay the night. If so, you'll be on your own. You're welcome to read through my medical books—something I like to do on rainy days."

After finishing breakfast, William pulled down the book Doc had used to show him how he set Mr. Mullen's leg. He needed to know what to do if he had to set one by himself.

A pounding on the door jarred William out of his reading. He arose to answer it.

Shug stood on the front step this time. "Master wants the Doc to come right away. The missus got an awful ache in her belly."

He invited her in, but she shook her head. Grabbing his macintosh and stuffing the heavy book under it, he tried to leave, but Shug stood in his way.

"Master says he won't let anyone see his wife except his brother."

"Doc is gone to help someone in childbirth. He may be gone for hours, even overnight."

The slave's eyes clouded with worry. Rain streaked her face. "I don't know. . ."

William rushed past her. "Dr. Peck told me to go with anyone who needed me, so let's go."

He ran part of the way, and Shug kept up.

She led him to the front door then left.

William knocked, his heart pounding against his ribs.

Mr. Peck opened the door. "You?" He closed the door in William's face.

Through the door, William heard the man hollering for Shug. "What's the meaning of this? I said to bring my brother."

Panting, the young woman answered. "He says the doctor had to go see to a birthing. It might take all day or night."

After another minute, Mr. Peck opened the door. "You may come in Mr. Chandler, and I'll ask my wife if she will see you." He almost ran up the stairs, leaving William standing on the rug, rain dripping off his coat.

William set the book down away from the wet coat then looked around. The house appeared fancier than he'd remembered. Gold lanterns lined the walls. An elegant rug ran the length of the hall. Elinor had grown up in luxury, a marked contrast from his humble farm cabin. His mind dwelled on the lovely girl whom he'd met here. When would he see her again? He found her so intriguing.

After several minutes, Mr. Peck came down the stairway. "My wife refuses to let you in her room. I'm going to send Joseph with the carriage to try to persuade my brother to come back to town with him. Where can he find him?"

"At the Wells' house."

Mr. Peck opened the door.

William lifted the book. "I brought Dr. Peck's medical book and will be happy to try to find something to help her sooner if she'll tell me what's wrong."

The man shook his head. "When my wife says no, there's no use in trying. You'd best be on your way."

William left then slogged toward the office, head down. He stopped by the post office to mail his letter—the one bright spot of this day. *I hope Elinor's day is going better than mine.*

◆　◆　◆

Elinor and her aunt rested while Betsy cooked dinner, giving Elinor time to process the afternoon meeting.

The other women had shared their efforts in gaining the vote for women and freedom for slaves—what Elinor wished for Shug and all her family. She told them about reading Phillis Wheatley's book. The women were astonished, and all wished to read it, so Aunt Charlotte promised to order and share it with everyone.

She and Aunt Charlotte stopped by one fashionable shop on their walk back home. Elinor couldn't concentrate on something as trivial as clothes after the heart-stirring conversations, so asked if they could come back another day.

Over dinner, they discussed the meeting. Elinor asked, "How often do they meet? They believe as I do—slaves are human beings just like us."

Her aunt nodded. "I agree and am glad to see you think for yourself."

"I hope I get to go again while I'm here."

Laying down her fork, her aunt smiled. "I'm glad you did. You added so much to the discussion with your talk about the slave who wrote a book. The Abolitionist Society meets once a week, but I have a friend who has a visitor this week, so she invited us to tea tomorrow."

"How nice. I hope it's as interesting as today."

Aunt Charlotte rubbed her temple. "I'm fighting a headache, so I think I'll retire early tonight, dear. Feel free to check out the library again if you'd like. I'll see you in the morning." She arose and walked toward the steps.

Elinor hoped she hadn't worn out her aunt with all the visiting. "We don't have to go anywhere tomorrow if you don't feel well."

"A good night's sleep, and I'll be fine. Pleasant dreams."

"You, too."

Elinor browsed the library before going to bed. Then, she tossed and turned as her mind wandered from what was going on in Washington to what was happening back home in Cynthiana. Was William missing her like she missed him? She planned to write him again in the morning since she had no idea how much longer they would remain apart.

Chapter Four

The sunshine on Wednesday brightened William's mood as he walked to the post office to mail Elinor another letter. He would write her each day unless she told him to stop, but he prayed that never happened.

Dr. Peck had returned home around midnight then left before William awoke. William had no idea about Elinor's mother, if the baby had arrived, or why Dr. Peck had been so late. He hoped to learn the details soon.

"Good morning, Doctor." A lady from church smiled. William was pleased to be addressed as "Doctor" even though he had a long way to go to earn the title. "Please tell Dr. Peck the Lanham family wish you both to dine with us this Lord's Day."

He nodded. "I'll tell him, and I look forward to it, ma'am."

She waved. "Don't forget now."

Nothing else to do on Sunday afternoon since Elinor was gone. Might she return by this weekend?

Doc stepped down from the mercantile's porch and approached him. "Hope I didn't wake you when I got home, William. Mrs. Wells' baby took his own sweet time and didn't arrive until ten last night, making my getaway after eleven. All the lights were out at my brother's house when I got back to town, so I waited until this morning to check on Clarissa."

"How is she?"

"Fine, same as the last time. She just had a little indigestion, so when Joseph showed up at the Wells' house, I sent a package of powders with him to relieve it. The children enjoyed seeing the horses and carriage, at least." The doctor chuckled then sobered. "Are you on your way somewhere, or can we go by the office and talk?"

"Coming back from the post office, so that's fine." He walked in step with his mentor.

"You've been writing your folks almost every day this week."

"Well. . .not just my folks."

"So you have a girl back home?"

"No, not back home."

A frown slid across the doctor's face, but he continued to walk.

William kept up.

When they reached the cabin, Doc washed his hands then boiled a fresh pot of coffee and cut off two pieces of sweet potato bread. "Mrs. Wells baked this yesterday morning when she was in her nesting phase before the labor began."

"Nesting?"

"Yes, like when a mama bird lines its nest with feathers and leaves before she lays the eggs. Lots of women get a burst of energy and clean house or bake before the little one comes."

William grinned. "I've got a lot to learn, and not all of it's from books."

"Right. A lot of it's plain old experience." Doc stopped. "Would the one you're sending letters to happen to be my niece Elinor?"

A breath whooshed out of William's mouth. "How did you know?"

"I didn't, just put two and two together, and it adds up to trouble."

William squinted. "I don't understand."

"My brother and his wife told me they thought you and Elinor were more than acquaintances, and they want me to put a stop to it."

"Our relationship is only in the budding stage, but even if it blossoms, you wouldn't stand in our way, would you?"

Doc chewed his upper lip. "I don't have a choice. I borrowed five hundred dollars from my brother to buy this cabin, supplies, and a horse and buggy when I first started my practice. I haven't been able to give him much over the years. He's never asked me to pay what he knows I don't have, but now he's asking me to do something for him—make you promise to never see Elinor again, or—"

"Or what?"

"Or send you packing. You have a week from today to decide. They plan to let her come home next Wednesday, but if you try to see her, I'll have to let you go. I could line up an apprenticeship with some other doctors I know from medical school."

"But they wouldn't be around here, and I want to see where my relationship with Elinor leads us. This isn't fair."

"Life isn't fair—another lesson you'll have to learn."

"May I at least write her about this so she'll know?"

Doc scrubbed his hand along his jaw. "They didn't mention writing, so as long as you don't do it after next Wednesday, I won't be breaking my word. Think about it and pray, and let me know your decision next Wednesday."

William stared at his mentor. "May I take a couple of hours to go walk and mull things over?"

"Certainly. Please give it some consideration. I would hate to lose you. You've been an excellent student and assistant."

"Thank you." William left, his heart pounding against the injustice of this whole situation. How could he choose between getting to know Elinor better and fulfilling his dream to become a doctor?

He shouldn't have to choose. What would she want him to do? He knew her kind heart would want him to learn to save lives. But at the expense of their chance to get to know each other better? He hoped she wouldn't want that any more than he did. *God, how can I choose when giving up either one may keep me from becoming all you want me to be and do? You have a purpose for me. Please show me in an unmistakable way how to proceed.*

He had reached the outskirts of town, so he kept walking. He slowed his steps and his mind, listening for God's voice but heard nothing. He headed back to the office.

Finding Doc still there, William sat at the table, his head resting against his hands.

"I prayed but still don't know what to do. You've been very kind to me, and I'll tell you my answer when I decide. Unless you need me, I'm going to write another letter to Elinor about this, so she'll understand if I don't visit when she returns."

The doc patted his shoulder. "You do what you think best. I'll let you know if I need your assistance."

William entered his small bedroom with dread instead of the usual anticipation of writing to Elinor. *How can I explain this to her without making her angry at me or her parents? Or both?*

◆　◆　◆

Elinor awakened early and didn't hear a sound in the house, so she sat down at her desk to pen a letter to William. She wished she would hear from him soon, as she debated if he would think her too forward if she kept writing before receiving a letter from him. He didn't strike her as someone who cared what society thought—one of the things that drew her to him. That, and his amazing green eyes, which took her breath away when they stared into hers. *Stop torturing yourself with his eyes and write the letter.*

She finished then tiptoed down the stairs and into the kitchen, surprised to find the maid. "Betsy, have you spoken to Aunt Charlotte this morning?"

Betsy nodded, making her cap bounce up and down. "Yes, miss. I went to her room when I arrived, since she asked me last night to come early. She told me to go on and fix you some breakfast, and she'll be down later."

"I hope she's all right."

"She has these headaches once or twice a month but is always fine as long as she gets enough rest the next day."

"What can I do to help?"

"Keep quiet so we don't disturb her. I'll make a pot of tea around lunchtime, and you can take it up. She's usually better by then." Betsy turned to the stove. "Your porridge is almost done, so go sit down, and I'll bring it to you in a few minutes. Would you like some toast and jam, too?"

"Yes, please." Still troubled about her dear aunt, Elinor sat at the table and prayed for her healing.

Betsy entered carrying a tray with a bowl of steaming porridge, toast, and some of Aunt Charlotte's strawberry jam. "Let me know if you need anything else."

"This looks good, thank you."

Betsy left Elinor alone with her worries. Aunt Charlotte had once taught her "turn your worries into prayers," so Elinor prayed—for her aunt's healing, for a change of heart in her parents, for God to show her what He had waiting for her when she returned home. Next, she added thanks for the food Betsy had prepared, and then she slathered on some jam and bit into her toast. Delicious.

The library drew Elinor down the hallway. She perused the shelves until she found her favorite novel by Cooper—*The Last of the Mohicans*. She'd read it countless times and always marveled at the courage of the two daughters who set out to join their father during the French and Indian War. How could she ever become that courageous if her parents seldom let her out of the house except to walk to town or go to church?

She settled into the window seat and began to read the familiar story, soon caught up in the action and the romances of Cora and Uncas as well as Alice and Heyward.

At the sound of footsteps approaching, Elinor stood and stretched. Betsy entered the library, carrying a tray of tea and biscuits. "Would you like to take this to Mrs. Bratcher?"

"Of course, what time is it?"

"Almost eleven. When you're finished visiting with her, come back down, and I'll make you some biscuits with ham and cheese."

"Lovely." Her stomach growled. *How could I get so hungry just reading a book?* She took her time climbing the steps so as not to spill any of the tea. After a knock, she entered at her aunt's cheery voice calling, "Come in."

"How are you this morning, Aunt Charlotte?" Elinor set the tray down on the table beside the bed. "I've been praying for you."

Her aunt smiled. "I'm much better than last night. Thank you for the prayers."

"Would you like me to come back later so you can eat in peace?"

"I don't want to miss a bit of our time together, so please stay." She patted the side of the bed. "What did you find to do all by yourself? Read?"

Elinor eased down beside her aunt. "You know me well. Cooper's Mohican tale."

"A tragic love story."

"Yes, but I always skim over that part, because I know I'll cry."

Aunt Charlotte smiled. "You are like me in so many ways. Your mother and I never had much in common, but I've always felt a closeness to you."

"And I to you." Elinor's eyes misted.

"Now, go downstairs and eat some food, while I do the same. Then we'll walk to Colonel Marshall's house. His daughter Elizabeth is just a little older than you and has a visitor from Cincinnati who is in her twenties. I thought you would enjoy their company."

"It sounds nice, but I don't want to tire you out and make your headache return."

"Don't argue with your elders, Elinor." A twinkle in her aunt's eyes told her the comment was in jest. "I feel fit as a fiddle and want to get out of this house. Please ask Betsy to come help me dress after she feeds you."

"All right. If you insist, but we must come home if your headache returns."

"Agreed, now what are you waiting for?" She shooed Elinor toward the door.

"Yes, ma'am."

Elinor found Betsy in the dining room with a plate of biscuits and meat and cheese. "This smells as good as it looks, Betsy. Aunt Charlotte would like you to help her dress to go out now."

Betsy crossed her arms. "I'll check to see how she's feeling before I get her dressed."

"Please do, as I don't want her to go if it makes her worse."

The maid returned as Elinor finished her lunch. "How is my aunt?"

"Seems to be better, and she's almost ready to go. You'd best get ready, too."

Elinor arose and went to her room to redo her hair then waited to escort her aunt down the steps.

Betsy stood by the front door with a thin shawl for each of them. They wrapped them around their shoulders, necks, and hands to ward off any freckles.

"Your servant takes very good care of you. I can tell you mean a lot to her."

"As she does to me. Her mother took care of me and my husband before he died, and

I couldn't have gone through that without her."

Elinor squeezed her aunt's arm. "I was so sorry to hear about Uncle Jackson. He always winked at me and had puzzles for me to solve."

Aunt Charlotte cleared her throat. "Yes, he was a special man, and I'm grateful for the years I had with him." She stopped in front of a brick house.

They climbed the steps, and Elinor knocked.

A servant opened the door wide and took their shawls. "Miss Key and Miss Beecher are sitting in the parlor." She led the way to a room similar to the one in Elinor's home.

The younger lady stood. "Mrs. Bratcher, I am so happy you and your niece could visit us today. May I present Miss Harriet Beecher, my teacher and friend." She opened her hand toward a short woman.

Miss Beecher nodded. "I am glad to finally meet the Mrs. Bratcher I have heard so much about from Elizabeth."

"And I am pleased to meet you and also to introduce you to my niece, Miss Elinor Peck."

"Please be seated." Elizabeth motioned toward a settee. "Polly will bring us some tea and cookies in a few minutes. Please tell me how the abolitionist meeting went yesterday, as I stayed home, awaiting Miss Beecher's arrival."

Elinor and her aunt went back and forth with details of the meeting. Aunt Charlotte told them of the book Elinor had read written by a slave.

Miss Beecher nodded. "Yes, I've also read it and was amazed at how the Wheatleys treated Phillis like a member of their family. So unlike the treatment of the slaves I witnessed at the auction yesterday on our trip through Washington." She shuddered. "Children were torn away from their mothers with sobs and screams. I had to force myself not to turn my head. Someone must do something about the inhumane treatment of the slaves."

Tears welled in Elinor's eyes at the idea of someone treating Shug and her parents that way.

Aunt Charlotte nodded. "I agree, and so do most of the women at our abolitionist meetings. Some think we need to advocate for women's rights, too."

Elinor proudly supported her aunt. "Most agreed our country would be a better place if women could vote."

"I agree," Elizabeth chimed in.

"I told my niece I doubt it will happen in my lifetime, but I hope it will occur in hers."

The conversation ceased as the servant girl entered with the tea tray. Elizabeth passed around the cookies then poured tea for each of them.

Miss Beecher's eyes searched Elinor's. "Do your parents share your views, Miss Peck?"

"We've never discussed it. We own three slaves, and my father treats them very well."

"Don't you see the incongruence of what you just said?"

Elinor blinked. "Pardon me?"

"Would you think it humane if someone owned you even though they treated you well?"

"I can't imagine how I would feel."

"That's part of the problem. Too many of us can't or won't imagine what the slaves experience each day. Until we understand what it means to be a slave, we won't be bold enough to do much except talk about it."

"I want to do more than talk about it. My slave is my best friend, and I plan to set her free once I'm married and can do as I wish."

Miss Beecher quirked an eyebrow. "And what if your husband doesn't allow you to do that?"

"I wouldn't marry anyone who would tell me what I could or couldn't do." Elinor sat up straighter.

Her aunt sighed. "Sometimes we don't know what our husbands will allow until it's too late. My Jackson was a good man, an abolitionist himself, but he was afraid to let me join. So I waited a year after he died out of respect for him, then joined."

Elizabeth asked, "What have you seen of Washington, Miss Peck?"

Elinor recognized her hostess was changing the subject. Her own mother had done it many times around the dinner table. "I only arrived Monday late. Then we attended the meeting yesterday. We stopped by a dress establishment on our way home, but I couldn't bear to think about shopping with everything about the abolitionist movement so fresh on my mind."

"Very admirable." Miss Beecher nodded.

The four ladies continued to converse of less controversial matters until Elinor noticed her aunt rubbing her temples. She stood, explaining about Aunt Charlotte's need to rest to get over a headache. "I hope to get to talk with you both again before I leave."

Miss Key arose and called for a servant to accompany them. "Please come back tomorrow, Miss Peck, as Miss Beecher has to leave on Friday morning."

Elinor accepted.

On their walk home, her brain whirled with all the new ideas buzzing around in her head. Could she make a difference in the slaves' lives? *I must do something.*

Chapter Five

Thursday, the sun peeking in her window awakened Elinor. She tiptoed down the stairs, eager to visit Miss Beecher and Miss Key again but hoping not to disturb Aunt Charlotte.

Betsy greeted her. "Would you like oatmeal and toast, or eggs and bacon?"

"Would eggs, bacon, and toast be too much trouble?"

"Of course not. Sit down, and I'll have them ready soon."

"First, I'd like to hear how my aunt feels this morning."

"She says she's better but wants you to go visit your new friends without her today. Her plan is to be up by dinner, so she told me to fix you an early lunch. Then you can stay over at the Key house as long as you'd like."

Elinor sat in the lonely dining room, which wasn't much fun without her aunt. She loved her parents dearly but often didn't understand them. Did most young people feel that way?

Betsy brought in her breakfast with the ever-present jar of strawberry jam. "Thank you, Betsy. Did you help make this jam?"

"Yes'm."

"My aunt and I plan to make some before I leave if we have time."

After breakfast, another Cooper novel swept Elinor away in time and place. Wrapped up in eighteenth-century America, she startled at a hand on her shoulder.

"Your lunch is ready, miss."

"Thank you." She followed Betsy down the hall to the dining room, where an appetizing plate of cheese and fruit awaited her.

"Would you like some milk to drink?"

"Yes, please. And won't you sit and eat with me?"

"Sorry, I have to do the dishes."

Elinor ate quickly, musing how the second-worst part of her punishment was eating by herself. The worst was her separation from William just as they were getting to know each other.

She carried her plate into the kitchen. "Is Aunt Charlotte awake yet?"

Betsy took the plate and added it to the dishwater. "No. I left a bell upstairs so she could ring when she felt like eating something, but I haven't heard it yet."

"I'll be on my way to the Keys' house, then. What time is dinner?"

"In the summer months, it's six."

"I'll return by then. Thank you for taking such good care of me and my aunt, Betsy."

The girl blushed. "You're welcome. You're as easy to care for as Mrs. Bratcher."

"Thank you for the compliment." She grabbed her shawl on the way out.

The trip to the Key house was short, as both dwellings sat on the main street of Washington. Elinor liked not having a chaperone in this small town. She slowed her pace to enjoy her freedom then sped up thinking about all she wanted to discuss this afternoon. She stopped by the post office and thrilled at receiving a letter.

Exiting, she held the thin envelope in shaky hands. The handwriting told her it wasn't from her parents. The Key house was near, so she stuffed the letter in her pocket and continued on her journey. Her heart beat loudly in anticipation of reading the letter after her visit.

A servant answered her knock and escorted her into the parlor where her two new friends sat doing needlework.

Miss Key stood and approached her. "We are so happy you could return. Since we're almost the same age, please call me Elizabeth."

"If you will call me Elinor."

"Of course."

Miss Beecher smiled. "Please call me Harriet."

The young women asked about Aunt Charlotte and then spoke of the weather and needlework, until Elinor could wait no longer to ask her question. "How could I find an abolitionist group near me? I've never heard of one in Cynthiana."

Harriet nodded. "Elizabeth, could you find me a pencil and some paper? I'd like to get Elinor's address to send her what I can find out about groups in her area."

"Certainly." Elizabeth returned with two sheets of paper and handed them and a pencil to Elinor. "Please put your address on both papers, so we can stay in touch, too."

"Thank you. I would love to correspond with you both." She wrote the information then handed each woman a copy.

After an enlightening afternoon discussing many topics, Elinor left around five, happy to have found some ladies who understood her. If only she could find like-minded women in Cynthiana. An image of William came to mind. She was sure he would understand. Touching the letter in her pocket, she continued to her aunt's house.

Betsy answered her knock. "Miss Bratcher is still abed but wanted to see you upon your return."

"Of course." Elinor climbed the stairs. Her letter would have to wait.

She knocked, and a soft voice answered. "Come in."

"How are you today, Aunt Charlotte?" She grasped her aunt's frail hand.

"Much better. I plan to eat with you tonight but thought it best to rest as long as possible. I am sorry my maladies have dampened our time together on your short visit."

"Short visit?" Elinor's heart skipped.

"Yes, I received a letter from your mother today saying they would send their carriage early next Wednesday, so you can be there for the dinner party she's hosting that evening. Your father has taken a new young partner at his office."

Mother and her matchmaking. But she would be home soon. "At least I'll be able to attend the abolitionist meeting with you again on Tuesday."

"I thought that same thing when I read the letter." Her aunt squeezed her hand.

Elinor returned the squeeze. "You rest now, and I'll see you at dinner in an hour." Her aunt nodded as she closed her eyes.

Elinor tiptoed to her bedroom. Now to open the letter.

Her hands shook so much it took three tries to break the seal.

Dear Elinor,

I was sorry to hear of your departure but happy you wrote to let me know where you were so we could correspond. Please forgive me for my mistake in touching you in public causing this situation. I'm sure you understand, I had no choice. Letting you fall and perhaps be injured is something I could never allow. I feel I have known you forever, although we've only been together four short times. Writing will have to suffice until you return, and I pray for that to be hastened.

Your forlorn friend, William Chandler

P.S. I will write every day until you return or tell me to stop.

She held the letter to her chest, then lifted it to her face and pressed her lips against it. He had called her *dear*. *Dear William*, who was forlorn at her absence and would write every day. She must write him again tonight.

◆ ◆ ◆

On Friday, William awakened thinking he must receive a letter from Elinor today. They'd met only a week ago, but her absence had truly made his heart grow fonder.

The scent of ham frying wafted under the doorway, causing his mouth to water. He washed his face then entered the kitchen.

"How are you today?" The doc forked slices of ham onto two plates then added some eggs.

"Tired. I didn't sleep well after writing to Elinor."

"I can understand it would be hard. Wish I knew how to make it better, but my hands are tied." Doc took a big bite of eggs.

William sighed then drank some milk. "You've been more than fair with me. I'm learning to trust God because I don't know what else to do."

"Always the best thing to do—let Him lead you."

"What's on the schedule for today? Since I may only be working for you five more days, you might as well keep me busy and help get my mind off my troubles."

"I thought we would do rounds together the next few days, so I can teach you as much as possible and also because I enjoy your company. William, if I had my druthers, you'd be my first choice to court my niece." He reached over and squeezed William's shoulder.

"I'll hate to leave you but will always remember what you've taught me about medicine and all your kind ways. I prayed to get the apprenticeship with the doctor God wanted me to learn from, and I'm glad you were the answer to my prayer."

"Me, too." Doc wiped his mouth then stood. "Finish up, and we'll head out to check on Mrs. Wells and the babe."

William gulped down his last two bites then walked toward his room. "I need to mail the letter to Elinor on our way."

"Sure." Doc put the plates in the dry sink, grabbed his hat, and then opened the door.

As they strolled, they discussed the details on Mrs. Wells and the delivery.

When they reached the post office, Doc turned toward the livery. "I'll pick up my buggy and meet you back here in a few minutes."

With a wave, William opened the door then handed the postmaster his letter, as he had the past four days.

The man nodded before glancing up. "Your name William Chandler?"

"Yes, sir." His pulse raced. "Do you have a letter for me?"

"No."

William's heart caved.

"But I do have two."

William stared into the man's twinkling eyes. "Two letters?"

"Sure do." The man pushed the envelopes across the counter.

He'd been debating what he would do if Elinor never wrote, if he never saw her again. "Thank you, sir." He sat on the bench beside the post office, tore open both envelopes, then found the letter dated the day after Elinor left, so read it first.

Dear William,

I hope you don't think it too forward of me to suggest our corresponding with each other, but I enjoyed our discussions so much that I hoped we might continue them while I'm away. I still don't know when I'll return, so it will give me pleasure knowing we can converse by letter. I attended an abolitionist meeting this afternoon with my aunt. The women here seem less concerned with class and race and want to stop slavery. I desire to help them, and hope to join or begin a similar group in Cynthiana. Are you familiar with the abolitionists? I will share more details of our meeting tomorrow.

He devoured the second letter, which was longer than the first. She related details of the meeting and how she'd met two new friends who agreed with her about slavery. One lady, a Miss Beecher, lived and taught in Ohio, and she and her family were active in the abolitionist movement.

Doc pulled the horse and buggy beside the post office. "Got a letter, I see."

William waved one in each hand. "Two." He climbed onto the seat.

"Better I don't know any details in case my brother asks, but I can tell they made you happy by the grin on your face." He shook the reins. "Giddyup now."

William pondered the letters the whole way to the Wells' farm. Elinor was interested in the abolitionist movement, which he and his parents were involved in back in Ohio. This information drew him closer to her in spirit. Had God brought him to Kentucky for this added reason?

At the farm, upon sight of the day-old babe, a lump formed in his throat. So tiny, yet his cry could wake the whole household. Would he ever hold a baby of his own?

Next, they checked on the broken arm and broken leg, with Doc pointing out ways to check for healing or infection. Their last stop was with an elderly woman who didn't have any physical problems. Doc said he stopped by to check on Mrs. Wiglesworth because she didn't have any family nearby. *God, help me be the caring physician*

Doc is—concerned about the body and also the soul, mind, and spirit.

On the ride home, William marveled at how much he'd learned in one day. More than many students might learn in a week or month.

That night over some rabbit stew, he told Doc how much he appreciated all of his lessons.

"I had a lot of good teachers, too, so I'm glad to pass on some of what I've learned. You have the heart of a true physician. Mrs. Wiglesworth would adopt you as her grandson if she could."

"She's a special lady. So spry for ninety-four."

Doc drew a paper bag from his pocket. "Yep. She even sent some molasses cookies and told me to keep them a surprise for you."

"When did she do that?"

"When she asked you to go fetch some wood for her stove."

"Sneaky lady. I want to stop to see her again before I leave."

Doc squinted. "So you're going to leave?"

"If I have to. I won't agree to not seeing or talking to El. . .er, Miss Peck, so I'd like to check out some of the doctors in the area. Have you contacted any of them?"

"No, I've only written classmates of mine from medical school, and the closest is in Louisville, about ninety miles away, but I'll try to make a list tonight of other doctors in the area for you."

"Thank you. Guess I'd better go write Elinor again since I have two letters to answer."

He stayed up until eleven, sharing some general knowledge of abolitionism in Ohio. With a promise to find out as much as he could about abolitionists in the area before she returned, he sealed the letter.

His heart overflowing with gratitude, William thanked God for a wonderful day. He fell into a deep, restful sleep, hoping he would dream of Elinor.

Chapter Six

Surrounded by many familiar faces at church on Sunday, Elinor thanked God for the people He'd brought into her life over the past week. She hoped to find some antislavery neighbors in Cynthiana when she returned.

As the congregation stood for the scripture reading, she listened to the minister recite a verse from Psalm 31: "Be of good courage, and he shall strengthen your heart, all ye that hope in the Lord."

She'd always been safe, surrounded by parents, neighbors, and slaves who loved her. Had she let her easy life keep her from developing the courage God promised those who hoped in Him? *God, please forgive me for my timidity. Grow me in Your courage, strengthen my heart, and use me to serve You and others. In the name of Jesus, amen.* These thoughts echoed through the days before her return.

On Monday, she went shopping to find presents for her parents and enjoyed a last visit with Elizabeth Key. She spent the whole day with Aunt Charlotte on Tuesday, including attending the abolitionist meeting. Afterward, she returned home to pack then enjoy her final meal in Washington.

"Aunt Charlotte, I can't tell you what a delight this visit has been. I've had my eyes opened to the evils of slavery, and met so many like-minded women who are working for the slaves' freedom. It's amazing there are only twenty slaves here out of over four hundred residents. In Harrison County we have more slaves than owners."

"Yes, Washington is a special place where people are open-minded, a fact that surprised me when I moved here with Jackson. I love the exchange of ideas and the care we show one another."

"I'm praying I can find some people in Cynthiana who feel the same way."

"I will add my prayers to yours. How do you think your parents will feel about it?"

"They might understand. But I'm compelled to do it either way, because I have to stand up for what I believe."

"I hope you will proceed slowly and with respect for your parents. I would love to have you here again, but not too soon." She chuckled.

"Thanks for the reminder. I'll write more often. Why don't you come for a visit?" Elinor clapped her hands. "I invited Elizabeth to visit soon. Why don't you accompany her?"

"A lovely idea. I'll speak with her the next time we get together." Her aunt squinted and studied Elinor. "You don't have to answer, but I wondered if a young gentleman could be the reason your parents sent you here?"

Elinor's face warmed. "It is. Some gossipy neighbors saw him stop me from a fall and embellished the scene, but Mother took their word over mine."

"I see. But don't you believe your parents love you and have your best interests at heart?"

"Usually, but they try to restrict my life—who I can see, where I can go, and always insist I be chaperoned outside the house."

Aunt Charlotte smiled. "I remember those days, too, my dear, but now I know my parents did want what was best for me."

"I'll try to remember your words."

"Are you going to tell me anything about this William? You're on a first-name basis already?"

Elinor sighed. "Not in public. Just when we're alone, and in our letters."

"So, you've been alone with him?"

"Shug was always there to chaperone."

"I see." Those two words showed Elinor her aunt didn't think Shug was a sufficient chaperone.

"Anything else you wish to tell me?"

"He's my uncle John's apprentice—very smart, and he treats slaves well, and he's tall and—"

Aunt Charlotte's eyes twinkled. "Handsome?"

"Yes, but he's so much more."

"He sounds like a special young man."

"He is." Elinor fanned herself with her napkin. "What time did Mother say the carriage would be here tomorrow?"

"Around ten, so you best get ready for good night's sleep."

"Good night." Elinor climbed the steps, the journey back home heavy on her mind. *What will the morrow hold? When will I see William again?*

◆ ◆ ◆

The rocking of the carriage put Elinor to sleep on the ride home. She awoke when the driver hollered, "Whoa!"

Pulling the curtain aside, she saw the familiar houses of Cynthiana through a mist of rain. She patted down her hair and smoothed her skirts.

Joseph guided the carriage close to the back door. He helped her out then steadied her on the wet path.

Shug greeted her with a broad grin. "Your parents are waiting in the parlor."

Elinor hugged her friend then climbed the stairs, aching in places she'd never ached before as she proceeded to the parlor.

Her mother met her with a hug, followed by extending her arms to separate them. "Let me see you. This is the longest we've ever been apart, and I've missed you so."

Father wrapped her in his arms, too. "We've both missed our ray of sunshine. How was your trip?"

"I slept most of the way, but now I'm sore all over." She smiled. "I've missed both of you, too, and have presents in my trunk."

"Shug has been heating water for hours, so she's ready with your bath and to help you dress for the dinner party tonight. Your father and I can't wait for you to meet Clyde Humphries, his new associate."

"Yes, Mother. I better go then."

"I'll have Joseph carry your trunk up."

"Thank you, Father."

Elinor climbed the steps, tracing her carvings with a finger. She'd missed her family and her home more than she'd imagined. She'd also missed William. How could she get word to him? Had he received her last letter about her return?

As she entered the room, Shug gave her a hug. "I've been so lonely without you."

"Me, too. Is everyone all right here?"

"Right as rain." Her friend helped undo her buttons.

The scent of roses hung heavy in the air.

Elinor slipped into the steaming tub behind a curtain, pink petals floating in the hot water. "Mmm. This is heavenly. Wake me up if I go to sleep."

"I'll see if your trunk is ready for me to unpack, then come back to wash your hair."

Since Shug planned to wash her hair, Elinor slipped under the water up to her ears. Did Shug ever get to enjoy a bath like this? Probably not. When Elinor had her own home, she would make sure of it. The memory of Aunt Charlotte saying a woman couldn't always do what she wanted in her own home if her husband didn't approve infuriated her. She'd never get married if that would happen. But William wouldn't be like that, would he?

Shug returned, and it took almost half an hour to take down Elinor's hair and wash it. After all the soap was rinsed out of her hair, Elinor stepped out into the towel Shug held for her. Her body didn't ache as much. *Lord, thank You for Shug and all she does for me. Help me to get through this night without making my parents sorry they brought me home.* An hour later, with her hair piled atop her head, and dressed in her newest gown of yellow silk with purple stripes, Elinor descended the staircase.

Father approached and kissed her cheek. He whispered in her ear, "You look lovely, my dear. Clyde will be enchanted."

She hoped not but forced a smile across her face as her father escorted her to the table, where he seated her next to her mother. Had it only been ten days ago she'd sat in this same seat in this room? Her world seemed topsy-turvy, like it would never be the same.

The man across the table stood as she entered. He was short but nice looking, with dark hair and eyes. His clothes looked as fine as any she'd ever seen.

Her father introduced them then told Dottie to begin serving.

"Miss Peck, your father tells me you just returned from a visit to Washington, Kentucky. How did you like it there?"

"I loved the extended visit with my aunt, but I did miss my parents and home."

"I was in Washington a few weeks ago, seeking to add a few slaves to my farm. They had a goodly amount, and I was able to buy three young bucks."

Her stomach roiled. He spoke of slaves like they were horses to buy. She couldn't speak.

Mother said, "I love shopping in Washington."

For once, Elinor was glad her mother changed the subject. She hoped Shug or Dottie hadn't overheard the tasteless comment.

Father swallowed a bite of roast before nodding to Mr. Humphries, then looked at

Elinor. "Mr. Humphries earned his law degree from Harvard University but wanted to move back to this area to take over the family farm. He'll be an excellent addition to my law office and allow your mother and me to travel more."

Mr. Humphries chuckled. "My father prefers to call it our plantation. He owns over two thousand acres in Bourbon County."

"Impressive." Mother smiled. "Elinor, why don't you tell us what you did while in Washington?"

Should she tell them about the abolitionists she'd met? Her parents might send her so far way she'd never get back. No. She had to stay in Cynthiana to join or establish a group here. God had revealed the evils of slavery to her for a reason. She would do what He led her to do here.

She sipped from her water goblet. "Aunt Charlotte had bad headaches part of my stay, so we didn't get out much. We attended church on Sunday, and I met several of her friends and attended meetings with them."

"I hate to hear my dear sister didn't feel well."

"Perhaps she could visit and let Uncle John suggest some remedies for her."

Father's excited voice answered her. "A superb idea. Write to her tomorrow, Clarissa, and tell her to come soon."

"Yes, dear." Mother turned to their guest. "Where will you be staying, Mr. Humphries?"

"My family also owns land on the west side of Cynthiana, so I'll stay in the old house there until I'm established enough to build a new house of my own." He smiled at Elinor.

She dropped her gaze. When would this meal be over?

Father told Mr. Humphries about several of the leading citizens he would introduce him to the next day. Finally, the men retired to the den to smoke.

Mother stood. "I'm sure you're tired, but I insist you visit with me in the parlor and tell me more about Charlotte."

They sat on opposite ends of the sofa. Elinor recounted the headaches often lasting two days or more.

Mother changed the subject. "Since Mr. Humphries wants to settle here, we hope he will ask to visit with you again. We expect you to be friendly to him."

"I'm very busy with my friends' wedding plans, so I can't get involved at present."

"Can't or won't? You know your father has forbidden John's apprentice from Ohio to see you?"

Elinor stood, startled by the news. "I didn't know. Why?"

"William is the son of a farmer, not a plantation owner and lawyer. Mr. Humphries can take you to parties around the area. He wants to be a senator someday."

"I have no desire to see him again." Elinor walked to the door. "I'm going to bed early and plan to sleep late tomorrow, so don't wait breakfast on me."

Her hands shook as she closed the door and climbed the staircase. What a mess. She wished she could return to Aunt Charlotte's.

Elinor turned and tossed in her bed, wanting the sweet release of sleep that wouldn't come. Her brain raced. Not only did her parents want her to see a slave-buying lawyer, they'd forbidden William to see her again. How could they be so cruel?

Arising, she threw open a window to let in a breeze. After lighting a lamp, she pulled her Bible off the nightstand and read from the book of Psalms until she finally found peace in the twenty-third psalm.

She fell asleep with the comforting words restoring her soul and preparing her for what God had planned.

◆　◆　◆

William gathered up his few belongings from the small room that had been his home the past month. The place he had planned to stay for three years. Tonight he must give Doc his answer, for William couldn't agree to not see Elinor again.

Carrying the cloth bag he'd arrived with, he opened the door into the kitchen.

The doctor glanced at his bag then motioned to the table, set for a late supper. "Please join me. I can see you've made your decision, and I respect you for it. Let's eat one final meal before you go. I'll miss your company and will send word to the inn if I hear from any colleague who wants an apprentice."

William sat down at the now-familiar table to a meal of greens and boiled eggs. "Thank you for all your kindnesses."

"You're welcome. What do you plan to do in this area?"

"I'm going to work for my meals and room at the inn by helping with an addition they're adding to the back. I hope to do odd jobs for others in town to earn a little more money."

"You're a hardworking man, and I'm proud to know you. I wrote an excellent recommendation to all those I contacted."

"Thank you. I couldn't have asked for a better doctor to learn under. You've taught me more in a month than many could learn in a year of medical school."

"You're going to make a wonderful doctor." Doc looked over the table at him. "I was going to take a delivery out toward Ruddles Mills tonight, the road I showed you yesterday."

William nodded as he peeled another boiled egg. "I remember."

"Since this is your last day here, and there are a few more hours in it, how about you do one last job for me?"

"I'd be honored to, sir."

Doc gave him further directions then extended his hand for a shake. "Use my buggy since you're still working for me. Tell the Coopers I'd like cash if possible, and you can keep anything you get. You've earned it."

"Thank you again, and I hope we'll still talk sometime."

"I'll make sure of it."

William took one last look around the small house then left with his clothes in one hand and his doctor's bag in the other, glad to have something to keep him busy this first night without Doc.

Chapter Seven

Mr. Cooper opened the door and welcomed William into the farmhouse. "You must be the new assistant Doc said he might send. I've heard mighty good things about you from him and others."

"Thank you, sir." He handed over a glass bottle. "Doc Peck told me to make sure you got this."

"Thanks. It's a new medicine that helped arthritis patients like my mom. She's been paining a lot here lately, and I want to make her days as comfortable as possible. Like she did for me when I was a young'un."

"I understand. Might I have a look at her while I'm here?"

"Follow me. We moved her bedroom downstairs last year so she wouldn't have to climb steps."

Seeing the diminutive lady, William winced at her bent back and neck.

She lifted her head a few inches, and brown eyes twinkled. "You're the new doc, eh?"

He winked. "And you're my new patient, eh?"

She cackled. "Sure am. And glad to meet ya."

He sat down, and they conversed for several minutes. Doc had taught him one could often learn more from a conversation than an exam. Standing, he lifted something out of his bag. "Could I listen to your heart with my stethoscope?"

"Looks like a horn to me."

He laughed. "It does. But instead of making musical sounds louder, it helps me hear your heart and lungs better."

"I like newfangled things, so listen away."

He placed the horn part against her back. "Take a deep breath, hold it, then blow it out for me."

She complied.

After listening, he said, "Your lungs are clear of fluid."

"That's good, right?"

"Correct. Now let me listen to your heart." He placed the instrument against her chest. "Your heart beats nice and steady, too. So the pain is your main worry?"

"I don't worry none. The Good Book says not to. But what my pappy called the rheumatiz does pain me right smart."

"Dr. Peck sent a new medicine for you to take three times a day, so try it, and let him know if it helps. Are you still drinking willow bark tea?"

"Yes, a couple cups a day."

"Good, keep it up, and Dr. Peck will be by to see you soon."

"You're not coming back, sonny?"

He sighed. "I'm not sure how long I'll be around."

"That's disappointing."

I agree. "Maybe things will work out, and I can come back."

"I'll pray on it."

"Thank you."

Mr. Cooper walked him to the door and pulled out a silver dollar. "I sold cattle today, so I have cash money. I figure a young doc like you can use a little cash."

"Thank you, sir, but this is too much."

"Nonsense. Your visit cheered Mother up, so it's worth it to me." He grabbed something off the hall table. "Here's a loaf of homemade bread she wanted you to have."

"Give her my thanks, and I'll come back to visit if I'm still around."

The man slapped him on the shoulder. "God speed."

William climbed into the buggy, the good wishes and promises of prayers lifting his spirits. He hated to leave this area and all the nice people.

Stars twinkled overhead. Elinor came to mind, and he wished he could stay in this area for another reason—the girl who'd won his heart.

God, You know what I want, but I'm putting it all in Your hands. Your will, not mine.

Stilling his heart to listen to God, he rode in silence until the horses spooked. "Whoa!" The horses stopped.

A moan of pain came from the woods. He grabbed his medical bag for the second time that evening then rushed toward the sound.

The waxing moonlight led him to a woman on the ground with a man kneeling beside her. "You gots to push, Nelly. Don't give up."

William coughed to warn them of his approach. "May I help? I've had doctor training."

The man's ebony eyes blazed. "White doctors don't help the likes of us."

"I'm an apprentice doctor, but I vowed to help anyone in need. Is your wife in labor?"

The woman's groan answered his question.

Not waiting for an invitation, William dropped to his knees beside her and grabbed her hand. "Squeeze as hard as you can while you push."

After what seemed an eternity, her grip loosened on his hand, giving them both some blessed relief from their pain. He nodded at the man and held out his hand. "My name's William, what's yours?"

"Henry. Can you help my Nelly?"

"It'll take all three of us. When another contraction comes, I want her to squeeze your hand while I check the position of the baby. Do you have a blanket we can wrap the babe in?"

The man untied a burlap bag and produced a blanket. William drew his knife from inside his bag then placed it in his pocket.

Moans pierced the air again. Henry grabbed Nelly's hand, and William pressed on her stomach. The pains were close together, and the baby was in the correct position. If Nelly could push a few more times, the child should be born soon. If someone came along, all three of them could be arrested. Or worse.

After a couple more pushes, William instructed Henry to prepare to catch the baby in the blanket. He needed his hands free to cut the cord.

One more push.

The whites of Henry's eyes shone brighter than the moon as he cradled the babe. A soft cry grew into a lusty one. "Your son has great lungs, Henry."

The man's face melted with wonder as he wrapped the cloth around him. "My son? Nelly, you hear that? We gots us a son."

Nelly reached out, and Henry placed the small bundle in her arms.

William grinned. "Henry, unbutton her dress so the baby can suckle. That should help expel the afterbirth."

Soon, the baby nursed while Henry watched over his family.

William kneaded her stomach several times then checked the placenta when it released, like he'd learned from Doc's books. Throwing the mess in a hole, he covered it with earth. They needed to depart soon and not leave anything suspicious behind.

He glanced at the happy family, mother and father leaning over and smiling at the child. The peaceful scene reminded him of a Nativity painting he'd seen. And like the Holy Family, this family would soon need to flee.

A dilapidated barn he'd passed back a ways came to mind, and William loaded up his bag then checked the scene one more time. A moonbeam fell upon his knife. He snatched it up and wiped it on his pants leg as he stood. "We need to leave, Henry."

"We don't have nowhere to go, just these woods."

"Nelly can't travel tonight. There's a barn nearby where you might hide until I find better shelter. My parents live in Ohio. If we can get you across the river, they'll see you on to Canada."

"Nelly, this man gonna help us get to Canada where we'll be free. God done answered our prayers good now." The big man scooped his wife and baby into his burly arms and carried them to the buggy seat. "I'll walk or run."

William climbed into the buggy then covered both passengers with a black blanket. He turned the horses back the way they'd come an hour or more ago. "You need to follow at the edge of the woods, Henry."

"Yes, suh."

Happy the moon now hid behind clouds, William drove slowly so Henry could keep up. When they reached the barn, Henry carried his family in his arms and settled them in the barn on some old hay. The barn smelled musty, not used much. All the better.

"We better set you up in one of those stalls over there." William pointed. "Stay low and quiet until I come tomorrow evening. I'll whistle five times like this." He demonstrated.

"Yes, suh. I'll listen for you. And we'll be quieter than a mouse."

"I'll be right back. I remembered something in the buggy." He jogged there and back. "Here's a loaf of bread a patient gave me. It should keep you from starving."

Henry's eyes widened. "Fresh bread? Glory be! But what will you eat?"

"The hotel has food. Do you have water?"

The man patted a leather pouch around one shoulder. "I just filled up at a creek a little ways afore the pains hit, so this should be enough for her to make lots of milk for our son."

"I'll be praying for your safety." *And for God to show me where to find help.* "See you tomorrow after dusk."

Henry nodded. "Thank you. Yous a fine doctor and a fine man."

"You're welcome. God had a hand in me being out tonight, and He's got us all in His hands."

"Amen."

As William turned to leave, Henry spoke again. "Me and Nelly talked while you was gone. We want to name our baby boy Courage for you and the others who showed courage helping us on our way."

William nodded but felt unworthy of the praise. He prayed all the way back to Cythiana, where he dropped off the buggy and horses at the livery. He didn't know any abolitionists here but recalled Elinor's desire to join such a group. Could she help him? Would she? She was supposed to arrive home today.

God, please continue to lead me on Your paths, and keep the slaves safe.

◆　◆　◆

Elinor was dreaming of heaven and of God preparing a banquet for her there. The banquet room glowed brighter than any light on earth.

She awoke, saddened about the dream ending. What was that sound—like something hitting the roof? Or her floor.

Standing beside the bed, she listened again. A rock landed a few inches from her feet. She tiptoed to the open window then peered down at the yard bathed in moonlight. What was he doing here in the middle of the night?

"Elinor, can you meet me by the willow tree? I need your help."

She'd never done anything like this before but didn't hesitate. "Yes." She wrapped a robe around her gown but left her shoes off. Sneaking down the stairs, she tried to remember which steps squeaked.

The wet grass chilled her feet, a new sensation, but she didn't stop. When she reached the tree, a shadow stepped out from under it. "William?"

He reached out and pulled her under the tree. "We can't be seen."

Warmth spread through her at his touch. "What's wrong? Did you get my letter about my father not wanting me to see you?"

"No, but Doc told me. I quit working with him because I wouldn't agree to those conditions."

"But you have to become a doctor."

"God will provide a way." He looked into her eyes and lowered his voice. "Do you know any abolitionists who would help me hide two slaves and a baby?"

Her heart stuttered. "Abolitionists, no. But my slaves will help us."

"We'll need a place to keep them a night or two until I can get them to Ohio."

"Shug and I found a hidden room in the cellar when we were little. Only the slaves and I know about it."

God be praised! Elinor has a hidden room. "Will your slaves help us even if they might get in trouble?"

"I think so. I'll ask tomorrow morning."

"Good, and I might need Joseph to help me get them here from a barn a few miles away. We'll also need to take food and water. Can you send word to me at the hotel through Shug?"

"Yes."

His face scrunched into a frown. "I don't want to ask you to do anything you don't want to do. This could get us all in deep trouble."

"I've been praying for courage to do what God wants me to do to help the slaves. You're an answer to that prayer."

◆ ◆ ◆

And you're the answer to my prayers in many ways, Elinor. He wanted to pull her into his arms, kiss her, and tell her he loved her, but that would have to wait. "We both better get inside. We have a lot to do tomorrow. Tell Shug to come to the back of the hotel, where I'll be building an addition."

"I will. I'm sure Dottie and Joseph will help, too."

"Would he know where we could borrow a buggy? I won't risk involving your uncle by using his."

"I'll ask."

"Thank you."

"Pleasant dreams."

"You, too." William nodded, although he doubted he could sleep.

He didn't. After walking to the hotel, he lay on the cot in his room and prayed and planned until the sun peeked through his window. He arose and wrote to his parents.

After eating breakfast, he measured and cut the wood for the hotel addition. Later, his stomach told him it must be noon, and a look at the sky confirmed it. Entering the back door of the business, he asked for a jug of water and two sandwiches. He would save one in case Shug couldn't bring any food. If Joseph couldn't find a buggy, William planned to run to the barn—maybe five or six miles each way. He and his brother had often raced to see who could run the longest.

As the afternoon wore on, his energy lagged with each nail he hammered. Shug's appearance behind a tree at the edge of the house bolstered his strength. He walked in her direction then turned his back and sanded a piece of wood as he spoke. "Did Elinor tell you what I need?"

"Yes, sir, Mr. Chandler. We's all willing to help—me and my mama and daddy. I'll leave this note from Miss Elinor behind this tree, and my daddy will be back with a buggy and food and water as soon as it's dark." She slipped away before he could thank her.

Grabbing his water jug, he sat down on the backside of the tree then unfolded the letter and read:

My friends are all willing to help and are cleaning out the room. You may bring the package tonight. Send a note when you know further plans. E

William marveled at Elinor's astuteness. He'd been too tired to think of telling her to disguise her message, but she'd done so anyway.

Time to eat supper, grab a nap, and be waiting for Joseph. Tonight would be another late one.

Chapter Eight

The pickup at the barn and the trip back to town went better than expected. William shouldn't have been surprised after all the prayers he and others had lifted up.

Joseph let William and the slave family out at the end of the alley leading to the Peck house then drove the buggy back to its owner.

After hiding the others under the willow tree, William skirted the bushes until he reached the house. Dottie opened the door before he could tap on it, then drew him inside. "Where are they?"

"Under the willow tree."

"Shug will go fetch them."

"But I—"

"Don't argue." She nodded at her daughter then bowed her head in prayer. "We need to pray them in."

He joined her in heartfelt prayer for Shug and the others. They didn't stop praying until the family slipped into the cellar.

Dottie examined the newcomers. "You all follow my daughter through that low door over there." She pointed then handed the male slave some food and water in a basket.

They followed Shug. William heard muted voices from the small room.

Dottie leaned in and warned them to be very quiet, especially from sunup to sundown, and to open the door only if they heard a special knock. She demonstrated the knock, then Shug closed the door on her way out.

William studied the wall but could no longer see the outline of a door.

A faint cry sounded through the wall. Dottie coughed for a minute then spoke: "If the baby cries again, we need to come up with some other sounds—drop a heavy lid or laugh or sing or something."

William nodded. "Hiding a baby does complicate things, so we need to act fast. Do you all know anyone who moves slaves in town?" Their eyes studied the floor. "I don't need to know names, just enough to help. Send word to me at the hotel. I mailed a letter to my parents to expect a package soon. If we can get them to Ripley, my dad will take care of the rest."

A smile of hope crossed Dottie's face as she pointed heavenward. "My Father will, too."

William departed, wishing he could have seen Elinor, but he knew their relationship would have to wait a little longer.

◆　◆　◆

Elinor lay in bed Thursday night, wondering what the morrow would bring. She hadn't heard anything from William. Her parents told her the lawyer would be visiting again for supper on Friday, and they expected her to take a walk with him afterward.

She fell asleep praying for God's leading in all the decisions she had to make.

The next morning when Shug came upstairs to help her dress, Elinor whispered, "Have you seen William? What about the slaves?"

Shug spoke against her ear. "Too dangerous to talk inside. Maybe we can walk outside later."

Elinor fumed but knew Shug was right.

After breakfast, she went to find Mother. "I need some pink thread for Shug to mend a dress. Can we walk downtown while it's not too hot?"

"No, I need you to stay around here today. Send Shug with a piece of thread to match then meet me in the parlor. We need to plan a party."

"What kind of party?"

"We'll discuss it after you send Shug."

After sending Shug on her errand, Elinor entered the parlor.

Mother turned, eyes beaming. "Your father told me Mr. Humphries has asked for your hand in marriage. We must plan an engagement party."

Elinor sank down onto the sofa. She drew in a fortifying breath. "But I hardly know the man."

Her mother walked over and touched her shoulder. "Most brides and grooms don't know each other very well. That will come with time, my dear."

She had to make her understand. "I don't even like the man. I can't marry him."

Mother stood and drew herself up straight. "You can learn to like him, and you will marry him if your father and I deem it best for you. Now—"

Elinor ran from the room and up the stairs. The rustle of silk told her Mother followed. She closed the door then threw herself on the bed.

Her mother opened the door. "We only want what is best for you, dear. You will be downstairs before six, ready for dinner, or I will send your father up after you." She left the room. *God, please give me the courage to do what needs to be done.*

◆　◆　◆

Elinor penned a letter to William then watched out the window for Shug's return. When Shug appeared, Elinor sped down two flights of stairs into the cellar. "Let's walk outside."

Shug glanced at her mother, who nodded. Once outside, she handed over the thread.

Elinor pushed the package back toward her. "I want you to exchange it for a lighter shade then take another letter to William."

Her friend rolled her eyes but didn't argue.

Elinor strode down the path.

Shug asked, "What's wrong?"

"Father's new assistant wants to marry me, and my parents approve. I refused. You must take this letter to William." She let the paper and her handkerchief fall.

Shug bent, pocketed the note, and then handed the handkerchief back to Elinor. "Then what?"

"Wait to see what he tells you, exchange the thread, then return. Bring me word as soon as you can. I'll be in my room."

As Shug left, Elinor prayed for God to work this out. She had done all she knew to do.

◆　◆　◆

William was planing boards so didn't see anyone until Shug appeared beside the tree. He inched his way over so she could hear him, then turned his back on her. "Is something wrong with one of our new friends?"

"No. Miss Elinor sent me with a letter." She dropped the note then moved away. "I have to go to the mercantile, but I'll return soon for your answer."

He lifted his water from the ground and sat in the shade of the tree for a drink. After opening the paper, he held it close to his chest.

> *W,*
>
> *I am so upset. Father's new apprentice has asked for my hand in marriage. I refused to consider it, but he's coming over for supper tonight. I do not want to do anything to put your friends in jeopardy, but if not for them, I wish we could run away now. The only thing I can think to do is refuse him and hope my parents will send me to my aunt's again. I trust you'll be able to find me after our friends are safe.*

His heart raced at her signature—*Your Elinor*. He longed to go find her right now and steal her away. She understood he had to honor his commitment to the slaves first, but later he would find her no matter where they sent her.

He entered the back of the hotel and asked the cook for a pencil and paper.

"No paper, just a pencil stub."

He took it. "Be right back." Behind the tree, he flipped her letter over and wrote his answer.

> *My dearest E,*
>
> *I am so sorry this is happening and that we might be separated again. I appreciate your unselfishness in putting others before yourself. Be assured I will find you wherever you may be. I pray it won't be long.*
>
> *Your W*

He left the note behind the tree, praying Elinor would be bolstered by his letter as much as he was by hers.

◆　◆　◆

"Elinor, come down here now." She jumped at her father's penetrating voice, then stood and straightened her skirts and her back. He could not force her to marry someone she did not like or respect.

As she descended the stairs, she noticed her mother in tears beside him. Mother's tears would not persuade her, either.

"Terrible news, dear," Mother sobbed. "That scoundrel has been sent packing."

Looking from Mother to Father, Elinor waited for more explanation before saying anything. *Scoundrel? Who?*

Father pointed toward the parlor. "Let's sit down, and I'll explain."

She followed them then sat beside Mother, who continued to sob.

"I stepped out of the office this afternoon but had to return when I realized I'd left some important papers on my desk. I could hear Mr. Humphries speaking. He was telling the man his plan was working to marry you, move out to the farm, then take your pretty slave girl as his own. He would beat you and her both if needed to keep you in line."

Mother wailed again. "Our poor baby. How could she have sent word to us?"

A stunned Elinor couldn't speak. She'd heard of babies born to slaves who were lighter brown, but it was a hushed topic. She remembered the women in Washington telling her a wife had no rights—their property belonged to their husband upon marriage.

Father stood and paced. "I told him if he wasn't out of town within the hour, I would tell Sheriff Jones of his plans. If he ever returned to our area, I would prosecute him myself." He took Elinor's hand and drew her into his arms. "I'm so sorry I let myself be fooled by his smooth talk and money. I'm happy you were able to see his true character. I promise I'll never bid you marry anyone you don't choose for yourself."

She kissed his cheek. "Thank you, Father, for your confidence in me. I'll let you know when I find the man I want to marry—someone honorable like you." *Soon, very soon.*

Two weeks later

Elinor awaited the arrival of William for dinner. He'd returned from the successful week-long journey taking the slaves to his parents' farm. Then Elinor sent word to her uncle, and he'd invited Father to the hotel for lunch a couple of days ago so he could see for himself what a hard worker William was. Father told Mother last night they would be entertaining William Chandler for dinner the following evening. He liked what he had seen and heard of the man and planned to give him another chance. He'd instructed his brother to reinstate William as his apprentice.

William arrived with two rosebuds. He bowed and handed one to her mother. "Thank you for inviting me, Mrs. Peck."

Mother smiled and nodded.

As William placed the flower in Elinor's palm, heat flowed from his hand to hers. "Thank you, Mr. Chandler."

"Two roses for two beautiful ladies."

Father nodded at William. "Would you do the honor of escorting my daughter to dinner while I escort my wife?"

With a grin, William crooked his elbow while turning toward her. "May I have the privilege, Miss Peck?"

"Certainly." More heat radiated between them as their arms connected.

Dinner went as usual, with small talk and several furtive glances between her and William, and some looks from Mother to Father. Once when Mother turned her head toward Dottie, Father sent Elinor a wink.

After dessert had been served, Father stood. "I have an announcement to make."

Looking first at William and Elinor, then at his wife, he continued. "William has asked for Elinor's hand in marriage, and I have given my consent."

Mother gasped then covered her mouth with her napkin and coughed. She looked at William then toward her husband. "I hope I will have time to prepare the wedding we've always dreamed of." She sought Elinor's eyes. "We couldn't be ready for months."

Elinor smiled. "I've always wanted a Christmas wedding."

Father raised his glass in a toast. "A December wedding it is. Congratulations to my daughter and the man who will make her happy."

William's gaze held hers. "I promise I always will."

Epilogue

December 1854

As Elinor Chandler climbed the steps of the modest house her parents had given her and William when they married twenty-one years ago, she remembered each addition they had added as their family grew and William's practice increased with the size of their town. She loved Cynthiana but worried about the divisions she saw growing between slaveholders and non–slave owners.

Shug was still her best friend and now served Elinor as a freewoman with her own house and family on the back of the property. William had agreed to her plans before their wedding. Today they would be giving the first of their five children away in marriage.

Elinor tapped on Elizabeth's door.

"Come in."

She held the package behind her as she entered. Her breath whooshed out at the lovely sight of her firstborn daughter in the mirror. When had she grown from the toddler to this tall, beautiful woman? "You know the saying, 'Something old, something new, something borrowed, something blue'?"

Elizabeth nodded.

"A present arrived yesterday in the post." She handed her daughter the package.

Elizabeth stood and drew her into a hug. "You and Father have already given me too much."

"It's a special gift from a special person. Remember the woman I took you to visit in Cincinnati? You named her Aunt Harriet."

"Of course, you called her the small woman with the big ideas."

Elinor laughed. "She still has big ideas and has written her second book, *Uncle Tom's Cabin*. It's causing quite a stir across the country. I wrote and asked her to send me an autographed copy and one for you as a wedding present."

Her daughter tore off the paper and read the inscription above the signature. "To Elizabeth, may you find the hidden courage inside you as your mother did when she was your age. Aunt Harriet." She wiped a tear from her eye.

"No tears on the happiest day of your life."

"I love you, Mother, and I so admire your and Father's courage. I will cherish this book and all you and he have taught me. I want to teach my own children to be as courageous as you both in standing up for what is right even when it is unpopular or even dangerous."

Elinor hugged her daughter again. "With God's help, I know you will."

Old-Fashioned Molasses Cookies Recipe

½ cup butter, softened
½ cup lard (or substitute additional butter or margarine)
1½ cups sugar, plus extra for dipping
½ cup molasses
2 eggs
4 cups flour
½ teaspoon salt
2 teaspoons baking soda
1 teaspoon cloves
1½ teaspoons ginger
1 teaspoon cinnamon

Preheat oven to 350 degrees. Cream butter and lard (or substitute) with sugar. Beat in molasses and eggs. In separate bowl, combine dry ingredients. Add to creamed sugar mixture and blend. Dough will be stiff. Shape dough into small balls. Dip into small bowl of sugar. Place sugar side up on greased cookie sheet and bake for 8 to 9 minutes. Cool and store. Makes about 4 dozen.

Rose Allen McCauley has been writing for over a decade and has four books published. She is thrilled for this to be her second novella collection with Barbour. A retired schoolteacher who has been happily married to her college sweetheart for over forty years, she enjoys their growing family of three children and their spouses and five lovely, lively grandkids! She loves to hear from her readers. You can reach her through her website www.rosemccauley.com or twitter @RoseAMcCauley and Facebook.

The Encumbered Bride

by Donita Kathleen Paul

Chapter One

Colorado

G iggles? Giggles did not fit with the pounding headache.

Girly giggles. His nieces? No, he wasn't at home. Horses. He'd been on a buying trip. Girly giggles did not fit with horses. Nor with the throbbing ache in his leg.

One side of Grant's chest felt heavy. On two points in that mass of searing pain, it felt like someone deliberately pushed fists into his sore ribs.

Did he fall? Yes! Off his horse. Yes, but something else. A cliff. He fell off a cliff? Was he even alive? Giggles and pain weren't a part of any heaven he'd heard described.

Not quite a cliff. He'd rolled.

"Get off him!" A bossy voice. A little girl, but not one of his nieces.

The heaviness lifted along with the points of added pressure.

"I'm suppose to watch for him to wake up. Lucy said he'd wake up." Younger, sweeter, still girly.

"Come back. Your baby doll woke up. Don't you hear her crying? She needs supper."

Grant tried to open his eyes. Leaden. Weighted down by pain and exhaustion. Never been so tired. Where were the little girls? Were they even real? He strained his ears. Rustling, whispers, giggles. Giggles didn't belong in a room full of heat and sweat and pain. Lots of pain. Dark pain.

◆　◆　◆

Cool water brought him out of the shifting tides of unconsciousness. His head swam. Dribbles ran down his chin and around his neck. Water. His tongue stuck to the roof of his mouth like cotton to a dung heap. A drink. One drink.

Why couldn't he open his eyes?

"He *is* smelly." That voice again. Bossy.

"Lucy said he's gonna die if he doesn't ever wake up." A loud sniff and a choked sob.

"He's not going to die."

"Lucy said."

"Deacon said he wouldn't."

"Lucy said."

"No more Lucy. Wipe up your spills."

A wet cloth dragged up his arm and down again.

Through sniffles, the younger voice spoke again. "Lucy said she won't have nothin' to do with him if he's dirty and stinky and gonna die anyway."

"Deacon won't let him die."

"Deacon's not here."

"Stop washing his face." Bossy again.

"This stuff won't come off." A rag dabbed at his cheeks. Water dribbled into his ear.

"That's whiskers. Man hair. Whiskers don't wash off."

Whiskers? How long had he been in this bed? Where was he? Deacon? Lucy? Were they the adults? Where were they?

"Minnie Sue, you not the boss of me."

"I am. You see anyone else here to be the boss?"

Big sniff. No answer. A rag plopped over his forehead, eyes, nose, and to his neck. Water dribbled with each swipe.

"Dip your washcloth in the bowl, and wring it out good this time. Do his chest around the bandages."

"That's hairy, too." A whine strained each word. "More whiskers?"

"No. Stop complaining."

The wet cloth swabbed at his collarbone.

"I'm gonna be four, and you can't boss me when I'm four."

"Wring that out more. I can always boss you, because I'm five. I will always be older than you."

"I'll catch up."

"Don't be silly."

The water actually felt good. His little angels might be sloppy at their job, but the cool cloth, the dribbling water, and the slight shifting of his arm relieved some of his discomfort. And if he relaxed, he might enjoy their gentle bickering. He liked spending time with his nieces and nephews.

"I'll hold up his arm. You wash the pit."

Big sobs. "It's hairy. Real hairy."

"Good Ole Bess, get a hold of yourself. This man is gonna die if we don't wash him up. You want him to die?"

He couldn't open his eyes. He couldn't speak. He could twitch. He'd twitched his toes and his fingers. Every other movement he'd tried so far caused pain.

He was in everlasting, horrible pain, and he was being washed by little girls. He'd almost rather die. But aside from the pain, his predicament was laughable. He couldn't laugh, either.

A soft wail. "You said he wasn't gonna die. Lucy said Deacon woulden let him."

"I know what Lucy said. Get some soap on that rag."

Grant heard no movement from the tearful angel.

The bossy one's sigh tickled the hairs on his wet chest. "I'll tell Mae you didn't help take care of the outlaw."

"He's not uh outlaw."

"We don't know what he is."

"We do. He's a cowboy."

"Could be! *Could* be a cowboy, not for *sure* a cowboy. You gonna wash Mr. Cowboy?"

"I do it."

Mae? The adult, maybe? Mae could be their way of saying Ma. Mae, Deacon, Lucy, Minnie Sue, Bess. Why Good Ole Bess?

A shudder tore his thoughts from mere names. Outlaw? Him? They couldn't think *he* was an outlaw.

He wanted to speak. All he got out was a grunt. He felt them jump away. He heard the bowl clatter to the floor and the splash of spilled water. He heard his angel girls run and a door slam behind them.

◆　◆　◆

Where were his little-girl angels? He'd been awake for ages. Hours maybe.

He still couldn't pry his eyes open, but he'd managed small movements. His fingers and toes worked. He'd managed to turn his head to the accompaniment of excruciating pain. He'd inched movement out of both arms and one leg. The other leg was tied to narrow boards.

Was it day or night? He couldn't hear a blessed thing. If people stirred beyond his door, they were doing it on tiptoe. Could silence drive a cowboy mad? Just a cowboy, not an outlaw.

From beyond that barrier of wall and door, boots clattered. Finally. Two thuds against the door, and it crashed against the wall. Sounded like the advance of soldiers storming a fort. The tramping across the floor could have been five or more men, but the footfalls were too light for adults. More children. How many? Surely not a dozen as all the noise would indicate.

"Be quiet! He's injured." A female voice he'd never heard. From somewhere outside his prison.

Not a prison, exactly, but he was trapped. Trapped more by his body than these jail-keepers.

"Shhh!" The hiss came from inside the room.

Boots shuffled across the floor. Yes, more than one pair. Two. One louder and pounding. One not so loud.

"You awake?"

Grant managed an "umm" and felt proud of himself. Communication. Soon.

"My name's Joe-Joe. Not really. My name's just Joe. I'm six." A boy. Friendly.

"I'm Buckeroo." He sounded like a buckeroo. "I'm s–six, too."

"We're twins."

"Are you a g–good guy or a bad guy?"

"Buckeroo, he can't answer that. You gotta ask one or the other, so he can grunt. And Lucy said it was hero or villain."

"Are y–you a hero?" He could tell them apart. Buckeroo stammered. "Are y–you a villain?"

Oh, he'd waited too long to answer. He concentrated on his tongue, his lips, even his teeth. "No."

"He talked," Joe-Joe hollered. He ran to the door and bellowed, "He talked, Lucy!"

"You be quiet in there. That man's sick."

"Not sick, Lucy. The fever's gone. Just injured. And he's not a villain."

"Good. Come get this broth."

He was thirsty and hungry. A few minutes later, he knew he'd been fed before. And probably by these two wranglers. The method was vaguely familiar. Buckeroo sat on the head of the bed, seemingly cross-legged. Grant thanked God that the boy had taken off his boots. Nothing that had to do with his noggin caused anything but pain.

They lifted his head, pillow and all, onto the boy's ankles. Joe-Joe put a cloth beneath his chin then spooned in broth. Warm, salty liquid seeped between his lips and covered his tongue with bliss.

"Wow! You're doing lots better, Mr. Cowboy."

"Almost n–no spills. L–lots b–better."

Footsteps, light and cheerful. "Don't get him all messy. Good Ole Bess and me cleaned him up." Bossy speaking. Minnie Sue.

Joe-Joe corrected Minnie Sue. "Good Ole Bess and *I*."

He scoffed with a humphing grunt that accentuated his superior maturity and wisdom. "You didn't clean up all of him. Charlie will come roll him. Then we boys do the hard stuff."

Grant had no memory of that. Where was the other angel? The tearful one?

The broth was good. Probably the best he'd ever had.

Minnie Sue's small hand pushed into his large callused palm. "Lucy said he talked."

"Y–yep."

Running footsteps. A small body fell against his chest.

"Wha–tee say?"

"Watch out, Good Ole Bess. You made me slosh."

"Wha–tee say?"

"He said no."

"Why?"

"C–cause I asked him if he's a v–villain."

The pressure left his side. Little feet tapped on the floor and hands clapped in glee. "I knew it. I knew it," Good Ole Bess crowed. "Our mister is a good guy."

"What's all the racket?" A new voice. Boy. Older.

Good Ole Bess ceased her stomping dance. Her little feet in light-soled shoes skipped across the room. Grant heard an *umph*. She'd tackled the newcomer.

How many were in his room? Five. All children. Lucy made six in the family. There was a Mae and a Deacon. That was eight. Adults? Children? Five children to his count. Lucy was too vague to pin an age on her. Where were the others? Parents? Were there parents around? Surely a grown person had set his leg, bandaged his wounds, and wrapped his head.

"He probably wants to know what happened to him. Anyone tell him?" asked the boy.

A dozen denials mixed in the air.

"Y–you tell him, Charlie."

"All right. I will." The boy moved closer. "You got shot in the head and fell off your horse. Then three men came along, took stuff out of your pockets, took your holster and gun, then rolled you over the cliff top. Joe-Joe, Buckeroo, and I saw it all."

"We st–stayed out of sight un–t–til they'd gone."

Joe-Joe poured more broth in his mouth with the spoon separating his lips. "Then we hoisted you in the cart, and Jangles pulled you home."

Good Ole Bess leaned against him again. He wished he could tell her to stop. The pressure hurt his ribs. But the comfort of her warm little self kept him from complaining.

He couldn't open his eyes, he couldn't do a thing for himself, but this little angel gave him hope. She patted his cheek. "Jangles is our goat. She gives us milk, but not now. She's with child."

Giggling, girly and boyish. Lots of giggling.

So a pregnant goat hauled his sorry carcass to a house filled with children and no adults to be seen or heard or spoken of. He had a lot of questions if he could ever get his mouth to cooperate.

Lots of questions.

Chapter Two

Grant looked at the ceiling through tiny slits, his eyelids straining to part. He guessed from the light in the room that it was morning. He couldn't even begin to calculate how many days he'd been under the ministrations of his angel children.

Lucy came to the door of his room. He recognized her scent, always something to do with cooking. Now the air around her wafted beef stew.

"You're awake?" Her soft voice soothed his anxiety. "I'll call one of the children in. They're out doing chores. More likely playing." She didn't approach his bed. "But they get things done while they play, so no need to fuss."

Rapid footsteps denoted her quick retreat. She never stayed near him for long.

Grant wondered if the mature Lucy ever fussed. She called the others children, but she was only thirteen. Minnie Sue had divulged that information, along with the opinion that thirteen was old. What would she think of her cowboy's twenty-five years? Ancient. He felt beyond ancient. He almost equated his aching body with dead, but surely dead would be more comfortable.

Good Ole Bess arrived with the expected bump against his side. The impact hurt, but he welcomed the angel who either laughed or cried.

Leaning over him, she giggled. "I'm not s'pose to tell you, you's ugly."

Her gentle fingertips stroked his scraggly whiskers. "I don't think you is 'cause you're our cowboy. Lucy says she's gonna throw up when she sees you."

"She didn't really throw up, but she gagged once." Minnie Sue's voice came closer as light thuds on the wood floor announced her entrance. He could tell who was coming now by the sound of their footsteps.

He saw Good Ole Bess wrinkle her nose and purse her lips. "Ew!"

Each of his angels had a variation of a reddish-gold mop of hair. The tresses on Good Ole Bess were springs of curls. From having combed his nieces' hair, he knew this could be problematic. Tangles lead to tears unless great caution was taken. But the girl's curls were washed and free of mats. Someone cared for her grooming.

Surely there was a person around older than Lucy. An adult, perhaps. Just one. He wished he could get his jaw to work, loosen his fat tongue, and ask all the questions that revolved in a frustrating pattern through his thoughts.

Buckeroo approached with a heavy tread and grunts.

"H—here's your b—bucket of w—wash w—water."

Did he stutter more because he was out of breath?

It must be close to dinnertime. The morning always ended with a cool, sloppy bath given to him by Minnie Sue and Good Ole Bess. He'd gotten over being embarrassed by this ritual. He had no shirt. The legs of his pants had been cut off. Splints encased one limb. The girls never touched what was left of his britches.

The boys had helped him twice to void the little fluid that passed through him. Most of the time, the pain obliterated any need for modesty. The bath was a treat. But after. . . Rolling to remove wet bedclothes constituted torture. He supposed the boys were as gentle as they could be. They washed his back from neck to his heels with the help of the two little sisters. He had yet to remain conscious. As they yanked the wet material from under him, he gave up trying.

He blocked out the thought of the bath's finale and concentrated on the cheerful prelude. The girls chattered nonstop and divulged scattered information, some of which might even be accurate.

Grandpa sat on the porch in a rocker with a shotgun over his lap. One day Grant latched on to that tidbit with relief. An adult. The next day, Good Ole Bess complained about having to restuff Gramps's legs because one of the goats had pulled all the hay out before breakfast. A scarecrow? On the porch?

He learned that Mae and three brothers were out chasing horses. That fit in with his memory about the Seady horse breeders.

He'd pieced together a timeline. He'd left his family's Wyoming ranch and ridden to Hopster in the Colorado Territory. Seady horses claimed the respect of the ranchers for two hundred miles to the north and east of the tiny town. He'd been a couple of days late. The Seady family had already sold their stock at the livery's monthly auction.

On the chance they might have other horses available, he'd gotten directions from the man who hosted the horse and cattle sales. The next day, on the trail to the Seady ranch, he'd been bushwhacked.

Lucy's voice carried from the other room. "You forgot to scrape your boots, Buck. Get out of here and take them off on the porch. Come back with the broom. You're going to get every speck of that muck off our clean floors, or you won't be eating dinner this noon."

"Joe-Joe's gonna be mad iffen I d–don't come back pronto."

"You think *I'm* not mad? He's going to have to stand in line. And I'm in line ahead of him since I serve the food."

Buckeroo shuffled off, mumbling about sisters and horses and needing more hay for the winter and someone named Stilling, who ought to be named Stealing. Grant's keen ears discovered something amazing. When Buckeroo mumbled, he didn't stutter.

He tucked that in his thoughts to cogitate on at leisure. He had plenty of leisure.

A rag of cold water hit him on the chest. He gasped at the shock, cringed at the onslaught of pain in his ribs, then relaxed as rivulets poured down his sides.

Minnie Sue clucked her tongue. "How come you always forget to wring out the first rag? He won't be comfy if his bed is soggy."

Good Ole Bess giggled and proceeded to push the sopping cloth back and forth over skin and bandages alike.

"You're getting him all wet," grumped Minnie Sue.

Good Ole Bess laughed. Splashes of water squeezed out of the cloth she held. "Of course I get him wet. He's taking a bath."

With a much drier rag, Minnie Sue wiped his brow, cheeks, and neck. Through the slits he had managed to keep open, Grant admired her honeyed hair, carefully parted down the center and captured in two neat braids. Her eyebrows and eyelashes grew dark and distinctive, setting off gorgeous blue eyes. If she matured to be a smiler, she'd have boys fighting to court her. Most often she frowned.

And who would guard these three beauties, Lucy, Minnie Sue, and Good Ole Bess, from unscrupulous suitors? And why in the world was Bess called Good Ole? The baby of the family had nothing about her to claim such a ridiculous nickname.

The sheets and blanket under him soaked up the excess water. The girls hauled the bucket away with no help from the boys. It must have been almost empty. In spite of the excessive splashing, Grant relaxed as pain eased out of his battered muscles. The bit of a breeze over the damp bedclothes provided some comfort in the warm afternoons.

◆　◆　◆

"Dinner's late," said Good Ole Bess from beside him. She'd taken off her shoes and tip-toed in. He'd heard her and wondered what was up.

"I got you a biscuit, 'cause Lucy makes 'em good. You get nothing but broth. That's not right. I get biscuit anytime I want. Open your mouth."

Grant parted his lips as much as he could. His curly-headed angel poked a small pinch of bread past his swollen lips. The passage was a bit rougher than the liquid tipped into his mouth, but his tongue caught the crumb and relished the taste. She'd even put butter on her offering, and that helped it go down. Grant closed his eyes and wished he could thank her.

"Don't go to sleep. You hafta finish 'fore the others come in."

He opened his eyes. He wanted to ask where they'd gone.

"They think I'm too little to round up the horses and the chickens and the goats and Toomany the sow, she's mean, and her babies. But I'm not."

Grant's lip twitched as if a grin might develop out of the swollen mess that was his mouth. Was his angel mean like the sow or too little? He knew which, but her chatter brightened his day.

Why were they gathering in the livestock?

Good Ole Bess smeared a chunk of buttery biscuit across his lower lip. He swiped it in with his tongue. Quite an achievement. Perhaps he would return to a normal, functioning man in time.

"We got black clouds rolling in from the plains and lightning way, way off where Hopster is."

Storm brewing. If only he could get up and help.

"We got a root cellar to hide in, but if a twister comes, I'm gonna hide under your bed so you won't be alone." She poked a bigger piece between his lips. "I won't be scared, if you won't. I'll sing loud. Maybe you could grunt. You're getting good at grunting."

One took compliments where one could get them.

Good Ole Bess sat up, moving her head out of his line of vision. She tilted forward again.

"You hear that?"

Grant listened. Thunder maybe. Far away. He hadn't noticed a flash of lightning.

Good Ole Bess hopped down from the bed, leaving a fistful of crumbled biscuit on his chest. She ran to the open window. Straining his eyes to the left, he could just barely see her small body hanging out.

"Smell the rain?"

Yes, he could smell it.

"That's not thunder."

The rumble came in a steady flow, no breaks. He strained to pick up clues. The trees outside rustled but not with the torment of wild wind. Not thunder. Not a tornado.

"Horses!" Good Ole Bess danced around the room, clapping her hands. "Mae's coming! And Deacon! And Robert and Tim!"

She ran from the room squealing and crowing. Gone for five seconds, she returned to throw herself against his side. She patted his cheeks then gathered up the crumbs. One hand brushed at what was left, spreading the butter around. He could feel it and smell it and would have laughed. But even the thought of laughing made his sides and head hurt.

"I won't go far. I have to stay on the porch when the horses come."

She ran off again, leaving her cowboy wanting to jump to his feet and run after her. Her excitement had energized him. He wanted to be on the porch as well. To see the herd of wild horses brought in, to see the lightning in the distance, hear the thunder mixed with the pounding of hoofbeats, and smell the rain. He rallied all his senses to capture the spirit of the outdoors.

Getting up. That had to be his next goal. He'd already opened his eyes. Big step forward. Talking would be nice. Moving would be better. He had to get up.

Chapter Three

G rant welcomed the sounds, smells, and utter chaos that flowed through the open window and the door to the big room. Someone was jumping on the porch. Most likely Good Ole Bess, if she'd put on her shoes. Minnie Sue, if Bess still had stockinged feet.

A horse approached the house.

"Mae! Mae! Mae!" Both girls hollered.

"Hello, pretty girls." A much older voice. Did his angels call their mother Mae? "Take Gramps inside, before he gets wet."

The scuffling sounds from the front door indicated Gramps was being dragged chair and all through the too-small entrance.

"Line him up." Minnie Sue ordered. "Just right! Or he'll get stuck."

"I know." Good Ole Bess huffed. "*You* didn't take the shotgun. You *gotta* take the shotgun."

A heavier set of boots thudded up three steps and across the porch.

"I got him, girls. How's my patient?"

"He's alive!" Minnie Sue's enthusiasm warmed Grant's heart.

His other little angel shouted, "He oped his eyes, and he grunts."

Unexpectedly, Good Ole Bess burst into tears. A wail carried her next words. "Charlie hurts him when he rolls him." Big sniffs. "I don' like that, Deacon. You should let us girls wash his back. He gets hurt real bad by the boys."

"Had to be done, Pumpkin. His skin would rot."

The three approached his room. This would be an adult. Deacon's voice was deep, his tread steady, and he moved with ease. Instead of three sets of footsteps, now only the heaviest and one of the lightest approached. Grant guessed he'd swept the baby of the family into his arms.

She was set down with a thump at the door. "Oh blast! I never should have left. Look at his bandages. Didn't anyone change them?"

Good Ole Bess renewed her howls with vigor. She'd subsided while carried by her big brother.

"I'm sorry, mister." A strong male voice. "I'll have you more comfortable as fast as I can manage it."

Grant slit his eyes and turned his head the little bit that he could.

Not an adult.

Not even peach fuzz on his chin.

Standard-issue blue eyes and brown hair so light it was streaked with yellow. A

Seady, but not a grown-up Seady.

Grant closed his eyes. Deacon was a boy. A boy on the cusp of becoming a man but still hollow-chested with none of the muscle of maturity.

Grant sighed. The deep movement scorched his ribs.

◆　◆　◆

Deacon had the stranger sitting in the front room. Mae looked at him out of the corner of her eye. Lucy had thrown down her wooden spoon and marched out of the kitchen and up the stairs. The door to her room closed with unnecessary emphasis.

Mae understood. Lucy had a weak stomach, and the sight of the bruises still in their purple glory all over the cowboy's face was mighty ugly. Deacon had changed bandages but left some of the more shallow scrapes open to the air. That wasn't exactly appealing, either.

Dressed in Tim's shirt and half of his pants, the man was decent. Lucy had complained he'd been near naked the entire time she'd been left in charge, and *that* was not right.

Maybe not, but corralling those mustangs had been top priority. The small herd had never been so close, and right up against the mountains where they could box them in. Now her family would have money for paying men to help harvest their hay. That would keep Stilling away from their door. She shuddered.

Stilling was bad news, and they tried to keep bad news off ranch property.

She'd needed both Robert and Deacon to handle the wild horses. Tim could do anything with an animal in the barn or in his smithy, but out on the range, Tim was clumsy. Clumsy in the saddle. A Seady! Well, he had other redeeming qualities. Maybe she should have left him to guard the house.

She shook her head and looked out the window to the barn. Rain had drenched every inch of the ground, every board of every fence, and all of their magnificent barn. The torrent had subsided to a heavy drizzle, and everything looked good. Smelled good, too.

Dear Father in heaven, thank You for that barn.

The structure was sturdy, massive, and uncomplicated. Unlike siblings.

Siblings were complicated. The frailty of Robert and Tim's relationship constantly wore at her skills of diplomacy. Tim would have felt like the unneeded twin if she'd left him behind. Small-boned but wiry, Robert thought Tim to have beat him to manhood. Tim, with no assurance generated by his muscular frame, envied Robert's skills as a cowboy and his affinity with animals. Tim had his own way with the horses, but the gift displayed dramatically in Robert.

They were both nineteen. Mae sucked in a breath and caught her lower lip between her teeth. She should be way past crying. Ma, Pa, and Uncle Boss had been dead four years. Aunt Sue birthed her baby and hung on just long enough to get Good Ole Bess a start before giving up.

With Aunt Sue's passing, Mae had raged. The only adult left didn't have to die. The others got washed away in a flash flood. Aunt Sue just chickened out on the challenge of running this spread and keeping Stilling from taking over. It had all fallen on Mae.

She studied the cowboy. Was he in pain? He sat stiffly in the best padded chair with his legs on the ottoman. Pale where he wasn't flesh-raw or bruised, sweat beaded on his forehead. His entire face puffed out like an overripe plum.

Pain? Yes, he had to be in pain. Not much of him wasn't battered. What wasn't purple was scraped raw, and some of him was both. No wonder Lucy, with her squeamish stomach, deserted her kitchen and ran.

Well, Mae could do the cooking. She picked up the wooden spoon off the floor and tossed it in the wash bucket.

Stew was already on the back burner. With the long-handled dipper left on the spoon rest, Mae gave the savory concoction a stir, poked a potato, and snitched a lick. A little salty, but the cooking potatoes should take care of that.

The tiny hairs on the back of Mae's neck tickled as they stiffened. She spun and caught the stranger's eyes on her. Or were they? His swollen lids barely provided a slit to look through. She dipped her head and focused on the large table between them.

"Bess! Minnie Sue!"

A door opened along the balcony above the common room. Their curly mops of hair topped the banister as their bright eyes peeked over.

Mae grinned up at them. The girls were really her cousins, not sisters, and sometimes she forgot she was not their mother. She'd propped the newborn in Aunt Sue's arms to nurse. But Mae was the only mom Bess had ever known. Mae had done all the changing, rocking, walking, and lullaby singing. In those days, she'd raged at God for taking away all the adults, then praised Him for giving her charge over the tiny ones. Her heart had broken and healed over the two little angels.

"Come set the table for lunch."

They raced to the stairs.

Minnie Sue's voice rang out over the sound of their feet tromping on each step. "Can we help with the cooking? Lucy doesn't ever, ever need help."

"You can help cut biscuits."

"I love biscuits." Good Ole Bess jumped from the second step to the floor. "I love gravy. I love stew." She twirled in circles to the kitchen side of the great room. Giggling, she collapsed on the floor. "I love biscuits, and I love you."

Mae scooped her up, holding the limp scrap of a girl under her arms. Spinning, Mae danced around the table into the open area of the common room, away from the massive black stove and the work counters. Good Ole Bess squealed with delight as her legs flew out. Minnie Sue bounced in place, clapping her hands and stomping her feet.

Mae's laughter bubbled up in an unusual display of joy. This form of exercise had been too long in coming. She was out of shape when it came to being frivolous. Her side ached, and she panted as if she'd run a mile.

If she never rode out on another roundup, she could tolerate the lack of adventure just fine. Household chores suited her so much more than barn duties. But she'd worked hard to convince her younger siblings that everything was just as she wanted. Nothing was going to ruin the illusion she'd woven around their happy home.

She finished her spin just before she bumped into her father's favorite chair. The chair needed a man in it. She flicked a glance at the one sitting there now. Absolutely not! The ranch needed a tough old coot to stand against the tirades of weather and the conspiracies of greedy men. Instead, the Seady family had a stubborn, scared girl pretending to be in charge.

Mae hugged Good Ole Bess and allowed the girl to slip from her embrace. Over the child's curls, Mae's eyes locked with those of the man propped up in her father's chair.

His stare between swollen lids caught her off guard. Surely, the broken cowboy didn't see through her facade.

Swollen lips didn't lend themselves to much expression, but surely the stranger smiled. Not much. A twitch at one corner of his mouth. A light twinkle in his bloodshot eyes.

Mae took in a sharp breath and turned away. Just because she wanted someone to come take her heavy burdens, relieve her of the onerous duty of keeping everyone safe and cared for, didn't mean God would send someone. And hadn't it always been in the past, that God provided strength within? Not a man from outside their small, close-knit family?

She mustn't imagine help where there was just another complication. She wiped her hands on the thighs of her denim trousers and turned to the kitchen. She'd promised the girls they could make biscuits.

Set the table and cook, Mae Seady. Do what you can do and don't dream. Whatever you do, don't dream.

Chapter Four

Grant glanced over at Gramps sitting in the rocker, one leg out straight, the other bent. A shotgun rested with the butt in his lap. Unfortunately, the muzzle propped in the crook of his arm pointed in Grant's direction. He eyed the black hole at the end of the barrel then grinned at the lifeless guardian of the household of children.

For three days now, he and Gramps had kept company. A little bit longer each day. Today, he'd sat outside this morning and now, in the late afternoon.

Conversation was nil. Fire blasted across his jaw at the twitch of a muscle. Eating qualified as torture. Opening his mouth more than a slot brought tears to his eyes. His big, strong cowboy image had crumbled over the past week.

And the old man? Well, the old man just wasn't much of a conversationalist. He kept his face toward the far distance, ostensibly bent on spotting any two-legged varmints approaching.

But Grant enjoyed the time on the porch. Minnie Sue and Good Ole Bess spent most of their time playing nearby. Both he and Gramps had turned down the girls' mud pies and cups of dirty "tea." Mae had taken over feeding them real food.

Lucy abandoned them for sewing and other duties that kept her out of the kitchen. Dressed as a man, Mae still made frequent trips to the barn. With her hair tucked under a beat-up old hat and feet shod in boots too big for her feet, she even walked with a masculine gait. In the house, she wore dresses and gravitated toward baking and stewing, and the brewing of all sorts of delightful concoctions for him to sip.

Her femininity kept Grant on edge, eager to make strides toward eating and talking, walking and maybe wooing. To Grant's way of thinking, her frequent presence was just fine. He loved the look of the oldest member of the Seady clan. Well, the oldest of an active crew. Gramps could hardly be counted.

Mae was easy to look at, saturated the home with the aroma of apple pies and fried chicken and any number of other culinary wonders. She sang while she worked. Strong songs of faith, sweet melodies of love, and rollicking tunes of fine and funny folk. The music pleased his ears. His ears were the best working members of his body. The rest of him improved daily.

He had all the younger Seadys identified by sight now. And he easily determined their dispositions.

Tim looked like a walking mountain, muscle and bulk bundled tightly on a tall frame. He ruled the smithy, where he tackled tedious aspects of caring for the animals. But he also created artful work. The hinges on the cabinets showed both skill and an artistic design.

Robert was lean, lanky, and loose-limbed. If he'd been built out of metal, he'd have clanked as he walked. The young man was made to be on the back of a horse. All the ranch animals seemed to claim him. The chickens followed him as if he'd hatched them. Toomany and her piglets squealed for attention when he walked past. The horses rubbed their chins against Robert's face like cats when he leaned over the corral. Grant noted how often Robert had to shoo the goats, dogs, and other loose critters away from his heels. The livestock's display of affection was comical.

Yet everyone turned to Mae for final say. Even Charlie, who had a tendency toward impudence and sloth, watched himself in her vicinity. And if Joe-Joe and Buckeroo landed in hot water, it was Charlie who had put the pot on to boil. He was a likeable kid all the same. Grant enjoyed his chatter as the boy helped scrub his back and change dressings with Deacon.

Deacon held a serious soul at the center of his mellow nature. This gentle, smiling fellow talked of Jesus as he worked on Grant's wounds. His spontaneous prayers often caught Grant off guard. Deacon gently preached as he guided his siblings' efforts to help. While he was different from anyone Grant knew, nothing about the young man irritated him. The phrase Grant had heard in church, "pleasing God the Father," came to life in the style of Deacon's life.

The hours on the porch presented an odd opportunity. Grant's mind conjured up all sorts of speculation about the Seady family. Physically, he couldn't follow anyone around to see firsthand the workings of the ranch. The setup kept him mentally alert. Solving puzzles had often been a source of entertainment with his close-knit family. One sister wrote stories that she read in the evening, challenging her siblings to unravel the mysteries she'd plotted. This ranch would have delighted that sister and the rest of his household.

Without his familiar confidantes, Grant mumbled his observations to his shotgun-wielding companion, but Gramps never commented on his children, his grandchildren, or the mechanics of running the horse-breeding ranch.

Of course, that was to be expected, but nevertheless, Grant stewed in his unsatisfied curiosity.

A fast-approaching horse from beyond the ranch buildings caught Grant's attention. Charlie galloped in from the hills to the front of the barn.

"Hey!" He pulled his horse to a sudden stop.

Robert, Tim, and Mae dashed out to greet him.

A short conference spurred immediate action. Mae and Robert hastened to the ranch house. Mae mounted the steps without a word. Her hands busily unknotted the hat tied under her chin. Her splendid head of hair tumbled around her shoulders as she passed him.

Grant wanted to grab her skirt, stopping her long enough to get answers. But his body wouldn't tolerate such an abrupt action. And Mae might not appreciate the interference.

Robert, scooping up Gramps, shotgun and all, charged after her. Grant held his breath, wanting to call out, demanding to know what was so urgent.

Could he help?

Help? He couldn't even get out of the way.

From the corner of his eye, Grant saw the little girls frozen in their playing house near the end rail of the porch. Both girls wore apprehension like a cloak. Their eyes turned toward the road.

Grant searched the yard for a clue as to what was going on. He'd seen Tim lead Charlie's horse into the barn. Now Charlie sat on the top rung of the pigpen as if he'd been sitting there for hours. He watched the animals below, but somehow Grant thought the boy's full attention was on the road that led to the Seady place.

Robert plunged out of the house behind him and surprised Grant by sitting in Gramps's chair. The breath caught in Grant's throat as he managed a sidelong glance. Robert was dressed in Gramps's uniform, faded overalls with suspenders over a green-and-blue plaid shirt, scruffy boots, hat pulled low on his brow, and the shotgun crooked in one arm.

"We're expecting company, Cowboy." Robert had hardly spoken two words to him since they'd returned from the roundup.

Surprised by the tenor of the boy's voice, Grant wondered if he always spoke on a stretched string. Or did tension squeeze a squeak into his throat?

Robert cleared his throat before continuing with a slightly lower pitch. "I know I don't have to warn you not to give us away. Just play along if things don't add up. I reckon we'll be telling you our secrets before too long."

A pale horse crested the hill on the road coming their way. A man in a city suit sat confidently in the saddle. Sunlight glinted off a shiny hatband circling his light hat.

Robert stiffened and stood. He hobbled to the top step of the porch, gazed a moment at the newcomer then turned, and with the steps of an old man, made his way inside. As he went in, Mae came out.

She wiped her hands on a cloth as if she'd been washing dishes. Gone were the britches and man's shirt she'd worn to the barn. A blue flowered dress hugged her trim figure, showing how young she was and how attractive she could be. Her golden hair was caught in some fancy braid and hung down her back. Tendrils escaped and framed her face. Soft brown slippers peeked from under the hem of a wide skirt. A white apron completed the look of a young lady interrupted in her normal chores.

Joe-Joe and Buckeroo raced from the side of the house.

"What do you want us to do?" asked Joe-Joe.

Mae turned from watching the man's approach and smiled at her little brothers. "Just do what you would ordinarily do. Don't let him see his presence bothers us."

Grant saw through the calm and pleasant expression on Mae's face. Tension vibrated in her breathing.

Good Ole Bess opened her mouth, her face composed to let wail in distress.

"Bess!" Mae spoke sharply. "He's a mean old man who'd take pleasure in your tears. Don't you give him the joy of seeing you cry."

Minnie Sue jumped up and dragged her little sister back to their dolls. "Your baby's fixing to cry, Good Ole Bess. You better rock her."

Mae snagged the glass from a table close to Grant's hand. "Buckeroo, be so good as to refill our guest's water from the well." She put a hand on Joe-Joe's shoulder. "Would you get a biscuit from the bread box, please?"

He headed through the door.

"On a plate, please."

"Yes'm." The door slammed.

Grant shifted.

Mae took in a sharp breath. "He'll soon be gone. We don't welcome visitors." Her words must have sounded stark in her own ears. Her eyes snapped to Grant's, then her whole face lightened with a warm smile. She winked. "Normally, that is."

She moved to the edge of the top step as the man pulled up to the hitching post a few yards away. Silver disks circled his hat. He wore a string tie around his neck. But unable to escape the heat, his white collar wilted slightly against his shaved chin and neck. A tailored strip of a black mustache accented his upper lip, and his dark hair must have been trimmed recently.

Grant's impression of the man fluctuated between dandy and danger. His outward appearance seemed too studied, like a piece of polished wood that didn't quite hide an interior riddled with blight. Termites? Dry rot? Greed and power lust?

"Good afternoon, Mr. Stilling." Though cordial enough, her voice didn't hold any of the softness that Grant craved.

"Good afternoon, Miss Mae. We've missed seeing you in town."

"We were there just ten days ago, selling horses."

"I missed seeing you. I meant to offer you a meal at the High Grounds Café. Surely you remember it's my dearest desire to spend some time in your company."

The visitor's sleazy smile and unbearable arrogance were just about enough to make Grant bolt from his chair. He sorely wanted to comment on the man's intrusion. To be able to stand and purposely position himself beside Mae as her protector would have sat well with Grant.

And he would have if it wouldn't hurt like all get out. But staggering to his feet didn't actually present a picture of dominance.

Grant understood why Mae didn't like this particular visitor. None of the Seadys were fond of him. On first acquaintance, he didn't like this Mr. Stilling, either.

"You are the finest woman the territory has to offer. It's a shame you're practically sequestered like a nun on this ranch."

Nope, didn't like Mr. Stilling one bit.

"It is my parents' wish that I don't socialize, and I believe I've explained that before."

"Ah, yes, the trip back East."

"Someday, Mr. Stilling. Someday."

The man nodded toward Grant. "Are you going to introduce me to your company?"

Mae's chin thrust forward, and Grant figured she would pass on that social necessity. Buckeroo came from the side yard, walking carefully so as not to spill the water. Joe-Joe appeared at the same time with a biscuit on a plate.

Mr. Stilling made a move as if to dismount. The sound of Gramps cocking the hammers on his double-barreled shotgun came from a window behind Grant.

"Not a good idea," said Mae. "You forget how particular Grampa Seady has become in his old age."

The man's eyes shifted to a point somewhere beyond the people on the porch, a point between Mae and Grant.

The screen door squealed again, and Lucy's light footsteps crossed the porch. She sat in Gramps's rocker, a piece of material in her hands, a needle ready to be plied. She nodded to the man on the horse but then turned a falsely bright smile to Grant.

Lifting the cloth for his inspection, she said, "Almost done."

A shirt for him? This was the first he'd seen of any such endeavor. What game were they playing? Why did he feel that the stakes were very high? Was this shyster about to shove all his chips to the center and call their bluff?

"Miss Lucy." Mr. Stilling touched the rim of his hat as if he acknowledged one of the ladies at a church function. "The schoolmarm sends her regards. Her offer to train you to be the next teacher still stands."

"Are you interested, Lucy?" Mae sounded sincere in her question.

Lucy spoke to her sister, not the visitor. "Mom and Dad need me here. I help with everything." She held up the shirt again. "I like sewing much better than lessons."

"There's a new seamstress in town. A woman from Cincinnati." Stilling looked at Mae. "Someone you could talk to about your visit east." His eyes shifted to Lucy. "I'm sure she would be interested in an apprentice."

Lucy ducked her head, suddenly absorbed by the next stitch she made.

Grant heard the slight edge in the tone of Mae's question. "Lucy? Lucy, would you like to do that? I'll talk to. . .our parents if it's something you'd like to do."

The look Lucy tossed at her sister said more than her words. "Of course not. Why would I want yet another person telling me how to do things? I like to experiment and make my own ideas show up in a dress." Her eyes turned to meet Grant's. "Sorry, but cowboy shirts don't offer much of a challenge. I prefer dresses."

The smile and slight nod of his head cost Grant less pain than the same movement would have a few days before. Deacon had his body healing nicely. But this family had his mind more confused than when he first woke in bed with little girls giggling all around him.

What parents?

Mr. Stilling broached the subject for him.

"I'd like to talk to your father and uncle about the riverside property. I'd like to lease the water rights."

Gramps growled from the window, and Grant detected movement, heard the metal barrel scrap against the wood frame.

"You'll find them up at the high-meadow cabin. Uncle Boss, Mom, and Dad left two days ago to set it to rights for the winter."

"I'll wait until they return. I've never been able to locate that outpost of yours."

"Suit yourself, Mr. Stilling. Now, if you'll excuse me, I'm behind in my baking."

Mr. Stilling looked purposefully at the laundry line visible round the south side of the big house. "Seems more like washing day with all those sheets hung to dry."

Mae said nothing. Her silence chilled the air. After an awkward moment, the man on the horse doffed his hat, reined his horse away from the rail, and trotted away from the ranch.

"Wh—what th—that mean, M—mae?" Buckeroo sidled next to his sister and put his hand in hers.

"It means Mr. Stilling is too interested in our family."

Robert appeared on the front porch, still shuffling and hunched like a man three times his age. He propped himself against the post holding up the porch's roof. "The only thing he's really interested in is our property. All we have to do is keep him at bay two more years until Tim and I turn twenty-one."

Mae jerked to a straighter posture. "Robert!" She indicated Grant with a quick glance.

"Ah, Mae, he's no threat. First, he can't talk yet. Second, he's probably grateful we saved his life, so he owes us, not Mr. Rich and Mighty Stilling. And last of all, he thinks you hung the moon."

He jumped out of reach right before Mae's hand could knock him off the top step. Laughing, he collapsed on the stoop. Through guffaws, he managed to say, "Mae, you've got a suitor, and I don't mean old moneybags. Tim and I'll have to ask Cowboy's intentions, but we'll wait till his jaw heals up some more so he can answer."

Chapter Five

Grant sat at the big table with a sheet of paper in front of him and a pencil clutched awkwardly in clawlike fingers. Mae hovered on the kitchen side of the table, paying more attention to him than she had in two days. Her actions betrayed anxiety. She didn't know what to make of him since her brother pointed out that he had a hard time keeping his eyes off her every movement.

The rest of the family sat around the table as well. Not for a meal, but because of the guest who'd ridden in midmorning. Of course, Gramps was napping, and the parents were conveniently off at the high-country cabin.

Grant forced his attention back to their current visitor. Unlike the other one, this man had managed to get in the house. The invitation, generously extended by Tim and reiterated by Mae, had surprised Grant. The law posed no threat, so whatever falsehood the family enacted had nothing to do with illegal activities. Why was Stilling such a threat then? The older man's presence caused caution but no fear.

The sheriff slouched in his chair opposite Grant. His hat hung on the top corner of the high-back chair, and his coat lay open to reveal the star pinned to his vest. A plate of cookies sat nearby and his hand cradled a coffee mug.

He'd come to deliver news and was pleased that his assumptions had proven correct. "As soon as Whit Stilling reported an unnamed, battered stranger out here at the Seady place, I put two and two together." He pointed to the paper. "Just write what you remember."

He took another cookie and slurped his coffee. Then he gave Mae a wide smile only slightly dimmed by yellowed teeth. "Sit down, girl. I'll tell you the whole tale."

Chairs scraped on the wooden floor as members of the family scooted closer, taking interest in the sheriff's account.

"You might not know the Biden brothers. Good-looking boys without a lick of sense. Mother died ten years ago and their pa passed last winter. They've been barreling into trouble one way or another since the snow thawed. They just don't have the smarts to be good at criminal shenanigans." He shook his head as if this were a sorry circumstance.

Grant thought it was. In fact, he agreed wholeheartedly. The Biden boys' activities had caused him a great deal of sorrow. And pain. And inconvenience.

"First thing those boys did was bring your horse and saddle into the livery and sell them to Max. Max comes to my office as soon as the Bidens are out of sight. With a knock on the head like you got, you might not remember, but you'd talked to Max the day before about the Seady horses. He told you that you'd missed the sale and gave you directions to the ranch."

Grant remembered up until the next morning while he followed the trail the liveryman had detailed. Something happened, and that something was the beginning of a blank place in his memory.

The sheriff continued. "Seems one or all of those boys were in hearing distance, because they decided you must be carrying money to buy horses. They'd plotted to relieve you of your funds and put it to their own use."

His pause for effect allowed the members of the family to dwell on just what those ornery boys had in mind.

Good Ole Bess wasn't as involved with the flow of the tale as the others. "Pass the cookies, please."

The listeners stirred.

Grant thought it inconceivable that everyone's attention shifted to refreshments. Good Ole Bess waited while the plate traveled past her siblings on the left side of the table. After she'd taken one, the cookies returned down the right side. Mae got up, replenished the plate, and put the milk jug in front of Lucy. The procedure for refilling drinks, coffee, and milk, plus supplying yet another helping of cookies, wrung the last drop of Grant's patience. He couldn't demand his right to know the end of the tale. He ought to be at least as long-suffering as the little girls, but he thought he'd explode with curiosity.

Finally, the sheriff returned to his story. "I found them at the saloon. Got there before they'd spent much money on booze and gambling." He winked at Grant. "Locked up your things in my office, 'cept your money. It's in the bank under your name. Found everything I needed to identify you. Sent a letter to your folks."

Grant groaned.

Mae's eyes grew wide. "Perhaps you can write a note to them, and the sheriff will post it when he returns to town. They must be worried sick."

Grant nodded. Father, Mother, three older sisters, four older brothers, and George the cook. Worried? More likely some of them were en route to rescue the youngest son. He could do without that. His ma would be beside herself. She probably led the search and rescue party.

"Getting the truth out of the Bidens only took time. They're too stupid to lie very well. Let 'em talk and they dig their own holes to fall in." The sheriff couldn't hold back the grin on his face. "For instance, I asked where they'd seen you last. One of them says he can't tell me 'zackly 'cause he wasn't paying much attention to where they were. And he tops that by saying he didn't know where he was 'cause he was too busy keeping track of where you were."

Mae frowned, not finding the story as funny as the older grinning boys did.

The cookie platter passed by again. The sheriff picked up another.

Was that an even dozen for the lawman?

He crunched a bite then pointed with the remaining crescent. "They said you were already hurt when they got to you. Dead probably. They said you fell off your horse when it got spooked by something. Then one of them pipes up and says all horses spook at the sound of a gun going off."

"It w—wasn't f—funny," said Buckeroo.

"We were there." Though Joe-Joe's voice didn't quiver, emotion sucked out its usual volume.

Charlie pushed his empty milk glass as far from him as he could. Grant noted his attempt at distancing himself from youth failed with a telltale milk mustache bristling with stray cookie crumbs. But his serious face and sober tone testified to the true feelings behind the scamp's usually happy-go-lucky expression. "Those men weren't fooling around. They meant to kill him."

"W—we h—hid."

Joe-Joe nodded vigorously. "Of course we did. Smart thing to do."

"Right!" Charlie searched the faces of those around the table as if seeking a second to his opinion. "If I'd had my rifle, I'd a shot at 'em and scared 'em off. But we were across the canyon on the east side in the shadows. And we couldn't run across and climb that steep drop-off and do a lick of good."

"And afore you knew it," said Joe-Joe, "they rolled him over the edge, and then we could get to him."

"We—we helped him."

All three of the boys telling the tale stopped to stare at Grant. He could read the anguish in their eyes. They'd wanted to rescue him before the men left, but what could three boys do against three armed men bent on cruelty?

Grant recognized their visible torture of being inadequate. Their distress pounded at him for forgiveness. He managed a nod and said, "Thank you," much louder and clearer than he'd have thought he could.

In unison, the boys released a sigh. Their liberation from guilt lightened the whole room.

Mae stood and moved behind the twins. Her hands on their shoulders must have been light, but Grant saw strength pass from her to them. "You saved his life by getting him in the goat cart and home as fast as you did."

Charlie swallowed hard, blinked hard, and nodded hard enough to knock the cowlick into a swagger as it shot up from the crown of his head.

◆ ◆ ◆

Mae stood on the porch and breathed in the cool night air. The stars glittered across the heavens, as if she could reach out and scoop them up like a sprinkle of sugar. They couldn't be reached, of course. A lot of things in life looked attainable but were not.

The cowboy had been completely incapable of writing out what had happened to him. The sheriff eventually understood he'd have to wait another week or so, but keeping the Biden brothers under lock and key was his intent. He had evidence as well as the testimony of Charlie, Buckeroo, and Joe-Joe.

Grant had managed to write one shaky line to his folks, saying he was on the mend. She'd taken the paper from him after watching him struggle to push that pencil in all the right directions. She hadn't realized how mangled his right arm and hand were. Compared to his battered body, the arm looked pretty good.

She'd written about the boys finding him and bringing him home. Of course, she didn't mention that her parents and aunt and uncle were deceased. Nor did she mention she'd gone off to round up horses. She didn't mention she'd left Grant with the youngsters.

At the time, she'd thought he was going to hang on a few days and then die no matter what they did for him. He didn't die.

For almost a week, he'd watched her from that hideously swollen, discolored face. His calm presence occupied far too much of her thoughts. She longed to sit and gaze into his eyes and, by sheer will power, figure out what he was thinking.

Now, she knew his name. Grant Winchester. He wasn't a down-and-out cowboy, but the son of a respected rancher. That ranch was two hundred and some miles north of them and did well enough to buy the best horses. The rancher was smart enough to know that Seady horses were the best. She knew the cowboy had family and a place to go to when he recovered.

He didn't have one reason to want to hang around the Seady place. How she wished she could create a reason. Wishing was as unprofitable as dreaming. Wishing. Dreaming. Bad ideas.

Mae closed her eyes to pray. But before she really got started, a thought struck her plea like a hammer hits a nail. Her eyes shot open.

Maybe praying had slipped into that mire of bad ideas.

Chapter Six

Grant tottered along, following Robert as the young man worked with the new horses. The finely crafted crutches made by Tim and Lucy gave him amazing stability. He leaned himself and the sticks against the railings of one of the training corrals. The carved wood with padded underarm braces looked better than he did.

Grant's face had faded from black and purple to a red and brown mottle, and now sported yellow and green as predominant coloring. The swelling had subsided to the point he could use his mouth for more than an inadequate portal for mushy food.

Chewing still involved pain, but he could talk. At least now his mumble had additional clarity as far as consonants and vowels went. Everyone understood him now. And when he got tired, his fingers worked enough to manage a pencil.

He'd spent the first week following Mae with no objections from the lady herself. The little girls giggled a lot. Lucy cast him tolerant smiles. But the young men in the family never missed a chance to tease, harass, and embarrass their sister and her suitor.

Mae's patience with their shenanigans amazed him. If he were in better shape, he'd be tempted to give them a lesson in respect. But looking through Mae's eyes, he began to see their incessant ribbing as love. Their jests were never mean-spirited.

Sometimes Charlie's immaturity bested him, and his humor crossed a line that the whole family seemed to understand. Odd, but Grant saw his own brothers' mocking in the little guy's jokes. Somehow, as the Seady family forgave and directed young Charlie's banter, Grant pardoned his own brothers' misdirected wit. Old resentment lost its edge.

As the days went by, Grant wanted not only to capture the lady Mae's heart but also to join this fun-loving family.

His parents had a mountaintop-high work ethic. This parentless family wore calluses into their palms, but they raised plenty of ruckus with tomfoolery as well. Every step of the horse business involved more patience, hard work, and determination than he'd ever seen. His family might have more material security in cattle, land, and houses, but this family had a solidity built on mutual respect. Even Good Ole Bess commanded respect.

The little girl raced across the open space between the house and the barn. She grinned her wide-open smile at Grant then hurled herself up the rails to sit on the split log second from the top.

She wasn't allowed to sit on the top yet.

"It's time to do my job." She handed the sack she carried to Grant. "Carrots and apples."

Grant had watched her do this before and knew what to expect. Robert brought what he called a second-stage horse across the paddock.

First-stage horses were ready to sell. Third-stage horses were fresh off the prairie, new catches. This one was a mare in the process of gentling. Minnie Sue and Good Ole Bess interacted with these horses on a daily basis but under supervision, rigid supervision.

The wild horses were not trustworthy yet. But they would be. The Seady method of breaking and training horses led to stock that sold for a cost far above the other horse traders' animals.

Grant chuckled under his breath. The Seady horses were like the people in this family. They became an integral part of one another. Horses became trusted, intelligent partners in making a life.

Robert cut the apple he drew from the sack into quarters. Bess held it out on a perfectly straight palm. The horse warily nibbled the offering. When the mare finished the first morsel, Good Ole Bess giggled, pulled back her hand, and rubbed it on the front of her dress. She shook her curls and beamed at Grant. "She's got whiskers but not man whiskers. Her whiskers tickle."

Robert placed a second quarter of apple in her hand. The mare relaxed and enjoyed the treat without nervous twitches. The third piece was held back, giving Good Ole Bess the opportunity to stroke the mare's cheeks, utter soothing words of friendship, and even give kisses to the velvety nose. Then the horse received another two pieces of the treat, again from the very flat, small palm of a child.

Grant had seen Minnie Sue and Good Ole Bess walk beneath the great horses who were members of the family's private stock. He'd seen the children brush the horses as high as they could reach. For Bess, that was the tops of their long legs and the underside of their bellies. The horses could have been pets like overgrown kittens or dogs. Except the horses behaved better than most farm dogs Grant knew.

His father had sent Grant to investigate these animals, rumored to be the best outside of Kentucky. As the youngest in the family, he'd turned into the adventurous buyer for the Winchester ranch. The more prestigious jobs had long been claimed by his older brothers.

Traveling suited Grant. He'd never yearned to stay at home. But now he'd found a home, a place where he'd like to kick off his boots each evening. This home promised to tie strings around his heart that didn't restrain him but, rather, anchored him.

He lifted his head to the sound of another horse approaching on the road from Hopster. He noted that Gramps had disappeared from the front porch. The rider coming to visit must be known to the Seady family. Grant squinted at the figure backed by the setting sun. As the man and horse descended the near side of the hill, he finally made out the figure. The sheriff.

Grant frowned. "Why do you suppose he's here?"

Robert patted the mare's neck and moved her away from the fence. He watched the approaching man for a moment. "Maybe he has a letter from your folks."

"The sheriff delivers mail?"

"Not usually. But that would be a legitimate reason to come check up on us."

"He checks up on you?"

"He knows."

Grant didn't say anything. "He knows" could refer to something other than the obvious.

He thought he'd ask the *most* obvious. "About Gramps?"

Robert laughed. "Yeah, Gramps. And Mom and Pa, and Uncle Boss and Aunt Sue. Everything."

"Why is it all such a big secret?"

Robert ducked through the rails, plucked Good Ole Bess off the fence, and gave her a little shove toward the house. "Training's cut short, Little One. Go help put cookies on the table for the sheriff."

Bess whooped, abandoned her sack of treats, and ran to the house.

"Because when Aunt Sue died, she was the last adult. Mae was only fifteen. There was no one in charge, and Stilling wants our land in a bad way, always has. If he knew there was no adult, he'd swoop in here with all sorts of lawyers and whatever excuse it took to buy us out."

"He doesn't know?" Grant grabbed his crutches as Robert walked away from the corral.

"Apparently, he has doubts. But no proof. He's been more persistent in the last few months. Something might have tipped him off, or he's just decided to cause trouble."

The idea of the slick and rich rancher taking advantage of this family gripped at Grant's stomach. "Trouble? What kind of trouble?"

"Horses run off by a cougar, only the cougar tracks weren't convincing."

Robert stuck his head in the open barn door as they walked past. "Tim, sheriff's on the way down the hill." He continued on toward the house, Grant following.

"Another time a hog took sick, real sick. Deacon almost didn't pull him through. Now, Deacon's no fool about medical stuff. You've probably gathered that."

Grant nodded. The pace Robert had set taxed his strength. He couldn't speak and keep up.

"Well, Deacon said he thought the porker was poisoned. And he found something in the slop that he couldn't identify as having come from the house. We buried that, but it was nearly the hog we had to bury."

◆　◆　◆

Mae smiled at the men and children sitting silently around the table. Silent, that is, except for the clink of forks and murmurs of "Mmm" and "Another slice, please."

Grandma Dolly's old recipe box yielded winners every time. When the family had lived in Indiana, their crops of tomatoes overwhelmed the kitchen garden. Consequently, the lady of the farm had concocted many ways to use the fresh produce aside from canning. Ever since, it was the tomato pie that received accolades of generations.

The sheriff, claiming one pie as his own, devoured the savory meat, cheese, and tomato mixture. "Arriving at dinnertime is no coincidence, young Grant Winchester." He looped a string of melted cheese around his fork to get the morsel neatly into his mouth. "Mae learned cooking from masters. And she's passing the skill down to these darling girls."

His gaze swept around the table. Lucy ducked her head when a blush pinked her complexion like the roses skirting the porch. Minnie Sue and Good Ole Bess laughed their loud enthusiastic bray.

"All we do is stir and pour." The smallest girl picked up her wedge of tomato pie and pointed it at her sister in the chair across the table. "Minnie Sue sometimes gets to cut."

Good Ole Bess's expression melted from triumph to umbrage. "I'm 'most four. I can cut, but nobody 'lieves me." Tears welled up and spilled in abundance down her cheeks.

Charlie snitched her gooey pie from her hand. Bess wailed louder.

"And that's why Good Ole Bess is called 'Good Ole.'" He held his prize out of her reach. "She can be counted on to be sympathetic to anyone's distress and especially to her own. Crocodile tears for anyone, anytime, and for any reason."

Deacon snagged the disputed piece of tomato pie and handed it back to little Bess. "You're wrong, Charlie. Crocodile tears refer to insincere crying done for show. Good Ole Bess can be counted on for real sympathy. Her tears reflect a genuine heart of concern."

Bess sniffed and tipped her chin up in Charlie's direction. Deacon received a damp smile and a smackery kiss on the cheek.

"I have yet to tell my tale of menace and mayhem," said the sheriff.

Robert threw himself back in his chair with a hearty guffaw, but Lucy and Tim grinned at each other.

"Sometimes"—Lucy's soft voice could just be heard alongside her noisy brother's laughter—"all the books you read show up in your speech."

The sheriff winked at her. "I've got a new bundle to share with you and Tim. Don't let me forget 'em. Wouldn't do to ride all the way back to town without dropping them off." He and Tim exchanged a look of mutual enthusiasm.

But the sheriff had business on his mind. "All of us will be needing solace as we unravel the quirks of the Biden boys. I've not got it all figured out yet." He winked at Mae. "I was distracted by a good meal, but I want to share my worries before I go back to town."

Tim put down his fourth piece of tomato pie and rested his elbows on the table. "You have our attention, Sheriff."

"Someone broke the brothers out of jail."

Mae sucked in her breath. "They're loose? Could they be coming after Mr. Winchester? Surely they know his money is safely in the bank."

The lawman's chin hardened as he wagged his head back and forth. "I was stumped. This was a slick job, not a bungled affair you'd expect from any of their cohorts."

His eyes pinned Mae. "I don't think they'd come after your guest." He paused to nod at Grant.

Mae took in how much progress Grant Winchester had made in visible healing, but he was still too weak to win even arm wrestling with one of the twins.

"Certain twists to the tale have come to light that have me puzzling over an entirely different possibility in their crime. In fact, I'm thinking they didn't come up with the original idea of robbing this man of his money." He laid a gentle hand on Grant's arm. "I've been doing some investigating, and the Biden boys were temporarily employed by Jackson Heeps the day of the last horse auction."

"I don't follow," said Mae. "What difference does that make?"

"My assumption had been that the boys overheard the conversation between Max and Grant, followed Grant, and robbed him."

Robert nodded as a notion hit him. "Someone put them up to the robbery."

Tim tapped a finger on the table. "And our first suspicions turn to Stilling."

"But he wasn't around, either," objected Mae. "Remember he said he missed seeing us the last time we were in town."

All the brothers chortled and nudged one another. Robert spoke up. "He said he missed seeing *you*. Didn't bother him much that he hadn't seen the rest of us."

The sheriff grunted. "It's not fitting that an old man like Stilling should come calling on a young lady like your sister."

Grant growled deep in his throat. "He didn't miss seeing me."

The slur in Grant's words caught Mae's attention. His speech had improved, although it still tired him to force his mouth to form sentences. Now he seemed in a haste to get them out.

Every day Grant's strength increased, and Mae's admiration for the wounded man grew as well. As he regained the use of his arms and legs, he helped her out in small ways, showing he had a big heart for being a partner, not just a guest. They'd shared a lot of conversations as he began to talk.

"I disliked Stilling on sight when he came to the ranch. But now I remember it was because of a run-in with him in Hopster, before I ever saw him here."

The sheriff leaned forward. "I'm interested."

"I was having dinner at the hotel. I planned to stay the night and leave the next day to come to the Seady place. He took a seat at my table without an invitation and proceeded to disparage the reputation of Seady horses. Said he was an old family friend, and since the elders of the family had stepped out of the running of the ranch, the quality of your stock had diminished."

Mae stiffened. "He said that? He actually said that! How dare he."

Tim's big hand covered her shoulder. "Calm down, sis."

Robert looked ready to lasso the city slicker. Every muscle tensed. "Doesn't surprise me at all."

Good Ole Bess burst into tears then stopped with a big sniff. "What's 'paraged mean? What's 'minished mean?"

Deacon scooped her up and placed her quivering frame in his lap. "It means he's talking ugly about our horses, sweetie."

Grant, who had waited patiently while the family sifted through the information, gave them all a half smile. "Anyway, everything he said was slick, no straightforward claims, just hearsay and insinuation."

He grimaced, much as he had when he'd overtaxed himself trying to demonstrate his strength was returning. Mae wanted to take his hand and encourage him to proceed slowly. With her brothers as witnesses, she clasped her fingers together and laid them in her lap.

Grant cast her a quick glance, their eyes caught, and she felt the zing of support she always received from him.

He continued. "All he said contradicted what I had heard from other sources. His manner turned my stomach in a way that made me think the Lord was helping me listen to his comments with a spirit of discernment."

Mae turned to the sheriff. "Why would Stilling interfere?"

The sheriff hitched a shoulder. "I've been watching him acquire land with ease, but I've never been able to catch him in direct thievery. He's power hungry. And land greedy. He's smart, but he's too fortunate in how he just happens to be at the right place at the right time to take advantage of someone else's hardship. It adds up to some kind of skul-duggery I just haven't been able to pin on him. He's dangerous."

The sheriff looked around the table, and Mae saw him calculating the salt of each member of her family. He stopped to study Grant for a moment longer than the others.

His gaze went on to rest somewhere between Robert and Tim. "If Stilling has set his sights on your property, and I think he has, just because it's one of the last bits of prime land he doesn't already own, then I'd wager he's got schemes in place to knock your feet out from under you. Driving away your paying customers would make it hard for you. No cash flow is bad when you have to hire to bring crops in."

"I remember back in Indiana," Tim spoke up. "The farmers all helped one another with harvest. I was too little then to do much, but I remember the excitement of the crews showing up at our farm." He grinned. "I remember getting to tag along to the neighbor's harvests." He paused and his grin spread. "Mostly, I remember moms cooking all morn-ing and all afternoon to feed all those men."

The sheriff's index finger stirred the crumbs remaining on his plate. He folded his hands across his slightly rounded belly and sighed, as if he regretted leaving the subject of food and returning to serious matters. "Your folks were here a full ten years before the flood, weren't they?"

The Seady children nodded in unison. Mae's eyes darted to their injured guest. "The flood" had a significance that they hadn't shared with Grant.

She saw the intelligent spark in his eyes. He'd made the connection. Her parents and uncle had died in that flood. That was the beginning of their saga as the family without a head. When Bess turned four in a few weeks, their success in beating the odds would have reached six months beyond her existence.

Did God hold their nemesis at bay for just this time? Perhaps they had a champion besides the covert support of the sheriff in keeping their situation a secret. Were the Seady children now the Seady family—a force to be reckoned with supported by the sheriff and a stranger?

Chapter Seven

Robert gave Grant a job dealing with the stage-two horses and their training. Grant chortled. He'd been given responsibility at one level of risk above the duties given to Minnie Sue and Good Ole Bess.

The girls sat on the rails of the corral fencing and offered treats, head rubs, words of endearment, kisses, and snuggles. Grant hobbled among the animals within the pen, offering treats, head rubs, body brushes, and yes, kind words, kisses, and snuggles.

At first, the horses regarded his crutches as a sign of evil intent. Gradually, they accepted this human with wooden appendages. Following the family's example, Grant moved slowly, spoke softly, and gave lots of affection in the physical form of food, grooming, spoken words, and soft, unnecessary touches.

Mae sashayed across the yard.

Grant lost interest in what he was doing.

The wind blew her flowered green skirt against her long legs, and the late-afternoon sun kissed red sparks into her blond tresses. No prettier woman had ever crossed his path. No angel had ever smiled at him the way she did. No soft rosy lips had ever begged for his attention.

And he still looked like assorted pieces of butchered venison, tied up in rags and hand-me-downs. He moved like a four-legged creature made up of old parts. Why she even took time to talk with him, he'd never know.

He'd been at the Seady horse farm for thirty-three days and still wouldn't be able to muster up enough strength to defend her against danger. He couldn't take her for a drive in the only buggy the Seadys stored in the barn. He couldn't ask her to dance at the Founders' Day Hoopla in Hopster. Charlie said not to worry about that. Last year was the first time any of them had gone, and just Deacon, Robert, and Tim attended.

Mae reached the corral and stepped up one rung. "Have any of you seen Charlie?"

Robert and Grant exchanged a look. A slight shake of the head answered their unspoken question.

"Nope," Robert answered. "Deacon and Tim are working with that stallion that kicked through his stall and injured a leg."

Mae looked toward the barn. "Charlie took Tuppy and the twins out with the cart to gather kindling in the woods. Buckeroo and Joe-Joe came back for lunch. They said Charlie decided to fish."

Her gaze drifted off to the small stand of woods a mile distant, toward the mountains. "He should have been home long since."

Robert had been soothing a nervous mare by gently stroking her back with a saddle blanket. He folded the heavy cloth and hung it over the top rail. "Fish don't bite much in the afternoon. He knows that. He probably had some mischief in mind." He chortled. "Or some laziness. I'll saddle one of the more amiable stage-two horses and give him a ride. Perchance I'll find our errant brother sleeping in the shade or building a dam where we don't want the stream stopped."

The wind swirled the dust. "I wouldn't worry, but—" Mae captured a long wisp of her hair the wind had freed. She tucked it behind an ear and nodded toward the range. "A storm's brewing over Higgin's Peak."

"No need to fuss, sis. He knows better than to hang around a draw when there might be heavy rain upstream."

"He's a careless boy." Mae sighed. Grant wanted to take all her burdens away. She squinted against the wind. "Charlie's not given to much thinking when he should be paying attention."

Minnie Sue climbed down the outside of the paddock. "Come on, Good Ole Bess. We know all of Charlie's hiding places."

"You girls aren't going by yourselves." Mae chased Minnie Sue and apprehended her with a hand on her arm. The quick little rascal had made it halfway across the open yard between the horse-training rings and the picket fence in front of the house.

She stomped one small, booted foot. "We'll take Joe-Joe and Buckeroo."

"I've got them weeding bean rows. They've neglected their garden chore for two weeks and almost got away with a third. And to make up for shirking, they're carrying water buckets to the late squash."

Good Ole Bess had pumped her legs hard to scramble down from her perch and catch up with her sisters. "I want to peek under the big leaves and see the baby pumpkins."

Minnie Sue shook her finger at Bess. "It's more important to haul Charlie outta trouble."

"I'll go with the girls." Grant let himself out of the gate and carefully latched it behind him. "I think I can keep up with them." He smiled first at Mae then at the two girls bouncing beside her.

"Pleeeease!" They spoke in unison, dragging the word out as long as they could hold. Minnie Sue ran out of breath first, leaving Bess with a triumphant smirk.

"Sure, he can go." Robert turned and walked backward as he headed to the barn door. "Take Tuppy and the cart. The girls know the way to the fishing pond. It's a bumpy trail."

In only a few minutes, Grant sat on the makeshift seat of the old goat cart, reins in hand, the two girls standing behind him. With their feet in the bed of the cart, they leaned against him on either side, each holding one of his arms. His healing leg ached only a bit. The grin on his face hurt a whole lot more, but he was so glad to be out and doing something useful, he couldn't stifle the smile.

Evidently, Buckeroo and Joe-Joe were making up for a whole lot of slipshod chores. They'd had to unload the kindling and stack it in the kitchen, before they even began in the garden. Neither one expressed any joy at being left out of the adventure of saving Charlie, wherever he was. But they didn't grumble, either. One look from Mae, and their expressions slid into masks of compliance. Not quite cheerful compliance, but pretty close.

Her last words to the boys were, "I want to hear some whistling while you work."

To those heading out to search for Charlie, she said, "Watch the sky."

Goat cart and horse rode out together, but Robert ran his frisky mare around to the other side of the stand of woods. Grant guided Tuppy through the high grass on a trail somewhat beaten down by earlier traffic.

"This is the way they went," announced Good Ole Bess.

"This is the way we always go." Minnie Sue pointed to a break in the tree line. "There's a swimming hole we go to when it's really, really hot. The water's chilly."

"It's really snow from the mountaintops."

Minnie Sue sniffed her scorn. "Not when it gets to us it's not. It's melted."

"But it once was snow. The same snow we can see on the peaks taller than Higgins."

"That's true," admitted Minnie Sue. "We aren't allowed to swim there alone, 'cause cold water can give you a cramp, and a cramp can make you drown."

"We gots lots of water."

"That's what makes our land so rich."

"Land can be rich?" asked Bess. "I thought only mean peoples like Mr. Stilling was rich."

"Rich means good for cattle and crops and stuff. Rich land means rich people want it."

"Oh."

Grant stifled both a grin and a chortle. The little girls' conversation had delighted him even before he could get out of bed.

The wind picked up and a sheet of lightning brightened the dark clouds miles away, hovering over the peaks.

"Mae doesn't like storms." Good Ole Bess hugged Grant's arm harder.

He suspected the girls didn't, either, but perhaps they weren't as clear on just why storms held a special fear for their big sister.

"We'll stay out of the gullies." Grant clicked his tongue and jiggled the reins against the goat's back. "And we'll bring Charlie home as soon as we can."

The goat quickened his pace as if he caught the urgency of their mission. Ruts and reaching tree roots jolted the goat cart once they passed under the canopy of thick aspen. The coin-shaped leaves clattered as the wind whipped through the forest. The air thickened with the weight of moisture in the coming storm.

"Call for Charlie," Grant instructed his two companions. "Then stop and listen for his answer."

"Charlie! Charlie!" His name bounced among the straight, white-barked trees.

Grant slowed at a fork in the sketchy path. Minnie Sue pointed to the right. "That's the way to the caves." The left branch looked to be used more often. "The stream, waterhole, and felled timber's that way."

"Charlie's supposed to be fishing?" Grant gazed down the beaten path to the waterhole.

"Yep." The girls spoke in unison.

"So let's try the caves first." He guided Tuppy into the higher grass. "Keep calling his name."

The tumble of distant thunder changed its tune as they moved closer to the caves and the foothills. A flash of light and snap of air masses colliding brought the girls clambering over the low bench to squeeze in next to Grant.

"I hope he's not in a gully." Minnie Sue's fingers dug into Grant's flesh. All Bess could do was nod, but since her face was buried in his upper arm, he felt her response.

"We're going uphill, bit by bit." Grant wanted to reassure them, but he hoped the reckless boy was on high ground. "The real danger is lower, where the water rushes off and joins together in cuts across the plains."

Bess jerked to her feet. Grant's arms snagged her. "What are you doing?"

"I heard him."

Grant reined Tuppy to a halt. They all three quieted, straining to hear above the wind playing havoc with the branches above them.

Bess sucked in a huge breath. "Charlie!" Her holler should have been heard all the way back at the ranch house.

"I'm here. Over here. I'm stuck."

Minnie Sue hit the ground first, on her feet and ready to rush off.

"Wait for me." Grant went over the side and pulled his crutches from the back. Good Ole Bess was beside him and holding Minnie Sue's hand by the time he was ready to go.

"Keep yelling. We'll follow your voice." Grant ignored the twinges as his muscles objected to hard use. Occasionally, the pain caught his breath, but he managed to keep up with the determined sisters.

They halted at the top of a ditch. The ground dropped away, and the debris showed evidence of a recent slide. Charlie sat at the bottom.

"Charlie." Minnie Sue's bossiest voice blustered against the wind. "What are you doing down there?"

"The side gave way, and my foot's caught in all this rock and dirt and branches."

"I'm coming." Grant did a quick survey of the area. "Stay here a minute, girls."

He moved over a couple of feet, sat on the edge, put his crutches above his head, and with a push, sent himself sliding down the loose siding of the natural trench.

After hitting the bottom, he gasped a couple of deep breaths before he could prop himself up and hobble to Charlie's side. Several rocks the size of bread loaves clustered around his leg and buried his foot.

Grant put aside his crutches and grabbed one to roll aside. Before he pulled, he stopped. The possible desperation of their situation blindsided him. "Are you hurt?"

"Not much. I don't think anything's broken." Charlie's nonchalance wasn't damaged. "I've got on my good boots."

"That's a blessing."

Charlie struggled to sit up straighter. "Not altogether. They're really Deacon's old boots he hasn't really given to me yet."

Good Ole Bess's cry could be heard from above.

Minnie Sue hushed her and then called down, "Is he broken?"

"Not too bad." But how was he going to get him up the crumbling ravine? He'd jumped before thinking. Caring about the kid had impaired his normal clear thinking. Not good. Charlie was the least likable of the Seadys, and even this kid had him entangled. The oddest part of the whole setup was that he liked being interwoven in this family.

He grinned up at the angels. "Can you go get the rope from the cart? We'll need it."

The girls scampered off.

"Let's get you free before they return. You can holler if it hurts."

Charlie clamped his lips together as if pure torture would not pry them open for even a squeak.

After the first two rocks, Charlie helped dig his foot out. Fire scorched Grant's ribs, and his leg screamed like he'd rebroken the healing bone. He knew a few moments of rest would put him right. At least, right enough to get back to the ranch.

Minnie Sue's head appeared over the lip of the ravine. "Here's the rope."

"Wait!"

"I thought you wanted the rope."

"Don't throw it down. Pass one end around a tree trunk then lower that end. Keep the other end up there with you."

"I can do that!"

While they waited, Grant leaned back against the crumbly side, stretched out and almost comfortable since he wasn't moving.

He glanced over at Charlie, who was dirty and tired but definitely not repentant for causing trouble. "What brings you to this part of the woods?"

"I was sneaking away from those two men so I could get back to warn the others."

"About what?"

"The fire."

"What fire?"

"The one that isn't going to be started by a lightning strike."

"Charlie?"

"Yep, it was those two troublemakers." He scrunched his face. "I think."

"Just think?"

"I heard them plotting, but I didn't actually see them."

"Charlie? Grant?"

Grant looked up where Good Ole Bess's face peered over the edge.

"Yes, little angel?'

"Minnie Sue and me, we smell smoke."

Chapter Eight

A little fear gives a big push." Many of his father's sayings rang true. And they snapped him to attention at the most apropos times.

They tied one end of the rope around Charlie's small waist. The rope looped around a tree, and Grant pulled as if it were strung through a pulley, hoisting the boy out. Charlie helped. The girls cheered.

Now Grant rested in the ditch with both ends of the rope at his command. Smoke swirled at the top. The need to get them all to safety gave Grant the push he needed.

"Charlie!"

The boy's tousled head of muddy-blond hair appeared over the edge, followed by his dirt-encrusted face. Even in these circumstances, he sported a cocky grin. "What next?"

"I'm sending up one of my crutches for you to use. Tie the rope to the tree. It's up to you to get the girls to Tuppy and then back to the ranch. Warn the others about the fire."

On cue, Good Ole Bess's keening howl rose above that of the wind. "You come, too. You come now."

Grant had already made a loose knot around one crutch and hauled on the opposite rope. "Now, Bess, it's going to take me awhile to wiggle out of this ditch. It's important that your big brothers come. The sooner you three get help, the better."

"Hurry!" Minnie Sue's command could have been to any of them, her sister, her brother, or her cowboy.

Grant could see her in his mind's eye as she went on. "Charlie, you wait and get the crutch. Give me your hand, Good Ole Bess. We can run fast. We'll turn Tuppy and the cart around before Charlie even gets there." Her last line was delivered as she left, probably over her shoulder as she dragged poor Bess behind. "Mr. Cowboy, we'll save you."

Grant strained his ears to listen to their departure. When he no longer heard their voices or Charlie's grunts, he collapsed, sliding down to sit against a fallen log. He held the second crutch in one hand and the rope in the other.

At least Charlie and the girls were on higher ground.

Pain from each of his healing injuries brought all his senses to a sharp awareness of reality. He'd already used what energy he could pull from his weakened body. He gritted his teeth against expressing his anguish with something that would surely come out as a scream.

Those buffoons had managed to start a fire. Perhaps the rain would fall in torrents and snuff the flames before they spread. Perhaps the torrent of rain upstream would gather and crash through this gully in a few minutes' time. Staying in the gully was not an option. Moving promised to be agonizing.

He closed his eyes. "Dear Lord, guide the children quickly and safely home. Give Charlie the determination to take his sisters straight to Mae without succumbing to any distractions. Don't allow him any 'bright ideas.' Have Minnie Sue use her gift of bossiness to good end. No squabbles to slow them down. Bless the goat. Make him cooperative. Protect them, Lord, from fire, floods, and those brutes loose in the area."

He opened his eyes and glanced around. "Help me get out of this hole in the ground. Amen."

"And the crutch? How am I supposed to carry the crutch?"

Grant undid the top buttons of his shirt and pulled the tail out. With difficulty, he managed to force the crutch under the shirt collar at the nape of his neck. He eased it down between his shoulder blades until only the padding rested against the back of his head.

He stood, holding the rope securely in both hands. "One more thing, Lord. The knot Charlie tied to anchor this rope? Please hold it secure. Amen, again."

The slick soles of his boots refused to grip the decomposing forest rubble. He had to slide his right foot back and forth seeking a root or rock that would hold his weight with each step up. Only his left leg would hoist his body upward.

Every effort hurt one or more parts of his body. Some headway up the slope hurt all of his body, every single muscle. A slip thudded his side against a nubby root and reminded him his broken ribs were still tender. Very tender. He thought that particular clumsy bump took them from bruised back to broken.

Vocalizing took his mind off the aches. Since he was panting, the tune he chose didn't much resemble the actual song. But the melody was one Mae sang as she swept, and somehow the strong beat helped him concentrate on making each effort in a timely manner.

Mae would be relieved when the goat approached the house. Without a doubt, Tim and Deacon would soon be on their way to retrieve the straggler. He hadn't made hero status on this endeavor. Grant shook his head as his pride raised its ugly voice in his brain.

As long as the children were safe, his self-image really didn't matter. But he had plans, and failing to get out of this gully would end them all. He renewed the vigor of his song and pictured Mae sitting at the top of the ravine, waiting for him.

He crested the ledge and found no alluring woman. Victory over the elements smelled heavy of smoke and sounded like wind swept before a crackling fire. Lying with his face in a cool, soft deposit of old leaves, Grant felt the hot breath of a giant on his back.

He twisted to a position where he could undo his buttons. If he'd had the strength to tear his shirt to bits, he wouldn't have bothered to wiggle out of the sleeves. Measuring time was a lost cause. Pulling one arm out nearly wasted him. The second was easier in terms of pain, but must have taken twice as long. Every effort required recovery, panting, and waiting for spasms to subside.

As the crutch fell away, he stretched out on his back. After a pause, he wrapped his shirt around his head, covering this nose and mouth from the smoke. He allowed his body another few moments of respite.

"Dear Lord, help me."

Grant managed to get to his knees. Then, leaning on this crutch, he unbent his mangled form and stood on one leg.

Wind kept the smoke moving. A real fire. He couldn't ignore that threat. Just where was this fire?

The sounds worried him. Thrashing branches cracked. Fire consuming wood crack-led. Grant heard both. He turned his back on the loudest and moved toward the last place he'd seen Tuppy and the cart.

◆ ◆ ◆

Mae swung up and into the saddle. Deacon and Tim had already followed Robert, but she had taken the twins inside, changed clothes, and given Lucy as many instructions as could possibly come pouring out of her mouth in that short time.

She looked at the house. She'd left Lucy terrified. Her fault. Hiding the fear of a storm had always been impossible for her. Buckeroo and Joe-Joe were confused and rebellious. Again her fault. She hadn't handled ordering them around diplomatically. They already chafed under the discipline imposed when she'd discovered how much work they'd let slide.

Lightning flashed too near the ranch home. The clap of thunder nearly unseated her. The horse sidled toward the barn. Mae could manage the horse. The rest of her life seemed to be unravelling.

She turned her attention on the woods. Like Lucy, she was terrified. "Oh Father, calm her heart. Mine, too."

To ride out with the others to look for Charlie, she labeled a necessity. No other option. No choice.

Another jagged finger of electricity stabbed the trees on the mountain side of the woods. Thunder raised goose bumps along her arms. The children needed her.

Only three were in the confines of the sturdy house. She needed to gather all her chicks. Robert, Tim, Deacon, and Grant all searched. Was another adult really needed? Grant was still an invalid. Well, mostly. And the little girls were the best in a crisis, but still little.

Mae was confused. "Father, I don't know whether to stay or go. I was sharp with the twins. They don't know why they had to go inside. It's not more of the punishment. Make them understand. I know this storm isn't Your punishment for me. It's just a storm. I don't know which direction to go. Guide me."

Storms beat at her in a place hidden deep inside. The rain battered at her confidence that she could withstand the elements. Not just weather. Life.

One torrential downpour took her security. Soft, gentle, life-giving rain bathed the hay fields. Harsh, destructive, cruel rain murdered her father, mother, and uncle. Must everything in life have a vicious side?

The smoldering heat of confusion fueled the hard black coal of fear. She could face this uncertainty daily, even hourly, or she could cast it off.

"Father," she yelled. The horse pranced beneath her, startled by the outburst. "Heavenly Father, I'm sick of the tyranny of fear. I know where to make my allegiance. I cast all my cares upon You. I'm rebelling, Lord. Not against You, but joining You and Your heavenly forces who care for me. You care for my family. If You are for me, who can be against me?"

Mae paused, tightening the reins to hold back the horse who pranced as if to escape the duty ahead of them. The storm pricked at the animal's nerves. Her rant provoked more excitement. One more stimulant pressed in on Mae and her ride. Smoke.

She turned the horse's head away from the ranch and rode out toward the storm at a gallop. Gray smoke billowed from the far side of the woods. Black clouds crested the mountain peaks and rolled downward. From the break in the woods, Tuppy emerged.

Something was wrong.

Surely, she should be able to see a taller person among the three in the cart.

Chapter Nine

Where's Grant?"

The simple question reduced Good Ole Bess to wails and prompted an eruption of nonstop explanation from Charlie and Minnie Sue.

Mae somehow understood it all. She got off her horse and handed the reins to Charlie. "You ride to town, get the sheriff and men to help stop the fire."

The rapscallion's face lit up. He jumped straight from the cart to the back of the horse. Before Mae could add all the precautions springing to her lips, he'd dug in his heels. He and the horse exploded into motion, leaving the others on the little goat track.

After a moment of watching her younger brother disappear at a breakneck speed, Mae sighed heavily and went to Tuppy's head.

"You, fine gentleman, you." She stroked his cheeks and the tuft between his horns. "You've served our family with pluck, but we must turn around and count on you one more time."

Minnie Sue jumped to the ground. She helped guide the cart backward into higher grass and then out on the barely visible path. "What are we gonna do, Mae?"

"Go back and get Mr. Winchester."

"You called him Grant before."

Good Ole Bess sniffed long and hard. "We call him Mr. Cowboy."

"She knows that, silly." Minnie Sue went to the side of the cart. "Where's your handkerchief? You've got slime running out of your nose."

Bess lifted the hem of her grubby apron to her nose, gave a big blow, then wiped up.

Minnie Sue shook her head. "Who's teaching you manners? One of the boys? Get down and walk awhile so that Tuppy can rest. He's gonna carry Mr. Cowboy."

Two more bolts of lightning broke through the sky before Mae and the girls reached the line of trees. The thunder rattled the earth. Good Ole Bess whimpered and clung to Minnie Sue's hand. The smell of smoke saturated the air, but the stiff breeze kept it from gathering into cloudlike mists.

"Where'd all the smoke go?" Minnie Sue tugged on Mae's shirtsleeve. "Where'd all the smoke go?"

"Burning clean." Good Ole Bess's voice sounded authoritative. She loved to watch her brothers build a fire.

"Uh-oh." Thunder punctuated Minnie Sue's ominous utterance. "That means the fire's caught good, not just messing around."

"We need water! Lots of water to douse it." Good Ole Bess stopped in the track, halting Mae, Tuppy, and Minnie Sue as well.

A flash of lightning above the leafy trees. An immediate ear-popping clap, and all three girls jumped toward one another. Tuppy drummed his front feet and backed up.

Mae soothed the goat with a hand on his neck. "There, there, Tuppy. The fire is still three miles or more away."

She reached out to herd the girls along, but Good Ole Bess had fallen to her knees.

With her hands clasped in front of her and her head bowed, the little girl prayed, "Dear God, we don't need all this noisy thunder. We do need rain. Just stop hollering about the storm and get to it. You can help us save Mr. Cowboy and put out the fire and make everyone be happy." She stood up, dropped down again, and closed her eyes tight. "Please. Amen."

A bubble of nervous laughter choked Mae. Her little cousin was right, but a tad disrespectful. "Yes, Lord," she added to the prayer. "Please give us aid where we need it. I thought the fire looked like it was headed to the hay fields. Our timber is wet from all the nice summer rains You've sent. That's Your doing. Thank You." She started walking, leading Tuppy. "We pray for everyone's safety, including ours."

Minnie Sue caught Good Ole Bess's hand again and gave her a tug. "And dear Father in heaven, make everyone hurry up!"

Under the canopy of aspen, grass covered ruts in the track. Mae put Good Ole Bess in the bed of the cart. That small amount of weight lessened the old frame's bouncing over the uneven ground.

At the fork that determined the destination of pond or caves, they found Grant crumpled into a heap. Not stretched out, but folded inward, his splinted leg stuck out to one side.

Minnie Sue reached him first. She patted him on the back. "You don't look comfy."

Mae rushed forward and landed on her knees beside his shoulders. Gently she lifted his head. Forest grime clung to his forehead. "Help me turn him onto my lap."

"Wait for me!" Good Ole Bess scrambled down and ran to do her share of pushing.

Grant groaned as he settled against Mae's leg.

She stroked bits of leaf and dirt away from his eyes, ears, and mouth. "Wake up, Grant. Wake up. Oh, please, wake up."

His eyes fluttered then opened. He gazed straight up into Mae's face. He still wore ugly signs of his encounter with the Biden brothers, but she thought he was the most handsome of any man she'd ever encountered. The corners of his mouth tipped up.

Good Ole Bess clapped her hands and bounced. "He waked."

Grant sent a swift smile to her and Minnie Sue, but his eyes settled again on Mae. "I'm surrounded by angels, pretty, prettier, and prettiest of all."

Warmth tingled in Mae's cheeks. The embarrassing heat had nothing to do with the hot breeze.

Minnie Sue slapped her hands against her thighs then stood. "We gotta turn Tuppy again. But this is the last time. I wanna go home."

She marched over to the goat. "I'm tired and hungry. I bet you're tired and hungry, too. And Mr. Cowboy is tired and hungry and hurting again." She turned to address her cousins. "Well, come on."

Fat drops of rain hit singly, plopping on the leaves above. A scattered few reached the small group of people and the cool forest floor.

Good Ole Bess jumped to her feet and did a short, clumsy jig. "Hurray! God says yes." She grabbed Mae's arm and pulled. "Don't be scared, Mae. This is God's *good* rain."

The ladies redirected the cart, while Grant struggled to sit and then stand.

"Oh!" Mae ran to him as he started to straighten his torso. "You should have waited a minute more. We're here to help."

His chest rose and fell in shallow gasps, and his pasty white pallor alarmed her. She put one of his arms around her shoulders and tucked herself in well to support him. They took slow steps toward the rear of the cart.

"Quarter-cup." Grant muttered as Mae's hands embraced his sides to maneuver him to a sitting position on the back edge.

"What?" She stopped to look him full in the face. He was very, very close. Him sitting, her standing put them nose to nose. His breath puffed against her cheek. Oh my, his eyes were a beautiful, deep brown.

"Quarter-cup." He smiled and moved forward the inch it took to press his lips to hers. The movement was faster than lightning. That small touch hit her with the full force of a monumental clap of thunder.

"Quarter-cup," he repeated with a silly grin. "Each raindrop holds a quarter-cup. When a rain begins with large, heavy drops, the storm will break and spill the sky on the land. But the bucket will empty quickly."

"Huh?"

He laughed, a low rumble in his chest. She knew because the palm of her hand rested right where his heart must be.

"Miss Mae, are you always so befuddled when a gentleman kisses you?"

Oh my. She'd been kissed. The peck had not been a mistake or her imagination. The girls! She'd been kissed in front of the girls? Her head swiveled as she searched for them.

They stood a dozen steps away, side by side, holding hands, staring, and grinning.

Minnie Sue whooped. "Mr. Cowboy's gonna marry Mae."

Mae leaned in, her body, if not her prudence, yearning for a hug. She straightened, jerked her hands down to her side, and backed away.

The clouds chose that moment to quit fooling around with a few drips. As effective as a bucket of water over her head, the dousing awakened her from her stupor. She hauled in a deep breath, whipped around, and stomped to the goat's head.

"Get in with your cowboy, girls. Make him lie down. I'll lead Tuppy."

She kept her eyes forward, looking toward the ranch.

She couldn't look at him. Her face went all hot again each time she thought of the kiss. The warmth also settled in her chest. Her lungs couldn't get air in and out in an efficient manner.

And the thought of fire and storms? Any whisper of impending doom had taken flight from her thoughts. All she could think of was the cowboy being jostled around in the small wooden cart behind her favorite goat.

Frequent use had worn down the grass on the last part of the track as they approached the house. The wheels of the cart slipped and slithered on a thin sheen of mud. Mae led the goat right into the barn. Good Ole Bess jumped down and ran to her side.

"Mr. Cowboy is groaning and wet. I'm wet, too."

Joe-Joe and Buckeroo burst through the opening, out of the soaking rain and into the relative quiet of the horse stable.

Buckeroo shook water off like a dog. "Wh–what's going on?"

Joe-Joe smacked into the cart and grabbed Grant's arm, trying to pull him out. "From the girls' room, we could see smoke and then fire."

"You aren't allowed in our room!" Minnie Sue's voice registered two decibels louder and an octave higher than her brothers'.

"L–Lucy s–said c–come l–look!"

"So we weren't doing anything wrong."

Mae rushed to Joe-Joe's side. "Quit pulling on him. Can't you see he's hurt?"

Joe-Joe dropped Grant's arm and stood back in astonishment. "You mean more hurt than usual? How'd that happen?"

"We"—Minnie Sue's voice commanded respect—"found Charlie and rescued him."

Buckeroo looked around then scratched his head. "If you r–rescued Charlie, wh–where is he?"

Good Ole Bess managed to speak before her sister. "Off to get the sheriff."

"The sheriff!" Joe-Joe's eyes widened, and his mouth fell open before he gathered himself enough to say, "Wow!"

Buckeroo let out a long whistle.

Lucy, with a shawl held over her head against the rain, skidded to a stop just inside the barn door. "What happened?"

Outpourings of explanation filled the air, but one word silenced them all.

"Enough!" Mae ran an eye over all of them, skipping the cowboy in the cart just behind her. "Buckeroo and Joe-Joe, unhitch Tuppy and make him comfortable. He's worked valiantly this afternoon. Give him some of the branches you cut from the willow tree."

She dismissed them with a wave of her hand. "Lucy, help me get Mr. Winchester to the house. The girls need dry clothes."

Grant, who had been strangely quiet, lifted a hand and with one finger turned Mae's face toward his. "I'm wet, too. I should have dry clothes."

Somehow, during the time she had detached Joe-Joe from the cowboy's arm and shooed him away, she'd moved closer. He must have boosted himself to a half-stand, still leaning against the cart.

His arm was around her waist. Was she holding him up?

His chest was bare. His wet shirt hung around his neck, over his shoulders, like a granny's shawl. Mae's eyes slipped, and she focused on the expanse of hairy chest level with her nose. Not like a granny in any way, shape, or form.

"Lucy!" Her call squeaked out on a breath of air. She cleared her throat. "Help me get Mr. Winchester to the house. Girls, run ahead and change your clothes."

Good Ole Bess's voice registered distress. "Can we help Mr. Cowboy get his dry shirt? He's hurt again. Bad."

A strong arm squeezed Mae closer into Grant's side. She couldn't help but turn to see his reaction. His eyes twinkled. She felt the laughter he suppressed. His fingertips wiggled against her side, urging her to giggle.

"Mr. Cowboy!" That squeak. She cleared her throat *again*. "No, Bess, Mr. Cowboy is strong enough to deal with his own clothes."

Lucy's grin should have split her face. She moved to Grant's other side. "We need to get you some hot tea for your throat, Mae. I think you're coming down with something."

Chapter Ten

The twins reported from their post at the window in the girls' room.

"No more smoke. Can't see the trees, either," Joe-Joe complained. "It's raining so hard, we can barely see the barn from Mae's room."

Lucy had given the girls a bath in the long narrow room next to the kitchen. Firewood for the house and kitchen lined the two side walls. A door to the outside and a door to the inside just fit between the stacks. A bathtub sat in the middle of the room and hung on the wall when not in use.

Grant sat in a chair beside the tub, doing his best to wash up in the tepid water. Buckeroo came in with a stack of folded clothes.

Grant recognized the material of one shirt. "Where did—?"

"The sheriff d–dropped off your saddlebag and a p–pack and your g–gun belt b–before he went chasing after T–Tim and Robert. He said 'at this point in time' p–putting the fire out was m–more important than catching the B–Bidens."

Grant nodded. "Right. Even three Bidens on the loose couldn't be as destructive as a wildfire."

"Exceptin' if you c–count it w–w–was the B–Bidens who started it."

"You've got a point."

Buckeroo grinned at the faint praise. "You w–want me to help pull your socks off?"

In answer, Grant angled his leg toward the eager boy. "Where's Charlie?"

"He r–rode out with the men. L–Lucy told him to s–stay, but he d–didn't mind." Buckeroo made a face but didn't utter any condemnation that might have crossed his mind.

With the twin's help, Grant changed all his clothing and washed most of his body. He was tuckered by the time they'd fastened the last button on his shirt.

Joe-Joe stomped his feet as he dragged the crutches in and thrust them into Grant's hands. "Get moving, Buck. Mae's cooking up a feast. She says all those men who went to put out the fire will surely come back this way. She needs to feed 'em, and we gotta do the little stuff she's too busy to do."

"Where's Lucy?" The indignant tone gave away Buckeroo's opinion of helping in the kitchen.

"Busy."

"M–Minnie Sue and—?"

"Asleep."

"Asleep?"

"On the sofa. Mae says there was just too much excitement for two little girls."

"M–man, I'm n–never letting you t–talk me out of d–doing chores again."

"This isn't part of the penance for shirking. This is extra."

"It's still y–your f–fault."

The boys stomped out of the room. Grant followed on crutches, clumsily maneuvering through the tight doorway. He beelined to the table before Mae could kick him out of her domain. He knew she'd liked their kiss by the way she refused to look at him. Women could be fun when flustered. Mae was adorable and fun.

"What can I do to help?"

"Drink this." She placed a mug of something hot in front of him.

He knew by the tinge of the liquid and the scent that this herbal concoction eased his pain. He didn't quibble. He needed something to take the sting out of his sore muscles.

Mae usually talked with him as she prepared the meal. Many days, she'd given over the chopping knife into his capable hands. This evening she handed him carrots, knife, and board, but she avoided his eyes and didn't speak.

Grant sipped the soothing brew to ease the pain, and chopped in a frenzy to mitigate his frustration.

"Small pieces," instructed the woman he loved. "We need this stew to cook quickly."

"Doesn't the name *stew* imply a long time simmering?"

"Not this time."

She whisked away the board and its small mound of carrots to slide them into her biggest pot. She returned an empty board and stacked potatoes at Grant's elbow. Within thirty minutes, pounds of finely chopped vegetables roiled in a beefy broth.

He downed two-and-a-half mugs of tea, and the greatest pain he felt at the moment was the distance Mae had put between them. Not physically—they were in the same room.

But her pleasure at his attentions had vanished. Maybe he was wrong. Maybe she hadn't liked the kiss.

She stood at the sink with her back to him, washing dishes.

Grant managed to stand with only a few scrapes of the wooden legs against the floor to announce his movement. Surveying the room, he saw the two little girls asleep, piled together on the fine cushions of a large sofa. The boys remained upstairs but hadn't reported on the amount of rain that blinded their view. Lucy had a book and sat in a chair near the front window.

With careful steps and only one crutch, he crept up behind Mae. He captured her waist with one arm and pulled her back against his chest.

She stiffened.

Heartened by the fact that she didn't yelp or pull away, Grant laid his cheek against the crown of her head.

She sighed.

He allowed his lips to nuzzle her ear, then trailed kisses down her neck.

She leaned back.

"Mae," he whispered. "You and I don't need to stew. We'll have years to simmer. If—" He leaned the crutch against the counter and used both hands to gently turn her around. "If you marry me, I promise we'll do some mighty fine cooking."

She tilted her head up. He took advantage of that tempting angle and kissed her.

He could have held her in his arms and continued the delight of touching, smelling, sensing her joy in being his love for as long as the family stayed occupied elsewhere.

She pulled back.

"No, Grant. I can't. My family."

He recaptured her lips. She slipped away with a slight move of her head. His mouth was next to her ear. Hers lingered near his.

"No man wants a woman encumbered by a family. Not just a sister or a brother, but *nine* people who depend on me. They *need* me."

Joe-Joe bellowed down the stairs. "Mae! They're coming!"

◆　◆　◆

Mae busied herself with bowls, mugs, spoons, and glasses. Hot stew, cold well water, hot coffee, warm biscuits, cold butter and milk from the root cellar. The room smelled of steaming clothing. The men had swaggered in, buckets of water dripping from their soaked shirts and pants. Two dozen pairs of boots lined up on the porch.

The storm had eased into a dwindling drizzle, but the tumult in Mae's heart kept her from focusing on anything. Moving through the motions of hospitality, she served the men. Their tales of a long ride and an acre of hay and a smattering of trees blackened by the quick flames and doused by rain only touched the fringe of her thoughts.

Like fiber in a loom, the warp and woof wove back and forth, in and out, and all the cross threads were Grant Winchester. She couldn't detach herself from his presence. She doubted she ever would be able to. Each interchange entwined their lives, weaving them into a single cloth. That's what she wanted.

Lord, there is no way. No way I can see. But I trust You. You can see the end of this trail.

Her prayers scattered and resurfaced as she took care of the mealtime routines, until an unnatural quiet settled over the room and grabbed her attention. Charlie stood beside the sheriff. Every eye was fastened on him. For once, his cocky air sunk under the weight of what he had to tell.

"I snuck up on them. I didn't let them see me 'cause I know from before—" His eyes drifted over to Grant. He swallowed hard but responded when the cowboy nodded his encouragement. "I know how mean they can be. They were angry. They kept saying *he* didn't take any of the chances, and *he* didn't want to get dirty, and *he* this and *he* that, just lots and lots of complaints about this man."

The sheriff's big hand rested on the boy's shoulder. "Get to the part about the fire, Charlie."

"They were supposed to set a fire so people would think a lightning strike started it." Charlie imitated the Biden brothers' voices.

"How we gonna do that?"

"Climb a tree and set the fire at the top where the lightning would hit."

"Lightning don't hit at the top."

"It does!"

"Not just at the top, you stupid—" Charlie stopped and looked around the room. "I gotta leave some of it out, 'cause Mae doesn't let us say some of the words they said."

Mae smiled at him. He was caught up in being the center of attention, but he'd remembered their code of clean talk. And his gift of mimicry. . .she could almost hear the rough men and pick out the different personalities.

"Anyway, they argued some about a tall tree or a short tree, a tree close to the edge, or farther in. And they wanted the hay to burn, so one of them wanted to skip the trees and just go set fire to the field."

Charlie turned to look at the sheriff. "Then one of them said, 'Mr. Stilling ought to be doing this himself. If he wants a fire done just the way he wants it, then he ought to set it himself instead of sending us to do it.'"

Again Charlie's imitation was humorous in its accuracy, but the meaning of the words sent chills up her spine. Her legs lost their starch, and she collapsed onto the nearest empty chair with an ungraceful, audible *thump*. The chair was next to Grant's. Charlie had been sitting there before being called on to give his account. Grant took her hand. She gladly accepted his comforting touch and squeezed his fingers closer to her palm.

"We can't track them." One of the men gestured toward the window and the heavy gray skies.

"No need," said the sheriff. "I know where they've been camping. When we quit the firefighting business."

A chuckle went around the room.

The sheriff continued, "I sent Rodgers out to check. He should be turning up here before too long."

Rodgers did show up after the men had devoured every cookie, pie, cake, and enough coffee to float them all out to their horses.

He removed his muddy boots before entering. "The Bidens have ridden to Stilling's ranch. I didn't follow them all the way, but there's no other destination out that way I could think of."

The sheriff grabbed his hat. "Then it's time to visit Mr. Stilling."

"It's late. Going to be dark in an hour."

"You can go home if you want, Dan."

Dan grinned with only half his teeth decorating the smile. "No way I'm missing this. Stilling practically stole my brother's land. I'd love to see him get trussed up like a turkey and locked in the hoosegow for eternity."

Chapter Eleven

Mae and Charlie flanked Grant as they rode out. When the sheriff said he wanted her young brother to come along, she'd insisted she was going, too.

None of the men had opted to go home. They didn't seem to be seriously considering what might greet them at the rich man's ranch. They rode easy in their saddles and made nonchalant comments about hunting and the weather. One man even mentioned the pie his wife was making for the church picnic.

Mae's thoughts were deadly serious, and as they came closer to their destination, her prayers became more fervent.

She'd been shocked to find that most, or maybe all, of the men who showed up to help knew the young family had no living parents. Apparently they'd conspired to keep the news from Stilling. The arrogant landowner had few friends in the area.

The wind had died down completely, the wet air hung about them but no longer wept, and high in the sky the clouds broke up. The moon periodically peeked through wispy stretched-out lengths of leftover veils.

The sheriff stopped his posse at the base of a long, rocky hill. "The ranch house is just over this ridge. Rodgers, scout the house and the stable. The rest of us will wait for your report."

Rodgers rode out, following the hill to the east.

While he was gone, the sheriff explained what he wanted done, should Rodgers come back to say the brothers were there.

Mae realized how much the men respected the sheriff as they listened and agreed to his tactics.

The scout returned with a grin and barely suppressed excitement. "They're there. And hopping mad. He left them to dry off in his kitchen. And here they are, in where all this great food is being made. No one offers them anything. They get dried off a bit and some servant moves them to a room with old furniture. Mr. Stilling has his dinner, taking his time. And now he's having a drink in his office. One of the servants, an old guy, asks if he wants the ruffians shown in, and he says no. He's in no hurry."

"How do you know all this?"

"Well, first I did some crawling around under the windows. With the rain finished, the windows are open. And second"—Rodgers winked at the sheriff—"the upstairs maid is being courted by none other than me. She works in the kitchen in the evening. I gave her our signal, and she snuck out to give me the details."

The group of men laughed. The sheriff held out both hands, palms down. "Settle and focus. Remember, this is no tea party we're going to, and the Bidens are dangerous."

The sheriff looked around his group of volunteers. "Split up as I told you. Block the getaway routes. Keep your eyes open. We don't want a gunfight, so keep your weapons out of sight."

Rodgers led three men to the back of the house. The deputy took three men with him to the bunkhouse to explain that the sheriff was going to have a talk with their boss and no interruptions would be tolerated. Two men went to the stable to guard the horses, keeping them unavailable should someone decide to take a quick ride that night. Others took points farther from the house.

Mae, Charlie, the sheriff, Grant, and three men took the front of the house. The Stilling household had made no attempt to obscure the people within from anyone outside. Of course, no one should have been outside.

Standing on the porch, Mae could hear the Biden brothers' complaints. Charlie's imitation of their voices was uncanny.

"Look at us, Mr. Stilling," the man shrilled. "We got holes in our clothes. Junior's got burned spots on his arms. The wind whooshed. The fire exploded in one of the trees. It hopped over our heads to more trees. We could have been killed."

"You ain't paying us enough to set fires."

"Fires is dangerous."

Stilling's soothing reply did not reach Mae's ears.

"Robbing that Winchester guy didn't work out real good. We got arrested."

"And I got you out!"

The sheriff chuckled. "Mae, you, Grant, Tim, and Smith stay out here. Robert and Charlie and I will go inside."

Mae leaped closer to grab his arm. "But—"

"No, Mae. There are three stupid men and one spoiled despot in a small room. You're too emotional. Grant's banged up. And besides, I just don't need more people to keep track of. Charlie is going to identify the Bidens as being in the woods, then I'll send him out. Boxer and Smith will come in. We'll make the arrests."

Mae hugged Charlie tight. "You do exactly what the sheriff says."

"I will, Mae. I'm not stupid like them."

The sheriff didn't bother to knock. He walked in with Robert behind him and Charlie next to Robert. Mae and Grant moved for a better view into the room. Neither bothered to hide. No one looked out the window. Those in the room now watched the hall door, spilling three new visitors into Mr. Stilling's office.

"Evening," said the sheriff. "Charlie, which of these men were in the woods by your house this afternoon?"

Her brother came to stand in front of the lawman and pointed to each of the Biden brothers.

Stilling took three quick steps forward and stood facing the sheriff. "What is the meaning of this? I'll not have you storming into my house. Take these buffoons if you must. If you have business with me, come to my office in town tomorrow."

"My business is with you, tonight. Charlie, go on now."

The movement was so swift, Mae didn't see how their positions reversed. Stilling was out of the lawman's reach and backed against a table. He held Charlie with an arm nearly strangling her brother. In his other hand, a small pistol pointed first at one person and then another.

The sheriff rested his hand on his gun but did not draw.

Stilling nodded. "Wise move, Sheriff." Waving the pistol in emphasis, he snarled at the Bidens. "Junior, take their firearms. You can have them. Leave. Go out the back door to the barn."

Junior stepped forward warily and took the sheriff's gun and Robert's rifle.

"Our money," the shortest Biden protested.

"On the table, and there's an extra three hundred. Take it and leave the territory. Go to California. Buy a gold mine."

With delight, the three men took the guns and the money and headed toward the back of the house.

Stilling pointed toward a door. "Open that."

Robert was closer and opened it without a question. Mae saw hanging coats.

"Get in."

The two men complied. Stilling shut the door, turned the key in the lock, and strained to prop a chair under the doorknob while dragging Charlie.

All the time he dragged Charlie around. The boy's feet barely touched the floor.

Mae shook Grant's arm. When had she grabbed him for security?

"Grant."

"I know. Stay calm. We'll rescue him." Strong and confident, he was close enough for her to lean against. "Mae, we'll always take care of our family."

Stilling charged out of the room and appeared at the front door. He held the gun to Charlie's head. Armed men materialized out of the darkness, standing in a semicircle, each about ten feet from the porch.

Stilling shook. Perspiration beaded on his face. He blinked several times then used his gun arm to wipe sweat from his eyes. One of the men took a step forward while the pistol was away from Charlie. Stilling saw him. His gun arm jerked. With a wild movement, he pointed at the bold intruder.

Mae's throat closed over a lump. The man was scared and senseless. He could pull the trigger at any moment. He aimed first at one man and then at another. Mae scarcely felt the movement at her side. The sound of a gun exploding dropped her to her knees. With her eyes riveted on Charlie, she saw Stilling jerk. He screeched. His gun fell to the porch. He released Charlie and grabbed his bloody hand.

Charlie flew across the space between them and tackled Mae in a hug. He jumped back and spun to face Grant. "You can shoot. You sure can shoot. Will you teach me?"

"You already know how to shoot."

"Just rabbits. With a rifle. I want to shoot a pistol."

"No!" said Mae. "Tim, let your brother and the sheriff out of the closet. I want to go home."

◆　◆　◆

Grant awoke to the sound of familiar voices coming from the great room. He swung his legs over the side of the bed and froze. Sharp pain reminded him of the last twenty-four hours. Every muscle in his body testified to each assault upon his being since he'd ridden out in a goat cart in search of Charlie. Every bounce in the cart, every bump in the ravine he'd encountered, every mile in the saddle going to and coming from Stilling's ranch, and the too-few stolen kisses from Mae on the front porch of her home.

That particular assault had not been painful except for having to stand when he was tired enough to collapse. He'd have to do a better job of wooing her today.

The voices in the next room lured him to his feet. The door muffled the conversation, but he knew it wasn't just the Seady family around the breakfast table. He took the effort to make himself presentable, minus a shave that would just have to wait.

When he opened the door, his mother popped in front of him and swooped him into a hug.

"We're here. We're all here. Mostly. We came to rescue you. But you don't need rescuing."

Grant looked around the room. No, they weren't all there. But interspersed among the ten Seadys, way too many of his brothers and his dad and a couple of brothers-in-law cluttered the room. He expected some baby-of-the-family barbs since they'd come all this way to pull him out of some sort of trouble. He hadn't needed a rescue in more than six years, not counting his encounter with the Biden brothers. Would he always be the tagalong youngest brother in need of older siblings?

His mother patted his cheek. "But you don't need rescuing. Charlie tells us you are the hero, rescuing him from the clutches of a madman. And Tim tells us you are marrying his sister."

Grant's eyes flew to Mae, and a sigh eased from his lungs when she nodded yes. Her face glowed. Every day she got prettier.

"We're going to stay for the wedding, dear." His mom glowed, too.

"Stay for the wedding?"

"Yes, dear. When is it?"

"Tomorrow," said Mae, just as he said, "This afternoon."

Mae weaved through all the people scattered around the room and came to his side. "Tomorrow, Grant." She squeezed his arm and rescued him from his mother's clutch. "It's only Saturday. Tomorrow, after church."

He looked into her eyes and saw the joy she was willing to share with him. There didn't seem much to say. So he kissed her.

That seemed to be exactly what she wanted to hear.

Donita Kathleen Paul has given up on retiring. Each time she retires, she finds a new career. This time she married an author from New Mexico and is resurrecting skills as a wife and homemaker. She's delved into romance, fantasy, history, and is toying with time travel. Writing will always be a part of her life. "The more I take time off to allow my body to relax, the more active my brain gets. I'm have way too much fun to stop."

Mountain Echoes

by Jennifer Uhlarik

Dedication:

To my beloved son, Zachary. I could not have asked for a greater blessing in life than to be your mom. You have been my constant companion, and there hasn't been a dull moment since you arrived. I love your heart for God, your kind spirit, and your wonderful sense of humor. Thank you for making my life so rich!

Chapter One

Virginia City, Utah Territory
Late October 1862

Lord, I wish he'd brought the boy last night.

A quick tug in Hannah Rose Stockton's chest stopped her frustrated pacing on the Pioneer Stagecoach Company's porch. She shot a glance heavenward. "Forgive me. I have no right to be upset when Dr. Tompkins was attending to a dying patient, but would You please make sure he gets the child here before the stage leaves?"

She sat on a wooden bench and scanned the street, burrowing deeper into her cloak to ward off the predawn chill. The hulking silhouette of the empty Concord stagecoach stood a few feet away, and silent buildings lined the street. All was still.

She'd been honored to be chosen by the principal of the California Institution for the Instruction of the Deaf and Dumb and Blind for such an important journey—to pick up their newest student, twelve-year-old Travis Alcott. However, the boy would likely be frightened about leaving his home. She needed time to befriend him, earn some trust before they boarded the stage for the three-day journey to San Francisco.

The door to the dimly lit office opened, and her dour, silver-haired traveling companion, Edwina Jamison, leaned out. "Hannah Rose, please come inside. It's hardly proper for a woman to sit alone outside at this time of day. Besides, they will have our breakfast ready shortly."

Hannah chafed at Mrs. Jamison's use of her middle name. Papa had been the only one to call her *Hannah Rose*, though she'd taken to calling herself that in order to draw on his strength and wisdom. It wasn't worth correcting the woman. "I'll be in momentarily. I'd like to pray before the day begins."

"God can hear you just as well inside as out, child."

She gritted her teeth. "Yes, ma'am, but I find it easier to pray without the clanging of dishes and the other passengers' conversations. I promise I'll be in momentarily."

Mrs. Jamison nodded hesitantly. "All right then, but hurry. I wouldn't want something to happen."

The door clicked shut, and Hannah rolled her eyes. "I'm thirty years old, Mrs. Jamison. Nothing will happen, and I don't need a chaperone." For goodness' sake, she'd traveled by wagon train from Illinois to California by herself. She certainly could've taken the stage from San Francisco to Virginia City without the opinionated widow's companionship. However, the principal had insisted, and if Hannah hoped to be considered for a promotion to a teaching position within the school, it was best to do as her employer asked.

Hannah closed her eyes. "Lord, forgive my uncharitable thoughts. It was kind of Mrs. Jamison to come along. Thank You for Your provision, even when I don't think I need it. Please allow the return leg of the journey to be as uneventful as the ride from San Francisco."

"Reckon it will be iffen I have anything to say about it."

Hannah jumped to her feet, heart ratcheting into a gallop at the deep male voice. Near the building's corner, a tall man's outline emerged, though she couldn't distinguish his features due to his hat.

"Couldn't help hearing you pray."

Her cheeks burning, she settled a palm against her chest. "I didn't realize I had company."

"Didn't mean to startle you, ma'am. Reckon we had the same thought. Enjoy a quiet moment before the day begins. I'll find somewhere else to choke down Alice's coffin varnish—err, coffee." He hoisted a cup, steam wafting from its lip. He turned toward the alley. "Just so you to know. . .I'm the jehu on this run. You got my pledge I'll get you safely where you're goin'."

She stifled a chuckle. How was anyone to trust stagecoach drivers when they were called jehus after the Israelite king known for driving furiously? She sat once more. "Thank you for the assurance, sir."

"Yes, ma'am." He headed down the alley.

At the far end of the street, a one-horse buggy turned toward her, the *clip-clop* of hooves echoing between the buildings. Hannah stepped toward the railing, craning her neck to see. A single lantern lit the path and illuminated two passengers, one smaller than the other. A child, perhaps? Her heartbeat quickened at the prospect of meeting her young charge. The buggy stopped, and a suit-clad man swung to the ground.

Hannah stepped closer. "Are you Dr. Tompkins?"

"Yes, ma'am." He touched the brim of his hat. "You're Miss Stockton?"

"Yes."

The doctor moved around the conveyance and motioned for a half-grown child to climb down. The boy shot a hollow glance her way, ignoring the man. She smiled and met his eyes, though he looked directly ahead once more.

"This is Travis Alcott, the boy I wrote to you about." The doctor guided the boy out of the wagon and bent to his level. "Say hello to the lady." He overenunciated each word.

Travis scowled and shifted away.

Dr. Tompkins shot her an apologetic glance. "Sorry. Since losing his hearing, he wavers between anger and withdrawal."

She resisted correcting the man for his exaggerated speech. She'd frown and turn away from such ridiculous behavior, too. Hannah smiled at Travis. "We will teach him to communicate again." She paused. "Has he eaten breakfast?"

"Doubt it. The boy's ma is long deceased. His pa stays too drunk to care for the boy properly, especially since Travis went deaf."

Hannah's eyes stung. How hard the child's life must have been. Thankfulness for her own loving parents washed over her.

Again, the office door opened, and Mrs. Jamison looked out. "Hannah, dear. The meal is—oh." Her gaze fell on the newcomers. "Is this the boy?"

"Yes. We were just coming inside." Hannah stepped toward the door, and Dr. Tompkins guided Travis inside.

After the introductions, Hannah shifted toward Travis. She smiled and gave him a friendly wave. "Hello, Travis. I'm Hannah Stockton." She pointed to her chest then finger-spelled her name as she spoke.

The boy's brown eyes flitted between her face and her hand, though before she finished, he looked away and inhaled deeply, seemingly caught by the scents of pancakes and coffee wafting from the next room.

Hannah touched his shoulder, and he whipped around, his mop of dark hair falling in his eyes.

"Do you want to eat?" She signed the question, hoping he'd understand the self-explanatory gestures.

Expressionless, he looked toward the door where the smells originated. Beyond it, the sounds of chairs scooting across the plank floor and the clanking of dishes filled the room.

"Why isn't he answering her?" Mrs. Jamison asked. "Your letter said he could still speak."

"He's capable of speaking, but he rarely does. Illness rendered him profoundly deaf, so he doesn't understand what's being said. Also, his father's neglected him. He's not used to talking much."

Hannah's chest ached as she studied the boy's hollow cheeks, smudged with grime. His clothes were rumpled and dirty. His coat sleeves were far too short for his growing limbs, and the hem of his pant legs were worn to tatters. One shoe sported a hole in the toe.

Lord, how long since this child's been properly cared for? How long since he's been loved?

Travis ambled toward the doorway and, after peeking around the door frame, bolted into the room beyond. Hannah scurried after him, catching up as he leaned past a burly, bearded man at the table who was passing a heaping plate of pancakes. She caught Travis's hand before he could grab a flapjack. The boy faced her, brown eyes hard.

"No." She shook her head then held up a finger. "First, wash your hands." She pantomimed the action then held up two fingers. "Second, wash your face." Again, she acted the required action. "Third, eat."

Rather than watch her, the boy scanned the table and moved after the circulating plate of food. One of the men on the end stopped him.

"Yer ma told you to do—"

Travis ducked the man's grasp, trailing the pancakes. All eyes at the table followed Travis. When he made another grab for the last few flapjacks, Hannah again caught his arm. This time, he jerked free, glared at her, and stomped a foot.

The burly fellow rose, drawing Travis's attention, and stabbed a finger in Travis's direction. "Son, I'm about to wear you out unless you start listenin' to yer ma."

Hannah threw her hands up. "Thank you, sir, but he's deaf. He doesn't understand. Please let me handle this."

"Travis!" From the doorway, Dr. Tompkins stomped into the room, Mrs. Jamison close on his heels.

The boy must have felt the heavy footsteps, for he looked at the floor then scanned the room, focusing on the doctor.

Again, Hannah held up a hand. "Please, sir, stop. If you expect me to transport this child three days to the school, we must build a rapport before we board the stage."

The doctor halted. Focus at the table shifted between her and Travis, expressions ranging from surprise to disbelief.

"You ain't his ma?" the burly man asked, incredulous.

"No. I'm taking him to San Francisco to attend a deaf school. Please forgive us for interrupting your breakfast. Carry on, and we'll try to stay out of your way."

The blond man on the end disappeared through another door on the far side of the room. Once he was gone, Travis headed toward the man's vacant seat and partially eaten breakfast. Hannah failed to reach him before he'd scooped the top pancake from the stack.

She smacked his hand lightly and guided him toward the washbasin near the door. Travis gobbled the syrupy flapjack in two huge bites. Behind her, the men murmured, some sounding none too happy at having to ride the stage with such an ill-behaved imp.

Heat warming her cheeks, Hannah positioned the boy's hands over the basin and poured water over his sticky palms. She placed the soap cake in his hands, though he dropped it to face the table again. Thankfully, the blond-haired man approached and caught Travis gently by the arm. He spun the boy, fished the soap from the basin, and proceeded to lather Travis's hands.

The boy watched the blond man without a fight.

"I'm sorry, sir, but Travis stole some of your breakfast," she whispered.

He chuckled softly. "I saw him."

She smiled, recognizing the voice of the jehu. Lantern light caught his deep blue eyes as his gaze met hers, and something akin to lightning crackled through her head and limbs. When he shifted, the sensation dissolved, and along with it, every coherent thought she'd had.

"Alice is cooking up more flapjacks for you all. She'll have 'em out momentarily."

Mute, Hannah nodded. *Say something.* "That would be perfect, Mister. . .?"

His smile deepened, causing his eyes to crinkle at the corners. "Finn McCaffrey."

"Thank you, Mr. McCaffrey." She offered a demure smile and took the towel he held out. "I'm Hannah Rose Stockton."

"A pleasure, Mrs. Stockton."

She busied herself drying Travis's hands. "It's *Miss*."

◆　◆　◆

The woman's cheeks flushed a shade of red to rival her fiery hair.

"My mistake." Finn opened his mouth to speak again, when the familiar form of a petite, brown-haired woman stepped through the door. At the sight of her, his chest seized. "Pardon me a moment."

Finn brushed past Miss Stockton and hurried toward the doorway. "Sam?" He caught Samantha Foster by the elbow and showed her into the empty office. "What're you doing here? Is everything all right?" His thoughts flew over the reasons she might come to the stagecoach office before dawn, and one filtered to the top. "Ezra?" He breathed the name.

"Papa's fine."

Thank You, Lord. He closed his eyes and rubbed at the tension knotting his neck and shoulders. After a calming breath, he opened his eyes once more. "What brings you out so early?" He kept his voice low.

"I need to tell you something, and I didn't want to wait until you returned."

Guilt flooded him. He should've spent the night at their homestead outside of town, but it was hard watching Ezra weaken each time he visited. "Sorry I didn't come by. Your news must be pretty important."

Sam hung her head.

When she didn't speak, he tucked a finger under her chin and nudged it upward until their eyes met. "So?"

Tears pooled against her lower lashes, and she swallowed hard. "I'm with child."

Finn blinked once. . .twice. . .his mind churning over the unexpected declaration. "You're *what?*"

"I'm *with child.*" Her voice rose a little.

Finn darted a concerned look toward the dining room. "Shh. I heard you. I just—" *Oh, God, help us both.* He gritted his teeth and dragged her toward the front door.

"Please don't be angry." Her words dripped a mixture of fear and concern.

He burst out onto the porch and shut the door so hard the windows on either side rattled. For an instant, he stood stock-still, fighting the urge to put his fist through the wall. A couple of deep breaths restored some control, and he pulled the young woman into his arms.

"I'm not angry at you." He closed his eyes. "That good-for-nothing husband of yours, on the other hand. . ." Denny Foster had drifted in and out of Sam's life whenever he saw fit. Of course, the yellow-bellied fool would choose a time like this to drift again. "Iffen the scoundrel was here, I'd wrap my hands around his scrawny neck and choke the—"

Sam shoved back from him, her eyes huge.

A shudder ran through him. "Oh, Sam, I'm sorry." *Lord, forgive me.*

Eventually, she slid back into his arms. "I'm scared, Finn. What do I know about being someone's mama?"

A sudden, sharp pain lodged in his chest. They'd both done without a mother's influence, though he at least remembered his ma. He rubbed Sam's back. "You'll make a fine ma, and Ezra and I'll help all we can."

"I haven't told Papa."

Finn's brows knitted. "You're gonna have to. This ain't something you can hide for long."

"I will, but his heart is so weak, I didn't want to cause him any further distress." She shrugged. "Besides, I was hoping you'd be there when I break the news."

Finn sighed. That conversation would require careful thought and well-chosen words. "I'll be wherever you need me."

From the direction of the corral, faint voices drifted their way. The clopping of horses' hooves punctuated the air. Probably the hostlers preparing the team. A quick glance toward the sky revealed the horizon had brightened to a light gray.

"Reckon I better get on my work. Gotta check the stage before we pull out."

Sam hugged him tighter, then released him. "I should get back to Papa anyway." Her attempt at a smile quivered and twisted into a grim expression, tears pooling again.

His mind raced to find a way he could stay in Virginia City and attend to the new situation, but getting another driver moments before a run wasn't possible. He matched her grim expression. "We'll talk once I return."

She nodded. "Please be careful."

Finn planted a kiss on the top of her head. "You know I will."

He helped Sam into her wagon and watched as she turned the team toward home. Once the darkness swallowed her, he retrieved a lantern from the office and began the inspection. Starting at the nearest wheel, he perused the hub and the spokes but shook his head to clear Sam's predicament from his thoughts. Again, he checked the front wheel and axle, the leather thoroughbrace that cradled the coach's body, and the back wheel and axle. Rounding the coach, Finn repeated the process. By the time he'd finished, the eastern sky had grown bright. The hostlers had the team harnessed and ready. The passengers waited on the porch, their bags near the rear boot for loading.

At the edge of the group, Miss Stockton stood beside her student, who stared intently at the team. She touched the boy's shoulder and made various gestures as she spoke softly to him. Hands crammed in his pockets, the boy looked away. Finn watched a moment longer. When the kid's gaze once more found its way to the team, he grinned. The boy appeared to like horses. He could relate.

From his own pocket, Finn withdrew several jagged chunks of sugar he'd broken from the sugar loaf at breakfast, then approached Miss Stockton. "Ma'am?"

She turned wide hazel eyes on him. "Yes?"

"I usually treat the horses to a little sugar before a run. Maybe the boy might like to help me?" He revealed the sugar pieces.

A smile parted her lips. "He'd like that. Thank you." She turned to the boy and gestured. "Travis, would you like to feed the horses?"

Finn placed a single piece of sugar in Travis's palm, and the boy's brows furrowed. Beckoning to the kid, he stepped toward the nearest horse. Eyes riveted, Travis followed.

Finn helped the boy feed each horse and stood by as he rubbed their necks. When the lead horse nudged Travis's chest with his nose, the boy loosed a deep belly laugh and gave that animal extra attention. Miss Stockton grinned each time Finn glanced at her.

Once he'd returned Travis to Miss Stockton, he gave the call to load up. While the rest of the passengers piled into the coach, the doctor took Travis by the shoulders and bent, nose to nose with the kid. "You mind yourself, son." He spoke in a slow, exaggerated way. "These ladies'll take good care of you from now on."

The boy scowled and shrugged out of the man's grasp. When the gent tried again to take him by the shoulders, Travis rocked back a step and darted down the boardwalk at full speed.

"No you don't—" The doctor gave chase and, three steps beyond, caught Travis by the waist. The kid's hat tumbled off, and his feet flew out from under him. A frustrated scream escaped the child as he writhed to free himself.

Something deep within Finn broke, and he lunged across the porch. "Put the kid down. *Now.* He obviously don't like the way you're talking to him."

"This is none of your business, sir." Dr. Tompkins hoisted Travis higher, causing Travis to squirm more.

"Beggin' your pardon, but my passengers are my business. I don't cotton to folks manhandlin' 'em."

The stage office door burst open, and shotgun rider Bob Racklin burst out, gripping his firearm in both hands. The man swept the scene with a glance. "Is there a problem?"

Travis's eyes grew huge, and his frame went rigid for an instant before he fell limp.

"Whoa, Bob. Put that thing away." Finn pulled the boy's scrawny form from the doctor's grasp and settled him onto the nearest bench. He laid a calming hand against the boy's pounding chest. "Everything's all right."

Travis darted a frightened look at each man, ending with Finn.

Bob lowered the gun. "Thought you were in trouble. . . ."

"Nothing I can't handle, thanks."

When Miss Stockton slid up next to Travis, pulling him to her side like a mama bird sheltering her baby, Finn stepped away. The boy didn't resist her nearness, though he eyed the doctor and Bob with distrust.

"Real sorry, ma'am."

"You have nothing to apologize for, Mr. McCaffrey." She cradled Travis's head against her shoulder and brushed the boy's dark hair back from his forehead.

The sight of her soothing the boy and the feel of his undernourished frame stirred memories. His own ma had held him like that once, rocking him, petting his hair. A lump filled his throat, and he shoved the memory away, not wanting to recall the haunting images that came next.

He retrieved Travis's hat from the boardwalk then checked his pocket watch. "Ladies, I'll thank you to climb aboard, please. Bob, let's get the strongbox loaded up. Time we get rolling."

Chapter Two

The paper in Hannah's hand trembled, and not from the rhythmic rocking of the stagecoach. She stared at the messy scrawl, the words blurring just as they had the first time she read them:

Oct. 20, 1862

As told to Dr. Albert Tompkins: Clyde Alcott hereby resigns all his parental rights and responsibilities to Travis Alcott, relinquishing them to Miss Hannah Rose Stockton, representative of the California Institution for the Instruction of the Deaf and Dumb and Blind.

Signed,
X
(Official mark of Clyde Alcott,
as witnessed by Dr. A. Tompkins)

She dabbed discreetly at her eyes then glanced to her right. Travis stared out the window at the scenery blurring past, just as he'd done most of the morning. She returned her attention to the letter.

Mrs. Jamison leaned nearer on her left. "Staring at it isn't going to change the contents, dear." Her whisper cut through the rumbling of the coach's wheels and the annoyingly loud conversations of the other passengers.

Hannah lowered the soiled paper and turned to her companion. "It breaks my heart that Travis's father would sign away *all* of his parental rights. Has he no interest in how his son will do at the school?"

"The doctor said the man signed the paper then stated, 'Good riddance. The kid'll never amount to nothin' anyway.'"

The pointed words pierced Hannah's aching heart. She refolded the page and tucked it into her bag with the other papers Dr. Tompkins had given them. She glanced again at the young man, who'd made no attempts to interact with either her or Mrs. Jamison since boarding the stage. "That's Mr. Alcott's loss. This boy will thrive in the proper environment."

"I do hope you're right, though I admit I'm concerned. The child's been nothing short of morose this morning."

Lord, has Mrs. Jamison no understanding of the isolation he must feel? "I think he's handling himself quite well. Imagine how frightened he might feel. He's been removed from his home, given over to strangers, and placed on a stagecoach taking him away from anything familiar. With no ability to understand our words, he may think we've plans to abandon him in the mountains."

Mrs. Jamison looked at Travis. "I hadn't considered how this must appear to him."

She hadn't considered? Such thoughts had consumed Hannah's mind. Before she could answer the woman, Travis perked up and craned his neck. At nearly the same moment, the stage slowed. Hannah touched his shoulder, and when he looked her way, she smiled.

"What do you see?" She opened her hands wide, as if in a shrug, then pointed to him and then to her eyes. Hannah followed the gestures with arched brows, hoping he'd understand her question.

His brow furrowed, though he looked out the window again without response.

"We're in spitting distance of town, ma'am," a burly fellow said.

Hannah offered the man a conciliatory nod. "Thank you."

After a moment, Travis turned and patted her forearm then pointed out the window. She peered out the window, catching sight of a roof not too far off. Hannah grinned at him, fighting the urge to draw him into a hug. He'd communicated, conveying there was something to see. A tiny breakthrough. As they got farther down the rutted path, a dusty town rose up from the earth.

Carson City.

The stage rolled between the buildings and tottered to a stop. After a moment, the door swung open and Finn McCaffrey smiled up at them. "Welcome to Carson. Iffen this is your destination, the Pioneer Stage Company thanks you for your business. Frank can help you retrieve your bags. I believe it's just you ladies and the boy who're traveling on. We'll depart again in ten minutes."

Once the men on the center bench had exited, Mr. McCaffrey folded the seat out of their way and looked at Hannah. "Ma'am?" His intense blue eyes radiated warmth from under his hat brim when he offered her his hand. Clinging to it, she stepped down and turned to find Travis was on her heels, scrambling out of the stagecoach with no assistance.

The jehu grinned as the boy trotted off a few feet to watch the hostlers change teams. "Looks like someone's ready to stretch his legs."

"Indeed. We all are."

He turned to help Mrs. Jamison, though he spoke over his shoulder in her direction. "Iffen you don't object, the boy's welcome to help me treat the horses again before we leave."

"Thank you, Mr. McCaffrey. I'm sure he'd like that."

Mrs. Jamison stepped down and thanked the jehu then hurried toward Hannah, drawing her off a little way from the coach. The elder woman turned twinkling eyes and a sly smile on her. "Quite a handsome one, that Mr. McCaffrey. Wouldn't you say?" Her tone was low, confidential.

Hannah swallowed the sudden lump that knotted her throat. Handsome, yes. Quite. Though after what she'd overheard of his conversation with the young woman in Virginia City, he was hardly the sort she'd wish to know too well. She hadn't meant to eavesdrop, though from her vantage point near the door, she couldn't help but overhear the young woman's timid announcement and his less-than-receptive response.

"He seems quite attentive to you, dear."

She shook her head. "His interest appears to be in the comfort of his passengers. Particularly Travis. Precisely as it ought to be."

Across the way, Finn McCaffrey casually sidled up next to Travis and nudged him with his elbow. The boy looked up, startled, but smiled at the man. It was a warmer reception than he'd given to either her or Mrs. Jamison thus far. The jehu placed something in Travis's left hand, and the boy looked at it then turned, wide-eyed, back to the driver. Finn McCaffrey looped an arm over the boy's shoulders and guided him toward the new team. As they reached the nearest horse, Mr. McCaffrey smiled warmly at her.

The older woman's sly grin deepened, and she patted Hannah's arm. "You're fooling yourself, dear."

◆ ◆ ◆

The stage rolled steadily up the steep, rocky terrain, high into the Sierra Nevada. The morning's chill lingered, though the sun beat down on Finn's shoulders, causing sweat to snake down his spine. He arched his back and scanned the narrow road they followed, slowing the team through the sharp, winding turns while keeping a good pace.

"You got something stuck in your craw?" Bob Racklin's unexpected question snapped his thoughts back to the present.

Finn glanced at his friend. "Pardon?"

"I been jawing at you for the past five minutes about this pretty li'l gal I met, and you ain't heard a word of it."

He slapped the backs of the horses lightly and scanned the rutted path. "Sorry. Not in a talking mood, I s'pose."

His friend snorted. "Nor in a listening one, I reckon."

He forced an apologetic smile. "Reckon not."

"This got something to do with Sam's visit?"

Truth was, his thoughts hovered in dangerous territory, only partly due to Sam's news. The scene with Miss Stockton comforting the kid outside the Virginia station rattled him just as much, and the two episodes together had awakened a giant that threatened to drag him to a very dark place. He was left scrambling to find a rock big enough to slay it.

Why'd the teacher have to be so blasted nurturing? He sighed. She'd unnerved him, and he was in a mad scramble to find his footing again.

The boy was fortunate. A kid like Travis needed a mother-hen sort. The kid seemed plenty smart. He'd need to be challenged, and a woman like Hannah Rose Stockton could push him to better things.

Not every kid was so lucky. He sure hadn't been. Not when his ma had been taken from him by the time he was eight.

They rounded a bend and drove between two huge rock outcroppings. As they passed through them, the path took a jog left, and the terrain on the right side dropped away. His heart pounded, and his muscles tensed. Beside him, Bob braced himself. Below the road, tall pines and boulders dotted the rugged landscape. To their left, a ten-foot-tall rock face rose sharply, several massive stones dangling precariously over the edge, ready to tumble down on them.

If there was any stretch of the road between Carson and Strawberry he didn't like, this was it, but once they made the sharp turn at the top of the hill, the downslope was less treacherous, and the view would be reward enough for the anxiety.

The path dipped then climbed again. He flicked the reins once more. "Git on. Let's move."

The team leaned into their harnesses, pulling hard, hooves rattling against the rocky path. They kept a decent pace, Finn nursing them along with an occasional hollered encouragement. The six horses negotiated the path like experts. Finally, as the road leveled momentarily at the top, Finn drew back on the reins, slowing the team to safely make the turn.

As they rounded the blind curve, a dazzling flash of sunlight reflected off a distant lake, drawing his gaze. Finn squinted, drinking in the majestic view before he called to the horses.

"Git!" He shifted his attention back to the road as he flicked the lines. The horses straightened after the sharp turn and picked up speed when the lead pair shied suddenly. Finn drew back on the lines to regain control, though before he could, a black bear lumbered out from behind a jutting rock and swiped a massive paw at the lead horse. The horse loosed a terrified scream as it reared, red streaks sprouting on its neck and shoulder.

Finn braked hard. To no avail. The chestnut horses plunged forward, crashed against the rock face on the left then rolled back toward the right and the steep drop. The coach lurched, tottered, and slid from the path down the steep, tree-dotted slope.

Chapter Three

P lease don't die! Please."
        The rasping, frantic words leeched into Hannah's consciousness, rattling in her pounding skull. Who on earth was speaking? She didn't recognize the voice.

Something grabbed her, shook her, and with it came a gut-wrenching cry. Every nerve jangled warning, and she covered her ears and pried her eyes open. Her vision landed on the blurry shape of a boy.

Travis. He'd spoken, voice rusty from disuse, but clear as could be—like the doctor said he could.

Hannah wrapped clumsy hands around the boy's wrists and blinked to clear her vision. After a second, he stopped shaking her, though his fingers didn't untwine from her dress bodice. Again she blinked, her eyesight clearing enough to reveal Travis's dirt-caked face marred with wet trails that stretched from his eyes to jawline.

What happened? They'd been on the stage going home, but. . . Memories were hazy at best.

She looked around. The whole scene was familiar, but not. The coach's door had become its ceiling. The cushioned seats of the stage now occupied the walls from roof to floor, rather than side to side. Hannah grappled to make sense of things, her thoughts moving like sludge. She attempted to sit up, though her legs had somehow become wedged under the center bench. Had they crashed?

Every movement was uncoordinated as she extracted herself from the tight quarters beneath the bench. Her back ached; her limbs trembled. No sooner had she righted herself than Travis launched himself at her, his spindly arms circling her torso. His shoulders wracked with sobs. She pulled him to her, her hand straying to his hair to brush it from his face, though her fingers contacted something sticky. He jerked away, and she pulled her hand back to find blood. Hannah pushed him back and turned his face to reveal a gash that trailed from his forehead to his ear, still oozing blood. Heart pounding, she found her valise nearby, pulled out the first cloth she laid hold of, and drawing the boy close, pressed it to the wound.

"Lord, what's happened here?" Where was Mrs. Jamison? She looked around the sideways coach. No sign of the woman.

After several moments, the torrent of Travis's tears abated, and Hannah pushed him away again. She checked the wound and, finding the blood flow had nearly stopped, she laid the cloth aside. Hannah smiled to reassure the boy, though she could use some reassuring herself. An unconvincing smile trembled on his lips.